THE BURNING ISLAND

ALSO BY JOCK SERONG

Quota
The Rules of Backyard Cricket
On the Java Ridge
Preservation

Jock Serong's novels have received the Ned Kelly Award for First Fiction, the Colin Roderick Award and the inaugural Staunch Prize (UK). He lives with his family on Victoria's far west coast.

JOCK SERONG

THE BURNING ISLAND

TEXT PUBLISHING MELBOURNE AUSTRALIA

textpublishing.com.au
textpublishing.co.uk

The Text Publishing Company
Swann House, 22 William Street, Melbourne Victoria 3000, Australia

The Text Publishing Company (UK) Ltd
130 Wood Street, London EC2V 6DL, United Kingdom

Published by The Text Publishing Company, 2020

Cover design by Chong W.H.
Cover image from iStock
Page design by Chong W.H.
Typeset in Adobe Caslon 12.5/17.5 by J&M Typesetting
Map by Simon Barnard

Printed and bound in Australia by Griffin Press, part of Ovato, an accredited ISO/ NZS 14001:2004 Environmental Management System printer.

ISBN: 9781922330086 (paperback)
ISBN: 9781925923520 (ebook)

A catalogue record for this book is available from the National Library of Australia.

 This book is printed on paper certified against the Forest Stewardship Council® Standards. Griffin Press holds FSC chain-of-custody certification SGS-COC-005088. FSC promotes environmentally responsible, socially beneficial and economically viable management of the world's forests.

Across the tripwire lines of country, we sit in the dark
waiting for the call to come or for a length of rope to unfurl.

OMAR SAKR
Sailor's Knot

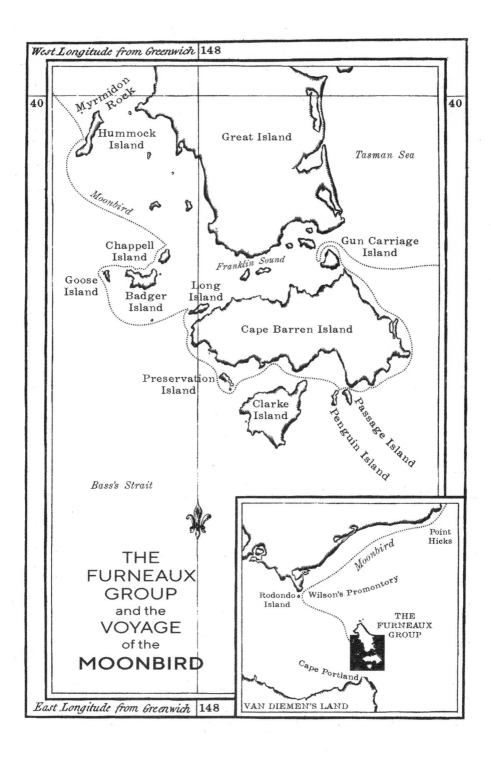

40

40

Myrmidon Rock

Hummock Island

Great Island

Tasman Sea

Moonbird

Chappell Island

Gun Carriage Island

Franklin Sound

Goose Island

Long Island

Badger Island

Cape Barren Island

Preservation Island

Clarke Island

Passage Island

Penguin Island

Bass's Strait

THE
FURNEAUX
GROUP
and the
VOYAGE
of the
MOONBIRD

Point Hicks

Moonbird

Rodondo Island

Wilson's Promontory

THE
FURNEAUX
GROUP

Cape Portland

VAN DIEMEN'S LAND

Eadem mutata resurgo

THE INDIAN

 I had been aware of the man in the corner of my vision for an hour or more.

Dark, but not a native.

He wore no hat and I could see that his hair was deep in retreat above his temples. A thin man, slightly stooped, with a delicate formality to his walk. I'd passed the rows of vendors and bought what I needed. Short conversations, greetings. Bargaining here or there—*surely that's the price for a dozen?*—slowing, shifting, turning. But always I could feel the presence out beyond my shoulder. The man never came close enough to hear or to speak: he merely kept in step as I moved.

And I am not someone accustomed to being followed. Lord, you'd die of the tedium.

In the sheds I bought myself a hock of mutton and a pound of potatoes. *No, Mr Ross, I am cooking for myself, same as last week.* Mr Ross shrank back into his shell, tortoise-man. While he wrapped the meat in long muslin, further out the dark man let the sides of his eyes inform him.

I forced a conversation with the woman who had broad beans. Veda, Vera, Thea. I didn't want the beans: I wanted to convince myself I was imagining things.

Still there.

He was not discreet. There was a stickiness to his movements that marked him out: I moved, he moved. While the crowd around us shifted and lurched, he was constant as a shadow.

I turned away from the market, out of the gloom of the timber sheds and onto the road. Sydney roiled about: raucous and uncaring, a stripling at forty-two years of age. Bullocks and horses splattered the dust of the street. Voices hailed and harangued; someone yelling about oysters. Scrapping children, the eyes of the old folk upon them, wondering in their breasts if these generations differed somehow for the accident of their birth. We do differ, down to the bones. And yet still we look homeward.

I turned back the way I'd come, stopped and drew out the hunk of mutton. Unwrapped it and made an elaborate show of winding the muslin around it once again as I looked directly at the man who shadowed me.

No, not a native. An Indian, I thought, though that told me nothing. The street swarmed with natives, with Africans, Bengalis, Malays. Even among the white faces there would be Americans and Welshmen and Dutchmen, and there perched on his wagon was the Chinaman who ran the Lion.

The man watching me was older, better dressed and much shorter than me. His remaining hair was a rich blue-black, his scalp smooth and unmarked, glowing in the sun. The face was lined with thought or care; there were years on his neck and his cheeks but he wore them comfortably, as time and not decay. His eyes were fixed upon me in a way that alarmed me.

I turned back to the market, found old Copsley with his firebox. He greeted me warmly but his smile faltered as he looked closer. I did not want to alert him, or cause a scene at this stage.

'I wonder if I could ask a small favour of you, sir.'

'Of course, miss.'

'Could I borrow that poker?' I cut my eyes towards it, on the bed of straw by the firewood.

His eyebrows shot up. 'This one?'

'No, the one beside it, with the hook-end. I need it at home.' He did not look askance at the odd request but simply went to grab it.

'No, I don't want to carry it around, not for the moment,' I said. 'Other things to do. But would you be kind enough to put it in the panniers on my mare? That's her, by the big tree.' I didn't point, merely indicated once more by eye. 'I'd be most obliged.'

'Certainly, miss.'

I turned my back without another word and came out into the street again. If this man intended to follow me, I would draw him away.

I visited some more of the traders, manufacturing small conversations. The eyes burned on me, out at the margins. Could I say it was open malevolence? No, I thought not. But it is troubling enough to be stared at.

When I was satisfied that Copsley had carried out his errand I returned to the mare, took the reins in one hand and slid the other into the pannier. Cold iron in there. Not made for the delicate hands of a teacher, but that was fine with me.

The mare, as always, made an ally of herself, stepping gently for home. When we stopped at the high wall around the barracks I took her muzzle and looked into her eye. The world was reflected there in the dark pool: the curving sky and the wall, bent by the lens, and there, only yards back, the Indian. I made a decision.

I walked the mare to the end of the wall and turned the corner. I slid the iron from the pannier and gave her a light smack on the rump so she continued down the road. The street was empty. The iron hung by my leg. I slipped into the small recess behind the corner buttressing of the wall and waited.

He came around, stopped just in front of me and I saw him assessing the unaccompanied mare. Just for an instant.

It was easy enough to bring him down. I swung backhand across his middle and the iron caught him low on his chest or high on his belly. The air came out of him with a bark and he dropped, allowing me time to lay a knee on him, right where the iron had got him.

I took his lapels and lifted his head out of the dust: an old, careworn head, and I felt a flush of remorse. But the eyes bored into me, huge now, even while his chest clenched and unclenched under my knee, mouth open but no breath passing, and I began to worry. I lifted myself off him but stood with the end of the iron at his throat as a warning. The mare had wandered back. She nuzzled at his hair while I waited for his breath to return.

I took his lapels again and forced myself to stare into his eyes. 'Lost, are you sir?'

He did not resist me physically but the dark, dark eyes lent an intensity to his gaze, a kind of searching. He had air now, he had speech, but it was strained.

'You are Eliza Grayling, madam?' His accent was not as I

expected it to be: flat, close to English but fading to something more local.

I saw no point in denying it. 'It's miss. And who would you be?'

The eyes worked around my face, searching. 'We must talk. There is much I wish to discuss.'

The mare stood above us, eyeing me softly. Her hooves made small, impatient shuffles.

'And you think following people around like that is a way to foster discussion?'

'Forgive me.' The searching eyes. 'I mean you no harm.'

I could see now that there was no threat in him, nothing in the way of physical power. There was only the haunted look of his face, and that was his concern, not mine. 'I'm walking up the hill to my home. You can join me or not.'

'Then I shall,' he said, and grimaced. I had hit him hard. 'My name is Srinivas. You may have heard of me.'

~

Well, I had and I hadn't.

Srinivas was the lascar, I was fairly sure.

I'd never heard the name, but there was a Bengali who lived at the centre of the stories my father had told me. He would be as old now as this man. It was the nature of my relationship with my father that in our long hours together he would become reflective and summon stories from his bones. One of them came from his time as a young lieutenant working as an aide to Governor Hunter, commissioned to investigate the strange affair of the *Sydney Cove*. An irresistible tale for a child—a distant shipwreck, the mysterious disappearance of almost all those who attempted the long walk to safety—salted with dark places and monsters. Clark, responsible for the ship's cargo, the bearer of unexplained wounds, who absconded at the earliest opportunity. Mister Figge, a shadowy figure in the tales, rendered compelling by the disgust, the horrified intimacy that animated my father when he spoke of him. The man was a tumour in him. He blamed Figge for the deaths of the missing souls and attempted to arrest him, whereupon he attacked my father with a knife and took off on a stolen horse. My father carried wounds, I understood, whose exact nature was not to be discussed.

Of all his tales, this one I could not ask to be told. He spoke of it only when he was morose, and then his gaze would drift, his voice would start at a murmur that scarcely shifted the silence. A man who had no wife, a widower in heart and temperament, a man with no one to hear him but an insatiably curious child. Later, as the drink took him, the account would be tinted with sarcasm and doubt. As I reached that age where children start their questions, my father would offer only fragments, the gaps filled by others and their rumours.

I never knew anyone else to mention Clark, but of Figge there were occasional whispers. He'd been murdered in the bush, or had found his way back to India, or even England. He was in China, he'd been hanged or impaled on a Gweagal spear or burnt alive. It was his skeleton that swung from the gibbet on Pinchgut, or turned up softened by the acids of a lime burner's barrel. He was a necromancer, a preacher, an alchemist. He was immortal, already reincarnated. He was a lightning rod for florid talk. When I listened to my father, I thought of Figge as some manifestation in the weather, a cataclysm that smote the men and violated the women and was gone.

The lascar boy, the Bengali, in my father's story had no name and Father spoke little of him. He was Clark's manservant, that was all. It was he who had provided the account of the long trek north from the *Sydney Cove* wreck that cast so much suspicion on his two fellow survivors. And I knew, too, that it was my mother who had drawn the story forth from the silent, terrified boy, which perhaps accounted for some of my father's anguish around it. At any rate, the story was full of contradictions, made worse by my father's frequently addled state in the telling. It confused *him*, even years later. And it certainly confused me. It formed some part of his wider grief: that much I knew.

~

As I walked up the hill, the provisions slung over the mare and the iron returned to the pannier, I waited for the Bengali to talk. It was extraordinary. This man, sunk deep in his middle age, was the legendary boy of those childhood tales. And yet I was no less disconcerted by his staring, by the smouldering intensity of his presence. Was he in his right mind? I felt sure he was quite profoundly disturbed.

Then he did begin to talk, prompted by some small invitation from me to do so, and it was as though a torrent had been released. The words rushed out of him, even while he stared.

'I suppose you may know, Miss Grayling, that I lost my father in the forest. I went back to the coast to find him.' This was the first thing he said, and it seemed stranded. As though it fell outside the order of the story he wanted to tell, such was his urgency in saying it.

I did know that the lascar boy's father was one of the survivors of the *Sydney Cove*. Now I learned that Srinivas had gone back south, when Sydney was done with him and he with them.

'The Walbanja came and met me. I knew from their faces, straight away. They took me to a place where they had buried him in a tree, bundled him, I suppose you would say. We wept together. They were very kind.'

The other lascars, his father's companions, had been taken in by the Walbanja, he said, and he was reunited with them. While he did not think they were *contented* with living in the forest, they were well settled with the natives by then, and the shipwreck was old history for them. They would not take Srinivas to the place where his father had perished. They had seen it, back at the time it all happened; out in a dark gully in the forest. They told Srinivas it was a dreadful place, a place they would not otherwise go. He stopped at this point in the story—we were again alone in a quiet lane—and took hold of my arm so firmly it hurt.

'Figge had led my father there and cut his leg so he would scream in pain, and the screams would lead them all to separate from the party and search for him.'

The horror of that day was vivid to him, even now; he carried it like a blade broken off in his flesh. The other lascars told him they heard his father's cries: they wanted to go and find him. But Srinivas had stayed with Clark, because that, his father had told him, was his duty. Clark had insisted on it, in any event. It seemed the boy's father bled to death, in dreadful pain, alone and cold.

Walking beside me now, older in all likelihood than his father had been when he disappeared into the forest, the poor man let out a strangled sob. He'd been tormented by that wretched day for more than half his life.

'Mr Figge took my father to a place filled with bad spirits, he said to me. I think about it…often.'

He released my arm and I saw the white points where his fingertips had pressed. The blood returned to them but left the crescents of his nails there. 'There is a rage inside me, miss. I cannot rid myself of it.' His eyes were holding me as he said it: they demanded my understanding. 'Rage is for the young. It is painful to live this way.'

I stroked the mare's muzzle while I thought. When we resumed walking, I saw my questions had been feeding his hurt, and his hurt was a wounded dog: offered pity, it might attack the hand of kindness. Silent, I left him the option of talking. In due course he took it, mouthing some Vedic voice in his head, it seemed, as much as speaking to me.

Years passed by, he told me, and some of the lascars, especially the married ones, left the forest seeking ways to return home to Calcutta, Kowloon, the places they came from. Others married into the tribes and built families: they invited the young Srinivas to stay among them and he accepted. The forest and the coast offered logic in a life unmoored and the Walbanja were gracious—and no one had any need of Sydney, he said. Something inside me rejoiced at this idea.

We were walking now among my neighbours, people who took delight even on an ordinary day in speculation about the towering spinster's activities. The mare whinnied a little, sensing my irritation. I saw one or two in their doorways and imagined their scandalised delight at this latest development: *The tall girl, George, you know the one, walking with a Hindoo. Deep in conversation!*

I say this because it is only me listening: fuck them, and fuck their smug, shallow gossip.

Srinivas spoke on and on, eyes closed but feet somehow never stumbling. He spoke of the arrival of the settlers on the south coast, taking up the land and turning it into industry of one kind and another. There was conflict, he said, and I took him to mean that the natives did not go quietly. The lascars, who had seen occupation before, knew the cards in that hand. They got work with the settlers, clearing cedar for timber; in time, they began to hire their own cutters and millers. Srinivas discovered a particular talent for finding ways to ship the timber north to Sydney. The planks came back from Sydney as handsome vessels that collected more timber, and the lascars—*former* lascars now—worked out that they could employ shipwrights on the coast and turn the timbers to good use where they were.

They made a success of it, he said. Old differences persisted— the Indians were never invited into the drinking, the shooting parties—but a basic level of respect was shown. It raises a question, he suggested. If each of us—and by 'us' I understood him to include me—came from the old world, from Dublin and Birmingham and Leith and Massachusetts…from Calcutta, perhaps, then how much of that is left behind and how much becomes this place?

'I walked that coast until my feet broke open. I do not wish to make grandiose claims, miss, but it is likely I was the first outsider to meet the Thaua. I sailed waters that Cook himself never found. But I will always be desi here, no matter my intimacy with the land.'

I was still wary of the wild anger in this man but I found myself warming to his sense of grievance. Perhaps one must nurse a grievance of one's own to fully appreciate another's.

His story meandered and stalled as we reached the Cooper property, Juniper Hall, perched on its rise and cut from a sandstone bluff at the back, a great fig tree towering over it. I led him along the path that skirted the main residence and ended at my quarters among the other staff. I tied the mare off, brushed her down. She dropped her head and ran her mouth over my hand: when I pushed back, she snuffled and shook her mane. It was a habit now, a paying of the fare for coming to town, though I knew her to love the walk anyway. I gestured to the Hindoo man that he should enter and he hesitated. When he relented, he made a point of removing his shoes.

Inside I stirred up the morning's coals, hooked the kettle on the idleback and swung it over the new fire. I cleared the clutter from the table to find space for his cup: fabrics I'd been sewing, plates with old food adhering, the books—Lord, the books. I watched the man's eyes wander over the space, taking in the chaos, trying to assemble something from it.

'I teach,' I said to him, by way of heading off the inquiry.

'Ah,' he replied. 'Your mother is a very clever woman. Something you inherited from her, perhaps?'

I must have reacted—did I bristle?—because he seemed startled at my reaction.

'I'm sorry,' he stammered. 'Have I...?'

'*Was.* She is deceased, Mister...Srinivas. Many years ago now.'

'Oh dear me, I am sorry. So sorry.' He dropped his head and when it lifted his face had crumpled. 'I did not expect...I knew her briefly. She was very good to me.'

My hands had taken to fussing with the bottles and glasses on the bench. All of this was ill-advised. A stranger in my house, a stranger tugging at strings tied to the past. As usual, I hadn't thought this through. 'Any other painful subjects you wish to raise?'

'I can only apologise,' he sighed. Waited. Came to a decision. 'Yes, there is one.'

'It was a rhetorical question.'

'I need your father.'

'Need him?'

'I need him to do something for me.'

I shrugged, determined to give nothing away. But the bitterness stung my mouth now.

'What sort of thing?'

'I have lost a boat, miss. A boat full of valuable things—livestock, timber and, most tragically, people. A crew, passengers.'

'Where did you lose your boat?'

'Bass's Strait. She was two hundred forty-three tons, a hundred foot long. The *Howrah*.'

'That's a substantial vessel, sir. Rather careless to...*lose* such a thing.'

He spoke again in a way that was addressed more to himself than to me. It seemed a habit of his. 'Maybe I should have expected this. It was passing through those islands...Where the *Sydney Cove* was wrecked.'

I poured the tea and watched him rotate his cup to set the leaves spinning. 'The Furneaux group?'

'You know the geography, then.' He was silent a moment, picking at a fingernail.

'What do you want my father to do about this?'

'He must go and find it. In his interest, as much as mine.'

'He cannot,' I said abruptly.

I'd startled him. He gathered his thoughts with evident care. 'Is your father, then, also...deceased?'

'No, he is...alive. He is no longer in the service of the King, so I do not see how he can be of assistance to you.'

The dark eyes indicated a change of tack. 'It is not the King's concern. Would you take me to him, perhaps? I should discuss this with him directly.'

'No. I will not do that, I am sorry.'

The visitor sighed. 'These are difficult matters, young lady. Difficult things to—'

'Very difficult, no doubt. But you see I'm not so very young. And I am busy.' I waved a hand at a pile of balled wool on a side table. The fowl had taken to nesting in it. 'I have domestic standards to maintain. So let us not waste each other's time.'

He smiled reluctantly, the first time I had seen the smile. It was gentle. 'You have your mother's spirit, if I may say so. A sad and lovely thing to behold.'

'And a long walk for the beholding.' The man made no attempt to get up from the chair he occupied. He had sipped barely half an inch from the tea.

'You cannot come here and make these demands—' I stopped myself.

I thought about it, too briefly I now realise, and was swayed by the affinity I felt for the man. A form of relenting, I suppose; one I should not have indulged.

'Oh, go on then—tell me why you must involve my father, or take your leave.'

~

He told me he remembered my father as a good man, though he was angry with him for a time. My father had promised him his freedom in return for testimony against Figge and Clark, then changed his mind and had Srinivas placed under guard. Seated in my kitchen after all these years, Srinivas said he could see that my father had been trying to protect him from the malevolent Mr Figge. The Bengali spoke that name with the faintest of shudders.

I tried to busy myself about the room, tried to make distractions. This story I'd heard in pieces, in moods, the leaden frame around my childhood, and much heartache besides. Governor Hunter was long gone, recalled to London, his name now just an inscription on a limestone slab; my mother was also in the ground. This story had belonged to me and my father, no one else. And this stranger had lived it.

As I reflected on this, the tale continued and found its way to the matter of the lost vessel. Srinivas knew something had gone wrong with it because it should have returned from Hobart, empty, by June. Things go awry with commercial voyages—even I knew that. Delays, disputes. Srinivas told me he was used to obstacles. But this delay was different, he said. There was no word at all.

Eventually a letter came through the governor's office. Some items from a wrecked vessel had been found. One of those strange symmetries: Mr Munro, a self-appointed leader among the sealers of the straits, had found them on Preservation Island, the place where, all those years ago, Srinivas's voyage on the *Sydney Cove* had ended and his ordeal had begun. He talked in a long-winded way, which I did not entirely follow, about how certain types of flotsam tend to reach shore when a ship breaks up, certain other types when it beaches and items are jettisoned, and so forth. Some sink and vanish, apparently, but some do not. 'One can tell a great deal about the catastrophe by the nature, and sequence, of what reaches shore.' I felt a sick certainty that he was referring to the bodies of the dead.

His eyes were elsewhere now, apprehending the demons that afflicted him.

Munro's letter did not lay claim to the discovery of a shipwreck: only to traces that must have come from a ship or ships.

Fragments of cabin fittings and a captain's sea chest containing correspondence and the ship's papers, which Munro claimed he had not read. It seemed to me that reading the ship's papers to identify the vessel would be the first thing that anyone would do, but Srinivas appeared unconcerned.

'I do not assume that he is able to read,' he said. 'In any case, I am satisfied by the description of the chest. It is my vessel.'

And indeed if, as he said, it was an Adige chest of the kind my father once owned, it would be unique: the ones I'd seen in other homes differed in all sorts of ways. Each was an individual act of craftsmanship.

I had taken a seat at the table as he spoke, and my eyes kept drifting to the embarrassing mess I had made of my small home. But Srinivas was fixed upon his tale and took no notice of what was around him.

Munro had made clear to him that, beyond these scraps of debris, there was nothing else. He'd thoroughly searched his own shoreline and those of the islands nearby, he said, adding that he was by reputation a trustworthy soul and, in recognition of that, he had been appointed the local constable, or some such title.

Srinivas looked at me now, an air of expectation about him.

'They all must have perished, then,' I said finally, at something of a loss. 'I am sorry. But these are common risks, are they not?'

'Yes, yes, of course,' he said, with something of the manner in which I would speak to the Coopers' younger child. 'But there are aspects to this, aspects that disturb me. This was a good vessel, in capable hands. There was no talk of storms. You eliminate the common causes—the weather, incompetence, an unseaworthy boat—and then you must look more widely. An isolated society of lawless men: yes, you would consider that.

Men who live off the sea, who might not be above committing a deception, an outrage. False lights, or…'

'This is wild talk,' I replied. 'There are patrols through those islands, everyone knows it. You need only ask them to carry out a specific search.'

He responded in a way I had not expected: he waved an irritated hand at his own face and told me no one would conduct a search at the behest of a Bengali. I hadn't considered this, but I knew immediately he was right.

'I have private means,' he said then, 'and I am long accustomed to achieving private ends.'

I had diverted him, and soon enough he returned to the thread of his story, to the other aspects of it that he believed to be *nefarious*. A striking choice of word: the sea took its share of vessels and lives every year; it was blind and indiscriminate. To hear talk of deliberate malice was something new.

A handful of sealers had turned up in port, said Srinivas, making splendid men of themselves, loaded with money. One such man, an islander named Drew, strode into a Launceston rooming house looking—and here Srinivas suddenly became awkward—for the services of a good woman. I nearly laughed: from all I'd heard, no one would seek a good woman in Launceston. But the point was that the man carried a fortune in cheques and heavy coin, and had no good reason for the possession of either.

This, I told him, was circumstantial. He was undeterred. 'Circumstances are strands in a rope,' he told me: it was their combination that mattered. When I asked him for another such strand, he told me that a cooked leg of mutton had floated ashore on Preservation Island. This time I did laugh, and Srinivas conceded a smile. 'They don't tend to sail the seven seas, mutton roasts.'

But his face quickly turned serious again, and he talked of rumours he'd heard: the use of lights to lure ships to their destruction. It had been put directly to him—he would not say where—that the crew and passengers had been murdered, the vessel plundered.

'The islands are wild places,' he said finally. 'A closed society. I cannot rely on anecdotes alone, because they tend to the outlandish.'

He meant no irony by this, I firmly believe.

~

When he was done, I drank my own tea in a gulp and set the cup down, said nothing in response.

'You remain unwilling to take me to your father?'

'He lives out of town.'

'Perhaps the next time he comes to town, then?'

'He doesn't—I take him everything he needs.'

'You're not making this especially easy.'

'I see no reason to. And it is in my nature to be uncooperative.'

'Yes. I see. Can I ask for your assurance that you will tell him about me? I can provide a vessel, provisions, everything. He will be well paid for his trouble.' His voice was pleading now. 'I feel sure he will want to help.'

'I will speak to him,' I said, finally. 'You have my word. I do not expect he will be able to help you.'

MY FATHER IN THE LEAF LITTER

I no longer make the long journey to my father's house.

I remember doing it that day because it was one of the last times: out along the ridgeline that tracked south-west into the open country beyond town, and then into the enfolding forest. I undertook it often enough back then, the hours of it, the mare and me alone in the trees. This time it was a Sunday in late November, and I went bearing a dozen eggs, a brace of dull-eyed fish and the request from Srinivas for an appointment.

The way out to my father's house began in the early morning as a road, but for most of its length was barely a cart-track. In its lust for expansion, the settlement was very quick to tell you what a road was, and the grandees were very quick to attach their names. This track had no name: it was an informality, an idea shared by others who had retreated to the hills. No signposts, no nameplates on the houses.

I was still unnerved by my encounter with the old Bengali.

The ferocity of his speech, the idea that emotional wounds could remain as bright and fierce over a lifetime as they were the day they were inflicted. I knew already that the wisest thing I could do was to keep myself and my father out of the reach of this drowning man, lest he pull us both under.

I was nervous now, in fact, twitching and straining to listen to every sound the bush made. When I stopped to eat, I crouched with my back to the trunk of a tree, peering out and even behind it. This was not my normal state. I climbed back on the mare with a look over my shoulder. The man's fixation was contagious, and now it was me with the wild eyes.

The mare threw her head and shied once or twice when we were deep in the hills. The contagion had afflicted her, too.

She knew the bend in the trail where the trees opened to frame a view over the valley, dull greens turning blue in the warm air. She knew to stop at the gateposts my father had cut from standing eucalypts. It was afternoon by now, his secret place hidden by the forest and the hours of travel. I tied her off by the gate that had failed in the winter and now hung askew from its post-hinges. Looping the reins over the timber was a formality. She knew to wait there.

The house was bark over a frame, a shingle roof. It was nothing to admire. Square, modest, at one with the surrounding trees because it came from them. Four apple trees, a pear, a persimmon and a fig, planted long ago in a time of industry.

The dog burst into frantic yelping before I'd passed through the gate and did not let up. She knew me well, yet she maintained this insistence on warning him of my approach. I had never understood why he needed a dog so large—or so vocal.

Soon enough my father would yell at it and the poor animal would stop. I had nearly reached the verandah when I realised he had not. Normally by this point in my approach he'd have sworn at her or thrown a tin, then stumped out to greet me. I studied her, lowered my body to a crouch. She had never rushed me, but the curl of her snarling lip suggested she would not allow me passage without word from her master. I looked up. No smoke from the chimney.

'Father?'

The dog cocked her ear at my inflection, as if she wondered the same thing I did. She was uneasy, and I could see now that she was chained. I felt sure the chain was short enough that I could pass her by and reach the doorway. Eyes on mine, she anticipated me. A bowl was upturned just beyond her bed of old blankets. She had defecated on the boards of the verandah, within feet of her bed. Her nose was dry: she was thirsty.

And now I saw that she was leaping in distress, not hostility. The chain jerked and its links rang. At the top of her rush the dog reached a paw in my direction and the chain yanked her back. She made a sound of pain as her shoulder struck the boards. I came forward slowly and stroked her. She whimpered.

The door had no lock and wasn't latched. I knocked and called once more and felt afraid again. I was four hours from town, enclosed in the forest. The dog's tormented state had worked some ill on me and the shadows all insinuated. I pushed the door and rushed in, wanting to confront whatever trouble it was that had taken root here.

He was on the floor, beside a fallen chair and half beneath the table. I took it all in as best I could, too much of it at first. A candle had burnt down to the surface of the mantel and charred it, though the fireplace below was cold and unused. And the filth—the indescribable squalor of the place—it took my breath away, the stench and the shock. My father had been living like this, again. I should have known, should have been here; I had allowed my own life to intervene. Not for long, but long enough for this to happen.

I kicked through a platoon of bottles, some standing, some fallen, to an outstretched hand. I felt his cheek: warm under the sharkskin of whiskers. In a surge of fright, I slapped him—an eye opened but saw nothing. A noise from his parched mouth, no more, but it denoted life.

I slid my fingers through the lank hair at the back of his head and tried to lift it. Stickiness: a wound between my fingers, blood congealed on the floorboards. The hair was matted by it, the collar of his old shirt stained brown. New horrors announced themselves: the powerful vapours of spilt booze and something worse. He had soiled himself, then. His trousers, normally secured by a length of cord that strung suspended between the points of his hips, were bunched around the tops of his thighs.

I kept a vision of this man in my mind, one that carried me through the glades of his decay. His dark hair swept back and oiled, his uniform, the firm jaw, the confident smile that creased his eyes. His hands that bore authority and tenderness on sculpted fingers. This was before his great losses, before he turned mad and volatile and unpredictable. Here now were those fine fingers, curled in the grime, stained by tobacco, scarred and blunted by life.

I hauled him up and onto a chair, a deep one with arms so he wouldn't fall. I filled a bucket at the barrel under his eaves, cleared the hearth of its refuse and lit a fire. He dawned slowly, murmured something. I found bedding, clothing, unused and tolerably clean. I tore the clothes from his body and the sheets from the bed and threw them in the fire. It roared and consumed the vile things. Once the water was heated I ran a cloth, warm and wet, over his sickened body and he stirred a little but still could not speak.

The sins and insults ran off him with the clouded water. The wound in the back of his head was a split—most likely made when his head struck the floor—its edges swollen, the bruise already dark and proud. He had done it some days ago, then. I could do nothing with it, only make sure it was clean and work the crusts of old blood out of his hair.

When the blood was gone, I took the scissors from the shelf in the wash-house, elegant ones with courting swans or herons moulded into the handles, an artefact from his life before. Blunt now, but sufficient. I snipped his hair until it was neat again. As I concentrated on his forehead, his eyes wandered out past me, somewhere in the indeterminate distance, pupils scrolling left and right to follow sounds.

Still he did not speak. I worked the scissors around the patches where the skin of his scalp was rippled and stretched taut. The places where it was melted. I knew them all. The hair grew sparsely over these places. Back when he cared, he would comb it over them. He winced once or twice when the blades caught in the knots. A good sign, I thought.

There was no razor to shave his bestubbled chin but I used a corner of the cloth to get the muck out of his ears. The dog began to make sounds again and I filled a bowl with water for her, took a knife, sliced open one of the fish and placed it within her reach. She leapt upon it and devoured it without regard for the bones.

I dressed him in clean clothes and found the pit in the clearing behind the house he'd been using for his waste: I threw in the bottles, the crates that held them, the gristle of old meals and the broken and filthy castoffs that littered the place.

The dog was barking again. I did not remember her being so needy.

He was clean now; the place was neat. I laughed to think it was neater than mine. Evening was coming down outside, a raucous crowd of birds and the soft padding of wallabies. I cooked the rest of the fishes, gave another to the dog and served plates for my father and me. But when I went to the armchair, I found he had fallen asleep. I took his cheeks in my palms and kissed his forehead, then heaved him out of the chair and onto the hessian of his cot.

And then I walked outside and threw every single bottle of his bloody rum at a tree.

~

It was while I was doing so that the dog started up again: urgently this time. I gave the last bottle fair aim and threw it so it tumbled forward in flight. It hit the trunk of the big gum dead centre and glass shattered brilliant in the late forest light.

I came around the side of the house, wanting to know what troubled the dog but not wanting a confrontation with my father over the bottles. It took me some time to pick my way through his overgrown garden, the mess on the ground that made the footing unsure. And it took me another moment to understand what I was seeing when I came to the end of the verandah: the back and shoulders of a man entering the house, my father with his hand on the doorjamb, waving an obliging hand to grant him entry. He had been asleep when I left him in there: maybe the man's knocking had woken him.

I stepped up and into the doorway, and there in the room was Srinivas. He looked at me strangely: part apology, part defiance.

'How did you get here?' I asked him.

'I followed you.'

'You followed me for four hours?'

He shrugged. 'It was not difficult.'

'Who do you think you are? You can't just—'

'There is no law against following someone, miss. It was very important that I see your father, and you were unwilling to take me to him, so I...'

Again that unworldly look in his eye, the infuriating combination of innocence and fixation. And more than that. In his right hand he held a bottle.

'Tell him to go, Father,' I said.

My father tipped his head in the direction of my voice. 'I'll do no such thing, Eliza. That would be the height of rudeness.'

'*Rudeness?* The man followed me out here!'

He was unmoved.

'I thought you were supposed to be a recluse! You live so far outside society that I have to spend my days travelling out here, and now this person comes barging into your home and you appear perfectly at ease!'

My father made a soothing noise and patted the air with his hand. 'Nobody came barging, dear. Why don't you, why don't you come in Mister, ah, Srinivas, and let's hear what you have to say.' He heard the thud of the proffered bottle on the table, and stepped backwards to the shelves I'd curtained for him with patterned cloth. His hands following a long-established domestic map, he drew out two heavy glasses he'd likely pilfered from an inn.

These sounds, the punctuation of so many conversations I'd wanted to escape. The trickling of the fluid, the way it stopped the room momentarily, its music speaking differing intimacies to any who heard. His hands sliding, mapping from bottle to glasses. Bottle down, glasses raised. This bloody ritual. I found a little-used lamp and attended to the wick, a task for my hands in the deepening gloom.

'How many years has it been, lad?'

Lad? Had they both taken leave of their senses?

'Thirty-three.' Srinivas was looking directly at my father. He was confused, I could see. My father was so adept at moving around his own small house that it was not immediately apparent to the Bengali that he was, in fact, completely blind.

'Thirty-three, thirty-three.' His hand found the glass and he threw back the rum, exhaled loudly and pushed the glass in the Bengali's direction again. 'Goodness me.'

'What happened to you, sir?' asked Srinivas.

'Oh, nothing *happened*. My affliction is entirely of my own making. I am blind, sir: as my daughter here is fond of saying, possessed of four senses and no sense. They tell me it was the drinking, but I've never been convinced.' He tipped the glassful down his throat again. 'Forgive me doing this...' He leaned forward out of his chair, following the sound of the Bengali's breathing, I suppose, and placed his hands on the man's face, tracing the contours with his fingertips, a look of faraway recognition dawning over his features.

'Ah, yes. Yes...it is you, yes.' His brows came down, as a sighted man might focus, and the strangest expression lit his face: a fervour, a ferocity I'd never seen before.

It suddenly frightened me how little I knew him. Every child, surely, expects that their father's world is built around them; that there could be no wilds unexplored because every-thing—everything—is devotion. But this was a man in primal state, utterly apart from me.

'He is back then? Figge?'

The Bengali nodded vigorously. 'I believe so. I do.'

My father sighed. 'Well, this day was always going to come, wasn't it.' He tipped back in his chair. 'So where is he?'

'I don't know.'

'Of course! Of course you don't know.' He pointed his head vaguely my way. 'He doesn't know, dear.'

'He is not even Figge anymore. I have been after him, all these years. Ports, towns, vessels of all descriptions. I have been a day late in places he has been, met the unfortunate victims of one outrage or another that he has committed. All of the horrors, sir. Depraved, pitiless—'

'There is no shortage of depravity about the place,' I interrupted. 'Can you really ascribe it all to this man?'

He thought about this for a moment. 'They all looked to be done for my attention, you see. A man who worked for me in the mill, his tongue cut out. Another, the stevedore, two years later. Blinded by means of a spoon, assailant fled into the night. A boy, a mere boy I had taken on: a stranger comes and offers him work. He returns, fingers crushed beyond repair and the stranger is gone. There were others, of course, that he did not allow to survive.'

'He would be old now. Same age as me.'

Srinivas lowered his eyes respectfully. 'He is not infirm. *I have missed him by only hours*, you understand. I felt his warmth in a chair he vacated at an inn. He eludes me easily, lieutenant, and I have come to understand why.'

They had launched into this exchange, this violent intimacy, without a word of the preamble Srinivas had given to me about his intervening years, without my father explaining anything about his descent from society, beyond the merest indication that liquor had blinded him. They were brothers, made siblings by their hatred and obsession over the absent man.

My father's face was fixed in grim confidence. 'It is not you, is it?' he said.

I did not follow his meaning.

'No,' said the Bengali. 'It is you.'

'You seek him, he seeks me. Ha! I have hidden myself well. More rum, if you please.'

I could hear it in his voice, the false note. The perversity of a man who would sooner have something to rail at than face the dreadful yawning silence of his own irrelevance. Were they just two wronged men at a table, the obsession of each feeding the other? Or had the Bengali led him skilfully to the crux of all that troubled him, and a man he could blame it all upon?

Srinivas poured again. He had not drunk any himself, but he was no less intoxicated.

'Why are you hiding like this?'

'Oh, hmm, shame, of course. Fallen a great distance in the eyes of the world. And...and not just about me, you understand.' He lifted his chin in my direction. 'I cannot have him gain access to, to others.'

The Bengali made a small gesture of resignation, a flipped hand. 'So you hide from him—but also you *seek* him, do you not? It matters not in the long run, you know. The hiding, the being seen. He has attached himself to your family.' My father was nodding along. 'What reason, who knows? But he is your curse, and he is not going to desist. There will come a day when he will stop bedevilling me, and it will be the day he finds you.'

'What are you both talking about?' I begged, but they ignored me.

'Time you went and found him,' the Bengali murmured, 'do you not think?'

'So where? Where do—'

'—provocations for years now. Gestures, harassments. My vessel—'

'What's that wha's thah wha—'

'—the *Howrah*. In the islands, Furneaux group, near Preservation. This wreck, lieutenant, these taunts escalated now to such a degree: the matter must be brought to a head.'

'And I...?'

'End it!' Srinivas pointed dramatically at my father, who of course could not see the gesture.

'Yes, I—'

'I will provide you with a vessel and master, all the necessary papers. You search the islands, interrogate the sealers, them at first, you understand lieutenant, and your inquiries will draw him to you. He cannot help but reveal himself!' The Bengali was leaning forward in his chair now, once again insensible to the reality of my father's blindness.

'And you...?'

'I cannot, I cannot.' The Bengali lowered his voice. 'This is the thing I have learnt about his games: if I appear, he vanishes. If I am there, he will stay in the shadows. It is you he seeks.'

'Of course.'

Mad or not, I thought to myself, *he is leading you like a sideshow gibbon.*

I saw an expression on my father's face then. It was unfamiliar, but I knew it to be elation. In the long, sad decline of his middle age, the Bengali offered him a purpose—one that dovetailed so exquisitely with his old rage and longing. The entire idea was abhorrent to me, but I had never seen him so happy.

I watched the Bengali, watching him. *And you*, I thought. *What is it that's burning in you?*

~

The following morning was Monday: I was due at the Coopers' residence to teach the children, but my absence would please them no end. Life had waited before for such moments with my father. It would have to wait again.

He was well enough by then to make bread beside me, but refused my entreaties to visit a doctor, as I had known he would. I avoided any mention of the bottles I'd destroyed: he would assume I had cleared them away, and I suppose the vaporous waft of spirits from the pile outside smelt no different to him than his house always did.

He'd had his fill from Srinivas, who'd left in darkness after refusing my father's entreaties to join us for an evening meal. I had made no such offer: I wanted to see the back of the man; I wanted the opportunity to talk to my father alone, ask him what on earth he was thinking. But he had gorged himself with lethal efficiency on the visitor's rum and was bereft of all sense.

There was no point in attempting conversation. I spent the evening as I had many others: waiting until he fell asleep in a chair, then heaving him onto his cot and arranging his head so he would not choke himself in his stupor.

Now his fingers found the dough and kneaded while I talked to him. He was quiet, mostly. I tried to work back to how I'd found him, before the Bengali turned up. I wanted to understand how he had ended up senseless on his floor with a starving dog and a cracked head but, as always, he told me I had misread the situation and it was nowhere near so dire. I waited after that, chose my moment.

'Are we going to talk about this…ridiculous idea?'

'Oh, yes,' he grunted as he worked the dough. He spread his hands on the floured table. 'We may discuss it, but there is no question about the matter. I must go.'

I looked at him in disbelief: he looked near the rafters somewhere.

'Papa, your poor head misleads you. This is work for a government cutter. You investigated a shipwreck once, many years ago, and it did not end well. It would be idiocy to dabble in this.'

He raised an eyebrow. 'Idiocy?' His voice lost its warmth. 'Is that how you address your father?'

I took his hands—they were tacky with dough. 'You are old now. You have suffered enough: you haven't been on a ship for many years…do I need to go on?'

'…and tell me a blind man is no use to anyone? Is that it?'

I said nothing.

'What Srinivas wants is beyond small matters like sight.' He waved an irritable hand. 'The having of eyes or ears or even clear wits is of no importance. Surely you can see what the lascar is trying to do, Eliza. He is giving me an opportunity. The taking of that ship of his? It can be the work of one man only, and he is a man who will easily evade a government cutter, if that is what he wants to do.'

'Then why doesn't Srinivas go and do it, if he's so sure it's this man behind it all?'

'You heard him.' My father had taken on a tone one would use with a recalcitrant child. 'He's been trying for years. Figge toys with him, evades him with ease, because it is not the lascar that he's seeking. He will reveal himself to me. Only to me.'

I felt a weariness come over me. My father was hopelessly fixated upon a man who had wronged him thirty-three years ago. He would be as old as my father now and quite likely just as enfeebled.

'Let me try to see it your way, Father. This evil man wants to get at you, for some reason that relates to the distant past. He can't find you, because you're out here. So he finds the Bengali and taunts him into doing the finding for him. The Bengali comes out here, because apparently *he* can find you without undue difficulty, and lo and behold, you've both played straight into the hands of this man. Surely the wise thing to do would be to send the Bengali away empty-handed, and thus bring the man's scheme to naught.'

'Hmm. He would not be dissuaded so easily as that.'

'How marvellous to have your very own nemesis.'

He extended his hand. It wavered in the air for a moment, then found mine and held it tight. 'Him that lures me, me that lures him. Ambush for an ambush. I will go, without question. Srinivas has given me the chance to correct something I should have put right many years ago.'

'Good *lord*! You cannot *see*—'

'It is immaterial. Immaterial. Just as he could slaughter a garrison, so he can be undone by a blind man: that is the nature of the thing. You cannot stop me, and you know it. Let this matter proceed. Perhaps it will result in some peace for all of us.'

It would be futile to assure him I suffered no lack of peace, and would quite welcome a breach of it; the argument continued for an hour or more. My reasoning, his stubborn insistence. How can you argue rationally with someone who refuses to admit the obvious? And what was his *peace for all of us*? I look back now and I wonder.

As the sun climbed into the middle of the day, he grew restless and I knew what would come next. With practised sweeps of his arms he explored the table, then the floor around him, feeling for bottles. His face darkened as realisation dawned. He stood, edged towards the wall, searching for the crates.

He faced me and the dead eyes managed to glare. 'The rum. What have you done with it?'

I held my breath.

'Where is the rum?'

'I took it away.'

'Where?'

'Gone, Father. I am trying to help you.'

He bellowed—pain or denial—and swung a fist at where the measurement of his other hand told him the wall was. The lining boards buckled but did not give. He cursed me for a damned whore and a horrible bitch and announced that my ongoing spinsterhood reflected the verdict of all of male humanity, that I was pious and barren and unworthy of the family name. He roared that my mother would never have dreamed of taking such liberties as I, ungrateful serpent, had taken. And through all of these insults I stood and cried and repeated that I loved him until he found a mug and sent it tumbling through the air to where my voice had told him my head was. And it missed by so very little that I fled his dismal shack, more in grief than fright.

The dog growled irritably as I crossed the verandah, my charity forgotten.

~

Srinivas reappeared at my residence early the following morning, waiting on the doorstep without a sound, so that when I rushed out to fetch kindling I nearly ran into him. The Coopers had no objection to me receiving visitors in my quarters, but no one ever came; thus my surprise. I must have muttered some reproach: *You might have knocked*, or something similar.

'But Miss Grayling,' he replied, 'I was not entering.'

'Fine,' I hissed. 'Come in, then.'

He inclined his head. 'If it is not too much trouble.' He was wearing a suit, and he held a package in his hands, bound with string.

'I am very pleased to have seen your father,' he ventured, as I indicated a seat. He sat himself down and placed the package on the table.

'I would vastly prefer that you hadn't, *sir*. And what right do you have to follow me all those miles? You're fortunate I wasn't armed.'

His hand rested unconsciously on the place where I'd laid into his belly. 'He will want to go,' he said, speaking, in that way of his, almost to himself.

I couldn't contain my frustration with the man any longer. 'He is blind. *Blind*. He cannot do any such thing.'

'That was an unexpected discovery, I must say.'

'Not if you've seen him drink.' I tried to break a stick to add to the kindling and the thing wouldn't yield, so I stood it against the bricks of the hearth and kicked at it, far too hard. The snapped half flew past my face. Over at the table, some internal adjustment was occurring. Srinivas peered at his fingers, curled and uncurled them. Then he looked up, directly into my eyes, in a way he hadn't done until then.

'You must go with him.'

'Oh, for God's sake.'

'You must, yes. It must be this way, it seems.' He nodded in fervent agreement with himself.

'I'm a tutor, Mister Srinivas. My work is cajoling the God-damned Cooper children into reciting their times tables. I'm not in the business of retrieving stray boats.' As an afterthought I added, 'And nor is my father.'

An eyebrow at my language, but his dark eyes remained calm. 'I am sure you're aware by now, miss, that the boat is only a part of this and not the entirety.' He pushed the package across the table to the corner nearest to me. I remained standing, poking at the kindling in its little pile.

'What's this?'

'The passenger manifest. Please...' He gestured for me to open it, and to my eternal regret I did.

Papers: a list, surname then given name. They descended alphabetically to *Molliner*, where the surname column became ditto and the given names read *Albert, Florence, Catherine, Jane, Sarah, Violet* and *Frederick*.

'It may help you with your—'

'Good Lord. An entire family.'

'Yes.' He lowered his eyes. 'Fine people. They had bought passage to Hobart. Albert had taken up land beyond Richmond, out in the midlands. Their possessions were to follow them— they remain in crates in a shed on my wharf.' He sighed. 'One feels a certain...obligation when a man entrusts his family to one's vessel and it founders.'

I read on down the list. Patient cursive, compiled out of bureaucratic routine, the writer having no way of knowing the weight of the words when these names became a list of the missing. Thirty souls, nearly half of them women.

I tossed the sheaf of documents onto the table.

'There is the...human tragedy of what has happened,'

Srinivas continued. 'But the matter has also caused considerable difficulties for the extended Molliner family. The chief justice has refused to formally confirm the deaths, so there is estate money that cannot be released. He has said that he requires further information to be obtained from the islands before he will attest.'

Options closing off. Voices inside me clamouring in one direction only. This man had a gift for subtle pressure.

'I am not asking you to endanger yourself, or your father. I am asking you to go and find out what happened. There will be other ways to apply force, if that becomes necessary.'

'I see it now. You believe that my father's presence in the islands will flush out the evildoer, and you are certain the evildoer is this Mister Figge, whoever *he* is. That is why it matters not that my father is blind. You are preying upon his deluded need for vengeance, with no heed at all for his safety. You have taken account of all these things.'

I do not know if I expected him to rush to a denial, but there was none. 'Look at what this man has done,' he said simply.

I followed his pointing finger to the manifest. 'There was a *shipwreck*,' I hissed. 'It was the work of nature.'

'I do not believe that, miss. And nor does your father.'

He stood, and took a long look at the documents. He did not move to pick them up.

'Perhaps I will return tomorrow.'

THE MOONBIRD

I would tell you, I would list for you the negotiations that followed. But they were arduous, and fated to end only one way.

It should have been clear. Srinivas was proposing a voyage that was futile and dangerous. There was no proof that this man from long ago was responsible for the fate of the *Howrah*. Even if that feverish notion proved accurate, there was no logical way in which my helpless father was going to bring him to account. Sending me with him was no further use, and would only endanger me as well.

But what purpose would be served by my setting it all out? You need only know that Srinivas, in concert with my obstinate father, wore me down. In the days that followed the Bengali's visit with the documents, the signs of their determination were everywhere.

A quartermaster from the wharves, a grave-looking Methodist, approached me at the Coopers' house, held his hat in his hands and declined to enter. He asked why my father, who was known to be sightless, might be seeking provisions for a voyage to Bass's Strait. He did not need to specify what was meant by 'provisions'—Srinivas had already made clear that he would victual the voyage at his own expense. My father was making an early bid to ensure that any intended vessel was groaning with rum.

A week later, Beckwith—the harbourmaster himself—relayed a message that my vessel was ready, and that I may wish to inspect it. *My vessel.* I had said nothing, been told nothing—much less signed anything.

Finally my resistance was at an end. I could not stand by and let my father sail off without me, and he had made clear that he would do exactly that if I did not join him. These are the times one takes stock. Ten years beyond a marriageable age, I had become something of a curiosity in the town. For those of recent acquaintance, those with memories that didn't reach back to the fire, I was an unappealing prospect: too tall to make a man look impressive, too fierce to make polite company. I was a vindictive harpy with an acid tongue who'd quite probably driven her poor father to drink. There was no prospect of change, either in me or in the attitudes of others towards me. If my life was to open itself to any change, any renewal, it would have to happen elsewhere. And an instinct deep inside me—something that felt like an itch—wanted to know what had befallen those children.

So I went, one spring Tuesday afternoon, to the wharves. Beckwith showed no surprise at my arrival. Behind the whiskers and the sharp eyes, I detected the echoes of conversations he had had with my father.

'Was hoping you'd come,' he told me. 'Owner's had her tied up here waiting for you. She's over here.'

He walked me along the timbers, under the swaying shadows of the trees that clung to the rock wall. The slime beneath us gave a metal scent to the air and the slick water made slopping sounds in the dark corners where the piles met the shore. Smacks and light brigs stood waiting; a clipper rested at anchor further out. There were more birds in the land behind us than over the water; given the air as a choice they still opted for the trees.

'Terrible business,' Beckwith said, out of nowhere.

'What?' The birds, scrawing at the air, made his words faint.

'About the *Howrah*. She left from here. Just over there, in fact.' He pointed. 'Lovely vessel.'

'All those people. Children.'

He nodded soberly. 'Odd how they prepared her, though. She took on the passengers but no one ordered any ballast. Must have ballast through the straits, you understand, especially if you're carrying people. Then they had the soldiers down here. Closed the wharf for a whole day. Lord knows what they were up to. Wouldn't tell me a thing. Here,' he said. 'This one's yours.'

My acquaintance with boats was cursory at best: that of a half-observant resident of a harbour town, glancing at the craft that bear news and people and commerce. I don't know what I had expected, but I must have assumed it would be something other than the boat he showed me now.

She was short, stout and sleepy-looking, and yet the very moment I saw her I felt a deep affection I cannot explain. She was the tired hound that wants to sleep on your feet: idle yet watchful. Able to tell the shadows of easy repose from those that should be barked at.

She looked nothing like her neighbours. She was carvel-built in heavy, dark timbers. Two short, thick masts; strange diagonal rigging. The hull was heavy, reassuringly so, rounding through a fat waist to a stern that was almost a teacup. The mainmast passed through a low cabin, while at the stern there was a modest quarterdeck.

I have no regard for the idea that it is possible to love an inanimate object. I will choose instead to say that this modest boat, perhaps eighty feet of her, was animate. And she was entangled, right alongside me, in a venture that made no sense. I felt she was on my side.

Beckwith was watching me. 'Shallow draft for island work,' he said. 'Gaff rigged. Double skipper's cabin aft, a front cabin— might be yours, I expect'—his eyes took in my height—'the bed's a little longer in there. Er, four singles amidships. There's a hold…I don't know if that's relevant to your needs…'

'It's…unusual,' I breathed. 'Not like the other ones.'

'She's a Danish schooner. Don't know how the owner came to be in possession of her. Sometimes they're confiscations, cheap sales. But those timbers, you take a drill or a saw to them, they give off a most glorious aroma, miss. Spruce, pine, I don't know.' The recollection of the smell transformed his leathery face.

A man who had been a boy, a manservant from an Indian river port, who'd lost a vessel and who also kept this beautiful one, so deeply European, here in a harbour that the rest of the world considered the farthest edge of the ocean. The Bengali was a knot in strange threads.

'Do you wish to look her over, madam?'

I did want to, desperately. But some voice inside told me to wait. 'What is her name?' I asked, as casually as I could manage.

'The *Moonbird*.'

'Lovely. Very suitable. I only sail on vessels with pretty names, you understand.'

He smiled and agreed, and I was turning to walk back

towards Beckwith's shed when I saw that a man was approaching us along the wharf. He was tall. Not young, but there was a vigour in his stride that projected confidence. Elegantly suited but practically shod, as his footfalls drew an echoing *clock* from the timbers.

He was lost in his own thoughts, or perhaps short-sighted: he only noticed the harbourmaster and me once he had drawn close enough for me to study his face. A strong face, half-smiling now under hair that remained thick but was more grey than brown, precisely cut. No whiskers, a clean, square jaw and lines that suggested the smile was a habit. My impression was that this man was more physical, his limbs more strung to a frame, than the bookish cut of his suit projected. Not handsome at all. His face seemed bent, somehow—whether by birth or accident I couldn't tell. Looking back, it is possible that this impression, this sense of an animal's body disguised, lodged itself deeply in me in that first instant.

Once he saw us, he raised a hand in greeting as if we were old friends. He carried a polished timber box under his other arm, with a brass handle and brass inlays along its edges.

He stopped when he reached us, placed the box on the ground and bowed before me, then shook Beckwith's hand. In a deep voice—an educated voice—he said that it was he who had booked the berth being advertised on the vessel bound for Bass's Strait. His name, he said, was Dr Gideon. 'Doctor Henry Fisk Gideon.' He explained that the box contained a microscope, that he was a doctor of medicine in private practice with a specialty in the teeth, and an amateur naturalist: that he wished to study and catalogue the creatures of the sea and its inshore littorals. He said all of these things in the easiest of tones, with the fluid warmth of a salesman.

Beckwith introduced me and explained that I too was to be a passenger, a private guest of the owner. The doctor seemed suitably impressed: he shook my hand, and for once a man's eyes looked down into mine, rather than up. Then the harbourmaster suggested we go below together and inspect the vessel, given that the doctor and I would be travelling companions.

So it was that I set foot on the *Moonbird* for the very first time.

Across the smooth deck that softly radiated the sun's warmth, through a hatch and down a short set of steps we entered the galley. I bumped my head on the low sill, as I would do almost daily in the coming weeks. The doctor saw my clumsiness and wove gracefully under with a smile.

'You could've warned me,' I muttered, but the smile did not falter.

The galley was small, freshly painted and functional, everything in its place. Every edge rounded, every hinge and screw-head recessed. No object sat on an open surface: each shelf was protected by a timber strip that would hold its contents in a swell. A tiny coal-burning stove occupied one corner with a vent to the outside air, the scorching of past meals carefully scrubbed away from the bulkhead behind.

A table hinged out from the wall and the harbourmaster lowered it and secured a retractable leg beneath it. Gesturing for us to sit, he began opening and closing a series of small overhead cupboards until, with a little satisfied *ah!* he produced a bottle of brandy and three heavy earthenware cups. I tried briefly to demur: I was an unmarried woman below decks with two men I barely knew. But the doctor would have none of it: with a broad smile he placed a hand over mine on the table and urged me to take a drink, since we would shortly be shipmates. The liberty of that warm hand was a shock.

'You must prepare your body for the rigours of life at sea,' he smiled.

'And must I leave common sense on the wharf?' I raised an eyebrow. A reflex of mine, to be cynical.

He was polite and amiable, and asked me about my family and my work. I told him that my father had been a lieutenant in the navy and had worked for Governor Hunter, but had retired some years ago to live in the bush. I could see in his eyes that he was doing the arithmetic: my father would be too young to have done such a thing voluntarily, to have relinquished such a position. But he made no comment.

Nor did he interrupt when I told him my mother had died when I was a child. It was the expression I always used: *she died when I was very young.* It conveyed the sense that I barely knew her, though I believed I knew her by touch and smell and soft words, and deep down in the well of my unseen soul, down in that darkness, I compared myself and my years to her ages and felt different kinds of pain every single day for her absence. These were the things I was accustomed to not saying.

The doctor was listening carefully, and I did not intend to give him any insight into the lives we were living, my father and I. So I threaded the tale away from sorrowful things and towards the Cooper children. Precocious but endearing, a girl and a boy. Their parents were indifferent, concerned only to see that progress was being made, that their little heirs were being equipped one day to return to Edinburgh society and make pretty witticisms in Greek. This glacial disdain of theirs for their children was another thing I never raised in polite conversation.

I could hear gulls outside. Beckwith smiled agreeably. He was a man adept at listening without taking up the conversation, and I'd momentarily forgotten about him. The cabin's sunlit interior put me at ease.

The doctor glanced at Beckwith, then back to me. 'And why are you coming along on this little voyage?' he asked me, smiling with the far corner of his mouth.

'My father and I have been asked to investigate the loss of a vessel in the Furneaux Islands,' I said, seeing no reason not to be direct about the matter. I explained to him that we had been visited by the vessel's owner and entrusted to act on his behalf. The mission felt important and worthy as I heard myself describe it.

'Such a notorious place,' he replied, fascinated; and he asked me the very questions that had occurred to me when Srinivas first outlaid his request. To my surprise, I found myself providing versions of the same justifications I had scoffed at only days before. No, there was no news of survivors, only flotsam. Yes, it was possible that there had been a sinister cause for the wreck. Did we have a notion as to who was behind the crime? No theory that was solid enough to advance at this stage. Again, I thrilled at being apprised of such serious matters, of answering the questions of the uninformed. The government cutter was inadequate to the task, I told them; besides, it would be instantly detected by the perpetrators—being flagged and loaded with soldiers—where a small private vessel would not. The two of them took all of this in with small mutterings of concern, but they did not offer any opinions.

In an effort to steer the conversation away from myself I asked the doctor about his circumstances.

'Oh, I am like all the others,' he laughed gently. 'A speculator, I suppose. I came from London two years ago, to take up a small grant. *Very* small,' he laughed again. 'Running away from sadness, a betrothal that was not all it promised to be.' His face fell: he did not want to go into details, despite Beckwith's urgings, because it would do no good now, and he had no wish to speak ill of his former fiancée. I thought that a fair position; not that I felt the need to say so.

Within a short period, he had established himself as a practitioner in Sydney. He had just published a book, the first of its kind, he believed, about the dietary benefits of fishes and seaweeds. It was the invertebrates that really fascinated him, he said. He wanted to visit the islands in Bass's Strait to collect specimens and to try eating any creatures he could find, measuring the state of his own health as he did so. The Plinian Society and the Dublin Herbarium had been notified of his work, he said, and were eagerly awaiting his specimens.

As he spoke with such enthusiasm, I studied his hands. They darted about then rested briefly on the table: strong, as I'd first noticed, the backs of them spotted slightly, rivered with veins and evenly tanned by the sun.

'You do your own fieldwork, Doctor Gideon?' I inquired, and he must have traced my line of reasoning. He answered with a smile, 'Yes, I do. I like very much to walk on the coast.'

He had been to Hobart before, had lived there briefly while he assessed which of the two towns might afford him the better opportunity to practise and study. The cutter that took him across had declined his requests to see the notorious Furneaux Islands, and had sailed through, leaving his curiosity unquenched.

As an amateur naturalist, I thought, this man was probably a pedlar of nonsense dressed up as science. But he was no fool. He had refrained from asking me about matrimony, an obvious inquiry of a woman who seeks to put to sea without any mention of a husband. It seemed reasonable to assume, therefore, that he might harbour designs upon me. I would need to watch him carefully.

But for any of the difficulties that could arise—with my father, with the sea, with the sealers or with the brutish man who might be behind the *Howrah*'s wrecking—this doctor could be an ally. Which reminded me to ask.

'Doctor Gideon, what do you make of the sealers? Would we be at risk from them?'

Before he could reply, Beckwith interrupted.

'Perhaps you read the papers, my dear? The island communities are as good as lawless. You would be well advised to conduct your investigations from the sea and never set foot upon the land. I can have this vessel fitted with one or two small cannon, lest they approach and you feel the need to loose a warning shot.'

The doctor listened to this calmly. He gestured towards the harbourmaster: agreeable in the very act of disagreeing.

'I am sure we can apply our discernment, evaluate the residents as we find them. As you say, madam—'

'*Miss*,' I corrected him. *Damn it. Slightly too fast.*

'Miss. The task is to identify what happened and who were the perpetrators, not to bring them in. Equally, the islanders are known for their refusal to abide external authority. I do feel we should take measures to protect ourselves. You might wish to consult with the vessel's owner, this Mister Sini—'

'Srinivas. Srin-i-vas.'

He practised the word silently, smiled again.

'—Mister Srinivas, about the availability of some strong hands to work the decks. They may double in defence of us if the need arises.'

There was an arrogance about this doctor, or perhaps merely a sense of assurance. I could see that it might become tiresome. But in a welcome contrast with the wild theories of recent days, here was a man who saw clear past the small hysterias. Here was a cool analyst, a level head: someone, perhaps, I could trust.

EMBARKATION

I took my leave of my employers, and told them I would be three weeks or so. I had worked without stint for them, occupied a role in their children's lives that was somewhere between tutor, governess and maid. They, and by 'they' I mean the wife, would have to reacquaint themselves with all of these roles. I saw no prospect that the Cooper children's Greek verbs would improve over my absence.

The children were tearful, the boy anyway. The girl asked me if I was going away to find a husband. I suspect she was glad to be rid of her oppressor: three glorious weeks of picking her nose without a slap on the hand. In an attempt to make a lesson of it, I embarked on a longwinded explanation of the geography: 'There is an open body of water which separates New South Wales from Van Diemen's Land, to the south of us. That passage is called Bass's Strait, and it contains islands, which are occupied by sealers. There are no natives there.'

The boy watched this performance, his nine-year-old face serious. 'That is where the lags go,' he said with authority, 'when they run away.'

~

The weather was perfect as late November became early December, and it was decided that we would sail on the first day of the Austral summer, December first. The night before, I walked the streets of the town, having wound back the chaos of my home so it wouldn't be painful to return to. I'd found temporary lodgings for the mare: she was an easy guest, the dear thing. I put the lid on the well and blocked the chimney. Everything I needed—which was not much—had been taken down to the wharf.

People sauntered arm in arm, or in conversational groups, or staggering drunken mobs. 'M'lady shoul' be promenading with a gennleman,' leered one such drunk.

'Let me know if you see one,' I answered. His friends laughed at him and his face twisted to a snarl as they dragged him off.

The streets were changing, and the people with them. More of them every year, arriving in boats, multiplying. White faces outnumbering the native ones now, and free settlers a majority over lags and soldiers. Babes in arms, toddlers at heel. Young people in love or in need of it. I had friends among those walking the streets, but I avoided their faces. I did not want to have to explain; what I was doing was inexplicable. I hurried on, found a quieter space at the wharf and the Danish boat waiting patiently there.

I spoke to her softly and I believe she heard my longings.

I said the weather was perfect, did I not? In fact the weather confounded us with its monotonous perfection. I could not remember the last time it had rained. Normally the spring brought with it soaking downpours that shook the roofs and flooded the streets, rains that splashed and drummed and cleaned the world; glorious thunder that voiced the heavens to the earth. But this spring, for the first time anyone could remember, there had been only sunshine. The wind came from the east every day, slanting only a little north or south. It never blew over the land or brought clouds. It was a slightly damp breeze at times, but even then the dampness was salted because it carried the mists of the sea over us. So insistent were the bright sun and maritime wind that it felt as if the weather had changed itself permanently and would never change back. Plants that had been lush and shiny now looked tired. They wilted and yellowed.

What did I feel that night, looking back to it now? I could say I felt a distant sorrow for the family who were lost under seas I imagined to be pitiless and cruel, though I'd never sailed anywhere. I saw those people sometimes in my imagination, suspended in the gloom, down among the rocks and kelps, snagged by their clothes and swaying in the current, their faces dreamily unmarked in death.

I could say I shared my father's thirst for vengeance against the nameless man who had wronged him so many years ago, and set his life on a course towards disgrace and ruin. I could say that Srinivas struck me as a decent man racked by obsession, and that his request was born of a perception that my father owed him something.

And each of these ideas weighed upon me that night, blinding me to the obvious choice, which was to stay clear of this madness. But the one that impelled me towards that wharf when there was still time and opportunity to stop, was the least of all justifications: I was bored.

I was heartily sick of a life that alternated between caring for my invalid father and making excuses for his calamitous fall from grace, and trudging to and from the Cooper estate to recite verses to the children. Matrimonial prospects—absence thereof—fed the mood. There is a particular ennui that comes with having assessed the worth of every eligible man for miles around and found them all wanting. They came up short, literally. Where to proceed thence?

It doesn't matter what the motivations were. Once I returned to the wharf in the morning, I was never going to turn and walk back up the hill.

~

I expected to find Srinivas at the wharf in the morning but there was no sign of him.

Beckwith was there, beside the amiable boat, lifting a large sea chest with another man. The other was as tall as me and thin, slightly stooped. His dark hair was precisely combed and his eyes were lost in shadows. The chest, decorated with chipped paint, looked to be made of tin. If it was his, it did not fit with his otherwise melancholy mien.

Beckwith placed his end of the chest on the ground and the man did the same.

'Miss Grayling,' he said, and gestured towards the man. 'I expect you will want to meet the *Moonbird*'s master. Mister Herman Argyle, I give you Miss Eliza Grayling.'

He bowed just a little, took my hand without enthusiasm and held it motionless. His grip was slight, though his eyes were intent upon mine. They were warm eyes, dark. Hiding something, but not particularly from me. He did not say anything.

On board, two short lads in identical grey slops, their faces indistinguishable from each other. They had either end of a folded sail, and the one at the end nearer to me lifted the load. Enough of Sydney's life and commerce passed through the hands of lags that the prospect of having a couple on board did not alarm me.

Just then the nearer one snapped the sail so a tarred cord whipped into the groin of the other, who looked thunder and burst unexpectedly into tears. He threw down his part of the load, turned his back and clutched at the site of the blow with both hands, hissing through his teeth as he kicked at a nearby stanchion.

The first man—his brother, surely—dropped his part of the load and came around to him, muttering soft words. He reached his arms out and embraced him. There was an irritated shrug and half a raised elbow in response, but soon enough the weeping brother had restored himself. Argyle stepped towards them.

'Angus, Declan, enough o' that.' He did not raise his voice.

The weeping brother eyed the other one and then appealed to the master. 'Fuckin started it.'

The other snarled, 'I'll feckin fenesh it too, ye pretty bitch.'

Ridiculously, they were still hugging. Then they tensed, their tenderness replaced by aggression as swiftly as it appeared. It was like watching toddlers. The master stood squarely between them. I realised I could barely tell the brothers apart. Thick necks, heads made of muscle, not bone. Short, robust limbs and heavy chests. By appearances at least, they were twins. But I was sure the one who'd wept had used sing-song Scots, whereas the other, the one who comforted him, spoke in thick Irish tones.

'Who's the tall bird?' the Scot asked the other under his breath. I pretended not to hear.

Beckwith spoke to my questioning look: 'Connolly boys. Dublin originally. The boy Angus was given away. He's, er...'—he pointed at his temple—'soft in the head, miss. Wound up in Stromness, brung up Orcadian Scot. Him and Declan here both got on the wrong side of it, both transported. Thing is, miss, they put em both on the same ship. *Marquis of Huntley*. Who knows, someone in the Home Office with a sense of humour. Started beatin each other the minute they clapped eyes an they haven't stopped since. Good workers, though.'

'A wonder they find the time,' I muttered.

'Young Declan's actually very good to the other un. But if they starts millin on board just let em go. Won't involve yer.'

Declan slapped Angus genially on the shoulder; they grunted and returned to their work.

Beckwith guided me below, where I found the large front cabin had been reserved for me. Of the four bunks amidships, the upper on each side had been removed and the remaining cots were curtained off: the master's on the starboard and my father's on the port side. A handrail had been installed from the bedside to the stepway at the foot of the cots. It led up the three stairs to the galley, to guide my unseeing father. His cot had been built up on a timber box at waist height, presumably so he could find it in the dark without having to stoop.

The Connollys, I learned, had rigged hammocks in the hold among the crates and casks, too cramped to swing without bumping the stores. A government-issue blanket had been thrown on each, their boots and some loose clothing scattered underneath.

That left only Dr Gideon, who had taken up the captain's

cabin because of his need for working space. Beckwith told me this in a reverential whisper. I was not invited to inspect Dr Gideon's quarters: clearly a man of such eminence should never have to put up with a woman traipsing through his private domain.

The boat smelt, not unpleasantly, of timber and resin and hemp, and the air in the small spaces below decks was dense and still. Sound from above did not penetrate far into this world: the timbers muffled it and the gloom created a sense of secrecy.

In the middle of the day I took the mare on her final errand, to my father's shack. I found him washed and shaved, a circumstance that filled me with optimism. A plate dripping on a rack told me he'd eaten. He made no attempt to bring a bottle with him, though I could tell through long familiarity that he had been drinking. The enormous care over syllables, the exaggerated precision of trivial movements like locking the door.

I was made to wait near the horse while he said goodbye to the dog. Someone would come by and feed her, he assured me, and she could not otherwise be persuaded to leave the house. She was no longer chained up, and she snuffled at him and licked and pawed while he told her he had work to do, an important journey, and that he would be back, that a good dog would watch the house and keep the badgers at bay. The dog thumped her tail on the boards of the verandah, pleased no doubt to have been assigned a role.

'And the porcupines,' he called over his shoulder as he came my way. 'Don't you forget the porcupines. Sneaky damn things.'

The dog did not try to follow us. She just watched, in the sad way of a left dog.

It was an effort, as always, to get my father into the saddle, though the mare was patient with him. Seated behind me, his hands were placed in a self-conscious combination of affection and distance: one on the back of my shoulder and one gripping the edge of the saddle. He knew horses well enough to be sure this would suffice.

He inclined his head just once, back to the house and the dog.

As I trotted the mare down through the streets, the knowing eyes watched us as usual. My father spoke to me over my shoulder. He was excited, fixed upon what he saw as his mission, and now I began to feel the resentment once again, listening to him. He had no idea that I would have to look after him out on the ocean, just as I was doing in the bush outside Sydney. Here I was again, married to the care of my father, on a ridiculous errand that promised both hardship and anticlimax. This fearsome adversary who awaited him was probably four feet tall and suffered from hay fever.

They could have one another.

~

Once I'd guided my father across the planks and onto the *Moonbird*, he edged his way carefully around the deck, running his hands over every fitting, every rope. His vacant eyes were enraptured, his mouth undone, as the workings of the vessel revealed themselves in the knots and shrouds and pulleys under his probing hands. Argyle had gone ahead of him and closed the hatches: the generous bulwarks of the *Moonbird* would keep him from tumbling overboard in the meantime.

I watched him for a while and decided he was happy. The master called me, said there'd been a delivery. On the table in the galley I found a letter. It bore Srinivas's name at the bottom, but the hand was female, I was sure, and the spelling was perfect, leading me to think he must have dictated it.

Miss Grayling,

I trust you are now settled aboard the Moonbird, and that you have been provided comfortable quarters. She is a beautiful vessel and will meet your needs.

I must apologise to you for my absences in recent days: my business required me. I have arranged, through Mr Beckwith, for two prisoners of His Majesty to crew the vessel and, in doing so, to provide you with a measure of protection. You may already have found they are spirited lads, but they come well recommended. You have my leave to be firm with them; they are under orders to abide all instruction from you and your father.

The master of the vessel, a Mr Argyle I believe, has been hired directly by Mr Beckwith, and I have not met him. I am informed he has sailed Bass's Strait many times and knows the waters and their islands to a remarkable degree.

I am informed also that there is a doctor of medicine who has paid for passage with you. His credentials are very impressive although, as with Mr Argyle, I have not had the opportunity to meet him. It is a matter for you—I am unconcerned—if he wishes to collect specimens. If you find that his studies are impeding your progress, I trust you and your father will take the matter up with him.

The vessel should have been generously provisioned. If you find that anything you require is not already present on board, please avail yourself of my credit through Mr Beckwith to obtain it.

Mr Argyle has been instructed to carry small arms. I recommend you acquaint yourself with their use, though I stress once again that I do not ask either of you to endanger yourselves in pursuit of anyone.

*Should you find the man who has taken my property,
you will have done the families of the missing, and me, a
great service. And if that man is the one I believe him to
be, you will also have addressed a longstanding grievance
in your father's life.*

*Be careful, I beg of you. You have my eternal gratitude
and admiration for what you are undertaking.*

*I remain,
Your humble and obedient servant—*

Such discordant words. *Taken my property*? Not 'extinguished innocent lives'? And the lack of specificity was peculiar. Had Argyle perhaps been given separate sailing orders? This letter said no more than *sail down there and see what happens.*

A shadow crossed the oblong of sunlight in which I had been reading. I looked up and through the small galley windows I saw my father outside, bent at the waist, his hands feeling their way across the panes, fingertips sticking frog-like on the glass as they memorised everything. His smile was child-like: he radiated purpose and energy.

~

We cast off that evening. The ropes slapped the water and were hauled in by the two convicts, and all that was steady and firm was gone, replaced by the uncertain will of natural forces.

Before we had even cleared the wharf, the doctor was beside me, apologising, his extraordinary face creased in confected chagrin.

'I have taken up the most spacious quarters aboard,' he said. 'I worry that this work of mine confers me indulgences that are unfair to others.' I saw in his expression the hope of forgiveness.

'See to it that you are productive then, doctor,' I retorted, and the hope evaporated: now he looked slightly wounded.

But then we were picking our way through the inshore lanes of Port Jackson, following the shoreline east then northward past Watsons Bay, where the natives had their fires on the plates of sandstone up high. Down closer to the water, the fishermen and the navy had taken over Camp Cove, sprawling in makeshift timber huts and warehouses over the tidal flats and the rocks. In among the small fishing ketches I could see native canoes slid up on the beach. For now, they mingled with the colony's enterprise, still maintaining their own.

As we approached the slow rise of South Head, I felt neither hunger nor thirst; only a strange kind of emptiness where a set of routines had been. What now? I wondered—do I make a meal or is one provided? When do I retire for the evening? Declan Connolly had gone through the crates and chests and sacks that were loaded during the morning, and found bread and fruit for himself and his brother. *Won't be long afore it's rotten*, he said to Angus. *Best be eatin it.*

I watched my father continue his exploration, his body responding to the *Moonbird*'s progress over the water. I tried to remember whether he was always this size, a head shorter than me and diminutive in comparison to the bulk of the Connollys. People diminish, in a real sense, with age. But perhaps it was the waning of my childhood adoration that made him small now.

The master had disappeared, and I realised I had not yet had a conversation with him. He was not at the helm: it had been entrusted to Declan Connolly, who stood there proudly gnawing at a peach with his free hand resting on the wheel, watching his brother caulking the deck.

Dr Gideon sat with his back against the rear wall of the wheelhouse, lit by the late sun. He was writing in a leather-bound notebook: he smiled when he looked up and saw me studying him, and each time he did it I made a point of looking away as though my eyes had wandered his way only momentarily.

With just enough breeze to fill the sails but not enough to raise a creak from the shrouds, we stayed close off the shore among the sweetest blues, where the green foliage and the sandstone tumbled to the water's edge. I had never passed this way by sea. Many times I had walked out onto South Head and sat by the signal station, on no errand but the urge to follow my nose, a habit my father told me I'd inherited from my mother. But unlike her, perhaps, I had managed to include my father in such wanderings. During the years when they were building the lighthouse, I took him out there on our old mare to watch the stone blocks of the tower rise from the convicts' mess of offcuts and dust. At least, I watched it. He did what he was doing now on the *Moonbird*—he employed the rest of his senses in deciphering the scene. At such times he could feel the glow of the sun or hear the tools and the insects with such clarity that I almost envied him his plight.

But now, viewed from this sturdy little schooner, the same headland wore different colours: lush growth and tranquil beaches I had never seen. They were the intricacies, the secret parts of what I was leaving behind. A world contained in miniature. The last of the local boats were falling away now. The islands, the mythical places I had been told about since childhood; they were drawing us to them, and that strange sense of inevitability filled me again. Whatever would happen there was preordained, a logical end to matters begun so long ago and never properly finished.

I was dwelling on such things when the master reappeared. I turned as he came up the short steps from below, and so great was my shock and surprise that for a moment I could not fathom the sight that confronted me.

Argyle's facial expression was unchanged, fixed in melancholy, but his simple trousers and linen shirt were gone. He was wearing instead a long, white empire-line dress, hitched just slightly in one hand to avoid stepping on the hem as he ascended. It was made from fine muslin with delicate sprig-and-dot embroidery on it and must have cost a fortune. He looked directly at me and took in my startled face. His own did not change.

'We will round South Head shortly,' he said. Behind him the slope of it had become a cliff as we followed it. 'The breeze will pick up. I'd be grateful if you'd assist the lads with the sails.' His voice was no different either; it issued from the shadows in him, though the setting sun lit the dress and the breeze caressed its folds. He took a chart from a small drawer under the helm and studied it, looking up at the landmarks to match them to the lines on the sheet.

The Connollys were securing the stowage of some casks. The one facing the master stopped his work and stared.

'Skipper's in queer duds.' By the lack of restraint in the comment, I guessed it was Angus.

Declan turned to look. A faint chuckle escaped him: confusion, not humour. 'Oh, this is goin to be a trip all right.'

'Mind your work,' I snapped, 'and not your opinions.'

The lad looked chastened. Argyle did not react, but moved past him to replace the chart in its drawer. His body fought the dress: it moved as a man's does. Above the straight-line bust, where a woman's chest might slope and swell into her bosom, were hard plates of muscle beneath his collarbones, a valley of sternum down the centre. The bodice was made to a woman's shape: the dress strained dramatically. Likewise his arms, flexing under the short, puffed sleeves, were those of a working man, bulky and thick.

From his position against the cabin wall, Dr Gideon craned his neck to see what had caused the reaction. He took in the sight calmly.

~

By late afternoon we were on open ocean, travelling well down the coast to the south. The land met the sea at a long, dark escarpment, a narrow plain at its foot. I could see the stacks of the colliery there, on the site where Srinivas and Clark and the imposter had made a fire from that first, foundational lump of coal. The ensuing stampede of coalminers was a part of the story I knew well, a part that reflected progress and industry. Unlike the darker pages.

No other sail blemished the perfect meeting of sky and sea, and the *Moonbird* rode heavy over the chop, smothering it with her reassuring bulk. Longer, deeper swells rolled under, lifting and lowering the boat as they passed beneath, heading for the end of their lives on the rocks and beaches.

My father started on a bottle of madeira around the same time Argyle draped a shawl over his dress. The Connollys had the sails tuned to the nor'-wester. A state of rest descended. I heated stew in the galley's tiny stove and set two places at the table—I assumed the rest of them would look after themselves. My father came without complaint and I sat him before the food. He kept one hand on the bottle—wary that I might take it from him—as he scooped food with the other.

'Where did it come from, Father?' I began.

'What?' He stopped and looked up. Oh, the tedium of these exchanges!

'You know what I'm talking about.'

'The bottle? Among the provisions,' he said casually.

'Remarkable. What stunning luck for you.'

We had played this corrosive game so many times. Pity, love and anger from me; resentment, love and anger from him. He would deny as a first line of defence—*What bottle? Who said I couldn't? Why is it your concern?*—then turn the argument on me, on my loneliness. If he was especially angry, or especially drunk, he would include a reference to my mother's achievements at the same age. Married to an officer—him—and raising a child, me.

I would flare and retort that the officer was now a recluse who depended on others for his survival, a man blinded and damned by his own deeds. And my mother was dead. And if my anger was at an incandescent peak, I might add that it was his foolishness that caused it. I would regret the words the moment I said them, even before he threw his bottle or his glass in my direction.

I did not even know whether it was true that it was his fault, since I had never known how the fire started.

It was a routine, a punishing exchange of hurtful truths and mere guesses that could never produce a victor. Apologies were rare, but they were always mine, never his. *Never.* The shouting fuelled him: he would drink on from the confrontation, enter a state where he was more animal than man, a sensory and heedless creature that craved and hungered and could not reason. He would piss himself, vomit, fall over, break things into shards. In the morning, all recollection would be gone along with the broken things, and contrition was only there as a cloud of

self-doubt, the drinker's vague awareness that they've done…
something. Lowered brows, soft speech. Never *sorry*.

The boat pushed steadily south and his drinking was only an hour old. In this state he could be agreeable company; warm and funny. Looking at him now, with the yellowing bruise on his scalp from the fall and a faint smile around his eyes, I saw a glimmer of the man I believed him to be. I loved him always but I loved him clearest when I saw the distinguished past in him.

'Are you happy with the master?'

He cocked his head as though my question was a faraway sound and crunched his face in contemplation. 'The boat feels right underfoot. Rides the short stuff easy enough. Course, that might be the boat, not him. But the rigging sounds tight, and those two lunatics are getting the sail orders right…when they're not threatening to kill each other.'

He laughed his sidelong laugh, sharp to the world's absurdity, and just for an instant it filled my heart.

'Have you spoken with the master, though?' I wanted to know what impression he'd formed, given he couldn't detect the most striking thing about him.

'Brief words, yes. He's…what am I looking for? Maudlin. Don't you think? Says the right things, sounds competent, but no spark. Mind you, that doesn't bear upon his competence at the helm.'

'What about the doctor?' I felt daring, reaching for a reaction from him that might accord with mine. My father took a large swig from the bottle, a sight that often set my teeth on edge. For now I could accommodate it.

'Seems serious. Urbane.' he muttered, more to himself than to me. 'His voice seems…What does he look like?'

'Oh…tall, well built—vigorous, one might say. Thick hair,

some brown but mostly grey. I would put him at fifty years, perhaps older. His face is…well, no one would call it beautiful.' I found that I did not want to say I thought him the more interesting for his disfigured features.

My father listened carefully. 'Yes. Hmm. Of what discipline is he a doctor?'

'Medicine. But he has an interest in diet, and he is taking up a grant of land, and he wishes to study edible fishes on our voyage. I fear such men can be terrible bores in a confined space.'

'Ah, hmm. I see. On the other hand, he may be capable of quite deep thought.' He drank again and sighed, so that the fumes gusted over me. He'd lost interest. At times I wondered if his wits were failing him, so brief was his patience for conversation. I took his dish away and washed it in the bucket of seawater by the door. I was about to leave him there when he called me back. He had a bundle of newspapers on the table before him.

'The doctor gave me these. He said they might be of relevance. Can you look?'

Folded copies of the *Sydney Gazette* ('Thus We Hope to Prosper'). Non-sequential dates over the past month. Advertisements, cures, diatribes, gossip…columns circled in pencil. The encircling hand had targeted stories about sealers in the straits: wild men, abductions, rapes and killings. The trafficking of native women and children, an antipode to the antipode we already inhabited, a place where bad men went to hide—from the law, or their obligations. Correspondents fulminated about a lawless society—surely an oxymoron?—led by a handful of powerful men. *Christianity and progress are all but forgotten in the islands amidst the stampede for fortune.* Such speculations led naturally into other discussions of the fate of the *Howrah*. Men there, men with Cornish ancestry who knew the art of wrecking. False lights, false hope.

It was a busy trade route between Hobart and Sydney, said the *Gazette*, and like a high bluff on a lonely highway, equidistant from origin and destination, the islands sat waiting: a hiding place and a natural setting for ambush. There were brigands in the islands, it said, banditti who were no less bushrangers for the fact that they rowed whaleboats.

I read it all to my father, who sat with his elbows on the table and fists rammed comically into his cheeks. He listened without comment, and waited until he was sure I had finished.

'Banditti,' he repeated. 'Exactly his thing. He'll be among them…not the same name, of course, something else he's adopted. We go from island to island, some'll be loyal to them, loyal to him, but some'll talk. As we go, we narrow it down, I think.'

'Father,' I ventured, 'perhaps you need to have an eye to other possibilities. Perhaps the ship just sank and nobody is culpable. Or there are brigands of whatever kind there, but the man you seek is not among them. Or he is, and the situation is so dangerous that we can do nothing but observe and leave.'

'Yes,' he hurried to agree, 'yes. Any of those, but…I am interested: the doctor must be aware of our aims?'

He had changed the subject as though he never even heard the contrary possibilities. 'Yes,' I sighed. 'I have spoken to him, in broad terms. That is why he's given you those newspapers, I suppose.'

He extended a hand towards me, sounding for the depth of my scepticism. It was a thing he did in lieu of looking into my eyes. I took the outstretched fingers and held them, poor foolish man.

'Sweet girl, why did you agree to come?'

I'd thought it through many times. I'd come up with

arguments for curious outsiders. But I hadn't yet answered him directly.

'Oh, the views, I suppose. Sea air. Thought I'd try my hand at scrimshaw.'

He smiled.

'I'm here to look after you.' I said it as neutrally as I could. It was hard to say because it implied, directly, that he was incapable of looking after himself. But he didn't fly into a rage, as perhaps he might have if he'd been much further into the day's drinking. In fact, his face barely changed at all.

'Do you feel you owe me anything?'

'No.'

No, there is nothing owed to a father who had stumbled and thrashed his way from one calamity to the next ever since I could remember. 'No, Father, I don't. I hope that doesn't sound disrespectful to you.'

I had learnt as a small child that powerful feelings—love, gratitude, pain—could pass between us unspoken, despite his blindness, or perhaps because of it. Some mysterious conduit remained. There was wounded pride in his eyes.

'If the time comes that you must look after yourself,' he said, 'you should do so.'

I could not know to what he referred. But he turned himself slightly so that he no longer faced me. His brow was inclined to the late sun coming in through the window now, as though he could see it as much as feel it, and it offered him solace.

THE WONDERS OF THE
WUNDERKAMMER

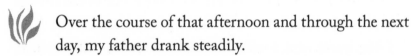 Over the course of that afternoon and through the next day, my father drank steadily.

You will say I should have stopped it happening, that it was my stated responsibility on this voyage to save him from himself. But anyone who has lived with such a man knows about getting between him and the bottle.

I tried. I watched him sliding through smiles and laughter, slurred words and stumbling, into staggers and falls and shouting and curses and silences and lost consciousness and revivals and more shouting and the aiming of blows at imagined assailants. I found rum among the provisions, commercial stuff, thank God, and Hollands gin. Not the rotgut again. I moved the bottles to other places I thought he would not look: I did not throw them overboard—not yet—out of consideration for the others on board who may have needed them to get themselves through long watches or for medicine or simply because it was a seafarer's entitlement to drink and not be beholden to my father's sickness.

But every time I moved the liquor he found it. He retained a fierce instinct for its whereabouts, this poison that owned and imprisoned him. I knew that my father loved me, but I had learnt many years before that there were forces in the world stronger than the best of love. The need for booze was one of them.

He fell asleep in the late afternoon and could not be roused, not even by another brawl between the brothers. Better in any event to leave him snoring in the shade of the cabin wall where Dr Gideon had taken the sun the previous day.

Argyle, regal in the white dress, announced we would anchor at Jervis Bay. Over the southward miles I watched the distant shoreline, wondering if this bay, or that, might frame the forest where Srinivas had found his home. I had no way of knowing where the Walbanja lived, or the Thaua, or where was the dark glade where his father had met his terrible end. I looked for a wharf or a stockpile of felled timber, but I saw very little evidence of human occupation, native or settler, even now. The place was wild and beautiful; it resisted taming.

The northern gate of the bay was announced by a towering cliff made of square blocks. So regular were their outlines that they could have been the work of some giant mason. To the south was an island, lower and densely wooded. A swell from the south-east pushed us in with a mile either side, no urgency among the men on the deck. A wide body of water opened to the north of us, flat and serene and impossibly lovely. It made a chalky blue-green over the sandflats, a blue of royalty over the deeps, shades of lilac and mauve where a haze blended the two, further away. And in the places where waves rolled gently over reefs, other colours would dare to intrude upon the chorus of those shades; a burst of orange and brown where the surge lifted kelp to the surface, an explosion of white as the wave broke and dissipated.

Argyle set us to one side of the expanse—the north, if I remember rightly—so we were slightly in the lee of the land and lying perfectly still on a motionless surface. I could see down, down to the silver backs of circling fish, down so deep that the smallest of them, way down there, might truly be the largest.

I slept soundly that night, my body set like a timepiece in synchrony with the tiny movements of the *Moonbird*, shifting minutely on the anchor line when the night air swayed her. I felt the boat cared for us in our individual plights, held us cupped somehow: carrying us, rather than being sailed by us. Argyle in the middle cabin, his faraway mien. My father, the collapse of consciousness turning with the hours into something approximating normal sleep. The Connollys, finally peaceful after the brawling day, slumbering in a welter of bruises, inseparably joined.

And the doctor, the doctor. In what world did he sleep?

~

In the early light of morning it was clear my father was sick.

I spoke to the master and with his consent I lowered the jolly-boat off its davits and took my father to the rope ladder, guided him down. A small brown spider scuttled out of the rowlocks, her home disturbed. I let her run onto my hand and deposited her on the rough braids of the rope ladder. Then I rowed my father to the beach and nudged the boat into the perfect white sand.

He crawled out with some effort, felt for the depth with a

pointed foot and took a few unsteady steps in the wrong direction, heading across the beach and slightly out to sea. I took hold of him and turned him: he accepted this without complaint, and stepped slowly out of the water and onto the damp sand. Here he turned and sat on his behind, exhaling loudly. 'Don't feel too flash this morning, love,' he said, as though ill-health had descended upon him from nowhere at all.

I sat beside him. My fingers found the stranded kelp, gleaming where the tide had left it overnight. Just offshore, I could see Dr Gideon on deck arranging his equipment. He threw a weighted net off the side and it made a satisfying *chrrk* on the surface.

'You must stop drinking the supplies,' I said to my father, as evenly as I could.

'Don't start again, my love,' he replied, then added: 'Was just a sip. Others had the same.'

'No, they didn't. No one else drinks like you do.'

He creased his face a little. 'Everyone drinks more or less the same, especially at sea. You're too young to know anything about it.'

'I'm thirty-two, father.'

A look of confusion crossed his face, then was gone. 'Well, you don't know, anyway.' He pushed himself to his feet with a grunt, threw off his trousers and shirt and edged forward in his breeches. The downslope guided him to the water's edge; he felt the shallows lick his toes, then walked confidently into the water. Some creature pulsed away as his feet advanced.

Once the sea had reached his hips, he lowered himself to chin-depth and submerged his head, shook it underwater and came up scrubbing at his hair. He had his back to me as he did this: the muscles of younger years hung slack from his shoulders.

Beyond him, Dr Gideon was hauling the net. The Connollys watched as he did so, pulling at folds of it as they came within reach but always with a hand clutching the shrouds. Both of them, despite their strength, were wary about leaning over the edge.

My father rolled over and floated on his back. I tried to feel that moment as he did: the cool salt water lifting him, the sky above registering not as brightness but as warmth. And his memory, feeding him some recollection of what the sky looked like, back when he could see it. I hoped that he saw a glorious memory.

~

When we returned to the *Moonbird*, a Connolly took my hand and hauled me over the bulwark. He held it a moment longer: I thanked him, called him Angus and he grunted that he was Declan. 'Doctor asked that you visit him in his cabin,' he said. His brother—Angus, I suppose—yelled at him from the windlass: 'Cannae work it, aargh,' and I saw my father and me in the two of them.

I made sure I stalled a little on deck before I went below. The gloom of the passageway ended at a glow where daylight entered beyond the open cabin door. I called out and the doctor summoned me, in that warm voice of his.

When I passed through the doorway my eyes struggled to take in the crowded contents of the cabin. The obvious things caught my eye first: small squares of sunlight from the stern windows landing brightly on a simple cot and washstand. A box near my feet, open and containing the accoutrements of medicine: weights and splints, paper packets containing bandages, lengths of silk and fine instruments. A row of shelves against the starboard wall: each fitted with a lip to protect rows and rows of large specimen jars filled with clear fluid, awaiting occupants. A couple of them were already tenanted with small fish and crabs, drifting faintly with the little movements of the boat.

There was a desk against the opposite wall and there, relaxed in his seat, was the doctor. He was smiling, studying me. He stood, moving like a much younger man, and indicated I should take the chair; sat himself on the edge of the desk. Around him were scattered papers and curious instruments. By the faint light of a wax lamp, a chart of a spray of islands was pinned to the timber of the wall in front of him. A jar stood empty, its lid removed.

'You wanted to see me?'

'Welcome, welcome,' he said, pushing the mess aside. 'I wanted to make us tea. Will you have tea?' Without waiting for an answer, he turned to a side table where a pot and teacups stood. He spoke over his shoulder as he poured. 'There ought to be some sort of petit fours, I know. But we make do, don't we?' I was still finding new objects in the crowded room, more laboratory than living space.

'I'm sure the convicts would agree with you. What does this do?' I pointed at a tall wooden box with an open top.

He followed my gaze: 'Ah! Viewing box. Look...' He flipped it over and I saw that the end opposite the open end was made of glass: a small windowpane had been caulked into the timber. 'One presses it into the surface of the sea and it affords a clear view of what goes on beneath. Water has the effect of distorting human vision, as you know. I am interested, among other things, in the difference between the human eye and those of the fishes. Consider: do they see clearly? It seems obvious to conclude that they do. But it is also possible that they see underwater the same way we do, but are more adept at interpreting that vision cerebrally. You follow? One is a function of the eye, the other of the brain. So we turn our attention to the anatomical structures of the eye and seek out the differences…'

He was determined to run on with this explanation. I was determined to test it. 'Do you mean the human eye or the fish eye?'

He laughed. 'It might be easier, aboard a small vessel, to obtain a fish eye, don't you think?'

I scanned the room again. 'What are the jars for?'

'Preserving spirits. Anything of significance that I can procure on our voyage will be fixed in fluid and sent to London for… greater minds to work on. You can imagine, Miss Grayling, how heavy those jars are. It took me forever to get them down here.'

'And this?'

I pointed at a strange object that stood on the floor in the gloom beside the far end of the desk. A glass orb, not quite a sphere, around a foot in diameter. It stood atop a brass cylinder, with a valve between the sphere and the cylinder operated by a small brass tap. The apparatus stood on a wooden tripod, and between the legs of the tripod there was a crank handle. The glass of the orb gleamed: in that dull interior plenty of things gleamed, but only this object did so in a way that suggested conceit.

'That? That is an air pump. I had it made from Robert Boyle's drawings. Are you familiar with them?'

I came closer. Peered into it. 'No. What does it do?'

He smiled. 'Perhaps we will have an opportunity to use it in our travels.'

My eyes roved further. Two pictures on the bulkhead behind him. The first was a lithograph depicting some terrible armoured monster: a bulbous abdomen and a narrow, pointed head lending it a shape like a comma lying on its side. Its backswept legs and mouth parts bristled with hairs like a fly, but it had no wings. In place of feet it had gleaming claws that hooked forward. It had a fierce, determined eye and what seemed to be a moustache.

'*What on earth?*'

He laughed. 'That, Miss Grayling, is a flea. It's a page from Hooke's *Micrographia*: I had it cut from the book and framed, I loved it so. The world we reveal with the microscope: all that power and rage in such a tiny creature.'

'A doctor with a penchant for fleas at close quarters. Nice.' Again he looked wounded and I wondered if I'd gone too far. 'And the chart? Why have you drawn on it?'

A long spiral had been traced over the map, its origin somewhere near Sydney, leading south-west then curving anti-clockwise, gently at first, through the south and then the east as it passed through the archipelago, becoming tighter and tighter as it wound its way into the heart of the speckling islands.

He waved the backs of his fingers at it. 'A fancy of mine…'

'What kind of fancy?' I had him now. I'd found a deeper topic, where he'd be unable to condescend.

'Spiral geometry. Sequences. Are you familiar with Euclid's golden ratio?'

'Not freshly.' I gave him half a smile. 'Remind me.'

'Brahmagupta'—he rolled the *R* extravagantly—'the man who brought astronomy to the Arabs?' He was seized by enthusiasm now. 'Binet's formula? You're not familiar…I'm sorry, I must not presume. You know of Fibonacci, the Italian? Five, six hundred years ago, he found a sequence that diminishes, or increases, I suppose, depending on how it is expressed—in conformity to a sort of irregular exponentiality. The golden ratio is one to one point six one eight, an irrational number, which is to say it cannot be presented as a fraction. So if you take Fibonacci's number sequence, any two of those numbers which are consecutive exist in a relationship which is more or less the golden ratio. It makes spirals, Miss Grayling. Isn't that beautiful? You see, it turns up all the time in nature: Fibonacci demonstrated its effect in breeding rabbits, but I think it might have much wider applications.'

'Such as?'

'We already know the sequence and the ratio appear elsewhere: the emergence of branches around a trunk, or leaves around a petiole, but I believe seashells might be another expression. We know they are involute, and that the creature makes the shell that way as it grows. But why are they doing this? In all of nature, everything forms for a reason...

'And then'—his eyes had closed indulgently but he opened them and glanced at me, fearful he had lost me to boredom or incomprehension—'consider the notion that the whelks and the turban shells are conical, whereas other shells are not: they merely spiral into themselves without projecting into a diminishing point. Again, Miss Grayling, why?' He didn't wait for an answer. 'Now the best possible illustration of this is the argonaut. I have never had one to use for measurement, but I believe the spiral will conform to the golden ratio, and the relationships between its coils will be Fibonacci numbers. So this is among the chief aims of my expedition.'

I sighed, holding it just short of a yawn. 'And the map? The spiral on the map?'

'Ah! Glad you asked. You would understand, I'm sure, that once you start to immerse yourself deeply in a concept, you see its embodiment everywhere you look. Consider the path I have plotted. This'—he stretched forward and pointed at the islands—'this is the path that your father and the master told me this morning that they want to take: to Wilson's Promontory and Rodondo Island, then down and into the south-western extent of the Furneaux group, around the south of Clarke Island and on into the Franklin Sound, thus surveying all of the major sealing settlements in one continuous line.'

'The line makes a spiral,' I said.

'It does. Sometimes when I look at it, I see a fish hook which continues in on itself to form a closing spiral. If I were to invert this chart, I believe you would see a bass clef.'

'Bass's Clef?'

He laughed, and I thought how easy it was to poke holes in this patrician exterior of his. We both looked at the chart and at the pattern of our plans. Then, without warning, my pleasure darkened and vanished.

'Doctor Gideon,' I said, 'the spiral can only curl inwardly.'

'Yes, in a fixed rotation that corresponds to an infinitely recurring pattern.'

Inward and inward, coiled upon itself and eternally tightening. It came upon me so suddenly, like the rushing water of a new tide: a desperate urge to leave the room, cancel the voyage, and drag my recalcitrant father off the cold carcass of his vengeance.

'But doctor, how will we get home?'

~

As the *Moonbird* ploughed on down the coast, each of us found our routines. So generous were her proportions that the usual complaints about cramping and stench did not apply: she rode comfortably over the swell as we made a south-westerly line towards Bass's Strait.

The Connolly brothers drank at the pace one might expect from two lags with a maritime history, but only within the bounds set for them by Argyle. That tenderness and volatility with each other: I'd watched Angus reef a line at lightning speed through a sheave block so Declan fell off a yardarm above him, then roll about laughing as his brother tried to thrash him with a cane batten from the jib. But they were scrupulous in doing everything Argyle asked of them, their combustibility held in the tenuous control of a sad man in a frock.

A moderate master, compliant crew. I thanked God for both these mercies. Argyle set them sail orders, kept them to a roster of cleaning tasks and turned them to any heavy work that might spare the rest of us. Pulling nets and pots and traps for Dr Gideon, guiding my father if he moved up or down between decks; Argyle was able to command them with an impeccable minimum of speech. He would place himself, whether consciously or not, at a higher point on the deck and speak slowly and clearly, once. When there was evidence of incomprehension he would simply stare, and Angus would wait for Declan's interpretation before the two of them did it their own way.

The empire-line was replaced the following day by a simpler linen dress. By late morning the master's upper arms were becoming pink with sunburn, but the dress was a practical choice given the heat of the day. It was shapeless and plain, but he'd combined it with tortoiseshell combs that kept his wavy hair back and revealed his face to be younger than I'd thought. He stood most of the time at the helm, not intervening in the boat's motion but watching the coastline off our starboard side and the wind scuffing the surface ahead of us in the south-east.

Argyle's hairy legs protruded under the hem of the dress and ended at his brown, bare feet on the boards. The watch he used for navigating was attached to a short piece of ribbon and pinned to the waist of the dress. I saw him writing: at first I thought he was diligent about keeping his log, but that only accounted for some of this work: much of it was done on writing paper. It was the horizon and the flat expanse of sea and the paper and him there, alone with his thoughts.

'Are you writing a letter home?' I approached him from behind and below: the scrape of the nib stopped and he immediately turned the paper over.

He did not look up as he answered. 'No. Just the business of the vessel.'

I came level with him beside the helm and I saw how his body was at ease in the dress, in a way it had not been when we first met ashore.

He looked up now. 'Yes?' One eyebrow stood high in expectation. I had no reason to begin this conversation, nowhere to take it. I imagine I must have sighed.

'I just wondered, I...I just wanted to say hello.' I smiled meekly but his eyes narrowed in stern examination of me.

'You wish to know why I am dressed this way, I suppose.'

His voice was not cold, as perhaps I have indicated, but warmed by some great animating complexity. I stammered the beginnings of a demurral but he cut me off. 'It's worth fifty lashes on shore. A small consolation I allow myself on board.'

Consolation. That word stays with me, even now. He chose it specifically. Not a freedom, or an opportunity, as one might expect of a man who has chosen to wear women's clothes, but a consolation. And telling me he'd be met with fifty strokes of course did not answer the question why: it spoke only of consequence.

I could hear my father in the galley below us, singing softly. The clink of a bottle. He was rapidly building up the map of the vessel in his mind, giving him freedom of movement and ever more access to the booze. I needed to keep moving it, or get rid of it. Argyle's eyes, which had been locked on mine, flickered slightly at the sound. He lowered his voice.

'What happened to your father's sight?'

'What do you mean?' It was churlish, but I could be opaque also.

'He was not blind at birth. He told me what your mother looked like.'

The words cut straight through me. I did not see it coming. I was looking into his eyes and then I could not see him for tears. But he moved, reached down into the galley and lifted out a stool, placed it beside me and shut the galley hatch.

'Forgive me,' he hurried. 'Terrible intrusion.' It was the most urgent thing I had yet heard him say.

I wept for some time, unable to dam the flow that had caught me by surprise. I was not in the habit of crying over my mother: I had steeled myself against it, devoted myself to carrying the old man through the remainder of his life, loving him despite himself.

'It was his drinking,' I said eventually. I wondered if he could hear us, even through the sturdy structure that separated the helm from the cabin's interior.

I decided there was nothing I could say that I would not also repeat to him. 'He was drinking so much, he was, was causing trouble. At the inns, in the streets. People remembered who he had been, that he was very senior under Governor Hunter and, you understand, that brought him a great deal of respect and also hatred. Macarthur's people, all the politics...Any old drunk is good for mockery, of course. But people laugh a little harder at a drunkard when they sense it's a fall from grace, don't you think?'

Why was I telling him all this? Why was I trusting him? Sometimes only instinct guides us.

'The people who cared would lead him home, clean him up. And the people who hated would get him locked up, and I'd have to go and have him released. Or they'd beat him. He was a fine man in his day, and I believe he could acquit himself in a fight. But they hurt him, they hurt him.' I was clenched up again, took a breath, slowed down.

'We made a decision. Me, the handful of friends he'd kept. We had him banned from the inns, and the commissariat were told not to sell him liquor. Most of the time they honoured the bans...But even then, we could not foresee where it would lead. You know the lags make stills in the bush and they bottle their own stuff. They call it rum—it's made from potatoes, mostly. He'd been buying it a week or so, that was all. He didn't appear for a while and I thought he'd just gone to ground after we had him banned, but he...They made a batch out at a creek-head, "Barrington's Old Farm", they called it. He bought a lot of it and he drank for several days and...'

I couldn't continue.

He looked at me and nodded slowly. 'Back-country stills...'

'He lost consciousness for a week. By the time he recovered his sight had gone. They caught the distillers and flogged them, as usual. Then the inns went back to selling him their stuff and he went back to drinking it. Macarthur knew, King knew. They were happy to have one of Hunter's allies crippled. Other people,

I suppose they took pity when he pleaded for it.'

I darted a look towards the cabin hatch. I had been told that a blind man will hear twice as acutely as a sighted one: I had gone further than I intended.

~

Later in the evening, Argyle had handed over the watch to Declan Connolly, and as I passed him doing something or other he said carefully, 'Miss.'

I stopped.

'Fine evening, miss.'

'Tis,' I answered. My expression must have demanded what his business was.

'Miss, don't mean to trouble.' His eyes were unexpectedly soft. 'It's my brother.'

'Angus?'

'Yes miss. Just makin sure you understand. He's a simpleton, see. Daft. Means no harm by the cursin an such.'

This intrigued me. 'You're very close, you two.'

'Have to be. He's a danger to hisself otherways.' A moment of evaluation in his eyes, a decision to continue. 'Found him on the hulks, when we was both taken down. *Connolly, yer brother's ere,* they said. An it was him all right. Wasn't gonna lose him then. I had to give a price to git him shipped with me on the *Marquis.*'

'A price?'

'Aye. Had to give these uns to the surgeon.' He pointed into his open mouth and I saw that all his teeth beyond the front ones were gone. He must have registered my shock. 'Sorry miss.'

'Not at all, Mister Connolly. Good to know about your brother, thank you.'

I placed this out of my mind: it was the master I wanted to talk to. He had gone to stand alone at the bulwark and from there he looked over the sea. My father was roaring drunk by now and could not have hoped to overhear anything. There was another matter that troubled me about our earlier discussion.

'Mister Argyle?'

He turned to look at me, more welcoming this time. I wanted to rush the words.

'You said you spoke to my father.'

'Yes.'

'And he mentioned my mother.'

'He did.'

'Did he tell you she is dead?'

'Yes, he did. Or I gathered it from what he said. I'm not sure, exactly.'

I held my breath for just a moment. Then: 'Did he tell you how she died?'

Again, the look in his eyes was faraway. A man who watches the sea during a rest from his work, which is watching the sea.

'I am sorry, miss. He did not.'

~

I returned to the cabin and found my father, as I expected I would, seated on the inbuilt bench that faced the table. Two empty bottles rolled on the bench beside his hip, and a half-full one stood on the table in front of him. The empties looked like they had contained madeira. The full one I could not tell, but it smelt strong.

His face rose as he struggled to recognise the sound of me. 'Eliza?'

I said nothing, stared at him. His eyes were tracking for small sounds and smells but the booze had dulled him. The damned weeping had started up but I clenched my jaw against it and gave no sign. He could not sense the run of tears. My father felt with one hand for the table edge, with the other for me. I let his hand waver in the air: I would not give him the comfort of soothing me. In the tips of the outstretched fingers I saw his hope die: the hand slackened and returned to the table.

'No. Not worthy of you, girl.'

He turned his body in the seat until he was curled like a wounded animal. He remained in that position as I watched him and grieved, and after a long time I saw that he was asleep.

RODONDO: INTO THE FOG

The next day we watched an island approaching on the horizon. There had been islands all along the voyage, and contortions of the coast that appeared as islands but weren't.

But there was a singularity about the one that loomed in front of us: a brutal bulk, high and sharp. As we neared, the great mass of Wilson's Promontory stretched southward out of the coast on our right, and the island drew threads of cloud from the low sky and teased them into mirages: the island was burning, the island was cut from coal or obsidian; the island was not there at all.

The world around us contained plenty else. The promontory was cloaked in great forests, and seabirds ventured out from it to soar high over our masts. Flatter islands came into view, porpoises rode the *Moonbird*'s wake and a million hidden fish erupted through the surface, flashing bright shards of flank and fin.

But it was the towering island that held the eye. During the morning it turned into a shark's fin, a hat, the wall of a forbidden city. When it could no longer play at illusion, it began to reveal details of itself: vertical ribs down its flanks like the baleen of a whale, a dark forest on the sloping heights above the vertical cliffs. The arc of the sun found new fissures and shadows, the escarpments stood higher and pressed their claims on the sky. The master kept the helm all day, eyes on the cliffs. The Connollys, bent to their work, glanced up as if to ensure it hadn't moved. Dr Gideon was on the deck with his journal once again to take advantage of the light. Each time he stopped writing to gaze at the island, the pencil rested in his mouth. Always, with him, this earnest need to appear learned.

Even my father appeared to sense the mass of the island. *What approaches?* he asked of no one—and indeed, the island was approaching us, rather than the reverse. Around midday, I made him and the doctor a small meal of biscuit and some pickled cabbage, with tea. The doctor looked up gratefully from his work and I pointed out that I was getting food for my father anyway.

By four, the island towered above us. Rodondo, Argyle said, named for an island in the Caribbean—at precisely the opposite point on the globe—which looked identical. The doctor concurred: it was not uncommon, he explained, for physical features on the earth's surface to be exactly mirrored in another hemisphere. Such equal distributions of mass kept the rotation of planetary bodies in perfect balance: thus an ocean might counterweight a continent.

I had no idea whether he was right, but I wasn't willing to take this at face value. 'Is there a boat such as ours, then, sailing about the northern hemisphere?'

He looked at me with absolute sincerity. 'I hope there is no other boat engaged in such sad inquiry as ours, miss.'

And damn him, just like that I felt ashamed to have been so flippant.

At five, the sun had fallen below the pinnacle of the island's mount. The temperature fell rapidly, and with the prickling of my skin I felt the first stirrings of fear. I stayed near my father, though he was already insensible. Argyle worked the *Moonbird* around into the lee of the cliffs. The breeze had died to almost nothing by now, a quarter mile off the south-western slopes, but he was careful.

At the bow, the Connollys carried out a sounding. No sooner had they called forty fathoms than there was trouble: Angus had snarled his hand in the line and he lashed out in pain, caught Declan by the shirt and pushed him against the windlass. Declan grabbed him by the face and squeezed hard: 'Fuck brother, will ye calm down.' The Scotsman's features were distorted by the iron grip, and foul curses leaked out one side of his squashed mouth.

The doctor wove between them, unworried. He was picking tiny crabs off the sounding line and scooping them into one of his jars, where the fluid immediately stunned them motionless and they drifted to the bottom. He was so absorbed in his work that he did not see me watching him. At such moments, I had noticed, the men forgot themselves. Engrossed by their work, or their arguments, their careful observance of a woman's presence on board fell away.

'Aagh me fuckin hand,' sobbed Angus. His brother had stood away now, looked wearily up into the rigging.

But over the sounds of shipboard life I thought I heard other noises.

Tiny, faint and hard to place, I thought at first they were coming from the galley, where Argyle was making food for my father. I wondered about the cliffs of the island, the flat expanse of sea between them and us. About our own sounds refracting, coming back towards us, altered by the sentient rock.

Shortly after dark we each settled into our place. I was restless; sleep would not come. Nature called but, out of concern that the men would hear, I could not attend the tiny head that was installed at the ends of the bunks. So I took myself up onto the deck.

The moon was out, silver on the calm sea. Stars all around, a puff of small cloud here and there. The island stood silent: a huge dark mass before us. Below me, a lantern burned, even now, in the doctor's cabin, although it must be well after midnight. I wondered briefly what he could be working on. What could please and intrigue a man so much that he would prefer it to the deepest rest of the night?

I took the second jib and arranged it around the small port in the gunwale where the boat access was, so that I had a screen, hitched my nightgown and lowered my backside into the gap. I could hear no other sound than the trickle falling on the sea far below: the only movement in the whole world. But once the stream had ended, silence fell heavily. Any sound now would have total dominion.

And so it was that a human voice cut the night.

A loud cry that was somewhere between distress and anger. Not calling to us, I thought. Perhaps raised in argument. It came, quite clearly, from the island. I looked that way and now I could see a pinpoint of orange light, flickering.

There were people on the island.

Argyle had insisted earlier that it was uninhabited. It had

no flat ground, he said, no place for settlement. And besides, landing a boat there, transferring materials and supplies, would be nigh impossible. I sat very still now, and listened. It was several voices, not just one. All male.

No one would live here by choice. Either they were wrecked here and needed our help or they were to be avoided. We had posted no watch overnight: the sea was calm and we were safe at anchor. I would not wake the master to tell him this. The inhabitants of the island could wait for the morning, and so could we.

~

At dawn the men were busy on the deck. The smoke from the previous night's fire was clearly visible, and it had been decided we would haul in close to examine its source.

The doctor had deployed a net behind us—he called it a pelagic trawl—and as the morning's faint breeze fattened the sails and we drew forward, the net fanned itself out in our wake, then sank from view. He said that he wanted to harvest what he could from the zone where the deep water of last night's anchorage sloped up towards the shores of the island. This, he said, was the most fertile water of all.

A sea fog was descending, enclosing us in a claustrophobic embrace with the island.

We drew close and shapes separated themselves from the rock, heavy timbers on the steep shore. No beaches, not even a scree of boulders. The Connollys made soundings as we neared: twenty-six fathoms, twenty-one fathoms, twenty-eight, twenty-eight. The island was a pillar: it stood stark without preamble upon the ocean floor.

Movement: a man, three men. Climbing, as much as they were walking, on the steep terrain.

Fog closing in. They had noticed us, stopped, were staring. I could see beards, clothes that hung loose and dark on one. Another was naked: certainly a white man, but naked.

Another man, further up. The fog closed tighter.

We were looking now at a thin splinter of the island, in which the men were contained. The dark flanks of the rock had disappeared in the mist, as had everything but a narrow corridor of sea between us and the cliff. Argyle was concentrating at the helm, in a navy-blue serge dress tied off with a bow over his middle. He wore a plain bonnet and matching slippers, perhaps in response to the early morning chill on the deck. He was a wind-vane in the breeze, the loose ends of the bonnet ties and the bow rippling in the air.

The small noises of our approach were muffled in the blankness of the fog. The Connollys called the soundings at the volume of close speech, and the mist absorbed their voices. They heaved the dripping line into coils at their feet then threw the plummet again. As we neared the rocks, the numbers diminished. At four fathoms, the smothered sounds of the island were reaching us.

Beyond our gunwales now, mere yards of water led to the wall of white where the air had compressed into miasma: dense, wet and featureless. It did not move, as one expects mist to move on the sea. It was heavy as the seawater. The sails and the master's ribbons had fallen slack. Dr Gideon beckoned to the Connollys and they abandoned their soundings to help him haul in the net: I could not watch, so transfixed was I by the closeness of the cliff and the suffocating fog.

I heard a heavy crash. I thought it was us, but there was no movement to suggest it. The sound must have come from ashore. Voices, laughing then silent. Who would laugh, here and now? And why did they not continue? Why was there no conversation? I was profoundly confused. The timber where I rested my hand—I was clinging to the base of the gaff—was slick with moisture.

The silence cracked a little once again, this time to reveal song. A man's voice, thick as tar through deep notes, then failing at its upper registers. The words unclear, the final line cracking hoarse, then silence.

I wanted to be gone.

I could not see the end of the bow from where I stood amidships. Still the damned whiteness. No sound for a long time, the boat creeping forward in the gloom. Over shallower water I felt more conscious of its lifting and yawing. I could not remember discussing why we were doing this. *Why were we here?*

Another crash and this time a scream. Pain, not fright. I could smell plants now, wet seaweed and guano. More sounds that could have been laughter. The spaces between sounds were too long, and their disconnection made them more unsettling.

Dr Gideon was on the deck, drying his hands on a cloth. He hung his head down, listening intently. The small wake of the *Moonbird* could be heard now, lapping on the unseen shore. The air was so still, the sea so oily, that these mere ripples rushed like unimpeded surf.

'You're looking out the wrong side,' he said quietly.

'It's plainly there,' I said, and pointed directly towards the noises.

'Fog refracts it,' he countered. 'It's off the other quarter.' He crossed to the far side. I followed him; he seemed certain, and as I did so the air moved and the light changed. More water appeared at our side, inky first then fading to paler green and I saw with sudden alarm that we were very close off the boulders; so close that I could make out shapes on the bottom in the clear water.

'Draft?' asked the doctor, an eyebrow inclined towards the master.

'Nine foot.'

We were using every inch of it. The lesson of those soundings was that nothing beneath us would happen in a gradient. The four fathoms could vanish and we would strike a boulder. They were everywhere: the previous day I'd seen Argyle weaving around them in what I thought was open water. In such calm seas, without whitewater on the surface to indicate their presence, they were even more dangerous.

I called to Declan, who had the helm, that he ought perhaps to swing her to port. I felt foolish even as the words left me—who was I to be calling such manoeuvres?—and he shot me a look of unconcealed scepticism. He looked to the master, who nodded faintly, and brought us round. As the rudder bit the water, the sky appeared over us and the fog receded. And what did I expect to see when distorted sound became vision?

I will try to describe what appeared, though a great many things happened at once.

The sudden spear of the cliff, so very close. Boulders dry and round marking a shallow cleft, not enough to call a bay. Tussocks above the rocks, overtaken on the rise by low, twisting timber and shrubs in lush greens that fed on the mist. Exposed columns of rock and then, higher up, great trees projecting out from the rock face and over us. A continuous run of vertical rock, perhaps fifty feet of it; between that and the commencement of the tree line there was a small, flat space. We were so close to the island now that it was impossible to see the surface of it—I imagined it was clear grass.

What I could see, as the last breaths of fog drew away, was a nest of small huts joined to each other to form a continuous roof. The timbers were of various kinds: boughs that appeared silver from immersion; planks and boards that were milled, some curved to betray their origins as the bones of ships. Iron bolts rusted in the air where the builders had neglected to pull them free. The structures huddled in a saw-cut ridge running horizon-tally across the cliffs; shrubs grown up over their low sides showed that these people had been here a very long time. But none of these things were my concern. What concerned me was the men.

They had pressed forward at sea level, six of them that I could see, but I felt certain there were others hiding among the shrubs and wreckage and boulders. Two men advanced in the water to ankle depth. A dull sound emanated, gathered mutters that blurred into one constant low and malignant stirring.

They were armed. Some carried clubs fashioned from scraps. One or two bore a hook or a crude blade of scrap iron. There were short swords that looked to be of naval issue. One of the men at water level had a rifle, and now I saw that another was braced higher, supported by a boulder, with a carbine levelled at the *Moonbird*. We had sailed deep enough into the small bay that they were able to cover us from three sides.

Nothing about their faces or any of the sounds from the island gave a clue as to their intentions. They just watched us.

The mist had lifted completely now. They must have piled their muck at the margins of their high platform, because clouds of gulls rose there, and the slightest breeze brought a terrible stench down the cliff.

I began to study their faces, their leers and scowls. Once, twice, severally I saw that the faces were scarred and misshapen, erupting in sores. Some were swollen around the eyes, or growths from within had devoured the nose. Missing ears, toothless mouths, lopsided clumps of missing hair. Some contagion had taken hold of them.

The horror of it now swept through us all. The master had brought a carbine up from below decks: he worked with practised fingers to tear open the cartridge and pour powder in the pan. The doctor stood close to the bulwark and braced his leg against it. His left hand held his notebook, his right hand a pencil, and he was sketching, or perhaps writing descriptions of what we beheld. The master was working the ramrod into the muzzle.

The *Moonbird* was only a chain's length from the shore these men stood upon. They wouldn't swim to us, I felt fairly sure, and if they did they would struggle to climb the sides. The greater danger was that we would drift further in and beach ourselves, having so little control in the lifeless air. The swells lifted the stern just faintly, then broke on the stones only yards in front of us.

The master laid the carbine on the boards of the forward cabin roof, and moved swiftly to the helm. He whispered to the Connolly brothers, issuing sail orders he didn't want heard from shore. Even poor Angus sensed the tension and was silent. Two, three full rotations of the helm as the master looked over his shoulder at the angle of the stern.

The doctor was obscured from view behind the cabin: he faced the main group of men where he stood. I could hear Argyle's orders to swing her clear, and the Connolly brothers working the lines. The movement on board had my attention for just a moment: long enough to miss what had happened in the crowd.

A man had darted forward from among them, a lad, I thought. The shape of him was lean enough to suggest there were not many years on him; or he was a grown man starving. Without warning, he leapt into the water with a great splash and set out towards us, making clumsy strokes with his arms, his intentions, hostile or otherwise, lost in his thrashing.

The men on the rocks followed his progress with the barrels of their weapons.

When the swimmer had covered about two thirds of the journey from shore, there was a rapid volley of fire. I could not make out who was firing or at what, but a split appeared in the timber of the mainmast only inches from my head and splinters struck my face. My father stood exposed forward of the mast: I leapt at him and dragged him to the deck. A shower of fist-sized rocks began to land around us as I peered over the bulwark, keeping my face between the pulleys.

The rounds were smacking into the surface and raising plumes of water, wide and long but closing in as some marksman found his range. Above me, Argyle was crouched low, trying to swing the rudder. The boom responded, sweeping inches over my head.

The swimmer was close when the ball struck him. It took him flush in the top of the skull and made a sound like he'd been hit with a timber. His eyes had been fixed on us in supplication as he thrashed our way, and by then it was clear he was trying to escape. But when the ball hit him it sheared away the crown of his head and the eyes were upturned by the impact, irises hideously absent. He slumped forward where he was. A brief and subsiding jet of blood; then his lifeless form floating face-down in the reddening water.

There was a great deal more yelling from shore, and a further round or two whirred through our rigging. The *Moonbird* had borne away by now and the gusts that swirled down the cliff filled our sails and swept us out of range. The dead man rolled over onto one side, sinking from view as the air escaped from the back of his shirt.

The firing ceased. We emerged from our various positions to meet in stunned silence in the centre of the deck, just aft of the foremast. Something had struck my father on the chin: he was bleeding a little. I sat him back against the cabin wall and dabbed at the cut with the end of my sleeve.

'Who were they?' he asked me.

I looked around at the rest of them: Argyle only a graven image, the Connollys breathing heavily after the labour of getting the *Moonbird* out of the lethal gully it was in and the doctor, to my surprise, calmly cleaning the barrel of the carbine.

'Did he…?' I found my mouth was dry. 'Is he…?'

'I'm afraid so,' the doctor replied pleasantly. 'I only wish I'd laid out a couple of those wretches before they hit the poor lad.'

'Your pocket?' the master asked him.

The doctor smiled and scooped out a handful of balls. Argyle counted them. 'You got off three shots in, what, forty seconds? Fine shooting, doctor.'

I hadn't answered my father. 'I guess they were lags,' I said to him. 'Absconders.'

Argyle looked dubious. 'They had working guns. I'd say someone's put em ashore from another vessel. An uprising or such. Sickness goin through em, by the look. But they been at those antics for a time now.'

'How do you know that?'

'Two o' them timbers on the rocks were inner sternposts,

and you only get one o' them on each ship. The doorway up higher? That was a keelson too big for both posts. So there's three boats at least weren't as lucky as us.'

As the others moved away, I leaned in close to my father. His face responded instinctively to my proximity. 'Father, that might be what you're looking for. A gang wrecking vessels. Should we not go back?'

His smile was gently scornful. 'You don't scare easily, do you? We're too far north, my love. And the man we're seeking, he's not so stupid as that lot.'

SEABIRDS AND SEALS

The master told us he would make a wide arc to the south-east, from Rodondo out to Hummock. It was open water, only a scatter of minor islands to the east of the route which he and my father had concluded were not worth investigating. *No sealers*, he said, and my father nodded judiciously. We would sweep down to the Furneaux group, eighty nautical miles, and begin again there.

The early morning had a faint drizzle in it. Tiny specks, a day that meant itself to be fine but had somehow leaked. This contributed to the damp over everything, which the master said was characteristic of the Tasman Sea to our east, and not of the Strait. As he told me this, he was removing the furred mantle he wore against the morning chill. The Strait carried dry air, he said, even when it was forced through by a cold westerly. I tried to imagine dry air between raindrops and could not.

The humidity clung to my skin and slicked the sails with

damp. The flies were huge and heavy and they droned in the air, trapped themselves in the close spaces below decks, where they would buzz aimlessly until swatted by a fractious hand. Rarely, but with great ceremony, huge flying ants would appear: the lost queens of some faraway hive, their drones searching frantically for them, not knowing the boat had carried them away.

Land masses in the distance appeared to float in the warm mist that clouded the horizons. Mountaintops hung in weird suspension. The sea darkened to slate blue. There could have been a storm in the far-off miles, the sky loaded with subterfuge, vague enough to hide a thunderhead.

The brothers were bickering. About seals this time, as we passed by Curtis and its grim neighbour, the Devil's Tower. The formation opened into two separate spikes as we drew nearer, bald granite spearing vertically from the waves. I could see, even at our wide clearance, that the rocks were a haul-out for seals. The swell washed heavy and blue over the weedy foot of the towers. I had by now become accustomed to the streaks of seal excrement, bleached in the elements, and the pungent smell of their bodies when the wind offered it our way.

'Stromness...' I heard. 'On the Scapa Flow.' It was Angus, a dreamy smile. 'Grey seals, right? But these uns are *red...*'

Declan grabbed his brother in a half-hearted headlock and started up a string of insults about selkie-folk. Angus punched lazily at his brother's shoulder. 'They's not seals. Seals're grey, can't fool me. An they got no ears.'

'So what're these then, feckin elephants?'

'Master'll know,' said Angus, as though bringing Argyle in would resolve the argument.

Declan only laughed. 'Him? Old Man o' Hoy in a dress?'

'Language.' Argyle scowled at them, an eye to me. The scowl

had the desired effect: they hadn't intended for him to overhear.

'They're seals, but of a particular kind,' came the doctor's voice from his favourite spot against the cabin wall. 'Pinnipeds. It means they have ears.'

As we left the tower of rock and the seals behind, the low sky over the ocean ahead filled with drifting black mists. Birds, millions of them, small and dark. We'd seen them over the water already, impossible to count in their swirling abundance, impossible to track an individual by eye. More like insect clouds than aggregations of feathers and beating hearts.

The *Moonbird* ploughed closer and closer to the great flock, and now the cloud of birds was parting, allowing the boat passage through the mass. They whipped past the rigging, darting and bending and making corners in the air. I could smell their bodies, distinct from the mineral sea and the lingering scent of the seals, life in those weeks being the exchange of one stink for another.

The doctor had rushed below decks and emerged again with a knife and a handful of fish, running the blade along them so their innards spilled and hung. He twisted the opened fish into a sheet of his fine netting. This he roped off with cord and slung overboard; a bouquet garni for the sea. He held the cord with one hand, and in the other waited a dip-net on a long pole. The great avian cloud formed a finger that pointed to the waiting bait: a cluster of birds circled in and stabbed at the gutted fish. The doctor pounced, swinging the pole down and the net caught a bird in the act of swallowing.

When he'd lifted it onto the boards, the doctor picked it up and neatly wrung its neck.

'Moonbird,' said Argyle, peering over his shoulder.

'Our namesake?' I asked.

'Indeed.'

'The natives eat them,' said the doctor, 'and so do the sealers. Made an industry of it. Full of oil, tastes like tar. These here, you see'—he pointed to the raised nostrils along the top of the bird's beak—'they have a sense of smell. Most seabirds don't. They go way out, across the Pacific, and come back to the very same burrow. Smell their way home.'

We looked out at them on the water, forming a raft that rose and fell and rearranged itself with every movement of air and water. A ripple through them would raise a thousand birds to the air, only to settle again en masse.

'Flyin sheep,' muttered Declan, and Angus laughed.

'Shearwaters, curlews, godwits...' Gideon was speaking quietly, just beside me. His voice had a dreamy quality to it, the sound of a man putting words to an inner vision. 'All of them are moonbirds because of their migration. The Pacific is the moon void of the world, as you know...No? The great crater formed when the moon tore itself loose from the earth, hmm? And every island on the rim of the void has a great migratory bird. This one is ours. So far they go, further than a man might sail in an entire lifetime, and they do it every year. Same burrow, same mate. They live many years and fly a long way. Multiply the years by the miles and they've flown to the moon, Eliza. Therein lies the name's origin.'

Eliza, he had said. No amount of scientific rhapsodising would excuse it.

'I am interested to know your thoughts,' he went on. I had a feeling he was not; that he was, rather, entranced by his own. 'Here in front of us you see the collective unspoken will that unites the birds. I've known fish to be the same; livestock, to a lesser extent. Somehow they surrender individual choice to something collective, and in return they receive the protection of collective thought. Imagine if humans lived like that—if we acquiesced all the time in what was being done around us. There would be no science, no discovery of new lands, no defence against tyranny.'

Good Lord, the pomposity of the man! 'And why do you suppose they might behave that way, doctor?' I asked.

He had his elbow on the bulwark rail, his chin cupped in his hand, and the breeze lifted the silver hair at his temples. He failed to sense the irritation in my voice, or he ignored it. 'I imagine it is the existence of predators. The individual is vulnerable, but the aggregated mass is safer. We humans don't behave that way because we have no predators.'

'No,' I countered, 'but we do have tyrants.'

'Surely not out here,' he smiled.

~

The doctor spent the remaining daylight in the galley. I could tell he was focused on cooking something specific, but he came up on deck and sought orders from each of us around sunset. The brothers were content to eat biscuit and pork with lemon juice, a diet I believe they would happily have subsisted upon when ashore. Argyle said he would join them.

My father could not be persuaded to take any food. He was slurring: it made me angry, it made me worried. But no matter the inversion of our relationship as parent and child, I couldn't very well force-feed him.

Which left the doctor and me. I was resigned to the biscuit and pork when he winked scandalously at me and said he would present me with something different. Again—*again!*—why was I not quicker in chiding him over these liberties? Back to the galley he went, and within the hour the others were fed and a peculiar smell wafted from the little vent: I couldn't say it made me hungry, but nor was it repellent.

I stayed on deck, as the evening was clear and warm. Argyle had gone silently below, the only occupant of a lonely world that spun in dark heavens. I would never have imagined a man could find such solitude in such close confines. My father was singing, tunelessly, and the brothers joined in now and then, before returning to their endless routine of insults and scragging.

The doctor returned as the moon was rising in the east. He was carrying a chopping board, and on it—poetically—was the moonbird he'd killed in the afternoon. He had baked it and splayed it open with a cut from neck to crop. Where the innards would have been, he had made a stuffing from biscuit, onion and lemon peel. The bird lay in a nest of chopped potatoes, as if it had landed on its back there and somehow burst open. The board tilted slightly as the doctor bent to sit, and a trickle of juice ran off the meat and onto the deck.

I gave him the *Bravo!* he was clearly expecting. He seemed pleased.

'Couldn't work out how to get all the damn—sorry, all the feathers out of it. Must be an old bird. I scalded it and they wouldn't come off, so I had to skin it.' He produced two forks from somewhere in his jacket. 'Here, let's see how it tastes before we get too carried away.'

We pulled at the greasy sinews, dark and wreathed in a thin layer of fat. I chewed tentatively and the doctor must have seen the look on my face.

'What do you say, Miss Grayling?'

'Something of duck…but the stronger flavour is cod liver oil. Somehow I think it is both fish and fowl.'

He pointed his loaded fork at me, choking laughter while he swallowed. Reluctantly, I smiled in return.

'Aah! There…a smile! You are *exactly* right about the meat. That's precisely what it is.' He chewed some more. 'Now, what is the science? What if this meat confers the benefits of both poultry and—oh, say, herring? Those oils in the fish that are so beneficial to the health? And what if they could be farmed and fed to convict workers?'

I looked at him deadpan. 'They fly.'

He burst out laughing, ejecting a string of meat from his mouth. 'Of course they do, you have me there. But there are ways. Aviaries…clipped wings, I don't know…'

'They also burrow.'

He could barely contain his mirth now. 'Oh, this is all too hard. I give up. We'll send the lags out at night with nets.'

We ate in silence for a while. I knew him well enough now to sense that a change of topic was coming.

'Where do you suppose you will find this man?' he asked suddenly.

'Who?' Wherever I had thought the conversation might turn, it was not here.

'The man you say is responsible for the loss of the vessel. I mean, he could be anywhere. These islands are a maze—that's why all the absconders are here, all the foreigners who don't want to be found.'

I knew it to be a question I should be capable of answering, and was not. 'You would have to ask my father.'

'But how does *he* know? Does he expect that some ringleader will leap out and reveal himself?'

I thought about that. The fish-bird was becoming less palatable as it cooled. 'Anyone who is capable of orchestrating a shipwreck is going to be someone prominent. It's not a thing you could do by stealth, is it? You'd need to recruit others, organise them. Such a person will nominate himself, I would think. He would stand out.'

'You imagine him as a kind of self-appointed deity. What about the rest of the sealers? Are they mere mendicants? They might not subscribe to the rules of society, but it doesn't mean they're savages before an idol. Surely they'd reject such a man.'

My father staggered down the stairs into the cabin, still singing to himself. He knew the rail well now. It was drunkenness, not his lack of sight, that had him stumbling. The doctor watched him go. He seemed terse after his comment: I hadn't expected him to defend the sealers quite so sharply, and while I had to admire his intellect, I was unconvinced by the argument. I saw every possibility that the sealers had thrown up the kind of charismatic leader who might devise such an incident, and such a leader would fit well with the character of the man who had attacked my father all those years ago.

'I shall return shortly,' he muttered now. He picked up the tray and its eviscerated bird, and followed my father downstairs.

I was left on deck by myself, just the night and the two Connollys playing cards nearer the bow. I knew the hands, the tricks: Declan was letting his brother win. I went to the rail and looked out at the night and saw the *Moonbird*'s wake glowing bright green in the darkness. The glow flared where the water was disturbed up close against the edge of the bow, then faded as the little bow-wave rolled away from the timbers and out into the night.

The doctor appeared at the rail beside me, smoking his pipe.

'It's enchanting,' I said.

'Not Ehrenberg...' He tapped an irritated index finger on

the rail, as though he was trying to dislodge something from his memory. 'Boyle! Robert Boyle has written on it. Luminescence... *animalcules*, he called them.'

'Boyle...the one who invented that pump you showed me?'

'Yes! The very same.'

I looked at his face, the bent and imperfect riddle that it was, and I saw the glow reflected in it. I wondered to myself why it wasn't enough that the glow was there and that it was beautiful.

'I have one more thing to show you,' he said now. 'Are you tired? Would you humour me a little longer?'

I shrugged and told him I could spare him a minute or two.

'I would appreciate it, you know. Too much of the work is solitary. Come, then.' He tapped out his pipe on the rail and indicated that we should go below. I followed him, past my father's curtained bunk, the doctor making an exaggerated shushing gesture with his finger on his lips. Out of the gloom and into his cabin, the curious assemblage of boxes and instruments, books and jars and skulls and feathers, a room inhaling more and more objects: not just the specimens, which were undoubtedly growing in number, but large items I was sure I'd never previously seen.

'Look!' He was peering into a tin bucket that was set on the floor beside the desk. He scooped his fingers through the water and brought up a most exceptional creature: an octopus of some kind, slightly bigger than his hand and wearing a white spiral shell where one might have expected to see its head. The shell was rippled and serrated in many different directions: there were no smooth surfaces but hundreds of small bumps that formed complex patterns, all of them leading back into spirals that complemented the winding shape of the shell itself.

Beneath the shell were two huge, iridescent green eyes. They could not blink, it seemed, nor change shape in any way, and thus gave no indication of the creature's displeasure at being handled this way. The tentacles were long and whip-like, and they sought out Gideon's hand and encircled his wrist. With several of its limbs occupied this way, the underside of the animal was revealed, pale and dotted with suckers, a small beak opening and closing like a feeding parrot. Those eyes shone out from within the nest of exploring arms, and I felt as though they were staring at me.

Gideon swept the tentacles off himself until they hung vertically below the shell. Then he took a firm hold of the animal around the point where its large eyes were, and pulled on it. It came free from the shell. Now I could see the head, a little narrower than I had imagined an octopus's head to be. He tossed the creature back into the bucket and it immediately inked, squirting jet-black droplets out of the water and onto a nearby pile of books. We watched it dart around the bucket before compressing itself into the angle where the bucket's sides met its base.

'Hmm,' he muttered. 'That's the first observation, then. Animal survives separation from the shell.'

He held the shell aloft. It was unblemished, white as quartz and slightly translucent, so that the yellowy light of the lamp passed through it and showed the shadows of his fingers beneath. Along its radial spine the tiny lumps were raised into little horns, each slightly larger than its predecessor.

'It drifted by the boat yesterday and I scooped it with a net. Lovely specimen, is it not?'

I agreed that it was. He used a small cloth to pat it gently dry, then placed it on a bookshelf behind the desk. Now he sat at an odd-looking occasional table beside the desk that I hadn't noticed before—another large item in the room that had appeared from nowhere.

It was not just a table, I realised, but a mechanical device of some kind, its function a mystery to me. The doctor bent and tended to it: adjusting a structure that resembled the base of a treadle sewing table, but with a leather bellows attached to one side. The nose of the bellows, pointing upwards, was connected to a tube that ran up and followed a metal arm to a box located at the user's eye height.

The device fascinated me because I knew instinctively that it was a product of the doctor's mind. He had not ordered it from a catalogue, nor commissioned an engineer to make it for him. It came from within him, a mechanical expression of the intricacy of his thinking. Having first dismissed him as a carnival hustler, I was now becoming intrigued by his abilities.

He pulled down on a polished wooden lever that lay against the vertical arm. A round blade emerged from a cavity on the underside of the raised box, and locked into position with a quiet click at the end of the lever's arc.

There was a slosh: the creature, in its boneless motion, was pacing in the bucket. He glanced at it.

'Remarkable organism, the octopus. Three hearts, circulating blood that is blue, not red. Why? Because it contains copper, in all likelihood to carry oxygen in the same way our blood does.'

I smiled and nodded, because I was fairly sure that was the reaction he was seeking. 'And if we accept the idea that the heart is the seat of the emotions, Doctor Gideon, what does one do with three of them?'

He laughed, sat before the table with his feet underneath and pedalled smoothly. The bellows started to breathe and the little round blade began to spin, fast enough that it emitted a whining sound. Using another timber lever, this one located on the side of the table, Gideon was able to lower the arm down to his working surface. He stopped briefly and directed a lamp that stood on his main desk so that it would illuminate what he was doing.

'Do you like it?' he asked. He gestured at the machine, his knees rising and falling, his face almost boyishly proud.

'To be quite honest it looks like a sewing table.'

He was crestfallen, and I felt instantly ashamed.

'That's because it started out as a sewing table. I added the saw mechanism and the adjustable levers, the bellows.' He gestured at them as if he could not comprehend why this was not impressive. 'It's a pneumatic saw—I know of no other example in the world. The blade operates at such high revolutions that it can cut through adamantine surfaces without the need to apply any force. Is that not remarkable to you?' He made a helpless gesture, clearly hurt.

Now he took the nautilus shell from where it sat on his bookshelf, placed it under the blade and put his spectacles on. I came closer. He was lowering the blade gradually using the lever, and with his other hand aligning the shell so that the path of the blade would trace its long axis precisely. As the blade came into contact with the shell the whining became a scouring sound, amplified by the cavity of the shell. He ran the shell through in one smooth pass, and a plume of white dust rose in the lamplight, powdering his jaw and settling on the lenses of his spectacles.

'This is the beauty of the saw,' he said. 'If I tried to pass a knife through this shell, no matter how sharp or careful, the shell would shatter.'

The two halves of the shell fell into his waiting palms. He

stopped his pedalling, brought the halves to his mouth and blew gently so the remaining dust inside was expelled in a little cloud.

'Ah!' he exclaimed as I peered over his shoulder. '*Now* you are interested. What do you see?'

I saw a beautiful symmetry: a spiral that curled into delicate miniature and then into infinity, one long, continuous chamber that narrowed and narrowed until it disappeared into itself. 'What do *you* see?' I asked him.

'I had expected to see chambers, as one does in the chambered nautilus of the Minoans. I do not think they are the same animal.' He paused, removed his spectacles and pinched at the bridge of his nose. 'I had planned to measure the chambers to understand how the ratio applies to their interior dimensions.'

He still had a hold of his nose, an odd mannerism. 'The head of the animal is clearly smaller than the interior space of the shell…a void inside, perhaps a buoyancy control: more air in the chamber and it floats, less and it sinks. But what would be the point of such a frail shell? Surely there's no protection in that…'

He pressed one of his square-ended fingers against the side of the shell and it flexed under the pressure. I thought it was going to shatter.

Then he pushed the halved shell away, placed a piece of thin timber board on the front edge of the desk, and retrieved the octopus—limp by now, the tentacles draped over his hand and dripping on the floor. The inking of the water had stained the animal a sad grey.

The unblinking eye watched me, maybe pleading, maybe only sad.

He took a scalpel in his left hand, swept his glasses back onto his nose with his right, then took hold of the animal and peered at it again. The returned stare did not disconcert him at all. 'Every argonaut we have ever studied has been a female. No one's ever seen a male. Or perhaps we have but none of us has recognised it. Might be an animal we know well, but the connection has never been made.'

'What are you going to do now?' I asked. He rolled the scalpel in his fingers.

'Dissect it,' he replied. 'And in the morning, fry it in biscuit crumbs. I do hope you'll join me.'

I laughed despite myself, then told him it was late and that I must take my leave. He pantomimed dejection, poking his lower lip out comically, and something in me responded to the foolery. I made a little wave across the cabin to him and backed out through the door.

In the tight passageway outside, my father was snoring softly in his bed, his head turned outwards towards me. Argyle's bunk was empty: another watch through the night.

I lingered there—why?—about to pass through to my cabin. The shadows, the warm smells of the timber, the faint movements of the *Moonbird*.

When I turned and saw the doctor come out of his room and stand behind me, just outside his doorway, looking at me, I realised what I had been waiting for. His eyes, bright with mischief, entreated my complicity.

My mouth was opening to demur, my breath suspended to wish him a second goodnight—and we were kissing.

I had not seen it coming: I had not known I was in his arms until I felt my whole body press towards his, the shock so great that I could not think of anything at all. I kissed him back, yes, I am sure of that. For how long? I cannot say. But then there was panic rising inside me: we were standing within a couple of feet of my father's bed. He must not wake to this. I gave a little shudder, and made to push the doctor away, but he clung harder. I turned my head; stepped away, felt his hands drop.

Just as I did so my father gave a snort, and woke.

'Girl?'

'Here, Papa.'

'What are you doing there?' He was climbing upright, pushing his blanket back.

'Just…just checking on you.' The doctor had made no attempt to retreat into his quarters. He remained standing exactly where we had embraced. His eyes were wide and darting, eyebrows raised, and mouth curled into the tiniest smile. Could this be amusing to him?

My father had found the edge of his bed and used it to drag himself to his feet. He stood up in front of me, a mere two feet aside of the doctor, who stood so perfectly still that even his breathing appeared to have stopped. My breath, too, had steadied.

Father came forward, tiny shuffling steps that measured the floor, hands outstretched.

'Eliza?'

'Yes, Father,' I said softly. Our ritual, so many thousand times.

His hands reached forward; the tips of his fingers searched the air. His right hand swept within inches of the doctor's jaw, but the doctor did not flinch or make a sound. Then one of my father's fingers made contact with my cheek, and the fingers of his other hand moved in unison to find the other cheek and there he rested them for just an instant. So lightly. I saw the confusion in his face as a faint light fell on his whiskers. The overworked senses adjusting to a suspicion about the space around him.

'Here I am, Papa.'

He swept both hands away from my face again and let them

complete a circle in the air. They came back without contact, with nothing to tell him, and his brow creased further; he did not believe them. His left hand rested on my right shoulder: the fingers of his right hand reached to my ear, picked a fine lock of hair and swept it back. I watched a tear form in his eye and spill free.

The doctor remained utterly still, all the life concentrated in his eyes.

My father patted my cheek gently. As he turned to find his bed again, he murmured, 'Sometimes I worry so in the night.'

THE NIGHT, GIBBOUS MOON

The flesh of the octopus-creature, though it saddened me to eat it, was delicious. I wondered whether it was wise to convey my enthusiasm to the doctor. He was watching for my verdict: in the end I smiled and put a finger to my lips to pretend I was still eating.

I sat on deck reading through the morning and into the afternoon. I had become accustomed now to the idea that the spaces below decks were too confined to spend extended time during the day. As comfortable as she was, the *Moonbird*'s cabins could be oppressive over long hours. Again I found the reading difficult, even now when there was so little motion under the hull. Out on the open water that separated the islands off the mainland from the cluster that would soon appear as the Furneaux group, the wind had died off and we were almost becalmed.

But the early summer sun was warm enough to offset the

morning chill, and the torn-paper sky full of promise. The surfaces of the *Moonbird* welcomed the body: timbers that were curved and sanded and had softened off under exposure to the salt wind and the sun. Fittings that made sonorous *plink*s and *thwack*s.

Argyle stood at the helm in a dress of coarse grey cotton, much like a servant might wear, and draped round his neck was a bright muslin kerchief. The brothers busied themselves in small labours about the deck. The doctor came up from below and brought his working board with him. I averted my eyes, even while I watched him. He claimed he preferred the light up here in the middle of the day, *good for fine work*, provided the wind wasn't too fresh. He kept smiling my way, trying to make a co-conspirator of me. The night before, I had concluded, was an aberration: a thing that didn't exist if I refused to let it.

He had kissed me. Not only that, I had kissed him back. Such things did not happen in my life, did not happen on land, and therefore must belong to some elemental slipping of the rules when one took to the sea. Very well, things were different out here. But having made an error, I didn't have to repeat it. That is, I *could* if I wanted to, or—

Damn it, he was looking again—that half-smile—and I feared the turmoil was written on my face. I smiled tightly back and looked out to sea.

When I looked again he was probing on the board with the scalpel, picking at a tiny bundle of pale flesh that could easily have been mistaken for fatty off-cuts of pork. Gelatinous, curled, in shades of pearl through to pink, a nest of fine tubes and little sacs and, at one end of the strange structure, the tiny black parrot's beak.

Occasionally he would stop and spray the specimen with a

mist of what I presumed to be seawater from a perfume bottle. He started explaining to me again, blithely, as though unaffected. He had isolated the digestive tract of the octopus, he told me, and what I saw on the board was *the part that lends most fascination*. It was the venom duct, he said, along with the glands that produced the poison. 'All cephalopods are venomous. And we know nothing of the properties of that venom.'

I could not think why anybody would want to keep and dissect the venom gland of an octopus, but he seemed almost childishly happy with his work.

'And I believe I now understand the shape of the shell,' he said. 'It is a *logarithmic spiral, spira mirabilis*, expanding at a constant ratio while remaining essentially unchanged.' Those lost eyes, enraptured. 'Cyclones, ammonites, galaxies. Constantly emerging into the world even as they replicate, a process known as *self-similarity*.'

There were disjunctions here I could not fathom, between admiring the incremental growth and the beauty of a creature; observing it in life, and then killing it and eating it, and finally studying its entrails. I wished now I had not met the strange and beautiful creature before he fed it to me.

~

In the evening my father was drunk again, though I hadn't seen him with a bottle in his hand.

Something was amiss, something was afoot. My long knowledge of his ways told me that he had a hoard somewhere, and I resolved to find it. I waited. I watched him in his phases: buoyant, funny and conversational, then morose. Moving about the deck— even dancing, in the full confidence that he now understood the layout of the boat—before slumping onto his backside and mumbling to himself. He was a drunkard, and a drunkard lives all the rampant madness of our dreams undisguised.

After we'd eaten the evening meal, he finger-traced his way over the timbers and through the rigging until he reached the bow, then propped himself up among the coiled ropes and began a muddled rendition of 'Spanish Ladies'. I picked up a lantern and went below.

Through the boards I could hear him on the deck. Eventually he would make his way back down to where I was: I had to hurry, but I had to be sure of what I was doing. Argyle was busy with his chart, the doctor with some other dissection. Angus Connolly was snoring in his bunk; Declan above deck on silent watch. My father, meanwhile, had mislaid his lyrical man-o-war somewhere between Ushant and Scilly. There was time.

I began with the small chest at the foot of his cot. Clothing, disarrayed. A razor and brush, his pipe. A brooch: a shell cameo in a delicate gold frame with a relief design of a woman's face, her hair garlanded with blossoms. I closed my eyes and felt it with a fingertip. I could not, no matter how hard I concentrated, discern the image without sight. But someone who had once *had* sight would use the fingertip to remember what they saw. Perhaps. The cameo called to me from a well of memory but that moment, whatever it was, hung like a phantom just beyond reach. I raised it to my nostrils but there was only the smell of old metal from the frame.

Another banging sound from above. I needed to hurry.

I plunged deeper among the garments and flinched in shock. My hand had found a blade: had I struck the edge as I'd struck the flat, I would have cut myself deeply. I traced along it in the half-light of the cabin and found the hilt, lifted it out. A dagger, nine inches long. Plain and ugly, flecked with rust along its spine, the honed edge bright.

I had heard from many people the tale of how the imposter Figge had stabbed my father. It was embellished by the vulgar with the epilogue that the attack had made me an only child: that the injury was of an unmentionable nature such that he could never again get a woman with child. So here was a weapon of lethal intimacy, a means of mortal violence available to a blind man. A blind man could not shoot, he could not hurl a missile or swing a club, but in close, working by feel, he could slip a blade between a man's ribs. For my father, who had felt the steel, a moment of vengeance in perfect symmetry.

Sounds on the deck, feet moving quickly. I could no longer hear my father.

The *Moonbird* lurched hard to port, so hard that I tumbled against the bulkhead and the lid of the sea chest slammed shut, narrowly missing my fingertips.

Voices above me, raised in alarm. A frantic winding of the gear. They had the ship hard over on her port side, straining. I tilted out of the cabin and clawed at the stairway until I was on deck. It was dark all around now. Declan Connolly thundered past me, coils of rope over his shoulder. He saw me, whites of his eyes.

'Yer damn father's gone over.'

I was shocked, but also strangely resigned: of course. Of course he'd gone over. The falls, the fights, the broken glass and the cooking accidents: he lived on the edge of calamity at all times. How could I have thought we would travel without incident on the open sea? I ran to the bow and saw we were curving back into the faint white aftermath of our own wake. Our hull was cutting phosphorescence again in the black water, confounding our vision out into the darkness.

The faintest glow of stars out there. Argyle was beside me, wrapped in a dressing-gown and sash, his eyes focused intently on the gloom, counting softly under his breath. Counting down. When he reached zero he called, 'Spill the mainsail,' and the brothers complied. The *Moonbird* surged as the wake caught up with us. Argyle called, 'Quiet,' and began counting again, forwards now.

The sounds of the boat's motion fell away and silence wrapped around us.

Impossible, surely. So much sea out there, and my father so weak. In all likelihood too drunk to call for help. But Argyle was perfectly still, strung like a hunting dog.

'There.'

He pointed forward, slightly off to our starboard side. I could see nothing.

'A landing pole or a gaff, perhaps, Declan? But be careful with him, please.'

I followed the direction he had indicated, over the slick dark surface to where it was broken by a tiny shape. Argyle ran to the helm and we veered towards it. As we drew closer I recognised the shape as my father's back, his body slumped forward so that his face was in the water.

One Connolly went to the port in the gunwale and the brother stood behind him and grabbed a fistful of the trousers between his buttocks so he wouldn't tumble in. Declan leaned out and swung the pole, and my breath shuddered for fear the hook on its end would sink into my father's flesh. But when the pole struck his back he did not react.

I thought then that it had been too long, too long. He had no more will in him than the strands of kelp that hung in the water nearby. It would take so little for the sea to finish him off, to leave me finally alone.

Declan began to twist the pole and the hooked end gathered a bunch of shirt. He laid the pole on the hull's edge and levered the near end down so that my father began to lift clear of the water. Angus was lying in the bay now. He reached forward as my father's limp form swung in towards the *Moonbird* and in one swift motion he had a hold of him. He hauled the old man onto the deck.

The water streamed off him and he lay there limp. Again, that crowd of feelings so at odds with each other. The terrible fear of losing him; the end of my central reason for living and, with it, a whisper of curiosity about who I might be now; relief that this mad escapade would end and I could go back to Srinivas and tell him his judgment was awry.

The men turned my father over, slid a cask under his belly and began to roll him, pressing on his back and thumping between his shoulderblades. He coughed and vomited: I took a bucket of water and sloshed the mess away. I admit I threw the rest of it over his face, and not because I thought it would rouse him, sodden as he was.

He shook himself, reached vaguely into the air in front of him and bellowed something; then he drew his feet up under himself, tried to stand, then toppled and fell.

The others wandered off, satisfied that the crisis was averted. They brought the *Moonbird* around to its original course and returned to their assigned positions: Angus and Declan to their hammocks, Argyle to the watch. I asked the master who had raised the alarm: he thought it had been the doctor, now returned below decks.

My father had sat himself up with his chin raised, a posture

I knew to mean that he was trying to orientate himself. Relief was curdling to fury inside me.

'You were very fortunate,' I said, as evenly as I could.

He heard the anger beneath my words. Looked pained for a second, confused. 'I don't know how I fell in...'

'I'll tell you how: you were rinsed! Where is the grog you're carrying? I'm going to put an end to it.'

Confusion again.

'I'm not carrying any grog, love. Just, just stay true to it, I beg you. We...find the man an then we'll, then we'll...' He slumped, retched, vomited again.

I turned away. Declan had roped off the gunwale bay: he couldn't go anywhere; it wasn't cold above decks. I decided he could spend some time reflecting on his idiocy.

I stormed down into the hold where the brothers were snoring in their hammocks. The provisions were kept in large wooden crates, roped down and braced between the ribs, and divided into their various purposes: dry stores, fruit and vegetables, water. I pawed through them all until I found what I was looking for: a few small crates of bottles and two casks. The noise of my search must have woken the convicts, because I could hear their exchange in the darkness behind me.

'What's she doin, Dec?'

'Ah, Christ a'mighty, the booze.'

They were powerless to intervene but they cursed me loud enough to ensure I'd hear. I took a crate and struggled up the stairway with it in my arms, banging on every step. When I got onto the deck I staggered to the rail and heaved it into the sea. Past my father, who did not miss the tell-tale clinking and splashing.

He turned his face my way, muttered the usual tired refrain about the serpent's tooth.

'We're not going back for *that*,' I spat.

I went back to the hold and repeated the process until I had removed every bottle I could find. The liar! Of course we were carrying booze. I watched the casks bob away into the darkness, took out some of the individual bottles and flung them as hard as I could, aiming them at the bobbing casks. It felt satisfying, as if I had lanced something that afflicted both my father and me.

He resorted to that stage of his bingeing that I knew well, sitting there mournfully on the deck, a blanket around his shoulders now, berating me. *The waste! The waste!* I had no idea about life at sea. I was a harpy, a shrew. *This* (whatever it was) *is what happens when you take women to sea.* My mother would be turning in her grave, *oh, mark my words.*

He didn't seem to be flagging, which was a worry. Normally by this stage he'd have woe-betided himself to sleep.

The frustration overtook me and I screamed, or shouted, I don't know, somewhere close to his face. It was the piling-up of everything: the ingratitude, the obstinacy, the insults, all of it. And for just a brief instant I thought I'd discharged the accumulated rancour. But his reaction robbed me of even that small pleasure. His expression shifted rapidly from bafflement to distress and he lowered his head.

'How many times,' I asked him. 'How many times must we re-enact this? Does it just go on this way until we both flag out and die?'

'Oh what, what? There is no re-enactment.' He swept his hands across the boards of the deck as though he wanted to draw a moat around himself. 'This is my life now, this is yours. No love in it. God's abandoned us and here we are.'

I had been standing above him, though he would only have

known it by the direction of my voice. Now I sat down at his side, suddenly exhausted. The words escaped me quietly. 'I do love you. I have always loved you.'

We sat like that and neither of us spoke. The boat slipped onward, closing in towards something we couldn't understand. The dark birds moved about us, specks of cold water lit on our faces, perhaps spray or the faintest rain, drips off the rigging, and here we were, two lost people on a voyage to nowhere.

~

'What happened to her?'

I thought he was asleep. The speckling damp had turned to light rain.

'To whom?' His voice was soft now; the rage had left him.

'My mother. Your wife.'

He sighed. 'Doesn't help to know.'

'Doesn't help not to.'

'There was a fire.'

'I know there was a fire, Father.' My eyes were accustomed to the darkness. I could see the pain on his face.

'What does it have to do with the man, the one we're pursuing?'

'It doesn't,' he began. 'Well, all these things, all misfortunes belong to large families.'

'Tell me.'

He waited a long time to answer. The night moved past us, but the demand hung there, weightless.

'They set fire to the house, in the middle of the night. You will ask me who and in truth I cannot say. But it had happened a number of times that year, to others, I mean. There was conflict. Could have been the Cadigal, the Gweagal, the Eora. I don't know, but the roof came down before we knew what was happening. It was…chaos. Terrible heat, smoke. I got you out. I went again but I could not get your mother out.'

I tried to imagine him, imagine my mother, *hated* so much by someone. 'Why did they burn our house?'

'Why do they do anything, Eliza? I can only say that it's not their way. It's something that, hmm…happened.'

'But why *our* house?'

He seemed distressed at this. 'Why not? Had to be someone's house.'

I could not tell what I was gnawing at. I knew only that there was something about him that resisted. Something he was not going to give me.

'What happened to her?'

'Don't, Eliza. You think you need to know it, but you do not.'

'*Please.*'

The lapping of the bow. The small strains of the timbers. Above us a dark silhouette against the sky: the doctor had caught a large ray and strung it in the rigging to dry. It caught the wind and flexed like a canvas jib.

He sighed as if I had asked him to lift a heavy weight, but he answered.

'The roof timbers came down on her. She'd never left the bed, could never have escaped. There was no one to extinguish it, nothing that could be done. So I waited, others came, neighbours, soldiers. We watched and waited till the sun came up and we could use tools to take out what remained. Your mother was… she was burnt beyond recognition. It was her, but…Why are you doing this to me? You need only to know that she is gone.'

In my heart she could only be beautiful. He was wrong

to think I was afraid to hear it. 'How do you know it was the natives that did it?'

'People saw them in the town that night. Said they were painted up. Word came back through intermediaries that it was them. It was no secret.'

'Is that what started you drinking?'

'Everyone drinks. Everyone sorrows. If life hasn't done it to you, it is only that it is biding its time.'

'Answer me.'

'I lost the best person I'd ever known. In the worst way I could imagine. Things fall apart after something like that, love. You have to understand…the pain makes you drink, then you drink to stop the pain.'

'There's none left on board, you know. What will happen to you?'

'Oh, it won't be good. Can we agree now, if it becomes too much…the doctor will have laudanum. And whatever I say to you then, it will be poison expelling. Do not heed it.'

'No.'

'Please promise me.'

'I promise.'

~

He refused to leave the deck, despite the damp. I found his bedding and brought it to him, covered it with a fold of sail. He was asleep very shortly and the image of him there, wrapped in the sailcloth, made me think of an engraving I had seen, perhaps in a book: a stormy sky, an angry swell breaking the ocean. A crew in a tableau of grief, committing their master to the sea.

I descended the steps to retire, leaving him up there, Argyle nearby on watch. There was a movement in the short passage-way. The doctor, the dim glow from a lamp in the captain's cabin just outlining his face. He was smiling a gentle smile of understanding.

'He has had a terrible time,' he said. I could not tell whether he meant the ordeal of going overboard, or whether he had overheard our conversation. 'Come, sit with me.' He placed a hand on the small of my back, and with the faintest pressure there he turned me and suggested the door to his cabin. I shrank away from the hand.

'It's very late…'

'You're restless. You will not sleep in this condition.'

I entered, despite myself. From the gloomy passage, towards the light, into the cabin, which was not a master's cabin any longer, nor a cabin at all, but was now a naturalist's chamber. A central table—where had he found a table?—was arranged with glassware: beakers, retorts, tubes and flasks. They formed a structure together, a tumorous skeleton. Around it he had rigged an ingenious web of strings and wires, which I supposed were there to hold the apparatus in place through the ship's rolling.

His desk was piled high with books and papers: the source of the light was an Argand lamp in a cleared space. One leg of the desk was darker and, as I peered closer, I saw that he had spilt the ink bottle and the slick had run off the corner of the table and coated the leg all the way to the planking of the floor. His clothes tumbled chaotically from an open chest by his cot, which was unmade. Garments formed a trail between the desk and the bed as though he had donned and discarded them heedlessly in transit between the two.

Under the sill of the window was a large wooden box on four short turned legs. There were drawers in the front of it, of odd shapes and dimensions, each with a small brass lock. The lid on its upper surface and the seams on its sides suggested the presence of folding panels.

I stood staring as he left to find me a chair. The jars of preservative stood in their gleaming rows on the shelves, but now several of them were occupied: a large crab, muscled like a circus strongman. A collection of tiny silver fishes that pulsed collectively as the *Moonbird* rode the swell, rising from the bottom of the jar and living briefly as a school, a swirling columnar vortex, then fading to the bottom before repeating the journey. A colourful ball in another jar that rose and fell also, tumbling and trailing a white coil behind it: a fish's eye. A tiny pale shark, skin rippled like a waterlogged thumb: it took me a moment to realise it must be a foetus, fine blood vessels visible through its translucent fins. My eyes were now avid for more perversions, greater extremities. Did the shadows conceal a severed head, air bubbles trapped in its whiskered mouth?

The collection drew me forward: unthinkingly I reached out and touched the curved glass of a large jar, behind which a small lobster sat neatly on the nest of its legs. The long, delicate antennae whipped backwards over its body to recede and vanish in the jar's uncertain lens.

'*Jasus novaehollandiae.*'

I hadn't heard him return. He stood in the doorway, strong and tall, a chair in his left hand.

'I am often surprised no one has thought to base a machine of war upon it. Armoured, spiked, almost devoid of structural weaknesses. Please—'

He gestured to the chair, which he had placed under the sternward window. He went and got another for himself, but stood behind it momentarily.

'What can I offer you? I have a little brandy which has survived your…pogrom.' He laughed gently and I found myself smiling. 'Or tea? A tincture of some sort?'

'Nothing, thank you.'

He shrugged affably and went to the desk, producing from beneath it a bottle and an array of smaller glass vessels. He poured spirit from the bottle into a small glass, then took a dropper and added tiny measures from each of the containers. A powerful chemical smell filled the cabin.

'What is it you're making?'

'Oleum vitrioli dulce. Brandy with a dash of vitriol and molasses.' He took a seat beside me, holding the glass between thumb and forefinger, his pinky extended daintily.

'Sulfuric acid?'

'Only a dash.' He grinned. 'Cleans the teeth.' He threw it down his throat and grimaced, then laughed. We were sitting backwards to the *Moonbird*'s path so that outside the panes of the window her wake made a silvery track on the sea. I hadn't been watching the moon but I thought, sitting there, that it must have been waxing because the night was luminous. The small peaks on the surface, somewhere between a chop and a swell, caught the light, mirrored it briefly before subsiding. The light behind us was yellow from the lamp, but the window's light was stronger: it cast a silver sheen on the surfaces of the mysterious timber cabinet. I looked over my shoulder, back towards the jars and their suspended agonies. His eyes followed mine.

'If the science makes no impact, I thought I might open a *Wunderkammer.*'

My unconcealed gaze, my carelessness. I needed to stake a position regarding this man, and defend it.

He was laughing again. 'I am joking. I do not subscribe to the idea that you should put specimens in a case just so people may gawk at them. People, you know'—he picked up a heavy crab claw from the surface of the desk and hefted it in his hand—'people do attach great prestige to naming things. They start with their own name, of course, that's human vanity. Then their patrons. Then they start settling their grudges by naming fat, ugly fishes after the people who criticised their work. And so the duke with his eight-hundred-year-old name finds himself immortalised in bulbous eyes and slime. So much fun to be had…'

He had me laughing now and he was plainly enjoying himself. 'What's this?' I asked, smoothing a hand over the top surface of the wooden box.

'Another of the parlour tricks that are integral to research.' He stood, bent over the cabinet and ran his fingers along the upper edges of its sides. The fingers stopped when they found latches. The unseen lid now swung back from the top surface. Its underside was painted in a delicate landscape scene: mauve hills and a cluster of natives in the shade of a foreground tree. There was lacquer over the image that shone with the lamp's reflected light.

I stood up and peered down into the cabinet. Inside were arranged an assortment of shells, some old and dull, others new and vibrant. The larger ones circled around the outside: whelks and cowries and clams, spiralling down to smaller snails and turbans, sand dollars and abalone, and vanishing at the centre through dozens of periwinkles and tiny maireeners.

'How do they not move about, with the boat?'

'I have created a gum adhesive. As you can appreciate, setting the very smallest ones requires some patience. And look…' He reached in and his fingers found the edges of the display. With a tiny wooden creak, the tray came up and then hinged backwards on articulated brass legs so that it stayed level and revealed another tray beneath. This was deeper than the first, designed with a series of platforms inside, coated in rich indigo velvet.

Upon the little terraces rested hundreds of small bones. Some were clearly the bones of birds, hollow and slight, and among an avenue of skulls I could see beaked ones. But others were more robust, despite their small size: the skulls of mammals, I supposed, teeth sharp and pointed or sometimes flattened for grinding. Beside each specimen there was a miniature paper label marked with impossibly small cursive. Roman numerals, Latin forms, abbreviations that assumed an understanding.

The narrow front edge of this tray was scrolled with botanical motifs: fern fronds and flowers. Unlike the upper tray, this one did not take up the entire width and depth of the cabinet: instead it occupied half the space. The doctor now lifted out a cover of black baize to reveal another tray of the same size, arrayed with dried animal scat.

Before I could focus on the strands of grass and tiny flakes of chipped bone embedded in each, he had lifted out the tray and revealed another level beneath, this time divided into two equal squares on the left and a square double their size on the right. The upper of the smaller trays held gleaming coloured beetles, while the one nearer to me contained spear tips, flaked from stone and razor sharp, of the kind I had seen the native children trading in the streets of Sydney.

I realised now that the trays the doctor was revealing were so elegantly thin that barely half the depth of the cabinet had been revealed.

'There is a pattern about it, I'm sure you have noticed.' His voice, inviting me to congratulate myself.

'Yes, but I can't explain it.'

'The side lengths of each tray are in a proportion to each other which accords with the golden ratio; that is, the long side is one point six one eight times the length of the short side.'

'Where on earth did you find this?'

'Ha!' He was delighted by my amazement. 'One doesn't go to a merchant to find a collector's cabinet with compartments arranged in a Fibonacci sequence. I had it made, to a precise set of specifications. There is a convict artisan in Newcastle named William Temple, who shares my fascination for the ratio. To be honest with you I think he is more occultist than cabinet maker. The inlays are rosewood, but that is only an aesthetic flourish. The timber itself, you will be interested to know, is red cedar, *Toona ciliata*, from the coastal forests of our colony.'

Cedar, the timber that the Hindoo traded. More coincidences: I had lost the thread of his explanation. I felt tired now, less enamoured of all this clever talk. But he was not done.

'Red cedar has insect repellent properties, you see. Which means I can put dried specimens in there without fear of infestation. That will become more important once we focus our efforts on birds and marine plants.' He cast a quick look at the slow dance of the floating objects. 'I do not wish to have all of my soft specimens in fluid.'

I yawned, and failed to conceal it.

'Of course'—a flash of chagrin—'how rude of me. You must be exhausted. Please, Miss Grayling, allow me to walk you to your cabin.'

As he spoke, he rapidly closed the various compartments he had shown me. When the two leaves of the lid were brought together, I saw that the top surface was vividly painted with countless fishes: a large shark across the top, followed by a schnapper, a dory, salmon and skate and many other smaller fishes that may have been painted from life, or equally, figments of my tired mind.

So the moment passed, and I would spend the night alone in my cabin.

But not asleep. The dance between us, our unspoken pas de deux, had not been brought to a stop by his agency or mine. He was angling, it seemed to me. Coiling around me like one of his spirals, and he was unhurried about that.

I would resist him, that was my most basic impulse. Because what I felt was unfamiliar and uncontrolled. The rational part of me, the part that always had its way, had taken a sideways knock and I was no longer sure of anything. I could find what it was that was stirring me; chase it down and master it. His mouth on mine; I kept summoning it, re-feeling it over and again. The mere fact I had never experienced this thing, that I did not know where it led, those were not reasons to shy away. I could control my addled father, the Cooper brats, any number of insensate animals. I could control myself, and I had done so for far too long.

To hell with resistance. I was an adult, of strong mind and will. I could take hold of this man. I could strip him down and devour him.

HUMMOCK AND THE
BOTTLE-ACHE

Two mornings later we were among the islands.

My father had decided not to bother with the Great Island: it was steep and mountainous, according to the master, with very little fresh water. The sealers had surveyed its coast over many years and found that it lacked haul-outs and therefore any worthwhile sealing. No one had bothered to base themselves there, let alone make a settlement of the place.

We lay wide of its north-western corner, where the light made great monuments of its granite towers. Off a headland a series of four small islands lay in a line from north to south, the first proud and conical but each subsequent one crouching lower in the sea than the one before it, so that they appeared like the vertebrae of some creature submerging or emerging.

Srinivas believed we would find our quarry in the outer islands, particularly among the southernmost ones in the Franklin Sound, that lay between the Great Island and its lesser neighbour,

Cape Barren. There was no gateway westward to the Great Island's coast that was not attended by them.

The master had elected to begin with Hummock Island, which the sealers had called Prime Seal until they slaughtered the last of the animals there. It was a long, narrow isle lying almost north to south, three rounded hills furred with pale brown grass. As we approached its northern end, a mile or so off, the master called for soundings. It was deep water—its colour showed that as clearly as the readings that the Connolly boys shouted—but Argyle kept calling for more readings while he frowned over the chart. He ordered a reduction of sail, then a sea anchor, and at length we were barely moving at all. The doctor and my father had both come onto the deck. The cloud was light above us and the sea quiet.

A shout, a shallow reading. The master swung the *Moonbird* into the breeze and told the Connollys to prepare the anchor. Within a matter of yards, we had come up from twenty-five fathoms to one. He waited for the wind to take us back off the edge of the pale rock that was now alarmingly plain to see below us. With deep green restored, he turned and found the doctor by the foot of the quarterdeck.

'Myrmidon Rock, Doctor Gideon. A high peak in a flat sea floor. Some creatures, maybe?'

The doctor set about dropping his various nets and pots. When he had them all tied off on sturdy lines, he produced a fishing reel and began cutting bait on a board. Within half an hour he had filled a basket with fish: long slender ones, spiky brown flat ones. I recognised the schnapper from Port Jackson, the same fish that glowed upon the lid of the doctor's curious cabinet.

When he was satisfied with the haul, he tipped it out on

the deck and sorted through it, a child among toys, assigning each flapping and crawling creature a fate. *Pin this one, fixative, sketch—no, the jars for that.* Heterodontus, *no, not you* as he tossed a small shark overboard. I watched—I tried not to be seen watching—his capable hands gripping the fishes as he studied them. When he was done, the process of anchoring and sail orders was reversed, and we crept towards the domes of Hummock Island as though careful not to disturb it.

We were to land on the western side, in the lee of the easterly breeze, and part ways to survey the island. Now it had come to the practical business of the voyage, I found I had little idea how we would carry out our task, what we would do if we came upon the wreckage of the *Howrah* or the remains of the souls aboard. What if there were survivors? And what were we to do if we came upon the wreckers? We had proceeded upon assumptions, and now they were firing questions back at us.

And there was a further complication: my father was unwell. At noon he began to vomit. Draped under the cathead, grasping it feebly to steady himself, he brought up a thick white substance streaked with blood. I watched the tips of his fingers as he heaved and retched and saw they were shaking uncontrollably.

I urged him to remain aboard and recover: in part out of concern for him, but also with an eye to the difficulty of managing him onshore. If he had been ill-equipped for vengeance before, now he was a clear liability.

As I expected, he would have none of it. Before we could ship the jolly-boat, he was in it, sitting bolt upright and defiant, staring into the void. God, the obstinacy of the man! I caught Declan Connolly rolling his eyes at his brother, who tried to reciprocate but could manage only a gargoyle face. At least my father had united them on something. Argyle and the doctor agreed to travel north and south respectively along the coast and to survey the whole island from its highest points. My task, along with my father, was to walk a loop through the middle of the island, which formed a low saddle. It remained unsaid, but was understood, that I would not get far with him in tow.

Nonetheless I packed a small bag of necessaries for both of us—warm clothes, a tinderbox and, as an afterthought, the leather satchel that held the *Howrah* papers Srinivas had given me in Sydney—and we ran the jolly-boat into a narrow cleft in the rocky coast. The waves were lapping high on the boulders, almost to the line where their orange coating commenced. There were no shellfish and no weeds attached any higher than the water: we must have arrived at the peak of the tide. The doctor stepped out with a line to secure us. Argyle helped me to get my father over the side and onto a small patch of sand. As his feet scrunched into the heavy white gravel, he grunted and shuffled our arms off him, his irritation plain to see.

At the top of the little beach there was a band of hard, dried kelp that crunched underfoot and then we were in among the tussocks, thigh-deep and prickly. I had to stay so close, at times I was under my father's arm and hefting his weight over obstacles. Birds flushed ahead of us, and slithering tails whipped out of view between grasses. I had grown up on a land carpeted with leaf litter and shaded overhead by sprawling, formless trees. Here, the riot was below the knees. Above was only the wide vault of the sky, met by the slope of the hills.

My father was groaning as he went, and disinclined to talk. When we had covered a hundred yards, we stood on a rise that revealed the great sweep of ocean to the east and west of the long finger of land, back to the *Moonbird* and away to Great Island. There were no seals to be seen and no sealers either, consequent on their stunning success at slaughter.

Gulls overhead, him failing beside me. The romantic vision of the wide world had fallen away now: there was nothing out here to discover, nothing to exhilarate. This was not the way I had thought our urgent mission would play out. And what if my father died out here? I looked at my feet: could I bury him in this rocky ground, no tools, no god, no congregation to hear the words? It would be just like him to expire somewhere so inconvenient.

'I'm looking around us, Father,' I said when he stumbled to a halt. 'There is nothing out here. The doctor is up there, up to our left.' His face followed the change in the direction of my voice. 'The master's along that beach to the right, to the south.' Again, he sensed the orientation. 'This is a waste of time, I believe. Why don't we go back?'

He bent over and clutched his knees, teeth gritted. One hand left his knee and rose to shoulder height, extended, and the fingers dabbed softly at the air. His face was tensed with listening, as the fingers explained something to him.

'Up there,' he said, with considerable effort. 'On the ridge line. Is there limestone coming out of the ground?'

'Yes. How did you know that?'

'Wind's coming from that way. Smells different with the air on it. Limestone makes overhangs, is where anybody'd shelter. We need to…*huargh!*…go and look.' He had vomited again. At least I would not be called upon to clean it off this particular surface.

But the word he'd used. *Look*. I thought, for the first time, that he was using it to mean *inquire*. But who was 'anybody'?

We pressed on, uphill now towards the reef of limestone he had somehow sensed. He fell more often as the ground inclined, catching his feet in the thick bases of the tussocks. He would tumble forward, cursing, then spike his hands on the needle-tip blades and curse some more, clutching his profanities between teeth gritted against the nausea.

We reached the limestone in the middle of the day. Both the doctor and the master had been able to complete their circuits in the time it took us merely to get up there. They were waiting at the entrance to a large cave. Argyle sat in silent contemplation, looking out over the blue expanse of the sea stretching eastwards, back towards Great Island. His soft cotton dress was damp with sweat where it gathered over his chest, and thousands of tiny grass seeds decorated the skirts as though the dressmaker had intended them to be there. He picked at them idly.

Up here, the wind had enough force to moan through the fissures in the rock and swirl my hair in strands about my face. I wished I had tied it: it was more than my fingers could control. The cave faced south-east and stretched back far enough to give shade from the midday sun as it receded into darkness. The floor was evenly worn, scraped flat and soft by wallabies. The badgers, too, had left their distinctive square droppings.

My father laid himself on the soft floor and began to shiver, despite the heat.

The doctor beckoned me further in. 'Feel the difference in the air,' he said, quietly. 'It muffles sound.' My eyes adjusted to the gloom as I walked further in with him. Now I looked back to the entrance and it appeared as a jagged tear, incandescent against the fabric of the dark earth.

'People have lived here,' the doctor went on, speaking quietly to himself. 'Very old, profoundly old.' He examined the walls as he strode deeper in, his fingers tracing irregularities in the surface. 'But not for a long time.' Now both his hands were pressed flat on the surface of the rock and he held one cheek to it, exhaling softly.

I was walking with him, deeper in. I should not have been.

There was a narrow cleft at the bottom of the cave's rear wall. He bent down and peered in, muttering into the darkness.

'How would they have got here?' My question broke his reverie.

'Oh, sea, perhaps. Or, the sea was lower—these islands were mountains once and one only had to walk over the plains to reach them. Divine punishments, you see. Or merely the slow change of the earth. Oceans come and go. Mountains too.'

He turned to me and his face was half-lit by the glow from the cave's entrance. The other half, in shadow, rendered him in a new and unsettling expression. He was serene, staring into my eyes and yet not seeing me.

Without taking his eyes from mine, he said, very softly: 'Your father suffers quart mania. It is the illness that attends the withdrawal from liquor.'

I didn't understand. He was often sickly after a binge, but what I had seen that morning, what the doctor was referring to, was something different. A low moan came from the entrance where I had left him, and I suddenly felt the need to rush towards him, away from this man who was a stranger all over again.

My father was cradled in the master's lap. The shivers had become convulsions and the rolling whites of his eyes bled with anguish. The thrashing gained in violence. The master looked around the floor of the cave and then at me and I was filled with gratitude for his tenderness.

The doctor, steely calm: 'It is coming on now. Find a stick, a piece of wood, something to ram in his mouth.'

There was nothing. It was as if no tree had ever grown up here. The only objects lying around, for reasons I could not fathom, were seashells. In desperation I took a large whelk and dusted the grit off it as the master prised open my father's jaws. Such cruelty to make him safe. I jammed the shell into his mouth so that the spirals of it sat between his teeth. But no sooner had I got my fingers clear of his lips than he ground down on the shell and it exploded in his mouth. Fragments of newly white shell landed on his chest and shoulder, and blood began to trickle from the corner of his mouth.

He roared in anger, fear, delirium. Violent waves passed though him, racked him, and he grunted in pain as they locked his muscles.

'How could you—let—this happen? *Aargh!* Get them off me! They will kill me! Fuck! Fuck! Fu—huh…poisonous ones, I know them. I know *all* of them, '*specially* these…'

He clenched his teeth again: his shirt was open and he was tearing at his chest with his fingernails. Long red welts appeared and began to bleed and to my horror I saw a curl of his skin under the longest nail. But he went again, this time horizontally, scratching repeatedly over the wounds he'd made.

'The young of them! Just as poisonous!'

'Take his arms,' said the master. He wrapped one of them underneath my father so that it was pinned by his own weight. A glimpse of his face: somehow determined and confident in its sadness and isolation. I grappled with the other arm but could not hold it down. My father's strength had become extraordinary: I had never felt it like this, in all the times I had picked him up, wrestled him down, evaded his blows. The thrashing had raised the dust of the cave floor and it covered his clothes and the hairs on his forearms. *He is my father, he is my father.* He got the hand free again and raked at his left eye. One nail caught the lower eyelid and tore it so that I saw a flash of the white under there, then blood, the brightest colour in the cave. Now he was weeping in pain, but it wasn't the eye. His hands had clawed themselves and he lifted them to his eyes and I realised that he believed he could see them.

'Pliers! My knuckles!'

The doctor was above me, bent forward and peering intently into my father's face. Suddenly his voice came: unhurried, untroubled. 'Strike him.'

I looked up at him in confusion.

'I cannot,' he said reasonably. 'It is better that you do. It may help bring him round.'

I trusted the eyes I saw then. And yet I hesitated.

'You must,' he said gently.

I turned back to my father, and once again I tried not to think of the face that had looked on me as a child, smiled upon me, loved me. I called inside myself to summon fury for his insults, his abuses. I needed it: I did not want to use it. It made me a stranger to myself.

I slapped him as hard as I could, laying the blow on his cheek where I thought I would do him the least damage. Something like shock passed across his face as his body rippled once or twice more and then was still. The blow had stunned him. It stunned me, for that matter, and it hurt my hand, although I had been weeping before the stinging even registered. The intimacy of the connection, the stubble under my palm, the recognition of having deliberately hurt the one you love most. The ragged sawtooth of his breathing abated, and now he looked almost peaceful beneath the damage he had done himself and the accusing red image of my palm on his skin. He was stunned or asleep or in some similar state: consciousness had burnt out of him and he lay still.

'Well done,' the doctor said over my shoulder. 'Awful thing to have to do.' He removed his shirt and bent down to pass it under my father's body. He tied it off over his small, round belly so that his hands were pinned in there.

'Mister Argyle, do you think you will be able to assist me taking him back down?'

They trudged out of the cave, the doctor leading the way with my father face-down over his right shoulder, and the master following close behind, grappling with his slumped and flailing legs. The doctor's powerful shoulders, the white hair on his sternum and the bright sway of the master's dress: I see them still.

They picked their way, grunting, over the tussocks, flushing out small birds. Down and winding down towards the jolly-boat, the afternoon tinting yellow around them.

At the cleft in the rocks where we had tied up, we found the little boat hanging from its mooring line: stern resting on the sand, bow wedged into the crevasse in the rock. The tide had emptied and left a sand flat that extended half a furlong or more. The sea level had fallen eight feet in our absence. Even Argyle, who had sailed these waters many times, seemed shocked.

'Lesson for next time,' he muttered, as the doctor lowered my father down the boulders and onto the sodden expanse of sand. We untied the boat and dragged it over the flats, beset by flies and covered in sweat, until a thin film of water appeared and began to lift its weight.

~

The *Moonbird* remained at anchor off the island while my father slept during the afternoon.

The Connolly brothers were playing cards again. Whist, though Declan seemed to have tailored the rules to make things easier for Angus. They were laughing uproariously one minute, cursing and cuffing one another the next. There was something strangely endearing about their antics: pups in a box. Each blow looked painful and would elicit howls of pain—*Aargh! Tha' wis ma fuckin snuffer!*—but watching closely I saw that they were not applying their full effort. The punches and slaps, the occasional kicks, were aimed at winning advantage or registering disagreement. Sometimes I thought Declan used them to curb Angus's antics. Any appearance of 'claret', as they called it, would result in ceasefire.

I'd been sitting on the quarterdeck, high above the water, the card-playing brothers below me. As I watched them, Declan threw a self-conscious look over his shoulder at me and I looked off to the sea. The master was watching all this in his silent way, working with a pencil on a chart. He had consulted briefly with me about our intended route: I had no idea what to tell him so he shrugged and continued with his musings. The doctor was absent, but then he reappeared bearing a bowl of rice he had cooked for me.

After a while the master returned with his chart, marked with pencil: a long spiral, just as the doctor had shown me. Great Island, with Cape Barren Island below it, formed a backswept exclamation mark, with the minor punctuation of Clarke Island below. Small islands littered the gaps between and all around.

'No point searching the Great Island,' the master affirmed. 'It's these ones—Preservation, Penguin, Passage, Gun Carriage— where they's settled.' He traced a finger on the paper from one

141

to another. The tightening spiral, islands that did not make neat points in the sea but floated raggedly upon it.

'Do you really believe these to be lawless people, Mister Argyle?'

He thought about the question. 'It is possible,' he ventured carefully, 'for people to live by the laws of the state and still be scoundrels. Not sure I swallow the stuff that the *Gazette* would have us believe. I've seen different laws down here, but not *no* laws.'

He said no more and retreated to his private world.

The afternoon sun was warm, and presently the doctor appeared, wearing a new shirt that fitted him well. He peered over the bulwark just below me, assessing the water. I sensed he was aware of me watching him.

He opened a hatch and took out a bundle of netting, threw it overboard. I watched it follow its weights down, a descending cloud in the green. A trail of fine bubbles surfaced in that brilliant clarity, and far below I could make out the shapes of the sand and the reef like forest and meadow under glass.

He had two ropes strung over blocks: once he was satisfied with the fall of the net, he began to operate them against each other, drawing the net closed and hauling it back to the surface. It came up streaming water and bulging with the sparkling struggles of tiny fish. It must have been heavy, but he spilled it over the bulwark without apparent strain, fishes no longer than a finger pouring like mercury over the boards.

He stood with them wriggling over his bare feet, and looked up to meet my eyes, confirming that he was aware of my gaze. He smiled at me: clear and untroubled.

I could find witticisms. I could look away, I could sneer. But then and there, in that sunlit moment, I wished to do nothing but see him.

The calm perfection of that afternoon was nearly enough to sweep away the thoughts that gnawed at me: the memory of the poor man they'd shot in the water, the distressing turn in my father's condition, the unknown horrors that waited in the southern islands. When I look back now, I see that afternoon as the hinge upon which everything turned.

Dr Gideon took another net from the same locker the first one had come from. This one was finer: a closer weave and a lighter cord. He needed no effort to lift the whole bundle of it with him, up into the rigging. He was so high above me that the blinding sun was no longer behind him but under him as he let the net fall. The top edge he retained, and threaded onto the gaff using a line of cord. Once satisfied with this, he clambered down to the boom and pulled the net taut, then corded it again.

When he was done, the net was stretched like a large transparent sail. It lilted gently in the breeze, just visible.

Back on the deck, he filled a basket with handfuls of the little fish and a few dozen wooden dolly pegs. His idea was opaque to me, but I did not want to pre-empt anything by asking what he was doing. Up he went: the same dance over the boom, this time pegging the fish one by one all over the net so they hung suspended and glinting up there, and my sleepy eyes saw it as something jewelled and diaphanous, the sequined veil of a bride.

He slung himself down and sat on the boards beside me, looking up happily at his work. 'Now we wait,' he said.

The parts of him continued to confound a rational whole: the fine, slender feet that showed no signs of hardship and had carried him so nimbly up there on the rounded timbers. The long whip of his body, barely touched by his advancing years, from the slender legs to the squared shoulders, the visible sinews of his chest. The thick hair that, but for the silvering at his temples, was a young man's; the damage to his face that was the only indication of hardship. No man I had observed could ape refinement if their body betrayed physical work: and no dandy could move with agility in high places. This man eased between both worlds and escaped definition.

I narrowed my eyes at him. 'And what are we waiting for, doctor?'

He lay back with his hands cupped under his head. 'Birds.'

The afternoon wore on. Time slowed and weighed drowsy on me. Nobody seemed to feel any urgency about their tasks: the brothers were fishing at the stern, and I could hear the master preparing food beneath us in the galley. The *Moonbird* sat serene at anchor, knowing unspoken things.

'Your father's bottle-ache will return,' the doctor said out of nowhere. 'That was not the ordinary sickness one experiences the morning after a bout of drinking. It was more serious, and there will be other bouts before his body purges itself of the liquor it has stored. It lives in the organs, takes time to leach out. And you have the paroxysms we observed today, the body resisting expurgation. Difficult for you.'

I didn't want to think about my father at that moment. I wanted to cling to what I felt: an antidote to the labour of being a daughter. I could be someone else if I wished it hard enough.

'The visions are interesting to me,' he continued. 'Formications, echoes from the deepest parts of the human soul, buried under the sediments of our behaviours, even our unspoken desires. Way down in the dark. The images are more commonly batrachians, but it varies. I thought he was referring to snakes. Was that your understanding?'

He looked at me, brows raised in inquiry.

'I don't know, I—'

'He must recover fully. If we reach the southern islands and he finds this man, these men, he seeks, he will need his strength.'

The sun was setting, out over the sea, casting brilliance towards us and lighting the rigging and the misty net in gold. Already, birds were careening into the net and sticking there, struggling and issuing sounds of distress. Most of them were small and swift-built, but there were larger ones too, some that I thought would be land birds and others that wore the colours of the sea. The whole net was trembling now, collecting the energy of their individual agonies.

At some point the master came by, looked without comment at the net and the birds, and said we would sail at dawn. The folds of the dress were clean again, dappled in that gentle evening light. His solemn face evoked goodness. I wanted so desperately to trust him, as I no longer trusted myself.

GRASS ELEGY

I had slept on the floor of the cramped bunkroom, elbows and knees uncomfortably pressed against the risers of the cots either side. I wanted to be beside my father in case the tremens returned and I was needed, but he slept deeply and so did I.

And this, I remember, is how the day declared itself.

Cries from above, running feet. An instant of terror that my father had gone over again; but he was beside me, already awake, feeling for the edge of his cot. The doctor's cabin door was open down the short passage: I do not recall him having stepped over me in the night, but there was no other way for him to come and go. Bright sunlight flooded in through every opening. I had learnt to feel for movement: we were still, though the dawn must have been long before.

My father, the cries. I did not know whether to aid him or run to the crisis—whatever it was—above.

Him, always him first. I took his arm over my shoulders and helped him up. He was still dressed, thankfully. With my hands on the backs of his shoulders I guided him to the short steps. His fingers found the handrail and he went up ahead of me, mapping the boat as he went. At the top he turned right and went forward, following the sounds. I went after him.

What struck me first was the intensity of the sun. The morning was cloudless, hot. No sails had been set. The net was still rigged above us but now emptied.

My father was rushing towards the bow, feeling for obstacles. A touch on the cabin wall, one on the bulwark, brushing his fingers over the bullseyes. The doctor, the master and Declan Connolly were at the apex of the bow, crowded together and looking down. Around their feet the anchor line lay in heavy coils, spooled off the windlass in a way I knew the master would not have permitted.

I rushed to them: my eyes followed theirs.

Below us, through the bottle-green water, the chain trailed away and pointed like an accusing finger at a human face. On the seabed, his lower legs obscured by a thick carpet of grasses, Angus Connolly was entrapped, tangled in the anchor line, eyes upturned towards the *Moonbird*. His mouth was open: his face frozen between terror and mere disappointment.

I gasped but couldn't speak. I could not look away, could not wrench myself from the eyes of the man on the sea floor. Through the emerald tint I believe those eyes still appeared blue, though another part of me thinks that could not be. He was unmistakably dead. There was no urgency in anybody on board: the staring eyes were lifeless.

Declan was hauling at the line, sobbing, but the combined weight of the anchor and its chain and his brother was more than he could lift. Argyle moved in beside him and put a hand on his shoulder.

'The windlass, boy,' he said quietly. The doctor moved towards it and made a motion to begin winding, but Connolly hurled himself at him.

'Was *your* watch, ye fucker!' The doctor reared back. 'What the fuck were ye doin? Sleepin, were ye?' He swung a despairing punch that flew wide. Gideon leaned back to allow the fist to pass: composed, even now.

'He's tangled himself, lad. Not a thing could be done.'

'It's never been his job! Not a once! It's *me* does the pick every single time…can ye not tell us apart, ye stupid prick?'

'Be calm, boy.' It was the master, at home in the sorrow, drawing a dark shawl around himself. 'Haul him in and we shall attend to him.'

When Declan Connolly began to wind the device, pouring his fury and pain into the work, the chain pulled taut around his brother's ankles so as to invert him and bring him feet-first towards the boat. At that very instant, when his head came around and began to trail, I will swear a glittering stream of tiny fish left his mouth like unspoken words.

~

The boy was buried on Hummock Island, on the side of a hill. Feet down and, according to the master, facing Scapa Flow.

Declan had cried all the way up the rise, cried in abandonment, in fragments of lament, among the hard breathing of the uphill walk carrying his dead brother's weight. He was talking to him, not to himself and certainly not to us. He chided his brother for the excesses, the carelessness that had led to this.

'Why'm I here, boy, puttin ye to bed with a shovel?'

He talked some more as he dug, poking at the earth with a length of iron from the *Moonbird*—it turned out we carried no shovel—then scooping with a cooking pot. He said his brother had tried to make an honest living. He'd been an ostler, even dug graves one year. Sure, he'd committed many misdeeds in his efforts to get by, but according to his brother he'd never crossed a decent man nor dishonoured a woman. Except a schoolmaster, whose name escaped Declan, who was probably honourable but who'd invited a flogging for his loads of pious shite. There were, of course, other words he used: his graveside profanities were so wildly out of place that they even elicited a tiny smile from the master, who swung at the ground with a sand anchor from the jolly-boat.

According to Declan, the judge who sent his brother down had a face like an arse full of carbuncles. The first mate on the transport was a turd with nostrils. Their overseer in Parramatta stank like the farts of an undertaker's wife. I looked at the shape of the poor boy, wrapped in his hammock, half-expecting his chest to start rocking with mirth. But his brother wept steadily as he tried to eulogise him, and the rest of us had not the faintest idea what to do or where to look.

'He loved sleepin out on the boat,' he said unexpectedly. 'Said there were no nights in summer up at Stromness. He loved the dark. Things ye take for granted, eh.'

When we were done, the men lifted him into the hole and his brother began to scoop soil over him as the master read from his bible. Seventeen years old, and he would not have recalled a day of freedom. The peculiar bond with his brother aside, had he ever experienced love? Did he imagine a future? Why did the Almighty create such a man, only to end his life thus? Now his bones would moulder under the windswept tussocks of a hillside on a sad island in an obscure sea, thousands of miles from whatever he considered home.

The birds called overhead and a dull band of drizzle swept through. I was shocked and numb: the lad had been so irresistibly alive, and now his mouth was stopped with this desolate soil. The granite boulders shone with a slick of new damp.

There we left Angus Connolly; his eternal rest proclaimed by a timber board.

~

Evening bore down upon us, an end to the cruel day.

I made the meal, eager for some mundane task to divert my mind. None of this was as I had imagined it: I had seen a man shot, a man I had never met, and in no connection whatsoever with our business. Now I had watched a man drowned, in the most ordinary of circumstances. And if we were drawing nearer to our quarry in a geographical sense, there was no sign that we were any nearer to flushing him out—or to understanding the task itself.

The drizzle continued, and as I crouched over the little stove I could see the doctor outside in the last of the daylight. He was walking the boom, plucking more birds from his mist net and depositing them in a canvas bag slung over his shoulder. They were a strange mix: small dun-coloured ground ones that had ventured offshore to the boat, seabirds such as terns and gulls and, out wide of the mainmast, a big gannet that flapped and cried in misery at its entrapment.

All of them went in the bag and I told myself firmly that this was science: a discipline that could spare no pity for a wild bird.

I chopped the carrots—still firm and not yet spoiled by the sea air. As I tipped them into the boiling water there was a faint tapping on the window above me: Dr Gideon, squatting on his haunches by the glass and smiling at me. He took a bird, one of the gulls, and wiggled its head like a puppet, making faces with its beak so that I burst out laughing, though I regretted it immediately. He stuck his head around the corner into the doorway.

'I'm no ventriloquist, am I?' he laughed.

'I don't know. I couldn't hear your voice.'

His face became serious, gentle, and he brought the rest of his body around onto the steps so he was standing in the doorway. 'You're sad about today.'

'Aren't you?'

I thought I saw doubt pass over his features, as if he were questioning himself. 'Of course it is sad,' he began. 'But there are lives…always…that will end before their time, in violent ways, trivial ways. Others—you, me, the master—there is a greater purpose and we prevail. You can only persist and perhaps say a prayer for these.'

I averted my eyes by stirring at the pot, which did not require stirring. '*Whose* purpose is this greater one?'

He appeared not to hear the question. 'There is much to discuss, I know. Would you consider taking your meal in my cabin, perhaps?'

His face was open, devoid of ill-intent or hidden purpose. The frankness of his gaze made me blush, and I cursed myself for it.

'Doctor Gideon, I am not sure that would be proper…'

'Of course, of course. I understand. In any event, I will retire there now to work on these birds, and if you care to join me, that is where I will be.' He smiled brightly and with a small

151

gesture excused himself. He brushed past with the merest touch on my arm and went down the short steps into the passageway that led aft to his cabin, tilting his shoulders slightly aside so the narrow corridor would accommodate his width. The gloom swallowed him.

I dwelt on his invitation for some time as I watched over the food. Yes, it was improper of him to have asked. But propriety had lost its way here. We had been living so close over these days.

I went to my father in his bed, intending to feed him but following some other instinct. He was awake and restless, but it was not a simple matter for him, as it was for the rest of us, to then go and occupy the living world. There were layers to rise through, visions to unscramble and sort—some into reality and some to cast back into the cesspit of dreams. I sat on the edge of his cot and made a spoonful of the soft vegetables, a little pork. He sniffed at it unhappily, making no move either to find the spoon or open his mouth.

'You need your strength,' I said.

He shrugged, dazed. His hair stood as though to walk off. I tried again. His fingers shook as he pushed the spoon away.

'It's good of you. Good of you,' he murmured. 'Leave me now, dear girl.'

I placed the bowl on the narrow shelf behind his head, hoping he might take it up when he felt more able. As I did so, a thought occurred to me: he had shown no further signs of the delirium tremens.

On the shelf, beside where I had put the bowl, I saw little talismans: the shell cameo I had seen in his sea chest, a clutch of tiny ear-shells cupped inside each other in descending order of size. And there beside the shells lay a glass pipette. I had never known my father to own such a thing. But then, I had never known him to be in such a strange state.

~

I sat beside him until he dozed, and then went back to the galley, took two bowls of food and returned to the dim passageway, the door to the captain's cabin that was now the doctor's. I knocked quietly so as not to wake my father who lay so close by.

That deep, sure voice of his, bidding me enter.

I knew the door latches on the *Moonbird* by now. Aiming to separate the worlds of my father and the doctor—but wanting neither to know it—I balanced the second bowl in the crook of one arm while I snibbed the door quietly behind me with the other.

He was standing behind the desk and I knew immediately that he'd seen me lock the door, but he did not comment.

Before him on the desk lay the birds, closed by death into teardrops, arranged into groups. A stack of the terns with their little black caps lay at the near end; two gannets were folded together like lovers. Finches in one pile, silver gulls in another.

There was no room on the desk for the food, but he gestured to the cabinet I had admired the previous day, took a calico cloth from a drawer and flung it over as a tablecloth. Then he picked up the two chairs and placed one at either end.

'Two hours until my watch,' he said. He made no comment about the fact that I had changed my mind.

I placed the food on our little setting and we began to eat. Behind him were the rows of preserving jars, their ranks now filling with all sorts of creatures I had not observed him collecting.

With their differing fluid levels, I fancied the jars would sound a chromatic scale if struck. He began to talk about the work: he had netted a fish that day—a *warty prowfish*—which he thought to be the only such specimen ever taken beyond Sydney.

I listened to him, nodding and making admiring sounds while the fancy took hold at the back of my mind that this eminent man was my husband, with whom I discussed such matters every night over food I had made him. His struggles for recognition, his breathless discoveries, the perils of his fieldwork…And I would catch myself thinking this way and scoff at my ridiculous self.

As he spoke and I feigned attention, I knew it wasn't the social standing of imagined matrimony that I desired. Had such a man been measuring flour or writing down lists of provisions I would have wanted him exactly the same. Matrimony was on a long list of desirable things that I had accepted were other women's pleasures. The opportunity had passed for them to be mine, and I had made my peace. Now here, on this boat, he had renewed the possibility.

He shovelled great quantities of food into his mouth without interrupting the flow of his observations, gesturing grandly with his fork. How did such a civilised man miss so entirely the business of table manners? A childish quibble: he was preoccupied. Suddenly he was up, throwing his napkin onto the chair.

'Look at this!' he cried, returning from the shelves with a narrow box made from heavy card.

Inside, upon a bed of sawdust, lay the strangest creature I had ever seen. It was a fish, I believed, but like none other: long and thin, the shape of its head was vaguely equine. I touched it with a fingertip: it had no scales but rather a hard, nobbly skin that was almost a shell; a cheek and a small dark eye at the end

154

of a graceful curved neck; beyond the eye a long snout, so thin it resembled a young reed, with a tiny, puckered mouth at its end. More musical instrument, it seemed, than biology. The body was covered in stripes and dots of many fantastical colours: purples and yellows and russets and whites. And protruding from the margins of the long body, in the positions where one might have expected to see fins, the beast appeared, like an ornamental shrub, to bear leaves. Two sprays also emerged from under the animal's chest, giving the impression of forepaws tucked under a kangaroo. The whole creature was perhaps ten inches long, but it contained all of the wonders of the world.

'What is it?' I breathed.

'A sea dragon. Not so rare as it appears, but a beautiful specimen nonetheless. They live on the sea grasses. Lacépède: damned Frenchman. Never left Paris, but he gets this lovely thing as his legacy.' His cynical chuckle gave way to a look of genuine wonder. 'I am torn, you see. The specimen as a whole will bring a very high price, but on the other hand I wish to dissect it.'

'Why?'

'Because I believe the animal is a vertebrate. See the elongation, the bilateral symmetry? Despite appearances it is a fish, not a relative of the crabs and shells. There is that desire, you understand, to take it apart and understand how it is composed.'

I looked at the wondrous thing and could muster no such urge to *deconstruct*. Why would one want to hear from each individual musician in the orchestra? Its beauty lay in its wholeness, in the impossible symphony of colour and shape. Divine writing had made nature from chaos.

'The colours fade after the creature's death. The beauty you see there will diminish.'

He stepped to the windows as he spoke, arms folded in thought. I was struck again by his unlikely physical strength, in a field that so valued thought over muscle. The silver light from outside fell on his face. I could smell the timbers of the *Moonbird*, the faint but inoffensive lingerings of the dead things in the room, and the sea. He spoke again, softly, inviting my trust.

'These are exceptional nights,' he said. 'Have you noticed, the sky is oriented off the stern such that we cannot see the moon? Yet all is light out there. The moon's not full, anyway, so whence comes all that glow? I suspect we are preoccupied with the moon and give too little thought to the role of the constellations.'

He took a cushion from the chair beside him and placed it on the floor. He sat, then finally eased himself to lie down with the cushion under his head. Now the light was all over him, making canyons in his clothes and great ranges of his powerful limbs. His face was healed by the light, unmarked and serene. I dabbed a fingertip on my tongue and extinguished the candle on the cabinet between our empty dishes. Now the light was stronger, the yellow gone from it. The panes of the window threw their shadows onto him; squares bent by the contours of his body.

I moved with the slip of inevitability to the floor and lay beside him. My arrival there did not cause him any surprise: his arm stretched lazily to find another cushion in the darkness behind him. I obliged him by lifting my head: he placed it underneath and then, after a time, his arms were around me, enclosing me in his world where the strange and wakeful night could intrude only in glowing and shadow. Deep in his chest and his neck I could smell him, neither fragrant nor sour but full of purpose.

He was kissing me then and it focused the whole of me into that one place as my fingers wandered the rough landscape of his cheek. My hair: his hands were in my hair and I could see it in the blue light spilling over his wrists and I exalted that *my* hair, the lure of *me* had captivated this man and I felt power and abandon in equal measure. He brought my hips hard against him and then took my waist in both his hands and lifted me so that I lay above him. I dragged downwards on his shirt, pressed a hand on his chest and the spill of his hair on the boards called some deep memory up inside me. His gaze drank me in; I understood that for him I was part of the mystery of this night. I was casting myself as a memory for him, to be preserved forever. Intoxicated by this idea, I drew the dress up and over my head and let the light fall over me.

I was in this state, fingers working buttons, when the reverie was shattered by the *Moonbird*'s bell. I heard the frustration hiss from my own mouth. I would talk to her, officious little boat, about having interrupted me thus.

'My watch,' he groaned. Perhaps I slumped a little, for he sat upright and kissed me on the forehead.

'Be patient,' he murmured to me. 'There is so much more opportunity.'

THE CUTTER

The master had made clear that he wanted to circum-navigate the great mass of Cape Barren Island, examining the offshore islands as we went. This was a plan he had devised in consultation with my father, and I found them early the next morning deep in conversation, the master explaining the nuances of the chart to him. I felt a strange resentment at this: over the entirety of the voyage so far, I had struggled to extract any conversation from Argyle, and here he was, engaged with my father, who had done little but make a buffoon of himself. Was I not an adult, possessed of intelligence and ideas?

The easterly light of dawn glowed pastel on a great cone that rose from the flat sea. *Chappell*, said the chart. By the time we neared it, the sun was strong and I could see the fat bodies of the seals hauled out on its rocky base. 'Snakes there,' said the master. 'Big ones. We won't be landing.'

The seals lolled and basked in their hundreds, perhaps

thousands, and as I watched them my father settled beside me, his face angled in their direction.

'No mistaking that smell,' he said, and before long, their grunts were audible also. The beasts covered the rocky flats, some even resting in the seaward margins of the tussock grass where room on the rocks was unavailable. Beyond them the ground was bare and speckled with burrow entrances that must have belonged to seabirds. The greatest of the mammals were perhaps eight feet long, and so thick in the body that any movement looked like a great effort. But even as I watched, battles broke out between the largest ones. Their agility under duress surprised me, their way of rearing up, barrel chests presented in belligerence, until they collided and shook, blubber rippling away from the impact.

These chieftains—I could not see them as other than males—wore great manes of loose fur around their necks and bared long yellow tusks in their roaring. They were blond and grey and bronze, and some had different faces—extraordinary bulbous cheeks spotted with sprouting whiskers, and long, drooping noses. These, explained the master, were sea elephants. Upon hearing this Declan, who had not said a word since his brother's interment, looked up from his work at the sheave block and muttered *dick noses*. His eyes caught mine: the words had fallen into an unhelpful silence that made them audible. I tried to keep a stern face as he grunted an apology.

We slid past under full sail, in close and eye to eye with the mistrustful beasts. Every sounding the convict called drew a reaction from them. They especially hated fourteen ('Four*TEEN!*') and they roared their displeasure at him. Connolly bellowed back, venting his grief at them in return. If they were damned I could not dispute he was damneder than they.

My eyes scanned the tussocks as we approached the northern tip, half-expecting to see the great serpents Argyle had spoken of: an Old Testament island, a pyramid of rock infested with venomous asps. Then we came down the western side: deep water and off-lying islands—rocks, really—through which the master wove a delicate course. To the west of Chappell, larger but much lower, lay Badger Island, and beyond it the smaller outline of Goose. Over several hours we drew slow circuits around these islands. Goose had seals; Badger did not. Neither showed signs of habitation, nor of wreckage. They were rocks that never changed, and things that grew and died beyond the care of the world.

When we had finished our survey of the west side of Goose, my father spoke. 'Goose is the westernmost of all these isles,' he said. 'If the *Howrah* struck here, or anywhere to the east of us, then the wreckage will have drifted east. The world turns and the winds prevail that way.' The master, who stood nearby in silence, nodded slightly.

~

The doctor and I had been circling around each other all day, exchanging glances but barely a word. Each time I caught the light on his face I felt a surge of animal lust that delighted and terrified me, and I castigated myself for all this foolishness. How could I care for my father, how could I discharge my duty on this voyage? The whole enterprise might be irrational, might even be ruinous, but I had come voluntarily and I had obligations. And yet here I was, a swooning idiot in the sun.

The boat ploughed her steady furrow, nodding up, nodding down. Patient mule that she was, she would have none of this nonsense and I should listen; I should take heed.

The master went about his duties in methodical silence. Connolly worked his grief into the ropes. My father disappeared below in the late afternoon, presumably to rest, to assist his recovery from the cruel withdrawal symptoms.

We anchored off Long Island, a barren mass of rock and tufted grass that lay only a handful of miles from Chappell, where we had started the long day. The sun slipped below the horizon behind us, the island to our east, and I watched Connolly at the anchor, wondering, I suppose, whether labouring over that particular piece of gear reminded him of his brother.

I had looked hours earlier at the master's chart. Each island bore its own curious shape: the only similarity was how jagged they were, none remotely circular. They grew and shrank back and added and lost their adornments as the sea rose and fell through the day. Goose was a long, tapering spiral like a whelk. Long Island reminded me of the sea dragon the doctor had shown me, but with tail and snout severed. An idle mind might spend hours making shapes out of their profiles, in much the same way one contemplated clouds.

The tussocks on Long were greened by a soak just near the seaward rocks, and as the dusk deepened Connolly took himself ashore in the jolly-boat with a cask to get water. He asked politely if I wished to come for the row, but I declined.

I had begun to think there were no people out here at all. None of the chaos and disorder we had been warned about: just rocks and grass, seals and birds and the moody sea that separated them. Maybe the *Howrah* had foundered through some careless error caused by sheer boredom. It would not have been the first time mariners had fallen victim to torpor.

After an hour or so Connolly came back and the master helped him winch the cask aboard.

The doctor glanced at them, preoccupied with some fixation of his, and made no movement to assist. Connolly was hauling line through a block to get the heavy cask up and onto the deck when he stopped suddenly and flicked the line through a cleat to hold it. He turned to look at the doctor and said a most unexpected thing.

'Eh doctor, would it kill ye to dirty yer precious hands wi' some work?'

There was a brief instant in which no one reacted, but I saw the doctor's face flicker through shock and fury before it relaxed into a wide smile. The master told Connolly sharply to control his tongue, and Connolly settled for glaring at the doctor with unconcealed hatred. The spiteful moment took a long time to pass.

The night came, and took up its regular rhythm: the master on his lonely watch, the doctor in his cabin, Connolly sleeping before his shift on deck. The clock was divided by one fewer, of course, with the loss of Angus, and the master had asked me, finally, to cover some of the watches. It did not trouble me. Restless thoughts kept me awake at odd hours, and it was a relief to turn those hours to something useful.

The sea turned perfectly calm; I could hear fishes breaking the surface. Yes, the anarchists and ship-wreckers of the strait were figments of an under-occupied press in Sydney: human carelessness was the disappointing answer to the mystery. Despite the late hour, I decided I would take the thought to my father. Perhaps it would prove an antidote to his fever for a mythical nemesis.

I descended the stairs and the stench hit me.

Someone had lit a lamp in the gloom so that I could see my father lay crooked in his cot, an arm draped over the side, fingers pointed towards an overturned glass on the floor. His face, the beginnings of a scrappy beard, was crusted with vomit. It had congealed on him, the fluid staining the pillow under his head.

The stink was of vomit, but more powerfully liquor. Where had he found it? Where, for God's sake, had he been hiding it?

I cried out for Dr Gideon: he came running from behind the partly closed door of the captain's cabin.

'Oh dear,' he muttered. 'Oh dear. Get me water. He will need to drink water. And you must'—he forced open one of my father's eyes and peered in—'*must* ensure he can breathe.' The doctor shuffled him across the cot so that his head draped downwards, and without a word of warning, smacked him forcefully across the back of the head. A gout of fresh vomit splattered on the floor. There was blood in it.

'Don't!' I cried.

'...his own good.' He struck another blow, the impact sending my father's lank hair flying.

'Please stop!'

I dived under the path of the third blow and clutched my father's head, weeping, smoothing his hair. I was covered in muck and did not give it a thought. I felt such sorrow, such grief for him that a thousand of these humiliations could not quench it. I looked up at the doctor and he gazed back at me—at me and my father—his face weirdly calm.

'Very good, then. Very good, my dear. I will let you handle it your way,' he said. *My dear.* His voice was barely more than a whisper. 'I will fetch the water, perhaps.' He left the bunkroom and returned with the bucket and a length of towel, and allowed me to attend to my father without further intervention.

I washed and towelled and combed his hair once again. Once again, I pulled the sheets off his bed and I took them out on the deck in the darkness and sloshed water over them and scrubbed them and rinsed them and hung them over the boom to dry and once again I remade his bed with clean sheets, working carefully around his unconscious form. While I had the sheets off the cot, I lifted the entire board that supported the bed so that I could look underneath for the hidden stash. There was nothing there: an empty cavity, devoid even of rat droppings.

Once again I made sure to put a glass of water by his bed to ease the tearing thirst that would attack him when he woke, and I kissed his tormented brow. Once again, he would remember none of this in the morning.

This hopelessness. It was the way I understood love. It had been so ever since I could remember.

When I was done I took myself on deck and dropped the rope ladder off the stern. Behind a screen of sail, I peeled away my reeking, soiled clothes and plunged with them into the sea. The cold water revived me, cleared away the doubts and the fears, and for ten minutes I was whole again.

~

My father made his usual way through the morning's uneasy truce.

I have been told it is the way of all drinkers to attempt restitution in the light of a new day. Having shaved by feel at the water cask, he made breakfast for us all, fumbling and crashing in the galley, but somehow producing pemmican and fried morsels of the fish which the doctor had been collecting. I sat at the top of the steps and looked through the windows at him to ensure he was in no danger from the stove. Several times I saw him raise a hand to the place at the back of his head where the doctor had struck him.

Finally, the anger got the better of me. I stepped in and closed the small door that shut off the galley.

'Where did it come from?'

He turned at the sound of my voice and, as he always did, he reached for my hand. I took his. I could not leave him stranded, feeling the air, and perhaps that was the genius of the gesture.

'Cut myself,' he said. He probed at a deep nick in the fold of his jowls. The blood had dried dark red on it. 'Fingers. Hmm, I don't know. Odd. Numb.'

He never nicked himself. Not even on the worst of mornings: this was new. But I would not allow him to change the subject.

'Where did it come from, Father?'

'Where did what come from, my dear?'

I sighed. 'The grog. Last night.'

His brows descended in doubt. 'What grog?'

'You can lie to the world but you can't fool me. You were drinking. Where did you get the grog?'

He squeezed my hand. 'What makes you think so?'

'Oh, there were clues. I cleaned your supper off your face.'

Again, the look of bafflement. 'Really? Must have been seasick. Thank you so—'

'It was dead calm last night. And we were at anchor.'

His face darkened to a scowl. 'And you have been a seafarer, what? A week?'

I gave up and returned above, to find Connolly had weighed the anchor and was now setting sails under the master's direction. The morning light showed a ruffling on the surface, a fresh wind from the north-west. Out at the landless horizon whence it came, a vague line of cloud was forming. According to the master, the long succession of fine days was coming to an end and a westerly change would be upon us.

The doctor fed a fishing line out off the stern as the *Moonbird* picked up speed. He had attached bright objects next to the hooks every ten feet or so: a spoon, a shaving razor, beads and even the shards of a glass my father had broken days before. Declan Connolly, watching the line, made a hand signal to the doctor every time he saw a big silver fish strike at one of the lures. The line was drawn in, the fish slashed through its throat and bucketed, and the process repeated.

We sailed west along the back of Long Island, aiming to round its western end and continue down the coast of the much larger island beyond, the one the master was calling Cape Barren. But before we could bring the coast of that island into view, there was a deafening blast. My first assumption was that my father had caused something to explode; but the master and Connolly were looking to the east.

As the boulders receded, we saw masts, a Union Jack, a high bow. Voices carried over the water to us from the direction of the ship.

'Government cutter,' said Argyle. 'Now what would they be about?'

A clearing pall of smoke explained the bang: they had fired a cannon at the shore. Our course took us closer: now there was laughter, cheering. Another deafening percussion, smoke and the crashing of trees on shore. Men had climbed the rigging with rifles and were firing intermittently; crews bent over the three cannons on deck. I could see the powder boys rushing up from below, bearing small casks. Swabbers mopped out the barrel of one gun while other men rammed the barrel of another. A breath of flame appeared before the detonation reached us along with more cheering in the smoke, and I could see now that they were aiming at a large boulder that stood on the beach.

We were still sailing towards the cutter, but either they hadn't noticed us, coming as we did from behind the corner of Long Island, or they didn't care. They emptied more rounds into the boulder, shearing great shards of rock off its face but more often bringing down shrubs behind it or causing eruptions in the shallows in front. The gun captain moved from one cannon to another, inspecting the packing before he pulled the lanyard on the gunlock. With each successful firing he would slap the backs of the crew, horse-faced and braying, and they would set to work again.

And now I saw that a man was waving frantically from the beach. He kept himself wide of the fire but shouted and pointed despairingly at the cutter and at the damage it was wreaking. Behind the man there was a low hut in the bush: it had not been hit, as far as I could see, but clearly the man felt he was in peril. I was beginning to think that those on board the cutter had not seen him, but even as I watched, a pillar of water erupted only yards short of him. He redoubled his protest, kicking at the sand now. The marksmen had turned their attention towards him and were laughing as they took aim. I dreaded a repeat of the moment at Rodondo, but it seemed the sport here was in terrifying him: sand sprayed up from the rifle shots encircling his feet. He retreated into the scrub to howls of laughter.

Argyle gave orders to reef the sails but not to cast anchor. We were half a furlong away, up behind their stern as they faced broadside to the beach. Their lookout had found us now, and had alerted his shipmates: the laughter died and their anchor chain rattled against the hull. Within moments, they had the cutter underway but we could see from the ripple of faintly breaking water ahead of them that the narrow passage between Long Island and the much larger island, Cape Barren, was blocked by a shallow bank. Their rudder came round and they tacked clumsily until they were facing us. For a moment I feared they would turn the cannons on us, but no one was manning the guns: all hands were in the rigging and suddenly the passage was a very crowded place.

As they came by, Argyle studied them through an eyeglass; I could see a uniformed man aboard their vessel doing the very same thing. Their crew now stopped their work and lined the near-side bulwark between the cannons so that the combined weight of men and armaments had the cutter listing drunkenly towards us.

All of them were silent now and staring: was this meant as intimidation?

'Please, nobody move or make comment,' said the master quietly. He was looking at Connolly.

The cutter edged by, the morning sun behind its sails. Only when it was well past us and heading north did the master give the orders to take us to shore.

~

The man's name was Jemmy Campbell. He was a miner, he said. His accent was recent Orkneys: an echo of poor dead Angus.

He stood barefoot and defiant on the low-tide flats, initially believing we were part of the recent assault on his home. He was short and wiry, his right ankle bent and marked with an old injury that caught my eye as we listened to him. He would put no weight on it, though it looked to have been there for years. The scar was the exact outline of a musket ball, and it must have passed clean into the bone. Both sides of his forehead were marked with deep scars, as though somebody had taken the time to disfigure him in deliberate symmetry.

'And how does a prospector wind up in these islands?' asked the master, drily. The man looked up and down the length of Argyle's muslin dress and did not answer.

His wife, a native woman, and small daughter, were sheltering in the hut and would not come out. He said his home was over east beyond the hills, and waved vaguely towards the pale mountain that spiked the horizon in that direction. 'Crystals,' he said. 'Nuff to fill a boat if I please ter.' He volunteered this in some mercantile way, I thought. Such a man might hint at riches in hopes of saving his skin.

He had a plan that involved sending quantities of gems to the governor: I did not follow why. As his fear wore off, he became boastful: he was, he claimed, the first and only miner in the islands. He asked us for passage to Preservation, where he had business to attend to. The doctor asked him if he needed to go back and tell his wife of his departure, but he demurred. 'Be back soon enough. Prefer to keep em out of bother in the meantime.'

As we took him on board he cursed all the while, and in my hearing, about the fuckin gummint and their fuckin eight-pounders. He swore the fusillade was nothing more than drunken troops entertaining themselves at his expense. I'd seen nothing to contradict that account, but of course I had no understanding of what went on in such a place. Then he moved on to the topic of his wife and his expression softened. 'Good woman, heathen or no. Saved me from my sinful ways.'

Argyle watched him struggling up the rope ladder onto the *Moonbird* as we waited in the jolly-boat, and delivered one of those inscrutable assessments he made above the pretty lace collar. 'Absconder. Wants a pardon from the gov'nor. No danger to us.'

Onward, to the south, the sky building.

Cape Barren appeared only a few miles long from north to south, but Argyle told me its girth was greater, that the island stretched further east even than Flinders. The mountains were extraordinary: great sheets of bare rock angled down from their summits, reflecting the sky and glowering with the changes in the light. Shadows and trees grew upon them, the going around of light and shade that was silent and older than time.

The cloud had appeared first in the north-west, but now it built further south, taller and darker. The wind came from there now, and the sea turned. Argyle was engrossed in the chart again, the paper folded over the rail of the quarterdeck.

'Ten miles,' he said. 'We put in at Preservation. Plenty of time.'

PRESERVATION

I knew of its fame. I knew of its role in my father's life, this tiny island that had delivered Srinivas and Clark and the hideous Mr Figge from certain death. I had perhaps expected cliffs and lethal currents and an oil-painting sky. I wanted some great drama to befit its reputation, but it was low and plain.

We sailed down from the north and the west and looped around the bottom corner of the island because my father insisted on visiting the site of the wreck. This suited the master anyway, as he wanted us to moor in the protected waters of the island's east side, out of the coming weather. He took us around the rocky southern end of Rum Island, barren and exposed. A handful of loose boulders guarded its coast, and Connolly stood alert at the bow with Campbell beside him, making hand signals to the master, who made small adjustments at the helm in response.

Campbell then guided us in, pointing out rocks he appeared

to know personally. On the chart, the island comprised two halves: a northern part that was roughly rectangular, stretched out like a cowhide with exaggerated corners, even furred like a hide in windblown grasses. The southern half was a long, irregular peninsula, much lower and coated in dark, stunted scrub.

Once we were around the rocky south end of Rum, the sea floor came into view: green patches of sand through the clear water, broken up by weed. This was what Guy Hamilton had somehow found all those years ago, a desperate man with his boat sinking under him, a fortune in rum and forty-nine lives at stake. I looked all around me at the maze of islands, sandflats and exposed rocks and felt the full weight of that achievement. He had skidded the bow of his dying vessel into a protected corner, perhaps not the most enclosed site in the archipelago, but safe from the brawling westerlies and only a short row from shore in two directions.

The sails were reefed and we lay idle in the shallows between Preservation and Rum. Connolly made soundings: three fathoms off the bow and six off the stern. In front of us stood a single exposed boulder, no wider than the beam of the *Moonbird*. Argyle studied the boulder, squinted west at Rum, north at Preservation and down at his chart. He stabbed a finger emphatically on the paper. 'This is the place.'

The doctor appeared now, carrying the timber box he had shown me early in our voyage. He requested the boat and it was lowered, then we undertook the painstaking task of getting my father into it. As always, his confidence outstripped his ability, and he attacked the rope ladder with far too much haste. But once we were in, the doctor pushed away from the *Moonbird* and rowed us a few yards clear of her shadow, then lay down the oars and dropped a small sand anchor. When he was satisfied that it had bitten and the little boat had settled, he lifted the box over the edge of the boat so that its glassed end sat on the surface.

'Miss Grayling,' he said, as though we had just met in the street. 'Press the end into the water and then look in from the top. You may wish to lift that shawl of yours over your head so that the daylight does not enter.'

I did as he instructed, and he moved himself to the other side of the jolly-boat so that my leaning over did not tip us too far. And thus positioned I stuck my head deep into the viewing box. The world inside was green, lit by unseen sources like a night at the theatre. We were suspended over a great timber bowl, and it took me a long time to understand what I was looking at.

In my ears I had the doctor's voice, telling me that Alexander the Great had once ordered a diving bell made of glass: 'It carried him beneath the seas and there he beheld a fish so great that it took three days and three nights to pass.'

My eyes were deciphering the wide green world below us. They fell upon a great pile of bottles and split casks and I understood: we were directly over the hull of the *Sydney Cove*.

I stared in wonder. After long moments I realised my father was asking me what I could see, and I knew that this was a moment of great significance for him. I spoke into the viewing box and heard my own words boom around my ears. I must have sounded strangely muffled to the two men.

'I see the hull,' I said. 'It stretches away to both sides of us. Disappears after a while, just the gloom, I suppose. The deck and the rigging are gone: only the, what do you, the feet of the masts remain in place. The tops of some of the ribs reach up near the surface in places. There's one just under us, Father!' It was whiskered with seaweed that the sun had found.

'In the bottom of the hull I can see piles of sand, very white, and bottles, and plates and timbers.' My father had his hand on my back, and I could feel him leaning forward as though for a better view of all this. The relics I could see were overgrown with clumps of sea grass. The thick column of the pump lay on the sand, the remains of the broken casks pinned beneath it. All of it was so clear I felt I could reach out and touch it.

A shadow moved over the sea floor from left to right and I gasped. A huge ray, gliding serenely over the belly of the wreck, inches above the cargo and the planks. Its long, thick tail trailed behind it and the tips of its wings pulsed like those of a bird in flight. It banked and soared away through a gap in the hull timbers, then disappeared from sight.

'May I see?' came the doctor's voice. I removed my head from the box and passed it along the side of the boat to him, then took up a position the same as his on the opposite side. The doctor stared into the timber box, his upper body hunched over the low side of the boat so that he looked comically as though his head had become stuck in the box. He was transfixed. Other than the ray, I had seen no fishes down there. I could not imagine what had captured his imagination.

~

When we were safely aboard the *Moonbird*, Argyle and Connolly set a light sail and inched us along the east side of Preservation until we were positioned at the neck where the narrow peninsula met the northern body of the island. The wind was well up now, and from the deck we could see over the top of the island to the west side, where the swell had leapt into life. We were protected from the breakers, but the wind passed straight over the island and whipped at our rigging.

The doctor stood at the bow, elbows on the rail and chin on hand, deep in thought. My father had come to life and was questioning the master about the chart; now he came to me and asked that I explain everything I could see. I tried my best: I couldn't know, in all honesty, if I was addressing the things he cared about.

I saw extensive timber buildings, strange ones that were built low against the wind and spread randomly as though they had been added one room and one pen at a time. I saw livestock: pigs and fowl and goats, so many goats that parts of the hillsides seemed to be moving about. Their bleating reached us on the wind, a high-pitched staccato multiplied hundreds of times over. Fences made of rocks and timbers gave the place a sense of order: squares and straight lines in a world of curves and points. Further away, on a rise in the land, I could see more of the same. The dwelling—if that is what it was—directly in front of us had an air of prominence about it, as though it occupied prized ground. Behind it there were fruit trees, December greenery in sharp affront to the muted colours of the islands. Rows of green corn stretched away to the west: more than it would take to feed this tiny settlement. These people were traders.

I told my father all these things, but he seemed impatient. Perhaps he wanted something from the rocks that would answer his decades of longing. He had parcelled his sorrows in a faraway place, and now that place was in front of him.

A dog barked over the goat chorus.

A man stood on the beach, watching us. From our anchorage a hundred yards offshore, I could see that he was well on in years, short of stature and dressed in clothes faded to colourlessness. He stood dead still, arms extended at right angles from his sides.

Strange thoughts were coming easily to me now: I thought he'd been crucified. It took me some time to understand that he carried a pole slung over his shoulders with a dark mass hanging from each end. When he saw we were slow launching the boat, he walked to a boulder and carefully placed his burden there, as though he did not want it in the sand he stood upon. Now he squatted on his haunches and stirred a hand through the glittering shallows.

Campbell stood high on top of the windlass and called through cupped hands: 'Munro!'

He looked up sharply, appeared to squint. We were close enough now that I could see a large dog, muscular and narrowing to its tail. It leapt about, barking excitedly but tethered somehow.

'That you, Campbell?'

Campbell waved and nodded.

'Good, sir,' called the man named Munro. He had the wind behind him and did not trouble to raise his voice. He waved some sort of assent and sat down, ignoring the dog, which jerked furiously at the rope that held it to a peg in the sand.

By the time we launched, the sky was dark with threat and Munro was looking up at it, then at Argyle, who stood in the boat as Connolly rowed with his eyes on me.

'Dear Lord.' Munro gawked at our square-jawed leader in his feminine garb as we nudged the sand. 'This is new.'

The dog was brindle, as tall as my waist and of no breed or perhaps all of them. It was beside itself with rage at our incursion, pacing back to the far end of its rope then hurtling forward to the near end, nearly whipping itself off its feet. The ferocious barking turned to a brief yelp of pain, and Munro picked up a stick from the sand. He waved it threateningly at the animal so it cowered and slunk back along the slack rope.

Campbell introduced each of us to Munro. He neither bowed nor sought to shake my hand, but eyed me bluntly. Then he turned and yelled over his shoulder towards the house.

'Louisa!'

There was no response, so he called again and swore under his breath. A woman appeared over the rise: native but dressed English. Her face was weathered like the rocks, her hair a wiry nest of white, dark and copper.

Behind her came another woman, then another, and finally a third. These three were slightly younger, their hair still a deep brown, bodies slenderer than the first woman. She eyed Munro before she looked to us, and remained standing at a distance with the others at her back.

'Isnae them, love,' he said.

On hearing this, the woman's entire demeanour changed. She received our greetings with a confidence I had not seen in the Sydney natives. She came forward and laid a gentle hand on my father, who was still sitting in the boat: he raised his chin and adopted his attitude of information-gathering. She had perceived his blindness from where she stood and now she helped him out of the boat and onto the sand. He thanked her formally and stood with a hand slightly raised until I came beside him and took it.

Despite his assurance to his wife, Munro's suspicion did not immediately pass.

'Your business here?' he asked abruptly.

My father spoke, which I was grateful for, because I did not know the answer. 'We are looking for evidence of a wreck. Some months ago.'

'Which one?' Munro narrowed his eyes.

'The *Howrah*. Hundred-foot barque, two-forty-three tons burthen.'

Munro's face was inscrutable.

'Ten-gun sloop of war for the Royal Navy,' my father continued. 'Converted over to trade. Dudman's Yard. You know them—they made a hundred or more. Flush-decked, sharp-bottomed barque.'

'Difficult thing to lose, you would think.'

'Quite so,' said my father. 'Especially with thirty people on board.'

'Hmm. You might've been told, I am the special constable for these islands.'

'This fella,' said Louisa, 'boss round these parts.'

Munro nodded. The title sat well with him.

'I was aware,' said Argyle, and again Munro cast a look over his garments as, behind him, Campbell shrugged.

Argyle went on: 'We're also aware you wrote to the governor about certain…items that washed ashore here.'

'Mm. I'd know of any such vessel landing on these shores. People come by, tell me what's so. And it happens I've heard of none such.'

Having said these words, his face changed entirely. 'Forgot my manners. Come away up. Need anything from the schooner?' He glanced towards me. 'Weather's coming in.'

I shook my head, indicating the small bag I had brought from the *Moonbird*, and we set off along a foot track through the pale grasses, feet squeaking in the brilliant sand, until, in a hollow between low dunes and boulders, the house suddenly appeared. It was more ably constructed than I had first thought. Some of the timbers looked to have been harvested from the low shrubs of the island: others had a furred appearance from rolling in the sea. The sea would provide all Munro's needs, save for water. Was there a clear line, then, that prohibited pilfering wrecks? Or causing them?

A door with a window set in it, a low sill that accommodated the short man but caused Argyle, and me, to stoop. More dogs about the doorway, half-a-dozen or more. Mongrels: large, stout, thin, mangy, a miscellany of God's forgotten beasts. One carried a bone, high and proud like an heirloom. There was no fury in them, not like the dog at the beach: if we had come this far, we must be here by consent.

Inside the house, a single room, dimly lit.

The fine fronds of the tussock grass were laid all over the floor, making a rich scent like hay. Little eddies of feathers had collected in the corners of the room and adhered to some of the surfaces. There was a cot against one wall, a heavy dresser cluttered with shells and glass and a hearth with a low fire burning. Stains on the hessian that curtained the window indicated this was where they cast their scraps.

A large wooden table stood in the centre of the room. Upon it lay a fowling piece, broken open and gleaming black, cartridges, a powder flask and a ramrod. I looked at Louisa, who had entered behind me, and she smiled sweetly. The inference was clear: if we'd brought trouble, we'd have been on the end of that gun.

Munro busied himself removing the gun and the ammunition from the table and swung a pot over the fire. He stood leaning against the stone of the chimney, his free hand on a hip.

'Louisa here is also called Drummerrerlooner. The other three's Mirnermanner, Pungerneetterlattener, and no one ken say it so we call er Sall, an then Tingnooterrer, what they call Tibb. So first two's with Kelly and Thomas. Tibb's stopping over from Woody.'

I had no idea what this meant. The women smiled shyly

and Tibb, who appeared the youngest, made an approximation of a curtsey.

'These uns is on a list, you might know. Man named Robinson, damned *evangelist*, sent his agents to search the islands for the wives. Wants to tak'em off us, make em into Christians, make em *European*, see. So you'll forgive me bein prepared.'

'Why would he take your wife, Mister Munro?' I asked.

'Int nobody ben *catchem*,' hissed Louisa fiercely.

'Louisa's *tyereelore*,' said Munro. 'All of em are. That's the word they use for themselves. Sealer women, come from Van Diemen's Land, from all about but mostly the north. Mostly speak South Seas pidgin. Some's taken by force, see; there'd be no sealing or birding at all in the straits otherwise. I'm pretty sure Sall an Maria were taken. They's never said exactly.' He lifted the pot off its hook and poured the water into a tin teapot, his voice constricted with the effort. 'You go back to the twenties, sealers everywhere here. Hundreds. Come from Africa, America, Poly-*nesia*. And if you got a woman can swim, can pack skins, grow the food, then you got an advantage. Can even read the weather, some of em.'

He moved about as he spoke, found old china cups here and there. He poured tea from a tin into the pot and swirled it.

'So some are taken, but not all of em. Louisa here come from Cape Portland, north-east mob. The big men there, see, them bungaras—'

'*Bungunnas*,' Louisa corrected him.

'—they got *plans*. Strategy. Givin up their daughters to these islands because they know what's coming on the mainland, maybe. Wanting to tie themselves more to here.'

Louisa stood listening to his account without comment, tying off an apron that looked to have been stitched from sacking. Her face was unreadable.

Munro poured the tea, began sliding cups across the table to each of us. These comments of his were retorts to arguments nobody had raised.

'We're man and wife, just as legal as you two are.' He was looking directly at me and at the doctor beside me, and I fear I must have blushed.

'Oh no, I—'

'Some of em, aye,' he continued over the top of my protest, 'come here by force. Kidnapped, sometimes there's a fight and they kill the husbands. But I tell you serious'—he stopped, apparently staggered by a fresh bout of indignation—'the man Robinson, the scoundrel, he's telling people we're "the African slave trade in miniature".' He spat the words, staring at each of us. 'Does she look like any man's slave to you?'

Louisa stood glaring, hands on her hips. 'Specially not Robinson's,' she said. 'He come round here, he won't make it out o' the boat...'

There was menace in the staccato speech. I knew now that as I'd placed my foot on the sand and stepped over the rowlock, that fowling piece had been trained on me, somewhere in the dune. How different our reception might have been. Life and death, strung from nothing more than the good fortune of having picked up Campbell.

'Mister Munro,' I ventured, 'do you have Kelly and Thomas stay here?'

He looked perplexed.

'Aye, I do.'

'But you say they took their wives, by force?'

'Dinnae ken for sure. Probably.'

'Why would you condone that?' I don't know what made me ask it; my father kicked me under the table. But I pressed on. 'Why would you allow such men here?'

He sighed heavily, as if faced with a halfwit.

'Islands, right?' He made a grouping motion with his hands. 'All stuck together, exactly like a family is. Can't separate em. This one's here, that one's there and nobody's moving. Best you can do is make sure everyone gets along.' He appeared to consider something for a moment. 'People here, they've killed men. Some deserved it, some didn't. Some's done horrors to the bairns. Now am I supposed to send em off? Have em removed? Work out which ones did the right killing? No. You get on, you keep going.'

My father had been silent throughout the conversation, his face following the voices. Now he spoke.

'Mister Munro, would you be agreeable to us taking a walk?'

Munro's eyes darted to his wife. 'Why would you be wanting to do that?'

'Doctor Gideon here is a man of science. He has driven us to distraction collecting his sea creatures on this voyage. It might do him some good to turn his efforts to terra firma.' He smiled benignly, and so did the doctor. Crafty old fox, my father.

'Well.' Munro shot another look at his wife. 'Why not?' It felt like the whole room had exhaled. Now he peered at the ceiling, fashioned from tacked-up hessian. 'But you might want to wait a wee while.'

We could hear the steady drumming of rain on the roof above us. Drips had begun to make their way through and down onto the tussock floor.

My father had been cradling his teacup in his hands. He placed it down to scratch at the scab that had formed under his eye. We listened to the *tyereelore* chattering and laughing, and my father's mood lifted in their presence. Their shyness had evaporated now and they were delighted by the company, as much as my father was by them. In the doctor and the master, I could detect no great change of mood.

After half an hour or so the rain eased and then stopped and the surrounding silence of the island returned. It remained a silence to me even when the gulls and the dogs resumed their perpetual contest outside, scrawing and barking, the spaces between the sounds deep and satisfying.

Munro stood and made for the door. On the wall beside the jamb at eye height there was a peculiar woolly ball, silver and grey. He grabbed it and I saw it was a fur hat that had been hanging on a hook. He punched it down over his head so that his hair and his ears disappeared under the pelt. Now the bristles were his hair, and it completely changed his appearance. I snorted to stop a laugh. The master almost summoned a tiny smile.

Munro's face said we weren't the first to laugh at it.

'Badger fur,' he grunted. 'Warm, but it itches like a bastard.'

I drained the last of the tea and looked at the cup. There was a ship's crest glazed on it.

~

So it was that we wandered out across Preservation Island in the gale: Munro reluctant and exaggerating his windward tilt, the doctor playing his role with obvious pleasure, stopping to admire a guinea fowl here and a plover there. He made notes and stooped to collect shells and seeds, depositing them in the pockets of his jacket.

Again I was left to guide my father, a thing I never minded

doing, but which was slow work. Before long the main party had moved ahead of us and we were alone. To our left, on a gradual slope that faced the northern arc of the sun, stakes of tea tree had been driven into the earth in rows of many dozen each, and between them were strung dark wallaby skins, stretched and drying in the sun. Anywhere else, the presence of rows and rows of stakes might signify agriculture: a vineyard or a hop garden. On these islands it seemed all the works of the land revolved around dismembering beasts and selling the parts.

My father's head turned a little that way, drawn by the smell.

He talked happily about the island, and what he considered the allure of the *tyereelore* women. I scolded him half-heartedly; they all had husbands, I told him. But it wasn't so base a motive: they were Sirens to him. The cultivated ground of the island was entrancing him too, the dramatic transformation from tussocks and boulders to gardens. I described the fruit trees, the crops and watercourses, rambling patches of parsley following the water. He stopped and sniffed the air.

'Pigs?' he said, turning his face upwind.

I could not imagine how he had picked the pigs out from the hundreds of goats swarming around us, but he was right. 'A sow and some piglets, I can see from here. Oh, and there's the papa. Fine porker he is.'

'Take me to him, little piglet.'

Such were his whims. We left the path we'd been following and took a fork that led to the sty. He listened to the snufflings of the little ones with a smile on his face. Their huge mother lay on her side, making gruff corrections when they strayed to explore the mud. The pen was open to the sky at one end, but the sow lay in a covered corner: on top of the fence palings, a section of very neat weatherboard and roofing had been added to the uprights. It was low enough that my father was able to rest his hand on it as he leaned against the palings.

I was so diverted by the piglets, their ridiculous play, that I forgot about my father for just a moment. When I looked back at him his expression had changed to one of intense concentration, and his hands were running along the edges of the roof. He put his nose to the wet timbers and smelt them deeply. The air only smelt to me of the mud and the fresh, sharp manure of the animals. But something else occupied him here.

'My darling,' he said, 'tell me about this structure.'

I looked at it helplessly: what was there to tell? 'It's a roof. About twelve, fourteen feet across. It has straight sides but a curve instead of a pitch.'

'What do you mean?'

'Like a flattened arch, can you imagine that? The timberwork is very exact—the boards join very tight.'

'A gambrel? A—er—mansard roof?'

'No, curved.'

'How tall are the sides?'

'Not tall. Two feet, perhaps?'

'How long is the entire structure?'

'Oh, fifteen feet, maybe eighteen.'

'Yes. And what fastens the timbers together?'

I came in close. 'Um…copper nails.'

'Any moss on it? Any lichen?'

I checked all sides of it. 'No.'

Voices, the loud laughter of the *tyereelore*. They'd circled back to us. 'Turn away from it,' my father muttered under his breath. I did not understand his meaning at first, but I followed his lead. They reappeared around a bend in the path, their hair damp from the drizzle. Declan Connolly lumbered along holding the front of his shirt as a sling. It was filled with bright yellow fruit.

'We are in luck,' said Campbell happily. 'Lemons!'

'Come,' said Munro. He was looking at us looking at the pig sty. 'This will interest you.' He led us across the back of his house, along a slight rise that overlooked the house and the sea, and the *Moonbird* weathering the gale. Out there she seemed forlorn, abandoned.

There were droplets on the fine points of the tussocks, and our footprints revealed the dry white sand under the heavy crust the rain had made. The cold wind flicked new droplets at us as we walked. Behind us, over the rise and further out to the west I could see the she-oaks bending to the wind, whistling softly.

This place belonged to the weather. People were incidental.

Munro led us to a shed made of planking, open to the east but walled in on the west side where the wind prevailed. Shrubs grew over the protected side, tilting away from the salt breeze. Inside were tall stacks of hides, rich brown in their centres and fringed with pale, ragged skin. They had been pressed into bales, a yard or more square: every hide was a living creature, every bale maybe a hundred hides. The smell was the stench of anything rendered: thick and sour and meaty.

I pushed my fingers through the fur in the stack nearest to me: the dark lustre of the top layer gave way to a surprisingly white undercoat that was warm and soft to the touch. Forty, maybe fifty of these stacks. Five thousand beasts. How could the seals breed fast enough to balance what was taken? I suppose gentlemen must wear hats, and felt must come from somewhere, and every hat in the world has its birth in the squeals of an uncomprehending animal being clubbed to death.

My father stood beside me, inhaling deeply through his nose.

The smells he was parsing must have been complex indeed if they conveyed the sight I beheld.

In the corner nearest to us, nearest to the daylight, the floor of the shed was covered in the same downy feathers I'd seen in the house. Great sacks, even larger than the bales of hides, stood in piles around the feathered ground. In the shadows were two cauldrons on wrought legs. Like the press, they were greased, smeared with gut and oil.

'Lucky ye're not here when we're boiling down,' Munro said, with a nod towards the big iron try-pot. 'Stinks to high hell. Mutton bird. The women call em *yolla* but it's the same, moonbird—as fer what you call your boat.'

Munro again cast an eye over Mr Argyle.

'Anyways the feathers and the oil go out, Sydney and Hobart, an we keep the meat for us.' He seemed inordinately proud of the enterprise. 'Main women's in charge, them *tyereelores*. The young uns we call *wanapakalela*: do all the pluckin and packin. Five hundred a day if they's quick. Try to do as much of it as we can this time o' year when the birds are skinny. If they gets too fat, they're harder to pluck and then the women get irascible.'

He beamed as he looked around at the splattered interior of the shed. No one knew what to say. Eventually he suggested we continue walking around the island, and I offered to take my father back to the house. He was tired, and becoming tetchy in the absence of drink: I could see it in the weather that crossed his face from moment to moment.

~

When we returned to the house we were presented with more tea, and small eggs on bread. I wondered if perhaps they came from seabirds. The feathers were gone from the corners of the room, and a large wood spider I'd seen in the corner of the ceiling had been banished, along with its collection of husked flies. Louisa had been caught out by our unexpected arrival, I realised, and had used our short absence to get the house up to a standard—perhaps one she thought I lived by. If only she could see my quarters.

I mashed my father's eggs into his bread with the back of a fork and touched his hand, bumped it slightly towards his cutlery. Gideon was concentrating on something, chewing urgently so he could talk.

'When we were walking,' he said to Munro down the side of his teeth, 'I saw two more houses over to the north of us. You didn't invite us to see them.' He gestured over his shoulder with his knife towards the rise of the island.

Munro hesitated, frowned. 'Cannae show ye there,' he said slowly. 'They's taken sick over that side. Whole family.'

The doctor was immediately interested. 'What manner of sickness, Mister Munro?'

'We don't know,' he replied. 'Want to keep the women and bairns away from em, in case it's catching.'

Gideon considered this a moment. 'Well yes, that's possible. But someone or something must have introduced the sickness to the island. Were the sufferers the only ones who came in contact with some visitors, perhaps?'

'No sir, not to my knowledge.'

'And why only one family? Are they unusual in any way?'

'No. They's normal folk, just raise the crops in season, do the birds and the odd seal...'

Gideon's eyes were roving distractedly around the high corners of the walls.

'Ye listening to me, doctor?' Munro turned to the others in the room: 'I dinnae think your man's listening to me.'

'What crops are they growing, Munro?' asked the doctor in the cold, terse manner I knew to be his thinking voice.

'Er, they do the beans in autumn, peas and rye in the winter, and some corn and vegetables in the summer…apples, pears…'

'The rye—do they store it?'

Munro looked baffled now. 'Course they do. We use it right through, feed for the pigs and flour for bread and…'

'And making liquor?'

Munro did not answer. If it was possible for such hardened skin to blush, I thought I detected a reddening of his features.

'Could we walk there?'

'Aye, you could but I dinnae believe it would be a good idea.'

'And why's that?'

'Every chance it's gangrene, doctor. Leprosy.'

Gideon thought about this for a moment. 'I doubt that. No. I would rather like to have a look, if I may.'

Munro shrugged. 'I suppose there's no harm in having a look. Louisa, would ye excuse me, dearie? And maybe juice they lemons while we're gone.'

Connolly and the master had already excused themselves to row back to the *Moonbird* and attend to the damage from the gunfight that had splintered us so long ago at Rodondo.

I looked to my father, curling and uncurling one fist on the table. The other hand, beneath the table, bunched the material of his shirt. I could make him walk with us, keep him away from the booze for another few hours. But it would be torture, and what would I have gained him?

He'd anticipated my thoughts. 'Darling, I think I'll stay behind if you don't mind. My legs are weary from this morning.'

His weak smile betrayed something different.

ST ANTHONY'S FIRE

I walked out there with Munro and the doctor, away from the coast and slightly north. The ground was open grassland, some shrubs and a waterhole to our right. The goats were all around us, advancing with their dreamy smiles then retreating at any sudden movement. The houses stood isolated on a rise, and as we drew nearer we could see children playing on an abandoned cart in front of them. We came to a dry-stone wall made from flat pieces of limestone. A finger-long lizard stood tall on the top row of stones, watched us and whipped into a crevice.

Adults had left the houses now and were headed towards us. They walked normally enough, and were dressed as I would have expected for islanders. But as they came nearer, I began to see the extent of their suffering. Their skin was covered in great red lesions: on some of them the boils were closed but on others they were weeping pus or had erupted and formed into scabs. A mother carried a tiny infant in her arms, the child's face peeling as though she had been terribly sunburnt.

The doctor introduced himself and they did likewise. I do not remember their names now. There was hesitancy in their muttered words. Shame, perhaps a taint of suspicion. I noticed that Munro would go nowhere near them.

Gideon was explaining that he was a man of divers learning, and that he wished to help if he could.

Now they were more inclined to talk: the sickness had made them outcasts and they were lonely. They told him it had started in the early spring; at first just cramps and flux. Then the suffering had taken all sorts of bizarre turns: the sores on their skin, strange feelings of numbness, terrible itching—even fits. But it was not until they began to exhibit ferocious manias that they were separated from the community. The anguished shouting, the delirium, filled the night and terrified their children. People did harm to themselves, swearing and racking and convulsing. The rest of the islanders had abandoned them, fearful of contagion.

The doctor was listening to all of this, as before, but only half-listening.

'So you say, you said to me, that the symptoms had advanced to mania *before* the patients were quarantined?'

The islanders took a moment to unpick Gideon's terminology, then agreed.

'And the infant?' he asked brusquely, addressing himself to the mother. 'It still feeds at the breast?'

She lowered her eyes and nodded faintly.

Until now, Gideon had been addressing them from a distance of perhaps ten yards: now he crossed the threshold of the gateway in the wall and stood closer among them. The sun lit upon the broad base of his neck, above the collar where the skin was tanned like leather. He showed no fear of transmission: he approached without hesitation a man who appeared to be the woman's husband, and with a cursory *May I?* began to probe at the suppurating wounds on his face.

'Perfectly safe,' he muttered in our direction.

We edged forward, none too keen to take him literally. Nor did the patients move from where they stood.

'Come,' he said impatiently, 'we have things to examine.'

He strode off ahead of us, following the faint foot-track that led back to the two houses and some outbuildings, adjusting his stride to walk next to the man of the house.

'Why do you grow rye here?' he asked him. 'Why not wheat or some other cereal?'

'It's tougher,' said the man, perhaps curious at the choice of subject. 'It don't mind the cold wind or the blowing sand.'

'So you sowed it when? May, June?'

'Aye, two weeks afore the solstice. Same every year.'

'I see. And what was the year like?'

He laughed bitterly. 'Terrible. Cold and wet, everthin come up late.'

'*Late?* Interesting…it was very dry in Sydney.' We had reached the houses, and now stood beside a small vegetable patch that had been carefully tilled and was protected from the birds by a fishing net strung across stakes. Bright young shoots of green speared in neat rows through the soil.

'Would you show me about?' the doctor asked.

The man led Gideon into the first house with his family, Munro and me trailing behind. Rough weatherboards on the outside, hessian sheets lining the interior walls. It was dark inside, basic and small enough to feel crowded. A hen bolted through underfoot as we entered. There were dried tussocks thrown on the floor here, too, and the planking was an odd miscellany of rough-milled timbers that looked local, combined with more finely cut ones that showed flakes of paint from previous lives. A handful of bottles and jugs sat on the mantel, and a central table, waxed to a shine, was dominated by the bulk of a heavy bible. There were blankets strewn on chairs. These were not affluent people, but I marked that once again the interior was neater and cleaner than my own home.

Gideon looked through the two bedrooms and then followed the man out the rear door to the wash-house and privy. Nothing appeared to catch the doctor's eye; nor did he appear any more interested when we passed through the second, smaller house. He was led into a rickety timber shed that contained tools: he examined them cursorily but said nothing.

At first, not knowing him, I had scorned him. Then I knew him—and I wanted him. At this moment he seemed unknown once more. Maybe he was several people, I thought now. Maybe we all are.

Bugs circled in a beam of light that came through a high gap in the wall; he watched them carefully but without investment: as if they could tell him nothing.

On returning to the vegetable patch, he squatted down and peered at the seedlings, asking what variety each of them was. Then, to the consternation of the family, he reached under the net and began pulling them out, one by one, sniffing at them and chewing one or two: when he ate a sour one he made a comical grimace and a small boy, the one who trailed behind the nursing mother, laughed. She freed a hand to cuff the child over the back of the head.

The doctor was led next to a series of pens and small paddocks containing the family's livestock: two pigs, a small herd of goats, a single cow and some chickens. He asked about each, about their health and their manner, how they were producing and whether anything tasted strange. The boy went straight to a russet hen and picked it up, stroking its feathers and presenting it proudly for our inspection. Nothing appeared out of the ordinary.

At the end of the path along the pens we came to a granary, a cylindrical structure made from flat slabs of granite, cleverly interleaved so that the whole structure was sealed. There was a large circular hatch on top of it, four or five feet in diameter and fitted with handles. At the front, where the man led us, a small door was built into the stonework down low so that the grain could be got out.

I looked carefully at the door as the doctor opened it: a normal cupboard door, mounted on its side so that it opened downwards and the spilling grain was helpfully cupped within. And it was, literally, a cupboard door: made by someone with the right tools and fashioned precisely, by a cabinetmaker. The timber was well finished. It did not appear to have originated in this rudimentary world.

The doctor scooped a handful of the rye grain and fished his spectacles from a pocket so he could examine it. He sniffed again but did not place any in his mouth. After a moment of thought, he tossed the grain on the ground at his feet.

'Anything else to inspect?' he asked the man.

The family looked at each other: mutters and shrugs. 'No, that'd be it.'

Gideon led the party back to the first house we had entered. He helped himself to a seat at the table, requested tea, and slid the family bible towards himself.

'Aah,' he murmured. 'You don't mind?' He had already opened it and begun leafing through before the man replied,

'Of course, sir.' He examined the dates of christenings inside the front cover, picked out various cards and pages of letters, and gave the appearance of reading them thoroughly.

The afternoon was dragging on. The man's wife built up the fire and began to wash potatoes over a bucket, dropping each clean one in a pot with a hollow thud. From a metal bin she produced a loaf of dark bread, placed it on a board and aimed a knife over it.

'Throw that in the fire,' said the doctor. He had not looked up from the bible.

'I—I beg your pardon?'

'You heard me. Burn it.' He turned a page, kept reading. The woman responded almost reflexively to the authority in his voice—albeit with a look of bewilderment—and lobbed the loaf onto the coals. It flared a moment, released an aroma that reminded me I was hungry and then settled to a slow smoulder. Gideon closed the bible with a thump.

'Tell me how you worship,' he said to the man.

If the man was shocked by the question, or by the burning bread, he did not show it. 'New Church,' he said, and I felt his self-consciousness. 'Got no minister available to us here, o' course. Make our prayers, read scripture when we can…'

'When you can?' the doctor interrupted. 'When you *can*? What does that mean?'

The man was taken aback. 'Lot of work here. Depends on the season, but sowing, harvesting…the animals of course, to feed, slaughter, take em out, bring em in. Wife here does the lessons with the boy. Get water, get…'

'So you attend to your Lord *when you find the time*?' He shook his head.

The man looked furious but did not reply. The boy had

gone to his mother and she was embracing him with one arm, holding the infant with the other. Her ravaged face bore misery and compliance in equal measure. And perhaps, I thought, just a tinge of scepticism. Hers was a life to be endured, nothing more.

'I will need to consider this,' Gideon continued. 'I am close to a resolution on the matter, but it requires thought.' And without another word he got up and walked out, leaving Munro and me at the table with the embarrassed family. Nobody spoke, and at length the baby began to cry. I excused myself and went outside to sit on the doorstep.

The doctor had walked away from the house, over to the near edge of the field, and was squatted on his haunches among the stubble of the winter crop. I watched him pick at the straws and hold a stem up to the light, squinting at it. He rubbed his fingertips in the earth, lowered his head in thought, then stood up.

He did not utter a word as he passed me in the doorway, but gave me a tiny smile.

'Very well,' he said loudly as he entered the room. The baby was screaming now. The family looked up hopefully; the mother fumbled under her shawl and fed a breast to the infant, silencing the racket. The boy was on another chair, picking at sores on his hands.

'The problem here,' Gideon began, sighing deeply, 'is impiety.'

He allowed the wave of shock to pass through the room.

'Sir, have you failed in your fidelity to your wife?'

The man did not wither under his searching gaze, but stood taller in anger. 'Never once!' he cried.

'Other women on the island?'

'No!'

'You sure?'

'I tell you again, never!'

'You ever...' He looked sidelong now. 'Have you ever been tempted by the stock?'

The allegation rocked him back as if the doctor had hurled a heavy object rather than a slur.

'What sort of man do ye take me for, sir? In front of my *wife*? And *child*, you ask this!'

The good humour never left the doctor's face. 'So not in body, perhaps,' he said. 'But your thoughts, sir, they have been impure at times, have they not?'

The man spluttered with indignation. 'I cannae see how this leads to burning sores and fitting and mad dreams!' He was so outraged that making an 'f' sound had caused him to spittle.

'Well, that's what you say. And I suppose you want us to accept that. But there is a pattern of events here that cannot be overlooked. The poor crop, your inattention to your sacred duties: scripture, prayer, *purity of heart*...and concomitant with that, the terrible pestilence that is afflicting your mortal bodies. Only a fool would disregard the connection.'

They waited now, breathless for deliverance.

'If you're New Church, as you say you are, you'll know that Hell is not a place God sends you to. It is a state of *being*, an internal and corruptive state that manifests in these sores and outbursts.'

He had turned the room. Their attention to him was desperate in its intensity.

'What can be done?' the man pleaded.

'You must begin by slaughtering the livestock.'

The poor couple looked at him in speechless horror.

'Yes, that is essential. Do not eat anything from them: make a pit and set the corpses aflame and then refill it, and do it all away from water supplies. And burn the stubble on the field out there. It will be dry enough in coming weeks. Take all of the grain in that silo of yours and throw it in the same pit with the animals. And when I say all of it, I mean every last seed.'

'What is the purpose of such destruction?' asked the man, defiant again.

'There is no way forward here but abject sacrifice to the Lord.' Gideon's manner had turned dark, and although I thought his performance to be a false one, I could not dispel the notion that he had access, inside himself, to deep currents we could not imagine. 'Exodus twenty-nine, sir,' he rumbled. 'You know the passages. I do not need to remind you of them. Jeremiah, particularly, tells us that sacrifice is worthless without an immediate turn to piety. Change your ways, all of you, or worse will come.'

Gideon stood, and he filled the room.

'Burn it,' he repeated. 'Burn all of it, and repent.'

He turned his eyes towards Munro and me, and those eyes were so convincingly filled with hellfire that I thought my own conscience to be under examination.

~

We ate at Munro's table that night.

My father had slept in the afternoon, and he seemed brighter now. To my surprise, he'd had no liquor in our absence.

Munro spoke approvingly of Gideon's performance in the afflicted house, and Gideon made modest demurrals: *it is a shame to have to say such things.* Louisa had arranged six bottles with cork stoppers by the door; lemon juice for our voyage, she told me with a kind smile. She and Munro served kangaroo that had been seared in a skillet on his wood stove, along with vegetables from their garden that would not have been out of place on a Sydney table. The other women fussed around us, set a table and tended the fire. Though it was not their house, they seemed at ease here domestically. The kangaroo meat was lean and dark, and they had made little effort to conceal its origin: tufts of skin and singed fur still adhered to the fillets. But it made a pleasant change from the various creatures the doctor dragged up from the seabed.

My father ate beside me. I passed things to him as his needs arose: the water jug, the salt. There was wine, too, Hobart wine such as the officers might keep. The things that floated ashore here.

'It's sad,' my father said quietly to me at one point. 'I could have stayed here.'

'What do you mean?' I asked him in return.

'They want for nothing here.'

The sound of the *tyereelores'* laughter cut across his words.

'But what do you mean *could have?*' I persisted. He merely shrugged. His fingers read the pewter dish they'd given him and found the food. He cut it, and ate.

Munro said nothing further about the meeting with his neighbours. Having ventured his endorsement of Gideon's dire prescription, he retreated into amiable silence. And because the discussion at the table moved on, I did not have the opportunity to seek my father's opinion. It bothered me still, seeing those simple people, suffering already, excoriated by the doctor.

Had he done it to impress me? If so, then I was complicit.

Louisa was telling stories of the islands, stories that revealed her to be deeply acquainted with them, though she was careful to make clear that this was not her country. 'When I'm ere,' she said, her hands making the geography, 'I ben callem Louisa. Back there, Drummerrerlooner.' The other women listened, nodding in silence. My mind turned it over: was it as simple as being known by different names in different places, or something deeper—stranger—than that? The fancy occurred to me that the places themselves might know her differently, the names being merely an expression.

Her people, she explained, came from Cape Portland, the nearest corner of *lutruwita* to where we were sitting. I did not understand that *lutruwita* was their name for Van Diemen's Land until she said: 'Only sixteen mile away'—pointing—'just over there on a clear day.' Her people were the North East nation, words she uttered the way I remembered saying *the United Kingdom* to the Cooper children. The nation was all but finished now, she told us, making it clear that she considered her future to be among the island wives.

I watched Munro watching her as she spoke: his gaze seemed to vary between pride and proprietorship. He never corrected her: in fact, it was she who several times told him not to use his hands, or directed him to offer his guests more meat or bread. Louisa was the *fingersmith* for the islands, he said proudly, and I was mystified by the term until he added that she had now delivered over a dozen children.

His confidence, I thought, emanated not from dominion over his wife but from his place in the island's society. He was their boss. The sealers sent all their trade goods through him and had done for years. They deferred to him in disputes, asked him to officiate when they married their women. He vouched for their credit with faraway officials, he investigated their misdeeds. His hands made gestures of authority as he described these things. Louisa eyed his cutlery sternly.

My father listened closely. I had watched him, as was my habit every evening, and somehow he was resisting the pull of the wine. He had taken a small glass, no more. The effort inside him must have been heroic. On other nights I had watched his hands exploring the table in search of the bottle, even in front of others. Now the shaky hands were firmly clasped in his lap.

'Where will you head next?' Munro asked.

'Oh, around Cape Barren,' said my father. 'A loop to the east and back around to Gun Carriage.'

'You fella careful there,' said Louisa, unbidden. 'Not like us, them lot.'

Munro shot her a look.

She saw it but continued. 'Just mean they's different. You ben know it, James. Always complainin bout them banditti an that.'

If it ruffled him slightly, Munro soon returned to his favourite topics. He was expansive to the point of tedium about civic matters. The need for wharves and anchorages. The infuriating payments levied upon the islanders to keep freelancing troops off their backs. The steady loss of seal numbers and the need for a report to Hobart about the decline.

The more he talked, the more I could see the fantasy collapsing before me: there was no anarchy out here. No lawless bands molesting the shipping. The murderers and wreckers and plunderers were a figment, a tawdry sensation for the Sydney press. The islanders were a diminishing community of men in decline, men who'd taken wives from Van Diemen's Land, mostly by agreement, and who made a modest living from hunting kangaroos, taking seals in their season and birds in another season. There were no laws that bound them, that much was true, but age and inertia were doing a fine job of keeping them civil. I had come to the view that there was no evil to be found out here. No Minotaur in his maze.

And then my father began to talk.

'Mister Munro,' he began, in a tone that made clear he intended a turn to formalities. He laid his fork down and turned his face to Munro, having fixed on his position through listening to him. 'What is that structure you have used to roof over your pigsty?'

Munro looked baffled for a moment. 'My pigsty?'

'Yes, the pen where you came upon my daughter and me earlier. A sow and six piglets. What is it, the structure that shelters them?'

I could see Munro weighing the question and considering how to respond.

'It's a piece of flotsam, Mister Grayling. Off the rocks.'

'Flotsam?'

'Aye.'

'Wreckage?'

Munro made an impatient motion with his hands. The atmosphere in the room had altered.

'Wreckage, flotsam…what the tide delivers, Mister Grayling.' He tried to laugh but an edge of irritation had crept in. 'Big tides here. Turn up all sorts o' things.' No one responded so he continued. 'We'd not have firewood if we didnae scour the beaches fer it. Y're supping with knives from a brig, cups from a brig. Crivvens, that chair beneath ye's from a sloop.'

The doctor looked down in amusement as Munro pointed a stubby finger at his seat.

'Yes,' said my father, 'but that roof. Did you make any inquiries as to where it came from?'

Again, Munro's face darkened. He did not respond.

My father continued: 'Eighteen feet by twelve, thereabouts? Can't be exact, of course…'

Munro only stared.

'South coast cedar. It has a smell about it. My employer is looking for evidence of a lost boat, the superstructure was added locally. Made of cedar.'

Receiving no answer to any of this, he continued. 'Hard for me, obviously, to assess these things, given my...' He waved a hand towards his eyes. 'But I would say the dimensions suit a cabin, likely a forecastle. A hundred-foot barque? It seems a reasonable inference...'

The old sealer drew a deep breath. Rage boiled visibly in him, but my father couldn't see it and he wasn't finished.

'A reasonable inference, *especially* when there's no moss on it. As one might expect if it's only been there a couple of months.'

Munro had heard enough now. He rose from his chair. 'You come to my island and you accept my hospitality, Mister Grayling. Eat my supper, and you make these—what are they, accusations?—under my roof. If you have something to put to me, then you go ahead and put it. But you better be damn sure ye're right.'

His face had twisted into an ugly scowl. The doctor was smiling faintly. My father, I knew, was feeling the air, deciding upon a course. No one spoke for a long time.

'A remote place, Mister Munro. Perhaps you have different means of getting by. Something drifts your way, you put it to advantage. Doesn't make you a wrecker of ships.' He shrugged. 'Doesn't make you a murderer.'

'Damn you, Mister Grayling! How do you dare utter that word in my home! Before my *wife*?' He was shouting now, but my father's voice remained quiet and still.

'It is not an accusation, sir. I am aware you wrote to Sydney about the captain's chest you found. But you must see that you have a problem. The government cutter that's been lurking about—drunks, fools. They will not form a complete view of this. If they find that cabin, and to be fair there is every chance they'll miss it, they will not ask questions. You'll be in irons, Mister Munro. You and your good wife.'

Drunks. From where I sat, I could see his hands trembling in his lap.

Munro remained standing there, holding the back of his chair, face scarlet with fury.

'Never, in all the years I have been here, have I refused a bed to passers-by. But you can leave. The moon is out, you will be fine to row back to your vessel and sleep there.' He spat on his own floor. 'Never darken my door again.'

His hands were on his hips, his face resolute. Louisa looked distressed. She had passed within hours from contemplating shooting us to sharing her home. Now she was back at a point approaching her starting position.

~

It was a long, slow process, getting my father into the jolly-boat. The goats had come down to the edge of the sand, where they stood bleating over our departure, a farewell that did not seem to imply judgment. The dog, thankfully, was elsewhere. I sat beside my father on the thwarts, absently rubbing sand from my bare toes with one finger. The doctor pushed us free, swung in with the water draining from him, and took up his rhythm with the oars. He watched me as he rowed, and he smiled slightly.

We could've done with that lemon juice, I thought.

The oars slopped; no one spoke. The dark outline of a stingray moved over the bright shallows as we passed. I was unsure whether I felt angry at my father for disrupting the meal and upsetting our hosts. Perhaps he had achieved something important. He was sober, alert. That had to count for something.

Once we stood firm on the *Moonbird*, my father felt his way to the far side and urinated. As he did so, he tipped his head in my direction: he could tell that I had hung back to watch him in case he tumbled over, and the supervision irritated him. But he let me walk him down the steps and into his bunk. Connolly had taken the first watch and the doctor remained on deck, so we were alone in the bunkroom. I averted my eyes as my father removed his shoes and trousers and eased himself into the bed. I waited until he was settled, then his voice broke the darkness.

'Munro said the moon was out.'

'Mm.'

'Was it full?'

'Nearly—it was rather lovely.' He'd reminded me of something. 'Did you know the moon came from the Pacific Ocean?'

'What?'

'The Pacific is the void where the moon was pulled from the surface of the earth.'

'Nonsense! Who on earth told you that? The moon is an entirely separate heavenly body.'

'But the…Oh, never mind.'

He fell silent. I thought he was asleep, but then he spoke again. 'Do you think he is responsible?'

I could see the profile of his face in a tiny splinter of moonlight that had found its way down.

'Munro? No,' I replied. 'I cannot say why, but perhaps…I think he has too much to lose. He controls the trade, he has the respect of whoever else is out here. It sounds as if he pesters the government rather than the reverse. Why would a man risk all of that? Why risk drawing attention to his wife?'

'Mm. But why did his letter to the governor describe the captain's chest in detail, and fail to mention an entire *cabin*?'

'Well, yes. But a timber cabin's no motive for such a terrible act,' I countered. 'If there was bullion on board, even rum, then maybe. But no one's said there were great riches on the vessel. No, I believe him to be innocent. So he has parts from the *Howrah*. It is reasonable to think that he scavenges the coasts of these islands, that people bring him things, that he trades. This is how they get by, we're told. It is a long way from there to suggesting he has committed murder. Really, no wonder he was so angry.'

He was quiet, listening intently. 'And if he had no involvement, what then?'

'Why can't we be satisfied that the ship met some misadventure of weather, or some error of human guidance? That it sank without the intervention of some outside agent?'

'But then,' came the answer from the bed, 'where are the people? Would no one survive? Bodies, there would be bodies...'

'Yes,' I replied. 'Or indeed, what if some of them were able to get away and they have launched a boat? Where would they finish up? We must ask the master about the currents, the winds. Perhaps you could say yes, *here*, or *here—this is where the floating wreckage or the survivors would cast ashore.* I think we are preoccupied with this idea of a malign force in these islands. It distorts our thinking. If such a person exists, it isn't Munro.'

Something else occurred to me. 'And if Munro has that cabin, why must we go on? Have we not found enough now to report back to Srinivas?'

I waited for a response and received one: a gentle snore. I sat awhile, feeling the secret stirrings of the boat. My hand rested on the rail of my father's bed, a perfectly rounded edge that felt firm and accommodating, like every other surface below decks. She made no odd creaks or bangs, the *Moonbird*; nothing rotted or broke. I had never seen the slightest evidence of a rat down here, despite the doctor's morbid menagerie. She watched over us, she shared all this, and she was somehow incorruptible.

With a gentle pat on his prickly stubble, I left my father sleeping.

On deck I found the doctor sitting alone.

He was on the cabin roof, making notes by the light of a small lamp. The decks, the rigging, everything seemed cleaner after the rainfall, and he sat straight and square-shouldered as he worked in the notebook on his lap, his back to me. I called his name gently so as not to shock him by my approach, and he turned and smiled.

'What are you doing?' I asked.

'Er, etymology.' He proffered the notebook, in which there were pencilled lists of Latin, Greek; his handwriting was a mystery. Lines and arrows linked the terms; circles marked firmly around some, others crossed out. 'I am supposed to be on watch, but as you can see, there's not a lot going on.'

'I'm replacing you at two.'

He smiled. 'Everyone may be replaced.'

I sat down, not so close as to appear forward. His comment sounded mumbled, and as I studied his features in the faint light, I had a sense his mouth was not the same as I had known it to be. Then I looked beside his hip on the boards, and there was a saucer with a set of dentures in water. I immediately diverted my eyes, but he was too quick.

'The price of an eventful life, I'm afraid.'

'Forgive me,' I said to him. 'They're extremely lifelike. I have never noticed...'

He smiled at this, without opening his mouth. 'They're realistic,' he said, 'because they're real.'

'Pardon?' I studied the false teeth more openly now. He watched me doing so.

He took them from the water and thrust them in his mouth, shaking the drops from his fingertips. 'They're Waterloo teeth—have you heard the expression? I had them made in Boston some years ago. The, er, the soldiers have no further use for them, if you take my meaning. They set them in porcelain. Very hygienic.'

How odd, I thought, that I did not find this off-putting.

'I hope the confrontation with Munro didn't disturb you,' he went on, his mouth forming the words more clearly now. 'It was unpleasant.'

'No, I am fine, thank you, doctor. My father is doing what he was commissioned to do, nothing more.'

A stillness in him. Waiting, somehow. Then he decided to speak.

'Did the Bengali man ever tell you what was on it?'

'On what?'

'The *Howrah*. The ship he has you searching for.'

I must have shrugged. 'There were passengers, but otherwise...timber, I presume. He is a timber trader.'

'You presume.' His voice lost its charm, but not its certainty. 'That boat wasn't carrying timber, my dear. The whole idea was that anyone with an interest would assume it carried timber, and leave it be. It was carrying sterling: British crowns to be used in the establishment of the General Savings Bank in Hobart. Big, heavy silver coins. Thousands of them, piled in chests. A consignment so heavy that it served as the boat's ballast.'

What? I scrambled for reasons he might be wrong. 'Why would anyone accost this vessel, if as you say it was thought to be a timber trader?'

'Someone must have found out.'

'How would they know? How do *you* know?'

'Because people *talk*. They can't help themselves. People who drink, especially, are fed by rumour.'

I fell silent, unwilling to accept the idea that Srinivas had concealed something so important from us. The doctor seemed happy to talk, as if unaware of how profoundly he had shaken my understanding.

'He is a clever man, your father. One can only admire his ability to'—he took my hands, one in each of his—'to imagine the world he cannot see.'

'Yes,' I murmured. I felt his hands, the closeness of his face. It was all I could feel.

'I see, in him, where you came by your steady nerves.' His face in the yellow glow of his lantern: calm, sure. 'He cannot hear us up here, you know.'

'Who?' I asked.

He saw my attempt at deflection for what it was. 'Your father, my dear.'

'My dear?' I laughed. 'My *girl*, my *dear...*'

He smiled that smile of his again, creasing his eyes slightly. 'You can always get up and walk away.'

He let go of my hands and I felt the absence of his fingertips. Then his expression changed again. He was alert now, looking out over the stretch of water that led back towards the beach and Munro's house. There on the slick pool of the inshore surface: a small rowboat picking its way out towards the *Moonbird*.

A single rower worked the oars. The hair, lit by the moon: it was Munro's wife, Louisa. As she neared the hull of the *Moonbird* she slowed her strokes and called softly to us. I came to the bulwark and called back. She found the rope ladder and climbed up to us. She had slung a large sack over her shoulders, and now she placed it on the deck at our feet.

'You fella take this,' she said.

'What is it?' asked the doctor.

'More from that boat, I think,' she said. 'My husband got it, same storm ben throw that cabin up on the rocks. Other men from Clarke help him lift the cabin up to the pigpen. Never showed em this.'

She pulled back the cloth that concealed the item, and there stood an Adige sea chest covered in fine patterns. It could only have been the one Srinivas said was mentioned in the letter to the governor.

'Money in it,' said Louisa, 'but my husband no touch it. Papers...you fella make em out.'

'What do you want us to do with this?' I asked. The woman stood back from it, as though it might taint her in some way.

'Nothin to me! Husband done nothin to nobody. Old man say'—she pointed vaguely below decks, indicating my father— 'they find this on im, they think...' She did not finish.

'How will you explain its absence?' asked the doctor.

'I say nothing, what he think? Think *you* lot bring em go. Can't help you that one.' She crouched, undid the latch that secured the lid. Inside I could make out a stack of papers. Louisa clutched a handful of them, held them up. 'Lookit,' she said. 'Aint bin wet.'

She was right. The papers lay flat in her hand without any sign of crinkling.

'Who did it belong to?' I asked her.

'Shipmaster. Munro read em to me one time: was the master's mail, belong im, you know. All the papers, manifest...'

The doctor had taken up a handful of the papers and was squinting at them. 'Letters between the ship's agents, bills of exchange...nine hundred, eleven hundred...fifteen hundred pounds.'

He put the papers back in the chest. 'I am worried you will be made to suffer for this.'

Louisa looked defiant under the great tangle of her hair. 'Not me you worryin bout,' she said calmly. 'Go down Gun Carriage, you hit some proper trouble, friends.'

She looked back towards shore. 'He sleepin now. Ol' fella sure rile im up, but. You lot get long time way from here. That ship gone now, see. Wan't us, wan't our island. Understand?'

I nodded. She climbed over the bulwark and was about to turn and descend the ladder when she looked back one final time.

'Don't come back ere.'

And she was gone. The doctor re-latched the chest and picked it up by its inlaid handles. 'This is your business, I suppose. I shall place it by your father's bed.'

I thought he was going to leave and I did not want him to. 'Tell me what happened with that family.'

He put the chest down, smiled vaguely. 'Family?'

'The ones who were ill. You told them the problem was their lack of piety.'

'Yes?'

I sensed he knew where I was headed with this but wanted me to ask. 'You are not religious, Doctor Gideon. Truthfully now, what was the problem?'

'Ah.' He smiled more directly and I loved the curl of his cheek where it met his mouth. 'I had a suspicion as soon as we arrived, when they said the harvest had been late and the season cold. The grain they had in storage had purple kernels in it.'

He watched me, all theatre now.

'St Anthony's Fire,' he said. 'Causes gangrene, fitting, madness. The more they ate, the worse it would have got. The others on the island had accidentally quarantined themselves from the real problem, the grain, by exiling the false problem, the people. It's not remotely contagious, even though it looks appalling. And once they stop eating the grain, they'll recover swiftly. Marvellous, no?'

'Then why did you rebuke them so about their observance?'

He shook his head. 'They're New Church. Swedenborgians. They do not subscribe to science. Had I said to them, *You have made a fundamental error in your handling of the grain and now it is infected with a blight which is harming you* they would have been indignant. Most likely they would have sent me on my way and thought us fools, and the problem would have persisted. So I appealed to their belief system: they took fright and will now do exactly as I told them. Burning everything that had been contaminated by the blight is not a perfect antidote, but it fits with their infernal understanding of misfortune, so they will carry it out faithfully.'

'The livestock? The boy's pet *hen*?'

'Unfortunate, but consistent with the necessary awe.'

'You lied to them.' Was I really arguing with him, or just… sparring? I no longer knew. But I saw the boy's face, his pride in that hen, and I turned away from the memory.

'I *persuaded* them, and they will benefit.'

He was right, of course; they would. But summoning God

and the Devil, and purporting to outwit both…I could only think it placed the doctor in a position of terrible power.

'Well, now,' he sighed, indicating the chest again. 'Can't leave this up here. May I propose we go below?' The frankness of his gaze was shocking to me. Not a hint of the modesty, nor the uncertainty, a man might ordinarily feel.

'Had you forgotten? You're on watch, doctor…'

'What difference is there between watching the bow from up here and the stern from my cabin windows?' He laid a finger lightly across my jaw, then bent to pick up the Adige chest.

'You think of everything, don't you?'

'Yes. Yes, I believe I do.' He twirled youthfully on one heel, balancing the wooden box. 'It is all ours, Eliza,' he laughed.

I did not understand. 'What's ours?'

By now I stood facing him and I saw the arched eyebrow. 'Everything. Anything.'

He did not lead me then. There was no need.

I made my decision, and went willingly.

THE BOWSPRIT ACHILLES

At dawn, the doctor slept peacefully beside me, his shoulder and arm protruding from under the blanket. A body I had taken and turned to my own pleasure. I exulted at the sight of him. The mysteries of him, the things that caused me fear, I had reduced them all to mere flesh wanting satisfaction. His secrets were vanquished along with his lust: now he was just a man.

Should I have felt different? Changed? The world felt a little different around me, perhaps; its colours neither more vivid nor less, but altered somehow. Its relative position shifted by no more than a degree.

The chatter in my head inclined to mockery and caustic asides. *Must we blush like a bride?* But I would push those thoughts away, indulgent of my new-formed self, and dwell for long moments on sensations I'd never felt, sounds I had neither uttered nor heard until those stifled, ardent whimpers filled the dark. The mockery would rise again: *Deflowered in my autumn! Ruined!* and I would cast it out with the memory of his hands, his weight, the wholly surprising flight from thought...

And so on.

Barely any of the conversation in my head involved the doctor who was, I congratulated myself, merely the agent of my pleasure: payment overdue for a lifetime immersed in the needs of others. It was a debt, I thought, not yet entirely settled.

~

In the days that followed, life arranged itself to a rhythm.

We were moving slowly, nosing in and out of tiny coves ringed by the domed boulders. Silver in the daylight, soft pink and gold in the dawn and the dusk, they were our constant companions. The oldest and highest of them were dusted in orange, a mysterious coating that spread over them and looked, up close, like old paint. Beyond the seaside boulders, every island grew the same: hills forested in the dry-stick trunks of she-oaks, khaki needles with yellow tips that whistled softly in the breeze.

Most of the bays were empty. Birds, an occasional seal, washed-up remnants of boats older and smaller than the one we sought. One bay, on the north coast of Clarke Island, contained a hut. A sealer named Briggs lived there with his wife and a gaggle of small naked children. Her name—I wrote it down to see more clearly the architecture of the words—was Woretermoteryenna. *Woreter. Moter. Yenna.*

We'd found Briggs covered from head to foot with blood: a nightmare vision that smiled and waved to us as he reclined on a sunlit boulder. He was watching his wife, further away, stalking a seal. What kind of maniac had we chanced upon? I was learning to look to Argyle when something disturbed me, and the wiry little figure on the rock did not perturb him.

Briggs, it turned out, was a reserved sort of man who'd chosen a life at the margins of the world. He did not invite us into his hut, and I sensed no other motive than that he did not want to open his home to strangers. He stepped down from the boulder to the flats that the retreating tide had made, and there he scoured a small pool in the gravelly sand with his foot and proceeded to wash the blood out of his hair and off his face and his hands. He had been flinching seals, he explained, 'bein work what's fit only for the worst of the lags'.

Only when he had completed this strange ablution would he shake our hands, but the smell of the gore lifted from him in the warm sun, the blooms of still blood drying on his shirt.

Briggs wanted to talk about his boy, as parents do, I suppose. The lad was thin, strong-looking, half-assembled on the edge of adulthood. He was named Dalrymple, after the river town in northern Van Diemen's Land. Dalrymple Mountgarrett Briggs, his father said proudly, baptised in Launceston and therefore: 'Bit Van Diemen's, bit Christian, lil bit Irish, eh.'

The morning was quiet, just the breeze through the she-oaks in my ears. We watched Briggs's wife approach the unknowing seal. She lay flat, clawed at the rocks to gain purchase and inched forward. Maybe it heard her. Maybe it was scent. It lifted its great head and studied the air with a wrinkled snout. Then it scratched itself and lay back down.

Briggs spoke again. 'She's his mother, but she still pine for the darky spirits.'

The woman had been so still that the small waves lapped on her feet and she did not remove them to higher ground. Small birds landed near her and settled. A crab edged from its crevice in the rock, unaware she was coiled there.

Then she exploded into movement.

Without warning she leapt from her hiding place with a length of iron in her left hand: the seal lifted its mighty head and bellowed and she brought the iron down with a wet thump. The shriek it produced was more human than animal: outrage and agony. The seal writhed and darted forward, biting at her like an enraged dog. But she was too quick. She brought the iron down again and again, each blow slowing the seal's movements, lowering its head. One swing of the iron broke open the arch of bone around its eye—another cracked its snout and the snout was bent down like a hooked beak and the bellows were smaller squeals now, some claim of injustice—*why?*—in there.

Briggs and I were concealed behind one rock, the others gathered further away.

'Tha' one's a clapmatch,' he muttered to me. 'Lady seal. Not so big, but they's easier to git. Pinnipeds is worth a pound each in Hobart Town.'

'Ah, pinnipeds,' I replied. 'It means they have ears, I understand.'

He looked at me blankly. 'Means they's got flippers for feet.'

His wife was working quickly now: blood slicked the rock and stained the water in the shallow pool that had been the seal's haul-out. Gulls bickered overhead: there would be shreds flicked clear from the carnage. Her arm upraised was a gorgeous thing: a braid of sinews that glowed in the sun. The downswing was its inverse, crushing horror. The head was beaten raw: impacts landing in a cloud of brilliant red around her legs.

Finally, the thuds stopped and we could hear her breathing hard. She bent to examine the seal. Satisfied that it was dead, she turned and looked towards us, smiling.

'Ken do twenny a day,' said Briggs proudly.

~

We sailed on, the stiff westerly days cold and persisting behind us.

The doctor had been fascinated by the killing of the seal: he wrote extensively in his journal about it, reading me passages and asking me my opinion. He thought the way Briggs and his wife killed a full-grown female, there was no way of knowing, until it was dead, whether or not it was in pup. (Gideon was puzzled about this aspect: 'Maybe they can tell?' he ruminated at one point.) Even if the mother was killed shortly after having pupped, he reasoned, the consequence was the same: the young ones would perish for want of food. And there was another thing, he said to me. The seals, harassed constantly in their haunts, would begin to abandon them. Perhaps this was why Briggs and his wife were stalking only one solitary female.

Armstrong's Channel passed under us, foam and blue, while we discussed such things, and I cherished the chance to question him about his ideas.

The passage between Cape Barren in the north and Clarke, lower and lesser, opened into a large bay. The mountains of Cape Barren framed it, vaulted rocks challenging the sky. To our right, the sea appeared open but shallow, and ahead was a low wall of land. I went to the master, his face a mask of concentration at the helm. That finger on the chart: two islands, long and lying side by side like fangs.

'Penguin and Passage,' he said, just faintly singsong on the Ps. He wore a patterned smock: little flowers on tawny fabric.

'Do we need to look?' I asked, because my father would want to know the same thing.

'Aye. Old sealer lives on Penguin. Dunno about the other un. It's just a, a tricky approach. We'll go round the top.'

'Going round,' he yelled to Connolly. The convict responded by taking the main block and tearing line through it. Work for a grieving man.

Penguin Island unfolded, sandy, grassed and dry and not a tree to be seen. Soon the familiar signs of habitation appeared: low roofs made of timbers lying on beams. The pickings, once more, of a society fed by the sea.

Round, further round.

Dunes, patches of brighter green where the freshwater soaks would be. A more extensive roof and a chimney, seeping a little white smoke and, suddenly, a gout of thick black. I saw Argyle's face change at this, an expression of surprise.

'Don't know why ye'd do that,' he muttered. 'Close enough you could come out and wave.'

He swung the wheel. Moments later, another belch of black from the chimney.

'All right,' he said to himself. Then aloud, to Connolly, 'Soundings!'

Connolly threw the plumbed line and began to call the fathoms. He was watching the line, looking up occasionally at me to see if I was watching him. We had curled around the top end of the island, and a sandy beach faced us as we nosed in. Behind us were the rocky shores of the other island, Passage. The space between the two was less than half a mile.

The soundings held at five fathoms, even as we inched in towards a solitary boulder that loomed off the beach. The shallow sand formed a spit out to the rock, the vegetation narrowing to a peak that followed the sand. A large gull stood defiant on the boulder's crown.

Argyle called the anchor as we came to a halt. The chain rattled out then pulled taut. A light surf swept the beach to our left.

Argyle called Connolly over and told him he wanted the doctor to bring medical supplies and the fowling piece. I asked the master what had agitated him.

'Smoke,' he replied levelly. 'More often distress than greeting. Best be sure.'

Again we launched the jolly-boat, leaving Connolly standing watch on the *Moonbird*, and my father below decks. The crossing this time was only sixty yards or so. The doctor rowed it, his back to the island, facing me. He smiled easily as he pulled the oars: either he knew there was danger and welcomed it or he was blissfully unaware. The master had the gun across his knees, his face set in stone.

We stepped ashore and Argyle stopped to listen. Not a sound, only the usual background of birds. The wind blew across the island towards us, bringing the smoke from the house, wreathing low with the gusts.

'Hello?' A cheerful holler from the doctor.

No response.

Argyle held up a hand for us to stop, turned his back and loaded the gun, keeping the muzzle low for the time being. With an eyebrow he motioned for us to continue.

This house was rougher, smaller. No garden, just a pen without livestock. No dogs. Two small boats turned over in the scrub, some fishing gear and a try pot. Along with twine from old hide bundles, they were the only evidence of work. Everything dry, bleached.

Argyle stood back from the door, the gun ready. The doctor opened it and went through. Not knowing what else to do, I followed close behind.

Inside was a cramped room with a table against one wall and boxes and sacks piled about. The daylight struggled in here but no lantern was lit. Evidence of lives like Munro's but with less order. The smell was of old food, smoke and bodies.

Warm bodies.

Two men lay on the floor, bound and gagged. One eyed us fearfully, his sweat picking up the filth from the earthen floor. The other writhed in pain, alone with it: a large iron hook was embedded in the muscle at the back of his arm and tied with a rope to the leg of the table.

I followed the eyes of the uninjured man, looking into the darkest corner.

There stood a woman. A native woman, dressed traditionally in strings and kangaroo hide, tall and fierce and beautiful. Her hair was cropped tight against her head, and beneath the hard domes of her shoulders, diagonal scars ran into the centre of her chest. A circlet of maireener shells glowed at her throat. Long high cheekbones made flat planes down to her jaw, and those planes caught a glimmer of light. Her mouth was proud, her brows cast shadows over hard eyes.

She stood with one leg forward, and a soldier's Brown Bess pointed directly at the two men on the floor. The barrel was so long that its muzzle nearly reached them. The detonation in here would be thunderous.

A cask of broken coal fragments lay between her foot and the hearth: it was she who had signalled us in, into her ambush. She held the weapon expertly, as I had seen the Corps do: one hand under the barrel keeping it level, the other wrapped around the stock with her index finger snake-alert over the trigger. Her eyes never left the two men.

'No further,' she said.

Argyle had come in with the gun raised: now he lowered

the barrel, held it out wide. No one spoke or moved. The room awaited her.

'Put your gun on the table,' she said calmly, and Argyle complied.

She walked towards it, keeping the barrel of her own weapon trained on the men. With one hand, she opened the breech and flipped the gun over, then banged it loudly on the surface of the table so the cartridge fell out. She hefted it back to Argyle.

The man with the baling hook in him groaned, and she looked at him quizzically. She took the rope that connected the hook to the table and pulled it tighter: he screamed. What had this man done to her that she would be so casually cruel? Satisfied that the rope was tight, she stepped over him and swung a graceful kick at the other man's backside.

He grunted, and she sank the foot in again. 'Waste of a good kickin, your arse.'

Then she came forward, stood within inches of me and looked over me from head to foot, her eyes exactly level with mine. She tipped her head to one side. Some sort of doubt appeared in the burning eyes, some lack of faith. We had not exchanged a word, but I disappointed her.

'Righto, stick insect,' she said to me. 'Off we go.'

~

We walked back the way we had come, back down the short path to the beach.

The woman's last gesture on the island was to pick up a log splitter that was leaning on a boulder near a pile of split firewood. She carried it ten yards to where the two timber skiffs were propped up, and placing the gun on the ground—within her reach and not ours—she smashed the bottoms out of both boats. When she'd finished she was slightly breathless. She dropped the axe and picked up the gun.

'Babies,' she sneered. 'Can't swim. So that's them done.'

On the row out to the *Moonbird*, she chose to stand at the stern. She did not once relax her stance, nor lower the weapon. Her every muscle screamed fury. The Brown Bess took up most of the space. As we approached our boat, Connolly leaned over the bulwark to watch our approach. He seemed baffled by what he saw, which was reasonable, I suppose.

'Let her aboard,' Argyle called calmly up to him. A brief discussion ensued between Argyle and Connolly. The master pointed out that the wind had come around ninety degrees while we had been away. The convict had set a stern anchor to prevent us swinging too close to the rocks, but the result was that the *Moonbird* now stood beam-on to the wind.

None of this mattered a great deal, but for the fact that her shoreward side was being slapped by an irritable chop. Connolly suggested we go round the bow and board her from the seaward side. The woman followed all of this without a word. Argyle took a look over his shoulder and altered his course so that he headed for the *Moonbird*'s bow. The doctor had seated himself in the bow facing us, with a glance, seemingly amused, for me. Gulls lifted lazily off the rigging as we approached.

We came under the bow, a part of the *Moonbird* I'd never seen from this angle. I knew there was a figurehead there at the top of the raked stem, a figure of a man. But I'd never looked closely at it.

Now I was looking at the doctor, who was looking up. No amusement now: he was staring at the figurehead in shock, his expression turning to something like nausea.

The carved figure was indeed a man, slightly smaller than life-size, naked and twisting at the hips. He was rendered as muscular, bearded, classical. His face mirrored the doctor's somehow, though the blank eyes, being carved of plain wood, revealed less. The figure was not squared to the line of the bow but twisted around, as though the man was writhing. One strong arm crossed his chest, the hand resting on the opposite shoulder. The other hand reached back and down, stretching towards something in particular.

We were in shadow now, under the sweep of the bow. It was suddenly cold.

One of the carved legs rested long against the hull, the other was buckled at the knee. The great thighs bulged in sculpted agony. The reaching hand was clutching at the ankle, the heel, and there the figure had been affixed to the hull by an iron arrow that passed through that heel. The doctor was taking all of this in and for some reason it seemed to unsettle him.

We came around the seaward side and the vision of the figurehead was gone. Moments later we were alongside the *Moonbird* and the doctor indicated with a swept hand that I should ascend the ladder ahead of him. I caught his eye: there was no trace of discomfort. I did not ask what had perturbed him so.

~

When she stood on the deck of the *Moonbird*, the woman became less concerned about covering us with the musket. She kept it in the crook of her arm while she assessed everything around her. Argyle, the doctor and I stood together near the rail where we had come aboard. I could see now that she had a string bag slung over one shoulder, and that it contained a handful of heavy items.

'I need to check my father,' I said to her. 'He is below.'

She raised her chin just slightly, indicating the stairway. 'Anyone else down there?'

'No.'

'Go on then.' She'd recognised that the musket was too long to allow her to do anything much in the close confines of the *Moonbird*'s interior, far less conduct an armed search.

I went below and through to my father's cabin. He had been sleeping: he was confused, and more so when I explained to him that we had been held up by a native woman with a soldier's musket. He roused himself and followed me up the stairs, his dry hand quivering in mine.

The woman stood tall in the centre of the deck, her back to the island. 'This ol man your father?'

He squared his face to the sound of her voice. 'You have come aboard, young lady, without invitation. Might not we ask who *you* are?'

Her brows shot up at this; more in amusement, I thought, than anger. 'Tarenorerer,' she said. 'Can you do that, eh? Ta-ren-o-rerer. Not so hard. Tommeginne my people, Emu Bay. Persecuted twenty-five years now by your lot.'

'Are you a wife?' my father interjected. 'Of a sealer, I mean?'

She glared at him scornfully. 'I'm nobody's *wife*, *luta tawin*! This body, only thing I own, and I'll be usin it for makin mayhem, you hear?' Her chest rose and fell once in an angry surge of breath. 'I'm hungry,' she announced. 'Make me some food, and make it *good*.'

~

I cooked her fish, some of the strange ones the doctor had netted, whose brothers floated, bug-eyed, in a jar of spirits below deck. She enjoyed the meal, sitting in the bow, legs crossed beneath her, implacable. I sat with her while she ate, and watched her patiently. As I suspected, her demeanour softened in my company alone and she talked more freely. Her eyes roved the horizon. It was not the sky that held her attention, though it was wide around us, shifting its light by the hour. Nor was it the sea. She glanced at its moving surface and I fancy she noticed things floating or things alive there, but although they might divert her eye—a flicker—her head never turned.

She was directed wholly forward and thus did not look back at the rest of those aboard. This interested me because it signalled a complete disregard for whether they might attempt to overcome her and seize the musket. Argyle had indicated to her in his gentle way that we were bound for Gun Carriage Island and this appeared to fit with her plans. She did not react adversely, at any rate. Her body tensed with impatience: everything about her posture demanded that we travel, that we arrive elsewhere and soon. She was in a hurry.

I watched her as she ate, and tried to divine what I could about her from the taut plane of her back. I discerned very little. I felt that an Englishwoman would reveal more of herself by being less naked. The small judgments and inferences that can be made from clothing, from hair, from ornamentation.

Mr Argyle had whispered to me as I fried the fish. He had heard of Tarenorerer.

'Worked in the north-east of Van Diemen's Land, among the settlers,' he said. 'Though I spose that term, *worked*…mean any number of things with settlers.' The moment with the gun made sense to him because they said of her that she'd been taught the use of firearms; that she then took that knowledge, the knowledge that placed us above them, and used it to teach her fellows. Who in turn stole guns themselves, and applied the new-found knowledge in earnest, putting Englishmen and Scots behind the bead for the first time anyone knew of. The trigger; the concussion, men in uniform falling bloodied. It took little of this in any town to found a myth. It had happened in Sydney when I was a child, when Pemulwuy ruled the night. Bodies left as they fell, eyes agape in horror at departed visions. Bodies arranged to terrify: impaled, dismembered, disembowelled.

In Tarenorerer's case, according to Argyle, the settlers responded with inevitable savagery. And they were hunting her.

Of course it was thus, I told myself as I took the food to her. Fear and hate subsist like stains, but paralysis only lasts so long before it is replaced by fury. In the moment of Tarenorerer's insurgency, as the natives forgot their place, we, too, forgot ours. Then everyone had to be reminded. The men gathered in the drawing rooms of the great homesteads. Dismissed the women, spoke their minds and vented their outrage. By morning, heads sore with drink, bellies uncertain, they formed hunting parties. Workers, convicts, sons and fathers: retribution, swift and sure.

These were the dark visions I conjured as I watched the woman eat her fish. When she was done, I took her plate and she thanked me gruffly. I took the plate to the galley and then I slipped down the passageway past my father's closed door. Into the doctor's quarters once again.

THE SYMPLEGADES

I woke in the small hours to the sound of the anchor chain against the hull, slid from the bed and dressed in the dark, then slipped silently from the cabin.

I had to pass my father to get to my own quarters. He slept lightly in the mornings and was an early riser, even when he'd punished himself drinking. I rehearsed again the things I would say if he stirred: that I had heard a noise at the stern and wished to alert the doctor; that I had wandered in my sleep…but he was snoring, turned away from the passage between the bunks, his streaked hair lying wild on his pillow. There was a stench as I passed him. Grog? No. Not exactly, and in any case there was no longer any on board. I had to keep moving. I went to my cabin and changed my clothes to avoid suspicion, then went above.

Tarenorerer was pacing the deck already. Dawn was far away, first light a mere suggestion in the east, but her feet padded the boards and her eyes were trained outwards. I came from the hatch behind her: she sensed my presence and looked around, cast me a dismissive glance and returned to watching the island. If I squinted, I could make out the sealers' house: no smoke from the chimney now, no sign of movement. They could not, in any event, come after us.

Connolly worked the windlass, eyes down and movements sleepy. When the anchor slotted home, trailing a garland of kelp, he waved a hand back to the helm. Argyle, dressed this morning in a simple blue cotton dress and shawl, was able to engage the mainsail with a flick of his hand that released a line from a cleat above him. There was just enough life in the air to nudge us forward. Tarenorerer broke from staring at the island and turned now to scan the horizon all around. When she came to look over the stern she tensed and skipped to the forecastle to gain a higher view. I followed her gaze but could see nothing yet, for the western sky was darker.

'Sail,' she said to Argyle. 'Back there.'

He turned as well, grimacing as the darkness told him nothing. 'What kind?'

She shrugged. 'Small, brig maybe.' There was no sign of the gun. I found myself wondering how authority worked here.

'What do you want to do?' asked the master, to my surprise. 'Do you wish to fall in with them?'

'No,' she said fiercely. 'We go.'

Argyle put a hand on the helm, calm as always. 'Very well, but where?'

'They be thinking we go south, round the bottom of Penguin,' she replied. 'That's the deep water, *tawin* always go that way.'

Argyle nodded carefully.

'So you go east,' she continued. 'Between Passage Island and the point.'

Argyle went through the fussy business of lighting the lantern that hung over the helm, then produced the chart from a shelf. He puzzled over it a moment.

'How deep?'

'Deep enough for this,' she said. 'Just the tide. Goes hard through there, whole channel empties out that way. We go now, we be runnin out with it. They's maybe too far back.'

For the first time, Argyle looked indecisive. 'It's very narrow,' he said.

'You got me and him on the sails,' she countered, and I heard the respect in the exchange. 'And her...' She looked at me, and there was no respect. 'Maybe just me and him. Get that doctor bloke up here. Get you through straight line, no tack, no gybe.'

The *Moonbird* was easing north while this exchange went on, the massive weight of the tide carrying us into the teeth of the gap. It was less than a quarter-mile wide and we were gaining speed towards it: the time for any change of mind was rapidly disappearing.

'Very well,' said Argyle. 'Miss, would you rouse the doctor, please?'

I went below and down the passageway, this time without the need to be furtive. My father was awake, struggling into clothes. I bade him good morning—the smell was all but gone—and knocked on the doctor's door. The handsome voice commanded me to enter.

He stood there dressed, hair oiled, smiling. His fingers fiddled with a cuff.

'You've come to summon me,' he said brightly. 'What's it to be, the rigging?'

'Yes,' I stammered. 'The master wants you up there.' I cursed myself inwardly. He asserted himself with ease, imperceptibly, when he wished.

'Very good. Let's get about it, shall we?' He surged ahead through the narrow doorway, brushing past me so that our bodies made contact. It was a liberty and he knew it. I watched his back as he passed my father with a nod and ascended the stairway. Damn him.

'You slept well?' asked my father from the edge of his cot. I had no idea whether the question was loaded in some way.

'Yes, fine thank you, Father. Do you need any assistance?'

'Shoes,' he grunted. 'Drive me mad.'

I tied the knots for him and spoke as I looked down. Even with a blind man, it is somehow easier if one avoids eye contact.

'You are still drinking.'

'Not your concern, love,' he said, as if he could cling to some vestige of paternal authority.

'It *is* my concern. It's me who cleans up after you. Me who worries. Who is giving you the grog?'

'You are not the only one on board this vessel who has my interests at heart. And if you worry so, then take me above. I am unwell.'

'You're always unwell.' I took his arm and draped it over my shoulders, guided him from the bed and onto the stairs. He felt his way up and I turned at the galley and looked around for food to prepare for us both, as the dawn light filled the small space.

He was out there, I could see through the little windows, trying at first to reverse himself into the break in the gunwale to attend to his toilet, then turning back the other way to throw up. He slipped and slumped onto one side on the deck, and I saw the master rush to his side and gently lift him to his feet. I did not rush to him myself. Had I finally begun to tire of his endless self-destruction? Or had the odd roll in the doctor's cot made clear to me what I'd been missing by devoting myself to my father? I went on making the food, sullen now. I made dough for the day's bread and left it to prove on the sill where the light would reach it.

Outside, the others hovered and picked at the rigging, bees tending the stamens: it made no difference—the boat was now sliding sideways into the gap between the island and the point. If we were thirty feet wide and the passage was three hundred, it would have been of no concern. But her sideways drift made the *Moonbird* more than eighty feet wide—and she had no grip on the water. Argyle's sail orders, and his quick hands on the wheel, were all but irrelevant to the boat's attitude. She wanted to bring her rudder around to the front, as though the stern was going faster than the bow.

I had no idea how one would resolve such a problem, but if it went, then there was no way to avoid hitting the sides of the passage. Connolly yelled to Argyle that we were caught in a roost; the master seemed well aware of the problem, but held his tongue.

Our new passenger, our pirate queen, was looking back across our beams at the entry to this funnel that had trapped us. I followed her gaze, and there to my horror was the brig she had spoken of, within a couple of hundred yards of us. I could make out men on its decks, a lookout in the rigging. I could see a row of small cannon in ports on her beam. There was no activity around the gun ports, but several of the sailors on deck were armed.

'Who are they?' I asked her.

'Who cares?'

I stared at her back: a large scar angled across her shoulder-blade, as long as a finger. It was depressed in its centre where a muscle had never regrown.

'All the same,' she was saying. 'Someone I stung, hey. Stung em good, all of em.' She paced again, like a prize-fighter. 'Batman maybe. Now there's one oughta be tied to a tree. Cut his filthy balls off...'

She strode up to the quarterdeck and stood with her legs apart, pointing a finger their way.

'Bah! Light yer little candles, *wadjella*!' She grabbed her breasts and shook them as she snarled. 'Why don't you fire them balls? You got balls?' She was shrieking now. 'Comin for you next, Mister Batman!'

There was a response of similar nature from the deck of the other ship. Someone bared a backside, someone loaded a Bess, but they would have known they were still out of range. The *Moonbird* was gaining speed all the time, not through any power from her sails but by the ineluctable force of the tide through the passage. She felt helpless to me, our calm and steady mare.

The sun was mounting in the east; the sea glittered but it did so with malice. The other boat had swung and was using her full sails to brake against the flowing water. I turned back to my father. 'Why do you lie to me?' I asked, the bitterness taking unexpected hold of me.

His fingers traced the rails around him, orienting himself even as we slid on into the gap and he considered my question. Experience and the compass of his body would have told him of our lateral drift.

'I do not lie to you, dear girl. If I keep small matters to myself, it is only in pursuit of some independence. Do you know how it belittles a man to be guided about?'

Now he was a wise man, now he was a fool. I was tied by pity and by obedience.

The *Moonbird* slewed further in, the rocks close enough for drying birds on the boulders to stare in disapproval. An unnatural eddy was forming left of the bow where she dragged against her will. I felt the tears rise once again and would not give in to them. He sensed it, damn him, and he patted my arm.

'This is deeper than last night's drinking, isn't it?' he said.

I looked away. 'Always has been.'

Argyle's instructions were rising in urgency. Connolly and the doctor were darting about the deck; even Tarenorerer joined them and was up in the foredeck freeing a fouled line. The other ship was closer but had more sail out. Its master was still trying to release it from the grip of the tide: to which we were willingly submitting.

My father sighed. The small, sad sound registered against the cacophony around us: sails and voices and water and wind. 'There are things I must tell you. About this voyage. Be patient with me. We will talk.'

I stood mute, grasping for the words to respond. There were none.

Argyle yelled a final order, one I did not comprehend. The *Moonbird* swung once more onto its other side, and we were through. The boulders waited either side of us, sunlit and gleaming with the wash of receding waves. Now there was open ocean before us, and the mountains of Cape Barren off our port side. Our pursuers had swung hard enough to avoid the flush, and were idling on the far side of the island. We had assisted the woman in her escape. Did that render us complicit, and if so—in what? Intuition said we had chosen the right side.

But Argyle was fixed with a new worry: our pursuers would only need to sail about four miles south, he said, down between Penguin and Passage, before they would round the southern tip of Passage and we would be in their view again. He studied the coastline through the glass, considered the chart. He told us there were three large bays on this side of Cape Barren: the first of them had a sharp nook in it. We could not outrun the larger vessel, but we could hide.

He steered us along a straight white beach, with the dull silver-green grasses and low bush behind it. Nothing out there: not a hut, not a stray timber in the tideline. At the far end I could see where the granite resumed, forming a short point that jutted into the sea. We came in close to it and followed the rocks, and very briefly I saw the gap: a cleft in the rock, a hundred yards or less in width. Argyle seemed determined to cram us into ever-tighter spaces.

The boulders on the point were bare: the ocean when raised to anger must wash over their extremities. But all was quiet on this morning; just the brush of the breeze behind us, ruffling the surface. At the mouth of the cleft, Argyle raced among the rigging, flicking cleats and releasing line through pulleys so that the sails dumped their burdens of air and we lost all power. When he was done and the *Moonbird* had swung into the wind, Declan Connolly took the long boathook, the one they'd used to retrieve my father, and pushed the clew of one of the foresails out so that it drew the other way. His voice barely above a whisper now, the master ordered him to prepare anchors fore and aft. I watched Argyle watching the foresail. It was now billowing backwards, reversing us gently into the gap. My God, the genius of it.

'Hold,' he called to Connolly, who waited with the windlass brake in his hands. There was a soft crunch as the rudder touched sand at our stern. The master had judged it within inches.

'Yes,' he said softly, and the convict released the anchor. He ran then to the stern and set the smaller one just wide to the starboard. We were pinned into the rocky cove with only yards to spare either side.

'Get all the sail down, everything off deck,' said Argyle. 'Everything.'

We did as he said, throwing bundles of spare sail into the hold while Tarenorerer went aloft with Connolly and tightly furled each of the sails. I began to understand the brilliance of what he'd done: we were a dun-coloured pile of timber set against rock and grass, with the morning sun low, directly behind us in the east. Only the sharpest eye could find us.

'Everyone down,' said Argyle, and we sat like spellbound children, peering out through the scuppers. My father looked bewildered, his gift for hearing and feeling of no help to him now. Soon enough the brig came around the southern end of the island, three miles or more from us. They were under full sail, racing, not searching.

'They think we've gone on around Cape Barren,' said the doctor.

My father addressed Tarenorerer with the question we all had: 'What have you done, that these people are searching for you?'

She raised her chin and narrowed her eyes.

'What have *I* done? Hah! Let's see. What have I done...'

She spread her long fingers on the timbers of the deck and counted them off. 'Well, I never put a ring around a woman's neck, see? Never *chained* her. Never sold no woman to sealer men, took her way from 'er country. I never made nobody work on the birding for no money, never had my way with another body against their will. Lotta things I never done.'

'Why are they so angry?' my father persisted.

She glared at him, realised the futility of it.

'I been spearin their sheep,' she laughed. 'Poor sheepies, fuck em—just take the kidney fat an leave em. That riles em up. Took some guns…Point a gun at us, some time you gonna get a gun pointed at you. You *wadjella* all very tough an mighty when you holdin the gun. Not much good when you lookin up the barrel.'

Connolly spoke up: the first time I could remember him ever interjecting in a conversation.

'Why are you sayin *you* all the time? I didn't do it.' He pointed at the rest of us. 'This lot never done it.'

Again, she flared. 'Not *your* problem, eh? Some other fella!' She scoffed and shook her head. 'Nobody ever done it, but it's gettin done somehow.'

I peered through the scupper again, and I could see the ship passing by to the south of us, heading north-east around Cape Barren. The master wanted to wait, to ensure our pursuers continued on their course. I asked to use the jolly-boat—I wanted to be away from the confines of the vessel—and I helped my father into it. The master said only that we were not to venture too far on foot, in case we had to make a clean exit. 'And don't stand on the ridge: keep the hill behind you.'

The sun was up warm and bright now, but I felt cold with dread. Connolly lowered us and I rowed the handful of strokes from the *Moonbird* to the apex of the V-shaped bight. On a small crescent of sand, I nudged us ashore and helped my father out again. He said nothing all the while.

'Shall we walk a little?' I asked him. He grunted his assent.

Up over the back of the warm gravelly sand, crunching

dry kelp underfoot. Through the soft beds of samphire that carpeted the gaps between the boulders; between the pinsharp tussocks and onto a thin soil made from their endless demise. I had no place in mind, just an uncertainty about when to begin talking. A rise that had a depression behind it: we would go up there and sit and face the sea. I led us that way, and when we topped the rise I looked down into the small bowl in the land and shuddered in horror.

A great pile of bones lay there, long, heavy and thick. Bleaching in the sun, skin stretched taut in places over them. I could see the divided bones of forelimbs, hips and the balls of long bones, and snaking columns of vertebrae. And skulls. A ripple of shock went through me until I saw to my relief that they were long and pointed and not human. But each and every one of them had been caved in. The shatters made straight lines where the iron had struck. Seals, in their hundreds, wrapped around each other, broken apart, scattered and piled. The older ones were bleached white. Newer ones were fawn, and some trailed the dry curls of tendons. Some were small, like the bones of children. I sighed and choked and tried to look away and could not: a large skeleton that contained, within its pelvis, itself in perfect miniature.

Heavy crows cawed from the mound, gleaming black against the bones. Previous generations of the birds would have been sustained by this slaughter: the descendants stayed on and they guarded the skeleton city with baleful eyes. The doctor would delve here if he'd come, taking samples and making admiring sounds. But I could only grieve, and I did not know for what.

We picked our way around it, and I clutched my father's arm more tightly than usual for fear he would fall into the grave. He must have smelt it—the stench was overwhelming—but he did not inquire. The ground sloped upwards and I stopped us at a smooth wide boulder in the sun, with the stink downwind of us. When we sat, I felt the warmth radiating into my thighs and I was a small girl again, lying on sandstone somewhere in Sydney, feeling that same slow warmth rise through me under endless sun.

'I need to know what happened,' I began. 'I need to know.' I did not know what else to say.

'The fire?' He seemed resigned.

'Yes. All of it.'

He turned his face so that the reflected light off the sea lit him, and his lank hair drifted slightly in the breeze. He was tanned deeply by the sun: I hadn't noticed it happening. He waited so long that I thought he might not speak at all. Then he began.

'You were born in the late summer and when I look back to that time there was this…veil of perfection over everything. Your mother was so beautiful. The centre of our world, even though you stole all of the attention. It was her. Feeding you, bathing you…beaming, just beaming. I had never loved her so deeply as I did in those weeks.'

He fell silent again for a long time.

'That night. She and I were in bed together. You were in your crib beside us. I was exhausted and must have been deeply asleep when I woke to a noise, not recognising it at first. It was very dark, but there was a glow from the roof. We were on fire.'

His empty eyes craned upwards to a ceiling he still saw. 'When I think back I cannot imagine how there wasn't time, but…The smoke was coming under the shingles, and the walls were just paper and hessian and tar, they caught so fast, and the room was filled with smoke. There was no *time*, you must understand.' He had turned his face towards me, pleading. 'I ran at the front door and it would not budge, even when I threw my entire weight at it. I was told afterwards that they had taken the iron handle from the well out front and wedged it across the jamb. I kept trying, three or four times, I ran at it and lost all those precious moments.

'I tried the back door. They'd piled rocks behind it. All of this, you see—premeditated. By the time I had given up on that door, everything was alight. You were still in the crib and I could hear you crying but I could not see you, the darkness, the smoke…sweet Christ, the panic. I shouted for Charlotte to take you and cover you and I believe…I believe she was trying to do that, when the ceiling began to come down and my hair was on fire, but then I found my hand was on the crib and I took you up in my arms…But your mother had fallen. The smoke, I suppose. I stood there and I had my precious daughter in my arms and my wife was on the floor and…the crib was on fire: I could not put you down. I did the only thing I could think to do and that was to run at the part of the wall that had burnt first and I threw myself at it with you under my arm and we fell through and we landed outside and there were people out there and they took you from me, and…'

He fell silent, knots of rage and sadness working their way through his body.

'Well. They did up a coffin and we buried her at the edge of the bush a mile away, a place she liked to walk. Timber plate to mark it, you've been there. And there were days after that I do not even recall.'

He fell silent. The crows swooped and fought where the bones were, sun on their blue-black feathers.

'It didn't take long for the drinking to start. Just to sleep at first. Then bottomless, endless. There were people…patient people—neighbours, staff from Government House, anyone I could think of. And the minute I knew you were in safe hands I'd go out and find rum.

'You cannot know the desire, the need…You cannot imagine the things that one will give up, one will trade, to be glowing again. To feel the world softer and quieter and calmer. Slower. Even the rages…the cursing and the fists, they are…something external to what is within, which is a state of total assuredness.'

'I have been drunk, Father, I think I can imagine it.'

'No.' The word cut hard through my sarcasm. 'I do not mean that. I mean having got liquor when you were without it. I mean having got it inside you, feeling its work. That is not drunkenness. Those first minutes, to know you are sated, reacquainted with a lover, and the whole universe and all its agents cannot undo the work of it. A sawyer will cut a hundred feet of timber—days of work—for a bottle worth two shillings and it's gone in an hour or two. A lag will risk the wheel, risk the flesh on his back. When I was roaring I would have given anything and betrayed anybody to get more.'

'No, you would not.'

It is possible to lock eyes with a blind man if you love him enough.

'You would never have betrayed me.'

The tiniest fragment of a question rose from the end of the words. It hung in the air and all of the years and all of our desperate need hinged upon it. He held my gaze somehow with his sightless eyes and I waited.

'No,' he said quietly. 'I never did. I never would.'

The world exhaled. Even the bloody ravens had waited.

'You know the rest,' he said eventually. 'I went too far. I

stopped asking the Almighty for His pity a long time ago, but the blindness was the work of God.'

'I do not...'

'Oh, not in the sense of retribution, or even grace. I mean it stood like a gesture—*Enough now. If I take your sight, you cannot rage anymore.* And I accepted it that way. A blind man can still drink, but he cannot fight, make a danger of himself on the streets. He can only linger in his despair and live out his useless days. And you were such a capable little thing, so bright and composed, working around your father's wreckage. You think I don't remember the sacrifices? Your refusal to count the cost, even when the cost was your chance of matrimony? You must know that these things are etched in my heart.'

I listened to all of this without a word. Some of it accorded with what I had expected. Some of it was new to me. *The doors barred as we burned within?* His sadness was already unbearable. I did not want to press him about the exact nature of his grudge, about who he felt had done this to him. To us.

Why had it come to this strange pass, to an ossuary above the cleft in the rock where our mare was hidden, for us to speak truly?

'Father, I need to tell you this: I don't believe he is here.'

'Who?'

'The man, Figge.'

He broke into a pained smile. 'You weren't born, you don't understand. How Srinivas suffered at his hands, how I suffered... we can *feel* him, do you see? Believe me, we are getting closer.'

'But what then? Even if you're right. It's not about finding the *Howrah*, is it? It's about you and the lascar settling your scores.'

His face creased into a deep frown. 'What's the, the, what? The *Howrah*? What are you talking about, my dear?'

Dear God. His poor mind now, too.

'The ship, Father. The one we're searching for.' I wanted to raise with him the doctor's assertion that she was carrying sterling; that Srinivas had deceived us in not mentioning it. But I saw now that there was no point: the realities as we already understood them were overwhelming him.

Realisation was dawning on his ragged face. 'Ah yes, yes, of course. Well, the motivation doesn't matter in the end.'

'Maybe not to you. But you've dragged me into this. Let me ask you: what if it harms *me* somehow? How will you feel then? More drinking and weeping?' I knew I had stung him. I felt both regret and deep satisfaction. 'You have made this man into a…a devil, a demon who wrecked your perfect life. And now you want to tear him down, as though that will put everything right. All those wasted years. Father, it's not that simple.'

'Of course it is. It is *exactly* that simple.'

'No!' I took him by the arm. 'Whatever it is you need to put right, *it is already inside you*. It's *you* who decided to be his victim. You who drank, you who forced them to pension you off. It's you who sought out the poison that made you blind. It hurts me to tell you these things, but the answer to all of this is still *you*.'

His face was fixed like the rocks in obstinacy. 'You want this to be more complex than it is, my dear. That is in the nature of women, I think.'

The old fool patted my hand. 'The solution is straightforward. We will find him, and if there is any chance presented, we will kill him.'

~

Argyle edged us out of the cleft in the rock, prised us out like a crab.

We followed the coast as the afternoon sun grew strong and the wind shifted to an onshore easterly that ruffled everything. Gulls and gannets followed us now and I wished they would leave us, for fear they would disclose us and our new passenger to whoever it was that gave chase. We came around a point and followed a long beach under the sheared rock of the Cape Barren mountains. Behind the sand lay a tea-brown lagoon, the stoppered mouth of a creek coming off the mountain. The dense trees in there swayed with the wind. Who owned it? Who would ever own it?

Tarenorerer had taken the master's glass and she stood on the deck gazing southward, legs athwart and the hard drum of her belly tilted slightly forward. She spoke quietly from under the brass cylinder, words I couldn't catch. I tried looking down the line of the glass to see what she saw. That way was open sea, and faint in the distance, lilac on the horizon, stood the shoulders of a low mountain. That was what she had fixed upon. And what, I asked myself, could hold her attention about a stretch of empty sea and the speck of distant land?

Should be burnin, this time o' year. Why them old ones not burnin it? When she lowered the glass from her eye I saw sorrow there, grief that had callused over. Perhaps it was these tiny glints of her pain, visible only in stealth, that drew me to her.

Onward, north-east, points and bays. The heavy hull of the *Moonbird* barely registered the chop of the sou'-easter. It was a world that sounded of rushing water under the bow and the small complaints of the rigging. Squeaks and knocks, the drum sounds of sails pulling taut. The warmth of the sun, that minor orchestra and a tiny swaying; all of it conspired to make me drowsy. I sat myself beside the steps, facing astern, and let sleep overtake me.

I woke, I don't know after how long, to find the doctor sitting beside me writing in one of his notebooks. He smiled when he saw me; it made us a conspiracy of two.

'Hello, you,' he said.

'What are you working on?'

'Birds again today.' He had stood another of his mist nets across two poles that projected over the stern. I could see something in it, small like a finch. A larger bird, white with a yellow face, hovered in the slipped air behind us.

'Gannet,' he said, and he tilted his book towards me so that I could see his drawing of the obliging bird.

'A fine likeness,' I said, and though I might have said it anyway, it was. He had captured in tiny strokes of a pencil the bold flight feathers of its wings, and the soft down of its belly, the dark eye. He touched the pencil to his lips.

'You were gone a long time with your father,' he ventured.

'Yes.'

'What did you discuss?'

'Oh, nothing. Family.'

His face took on a thoughtful frown. 'You know, he really is endangering himself—'

I must have raised an eyebrow.

'—with his drinking. You must make every effort to stop him. The tremens back at Hummock Island, that was a warning sign. Once it is chronic enough, it can endanger the, er, the mesentery. Very painful. And sadly it may end in sudden death.'

'How much do you know about his drinking?'

He grimaced. 'My dear, I would not have raised this, but I

have several times now had to put your father back in his bed, and indeed to clean up after him, when there have been excesses.'

'Oh my. Was this...lately?'

'Yes, this past week.'

'But I, I threw all of his grog overboard. You saw me do it. Even the ration for the others—there is nothing left for him to drink!'

'He is finding it somewhere, I regret to say.'

My hands were pressed on the warm timbers of the deck, either side of my hips. He looked down now at my right hand and placed his on top of it. Nobody else could see the gesture, hidden as it was by my body and his. There was a ring on my index finger with a small stone set in it. It had been my mother's, a gift my father gave me when I turned twenty-one, too many years ago now.

He rolled his thumb over the stone and toyed with it and I felt all sorts of suggestions in that small gesture, delicate enough that he did not even disturb the finger it rested upon.

~

We anchored in the evening off the north-eastern side of Cape Barren, away from the cover of the mountain. There had been no further sighting of the sail, and Argyle had come to believe that whoever was pursuing us had been deceived and had now continued north. I prepared a meal in the galley, golden light making shadows of the guano and salt crystals on the panes. The doctor's fish again, this time one that he called a wrasse. It was heavy flesh, greenish and tended to mush under the knife. But I was able to fry it, and a few onions disguised its poor character. Supplies were running low now—if we didn't catch more fish soon, we would be down to pemmican. As I handed a plate to the doctor, he leaned in close to me.

'I am going to operate the Boyle device this evening. Do you wish to come and observe?'

I eyed him sidelong. 'Will you be inviting all of us?'

'I was hoping it might just be you,' he said, his face lit with honest appeal. 'If you would like?'

~

I waited several hours on my bed, trying to read by lamplight. I closed my eyes awhile and opened them. There was no rush to visit the doctor: he would be working his secret rituals throughout the night, impervious to time and fatigue. I was restless. I went above.

The night was glorious, clear and still. I thought I was alone at first, the lines of the timbers and the rigging making silhouettes against the bright starlit sky. But then I saw that once again Tarenorerer was out there too. She had been assigned poor Angus Connolly's hammock, but I had never known her to use it: she seemed to live all her hours on deck. She was standing alone in the dark, one hand on the shrouds to steady her, looking up to the heavens.

High beyond the tips of the masts, infinity stretched from horizon to horizon. Aside from the minor rocks that lay dark on the sea, we were suspended between two curving worlds: the stars above and the depths below. The surface was calm enough to reflect the galaxies, so that it looked as though the universe swirled all around us above and below, as if *up* and *down* had ceased to exist and only *all around* remained: the *Moonbird* was aloft and freed of its own weight.

And directly up there, where Tarenorerer was looking, the Milky Way stretched across the sky, more detailed and vivid and terrifyingly vast than I had ever seen it. I dared not breathe, for fear I might distract her, might break the trance of that moment and its eternal assurance that we and our cares and our tiny boat were nothing, a floating dust mote in the stillness.

Looking down to the woman before me I saw ceaseless motion. Her head twitched between points and when it turned far enough I could see that her eyes, too, were darting about. She was following movements I could not see: happenings, events, I did not know what, like anyone else watching boxers or shoals of fish or children playing. Her face was reacting with fright, amusement, wonder and sorrow, tiny changes but unmistakable ones. Her free hand rose involuntarily once or twice as if something startled her. But for all my squinting and staring I could see only the beautiful speckled stillness.

She turned, after a long time, and strode directly to me: it was clear she knew I had been behind her all along. She looked into my eyes, as few others can do, and the stars lit her proud cheeks.

'Got made up there,' she said to me. She pointed a finger into the heart of the Milky Way. '*Toowerer* made the sun, and them stars made us. An you lot never gonna *un*-make us.'

~

Nothing stays fixed in time, and nor indeed did that moment.

I went below, shouldering my misgivings down the stairs. The doctor's cabin was once again candle-lit, and the strange pump contraption stood on the desk. He welcomed me, poured tea and motioned that I should sit. As I did so, he latched the door behind me, having checked discreetly around it in the direction of my father's cot.

The glass sphere reflected the candle's flickering and the glow of the central lamp. From in here, the starlight had retreated to darkness outside; we were dry and warm, afloat on the inkwell sea. He unscrewed a wide lid on top of the sphere and reached across the desk to where a crumpled heap of muslin lay. The cloth was moving. There was a stone placed over it: he removed this and reached in, removing a bird he'd trapped. It was the small one that resembled a finch.

It made a chirruping sound, loud in the confines of the cabin, and twitched its frightened head from side to side. Both sides of the head were a delicate cornflower blue: its neck and folded wings were glossy black. The doctor held it tenderly in his curled hand, then swept it over to the sphere and dropped it inside. When he had done so, he replaced the lid. I could see now that the plumage of the bird's belly was fluffy and white, and a handful of straight, rigid tail-feathers stood vertically from its rump.

The bird tried flying but the space was too small and it slid about on the downslopes of the sphere, wings beating forlornly. The doctor grasped the valve at the neck of the device, below the sphere, and began to turn it. I did not fully understand what I was watching but the apprehension was growing in me.

'What are you doing to it?' I asked.

He was concentrating: he answered distractedly. 'The valve removes air and creates a vacuum inside the flask.'

'But the bird...'

He shrugged, smiled. 'I can't very well mount it in the cabinet if it is alive.'

I found myself watching in fascinated horror as the bird

circled once or twice then wobbled drunkenly on its twig legs, failing to find purchase on the smooth glass. The doctor watched too, his face a mask of detachment. The bird tipped onto its side. Tiny feathers around its neck, shades of blue and black, trilled with the shudders of its body. All of the animal was just a heart now, that spun erratic with the strain. It rolled onto its back, one leg kicked and it was still.

The doctor unscrewed the lid. He wrote in a notebook as the bird lay on his other palm. *Superb Fairy Wren, male. Sexually mature...*

'Good.'

He looked up, and must have registered the disgust in my expression. 'Dear girl, the bird might be five years old. A falcon will kill it within a year. The bones will rot in the grasses on one of these godforsaken islands, and for what? You and I have just ensured this little creature will delight and inform for centuries to come. These are the pains and the pleasures of science, are they not?'

He removed his jacket, stretched himself into the space of the small room. I felt a deep languor, a desire to be done with the evening and recline. He must have sensed it for he took me firmly by the hands and led me to the bed.

'Please,' he said, 'make yourself comfortable. It is the greatest honour I can imagine to have you in here.' The words were soothing, as always. But smaller voices in me said that he had just killed a living creature to impress me. That my father would be sleeping outside the room, that he must know by now what had been going on.

There were so many competing forces at work inside me now. That tiredness that seeped all the way to my bones, the hot tea spreading warmth in the centre of me, an ache for his hands and his mouth that was new and frightening. And harder voices: responsibility, fear of being caught, a horror that any of this was happening at all.

In the shadows on the far side of the room the doctor was removing his clothes, item by item, unhurried. He was placing them on a chair, draping and folding with half a smile on his face. And now he walked to me; naked and tall, dusted silver, and the voices of complaint were turning to alarm and open mistrust, but other voices quashed them and I took him to me.

I was pressed against his body, held there by the strength of his hands. My cheek was somewhere on his sternum but I could not hear his heartbeat in there and I looked out from his embrace and saw the globe of the air pump, our reflection on the curving glass. We were distorted, long and strange, his flesh all golden in the lamplight and my face a hollow of confusion. And in that moment I did not recognise myself at all: we were smears of light, phantasms in the dream of some girl who was yet to be born.

I pushed him and ran him back towards the bed where he fell easy on his back, and I climbed him and tried imposing my will by enfolding my legs over his, gripping hard to make a vice that would hold him. I hauled my skirts and saw my thighs, and for an instant I thought them powerful.

But the shadows and the uncertain light crossed one another and made confusing shapes that cast a mad glare on his face and found ugly sinew in his body. And this was not the romance I had wished it to be but a wrongly drawn map that led down an unknown road.

GUN CARRIAGE

We came in the night.

Gun Carriage Island was a wide pyramid stacked against the starry sky, a sloping plain at its base. We had approached from the south-east, from the top corner of Cape Barren, along a small channel that led out to a sand spit and then on to the separate mass of the island.

It was shallow in the channel, Argyle said. He was dressed in dark hues that night: a bodiced jacket with velvet buttons and three-quarter sleeves. The skirts below it, also dark, hung halfway down his shins and he was barefoot, as usual.

I stood at the helm with him, my father at his other shoulder, us and the night. The wariness about pursuit had dissipated and the sea was gentle. But there was an unspoken foreboding between us.

Unspoken until my father gave voice to it.

'This will be the end of the road,' he said. I saw nothing out there that indicated it, yet I could not bring myself to disagree. Everything had become terminal: his obsession, my entanglement with the doctor, our search for the missing ship.

Argyle stayed wide at the island's first landfall, keeping us a hundred yards or more off the coast. There was surf breaking in there, surging chaotically at a coast that lied about its own contours. A long beach made a convex arc away from us, tailing off to the north-west. The mountain slowly rotated in response to our progress, showing new facets to the moon. The island ended at a wide triangular point that faced exactly north, and Argyle hewed close to this as shoals appeared on our outside.

He snapped the *Moonbird* around it, calling orders to Connolly. Tarenorerer sat in the bow throughout, watching, lost in thought. She had shown no sign of further aggression since the brief pursuit, only a kind of sad contemplation that was impossible to understand.

The water on the western side of the island was deeper. I knew this not from Connolly taking soundings, but from the way it moved under us: slow and pulling in strong currents, slipping our stern now and then. No swell here, no breaking waves; just a silent rocky shore that ran south for a mile, boulders standing vertically on the island's edge like gravestones.

It was as we came down this coast that I first heard the music.

I fancied I had imagined it at first. Voices raised in song— something that might happen at sea. Something old, unpolished but tuneful. Mere drifts of sound, the wind took them away then offered them again and I strained to find the melody. Then of all the sounds that rose from this bouldered world, of water and air in motion, of birds and whispering grasses, the one I least expected to hear: a piano.

Tarenorerer had heard it too. She stood; inclined her head to one side.

The rocky coast had ended and given way to a placid beach. No surf here, just the deep sandy sea floor rising to the shallows. The sound of the piano had stopped and so had the singing, replaced by loud, raucous voices. Conversation, argument, laughter. In the hollows behind the beach I could see lights now. There was an orange glow that I took to be a bonfire, and specks of yellow that must have been lanterns.

The others gathered on the deck and we studied the shore in silence. A signal fire appeared: men illuminated, standing around it. We went through our ritual of anchoring, ensuring we left the *Moonbird* beyond wading distance from the shore, lest these people prove hostile. I packed my shoreside bag once more: warm clothes, a tinderbox and the leather satchel containing the *Howrah* papers, which now included those from the Adige chest Louisa had handed me as we left Preservation. The doctor made a pile of his provisions: as well as clothes he had brought a net, instruments and jars, and the ever-present preserving fluid, a small cask of it.

Tarenorerer brought the fowling piece, along with ammunition and powder. No one was going to argue with her about the tact or otherwise of carrying it into someone else's settlement.

We rowed the short distance to shore and I felt the familiar crunch of the gravelly white sand under my feet. The ground steadied itself by tiny adjustments. As I guided my father out of the boat and onto the beach, I wondered how many more times he and I would perform this ritual. The familiar smell of him as I was close and lifting, sour and old. Filled with knowledge, if still unwise. It was an instinct he himself had honed over the years of his blindness, the ability to read stories into smells.

The men on the shore were sealers: scruffy, strong, affably drunk.

'Good time to come in,' one of them said under his beard. 'Smith's daughter's playin the piano.'

None of them thought to ask what we were doing there. None of them inquired after our welfare, or how many of us there were, whether the rest of us were armed or just the native woman who glared at them without speaking. A pack of ribby dogs wove around each other on the dry-kelp sand, eyeing us.

We were each offered a drink from a short cask. Then there was some explanation I half-followed about the rum coming in as payment for skins, twelve hides to the gallon. The man who mentioned the piano and the girl spoke up again, nodding towards the cask that Gideon was carrying.

'Ye goin to share that around?'

Gideon looked down at the cask and laughed a little. 'I think this stuff would rather change your evening, sir.' He did not explain further. The man wasn't deterred.

'Ye got pipe baccy?'

Again, we had nothing to offer. My father, of course, had accepted their offer of rum and was already tipping a glass of pungent spirit.

At the top of the beach, and before the sand gave way to thick grasses and boulders, two men stood waiting. We were introduced formally by the men who had brought us up. The first of the pair was a Scotsman; his name was John Smith. Hard-faced and somewhere in his forties, I guessed, his hair and whiskers were a fair kind of brown and his manner was authoritative.

'First man to make a home on Gun Carriage,' one of the men said proudly of Smith. 'Ten year ago.'

John Smith, I laughed to myself. What other name would a man use if he'd run away to an island?

The drinkers who introduced us had wandered off, taking with them an invalid who plodded along with the assistance of two canes. Smith led us into a narrow pass between the great boulders, the lantern's light glittering off the feldspars and throwing crazy shadows against the rocks beside us. The granite formed a low wall and a gully that was out of the breeze. And in that small space was a sight that defied belief.

A crowd of men and women: perhaps three or four dozen. Every one of the women was *tyereelore*, and the men had the distinctive look of mariners: rough hewn and clothed practically, faces weathered and pocked. They stood and they sat and even reclined in the bowl of the ground, making loud conversational groups and audience rows. Over their heads a rough shelter had been constructed from crossed timbers: cut saplings and the weathered planks of ships. Dried tussocks had been piled on these to form a thatch. Here and there the night sky showed through gaps, its blackness made more profound by the light on the ceiling. For under the beams, wires and ropes had been looped across the space, and under these were strung lanterns. They were low enough to avoid any chance of them setting fire to the timber roof, and this put them in the way of the occasional head. They swung gently on their tethers so the rich yellow light pulsed and moved against the timbers, casting a honey glow over everything.

There were dogs under tables and chairs, dogs loping across the open space in front of the piano: tall, slender animals, placid in this environment but built for speed. Once I began to notice them, I found that they were everywhere, outnumbering the humans. In the centre of the amphitheatre a fire burned brightly in a hearth of circled rocks. And behind the fire, on a convenient rise in the ground, was a timber stage.

On it stood the piano. It was a small, box-shaped instrument, undecorated, and a girl was sitting at it.

She was serene, a still point in the crowd. Her hands rested in her lap, her long hair was tied in ribbons, and she wore a formal dress and shoes. I thought her to be about fourteen, a picture of mysterious beauty such as I'd never imagined could exist in the strait.

A narrow ledge hinged out from the front of the piano, and the papers upon it fluttered slightly in the breeze. A woman came up behind the girl and placed a solicitous hand on her shoulder. The woman was a native, short and strong, with a nest of copper-brown hair. She wore a warm dress made of hides with reddish fur: kangaroo, I thought. She spoke softly to the girl, bringing her face close, and tucked a strand of hair behind the girl's ear as she did so.

Her mother. Their faces were identical, though the girl's skin was lighter. The girl pointed at the sheet music, her face upraised with a question. I stood transfixed by the riddle of it: how could the native woman know the music, the instrument? How could she have taught the girl? But if she hadn't, who else could have done so? And the greater enigma: how had the instrument got here? It was wildly out of place, an impression heightened by the presence of the upended carapace of a great lobster on top of it, affixed on a pile of wax. A lit candle had been placed inside so that it functioned like an orange lamp.

I accepted a mug—rum, unwatered—from the bearded man who'd appointed himself our guide, and crept forward in the crowd, heedless for a moment of my father and the doctor. Picking my way through clear spaces, I was able to approach close behind the girl and her mother. I could read *J. S. Bach* at the head of the sheet music. And on the varnished timber of the piano, just below the paper, the words *Pleyel et Cie* embossed in gold.

Aside from the Greek, I had taught the Cooper children elementary French. These words didn't come from the basic grammar we'd studied, but they were naggingly familiar. The crowd pressed and I shrank back among them, away from the pianist. I could smell cooking fish, smoke from the fireplace, crushed grass and liquor. Declan Connolly had a mug in his hand, and already, so soon, he was staggering. I had not seen him drinking with any great relish thus far, even prior to my efforts to rid the *Moonbird* of booze. Perhaps I had forced him into unwanted abstinence and he was making up for it now.

Someone broke a bottle, away in the background. There were calls to hush.

A single note rang out in the night, a solitary raindrop of sound that hung there and faded, before it was followed by a torrent of notes and chords.

The girl's fine fingers evoked a world that was not the island, but maybe a Europe they'd all forgotten or never seen. The sound had a soothing effect on the men in particular. They stood and swayed and closed their eyes as the music washed over them, rising in crescendos and receding into the slightest brooks of faint melody. The girl's body rocked forward when she pounded, and arched back from notes that were only whispers. Her eyes were closed, as though all present saw the same thing behind their lids; and for once my father saw it with them.

I found space on a plank and sat myself down. Sparks flew from the fire as a native woman tossed on a split timber. The music swelled again, melancholy and perfect. There was so much to understand in this confusing place. Something about the piano. Something I could not shake. Their rum was strong and warm, and I was not used to it.

I put the mug down and reached into the small bag I had brought ashore. Down among the clothes I felt the leather satchel containing the ship's papers, and I opened it, squinting to read the fading cursive records of the *Howrah* under the erratic light of the swaying lanterns.

The passenger list, the insurance papers.

The cargo manifest.

I traced a finger down the list: *Tea Chests, Sundry* and *Velvet Cloth In Roll...*

The music wreathed around me, so lovely. Intoxicating.

Another document came to hand. It had been folded and unfolded many times.

Shipped by the Grace of God, in Good Order and well-Conditioned...

I knew the next words before I saw them, drawn like clouds in billowing cursive: *Cottage Upright Piano, Pleyel et Cie.* According to the bill of lading it was to be delivered by the vessel *Howrah* to the Port of Hobart eight weeks ago, *the Danger of the Seas solely excepted.*

I stuffed the document back into the satchel and looked around guiltily to see whether I had been observed. But the audience was transfixed by the girl. She was neither Sydney nor Hobart, nor Aborigine nor Briton. In some way she was all of these things and in their combination something entirely new, wringing loveliness from a stolen piano, a dead family's furniture.

She was singing now, paeans of love and loss, and her voice was unaccountably old with the music, sad and strange. In a corner, Connolly sat alone with his drink and wept. I looked at my father, sitting on an upturned cask with a mug between his feet. His face was tilted up as though the sun shone on it, and I saw hope there. In that moment I was aloft on his shoulders and he was beaming with pride at something I had done. It was him and me. Not bound by dependence, just him and me.

He was at peace that first night on Gun Carriage, unburdened of the painful secrets he'd carried so long. He was drinking: so there would be sickness and recriminations in the morning. But for once I had no energy to fight it. All this time, fighting him over what I thought was his welfare, I'd been denying him solace from the demons in his mind.

~

We were introduced to many people that night. Bearded men: that is the image I see now. Long, unkempt beards they would fiddle with as they talked. The men wore any old combination of clothing and skins. On their feet they wore strange sandals strapped in place by hide thongs. I saw no evidence that anybody cared for their appearance, only warmth and practicality.

I found myself caught up in a conversation with a man named Tucker, whom I instantly disliked. He was overbearing, physically close and malodorous. He said his wife was a Hindoo: there was no sign of her but I instantly worried for her. As if sensing my discomfort, the *tyereelore* took me in hand and made me busy in domestic ways, in unspoken assumption that I was someone's wife.

They were unlike any women I had ever been in company with: garrulous and kind, but *hard*, in a way I could not fathom. They wore the same furred dresses I had seen on the girl's mother. They drank like the men. When they squabbled they had a tendency to grab at one another. But they were also solicitous

261

about small things—they tended well to their children, of whom I counted around twenty, including babes at breast. They were wilder than the Cooper children, and fearless before the authority of the adults. If they transgressed, the women roared at them and they scarpered with squeals and giggles. I saw them in corners and shadows, gorging on stolen food or curled around each other for warmth or sleep. As the evening wore on, they gradually disappeared to bed, and the women abandoned themselves to the revelry. A handful of the adolescents remained up, drinking with their parents but wary about inserting themselves into conversation.

One woman among them did most of the talking. She had parallel scars on her arms and legs, not evidence of trauma but ones that had been cut by her, or for her. *Cicatrices*, they called them back in Sydney: I did not know if that was the word here. Her name, she told me, was Pleenperrenner. She said it slowly, dealing the syllables like cards: *Pleen. Per. Renner.* 'You met my husband,' she said, and seeing my blank look, she added, 'The mayor. Of the island.' She studied me as she spoke, saw my continued confusion. 'I'm with Mister Smith, the Scotsman. Your lot call me Mother Brown. Maybe try that.'

There was no reason for the party, Mother Brown told me. No occasion. They argued about whose idea it had been, but they agreed it was spontaneous. They wanted the girl to play the piano.

They were eager to talk about their lives, and interested in mine. A woman named Poll was the wife of Charles Peterson, the invalid I'd seen on the beach. Another woman, heavy, with hair in matted pipes, said her husband called her Peacock, but that on her country she was Ghoneyannener. I asked her where that country was and she lifted her chin to the south-west. 'Port

Dalrymple,' she said softly. 'Leetermairrener, my people. Stoney Creek nation.'

'Do you miss it?' I asked. I don't know what I meant by the question. It was something my parents' generation would ask each other—*Do you miss Birmingham? Have you heard from Leith?* Peacock looked at me gently, the same way I would look at the Cooper children when they came up with some gemstone of sweet naivete: 'Hasn't gone anywhere, honey.'

Peacock had an easy intimacy about her and an endearing habit of placing her hands on mine when she wanted to emphasise something. She told me the islanders lived by hunting kangaroo, which they did all year round, and by birding and sealing, which had their particular seasons. Gun Carriage was the heart of the islands, she said, the place where most of the men had settled, and from where they did their trade. They knew Munro and respected him, but he was an outpost to them, retired to his chosen patch of rock at Preservation. He was the necessary avenue for their product, nothing more.

I tried to imagine these people as wreckers. As they spoke to me, as they listened to me, I tried to picture them setting false lights, murdering survivors, stealing cargo. The evidence— the cargo—was there before me, but nothing about Peacock's wonderful brown eyes suggested she would condone such barbarity.

As the *tyereelore* spoke to me, I found myself looking at the hands that held their drinks and, occasionally, hunks of bread or butchered meat. They were often large, but always scarred and knotted. Their nails were chipped and broken and bruised. The skin peeled away in painful-looking curls from the sides of the nails, and bled where the runs ended. My hands were similarly pitted, but only because a lifetime indoors had rendered them defenceless against the elements. Theirs, I could see, were permanently battered.

They did much of the sealing work, they said. They did the flinching, the flensing of blubber. If there were tasks that required swimming, like retrieving a mooring, they did those too. 'We look out for each other darlin,' said one old woman.

Tarenorerer blended in among the *tyereelore*, laughing raucously. She had shed the fearsome exterior we'd seen. She was one of them in this place: a Van Diemonian, in their speech *palawa*, but I could imagine that she was separate too: she had not relinquished her native life, and I had the strong feeling she would sooner shoot one of these men than marry one. She had taken our vessel with a gun in her hands, but it no longer mattered: she had what she wanted, apparently, for the time being.

I was watching her thus when Peacock came and sat beside me again. 'That there's a rare one,' she said, as we both watched Tarenorerer. 'You wondering what you got, hey?'

I admitted that I was, without making the obvious point that it was she who had got us.

'She been taken, all the time. No matter how much she fights, always taken again. Black people took her, Port Sorell mob, back when she was a little girl. An they sold her to the sealers—Hunter Island men over west, Bird Island over here. Catching seals, catching mutton birds…wasn't like now—this was back in the wild days. Made her a slave, made her work, lie down with them at night. She didn't just take it, but. She *waited*. She waited and she watched. Learned *wadjella* language, how to fire them guns. All that anger, buildin up in there. Make her heart go dark as night, right enough.

'She got mixed up with a bad fella, call im Norfolk Island Jack cos he been a lag over there, see. Used to call her Mary

Anne, and by Christ almighty don't never call her that. But she got away, two years ago now, went back to her country, back to the Tommeginne, cos she never let em go. She talked to the people, men, women, an she said we gonna take the settlers down. An she *meant* it. All that bad treatment, all them beatings, she wanted to take it out on the squatters, an the troopers an…she didn't *care* who, long as it was white men.

'*Here's how to use the guns*, she tell her people. *Go kill the bullocks an the sheep.* She not stupid, see, this one here. She knows it's a feed, but bigger'n that, it makes the white man mad as hell, an then he come out for a fight. Get the *luta tawin* in that little bit o' time after they fire their guns an before they can reload em. Stand up on a hilltop an laugh at the whiteys and tease em. *Come on!* she say. *You come up here an get yourself speared.*'

I thought of her shaking her breasts at the brig that pursued us.

'So Robinson's men ben chasin her, ben lookin for her. An I don't think to make a Christian outa her.'

'I don't understand,' I found myself saying. 'She's at war with the settlers but you women are here of your own free will. With the sealers. Is it war or isn't it?'

She shrugged and laughed. 'Survival, honey, any way you do it. Her people, my people, they all been comin up to these islands forever. *Lutruwita* got its seasons, these islands ere, we call em *tayaritja*, they got their seasons too. Seals, birds, eggs. So there might be settlers with guns in *lutruwita*, might be bible men out here in boats, but we be here anyways, without all them lot pushin us around.'

I looked around myself, at the men and women. 'Were any of these women brought here by force?'

265

Peacock's gaze followed mine. 'One or two. Mmm hmm.' She looked at me with something approaching pity. 'You don't understand it cause you want a simple answer.' And she shrugged with tired patience.

~

I moved to a smooth boulder under a low part of the roof where I could lean back against the encircling grasses and take in a full view of the gathering. They fascinated me, all of them. The rum was affecting me, I knew, but I would be fine if I could just sit and watch awhile.

It was when I was seated on that rock that Declan Connolly saw me. I knew in an instant that he was drunker than I was. He locked his eyes on me and staggered a little. Instinctively, I looked to my father, who was further away. He was deep in conversation with several of the men.

Connolly was coming towards me now. I looked up at him, as sunny as I could muster. He stopped when he reached me and stood there, staring until I became uncomfortable. He slurred something and I begged his pardon.

'Yer makin a big mistake wi' that man,' he said. I felt like his bulk had closed off the rest of the place.

'Whatever do you mean?' I asked. He could not know. Surely he could not know.

'Said yer makin a mistake.' He was not smirking or sneering, and looking back at that instant I do not believe he intended to frighten me. 'Coulda been me.' He shrugged helplessly. 'Coulda.'

'Mister Connolly, you have had too much to drink...' My consonants were sliding like his.

He leaned forward, his face a grimace in search of the emphasis he wanted. 'Anyway, thas, that's nothing. It's not. All right, fine. But not *him*.' He looked around wildly. 'That doctor isn' right in the *head*.' He pointed at his temple as he said it, then leaned back, watching me for a reaction.

I must have looked stunned. He leaned in again.

'I'm a goo' man, Miss Grayling. Fair man. Know I done some things, but I know right an wrong. Three years I'll have me ticket. But *him*...'

To my horror, he began to cry. He wiped fiercely at his eyes with a sleeve and looked around.

'Mister Connolly, you're repeating yourself.' It was a cold thing to say.

'All wrong, what you done. That man's a curse...'

A curse or *accursed*, I could not tell. There was background noise; and he slurred.

As he said it, he looked around and my eyes followed his. And we both simultaneously locked eyes with the doctor. He was standing ten yards away, with a clear line of sight through the thinning crowd. He looked at Connolly: he looked at me. His face did not change at all, and he held the gaze until we both had to break off and look away. Had he scowled, or shown temper in some way, it would have been expected. It was the calm in him that disturbed me.

Fuck him, whispered Connolly, and he stormed off.

The doctor did not approach me, and for some time I gazed uncomfortably at my lap. When I looked out over the crowd, the men had pushed the piano onto a pair of long timber skids and were hauling it back towards the complex of houses, as if they bore some kind of sarcophagus.

The doctor loomed in my vision now, occupying the space

267

under the low roof. I knew the grog had got to me—I cursed my carelessness—but if the doctor had been drinking, there was no sign of it.

'So lovely,' he was saying. His smile was wide and generous and welcoming.

'The place?' I asked, confused. 'Oh, you mean these people.'

'I mean neither,' he purred. 'I mean you. To make such a lonely voyage and to have you beside me. Was the convict troubling you?'

'When?'

'Just now, when you both looked my way.'

I feigned surprise, poorly. 'Oh no. Not at all.'

'Good.' He paused, smiling. 'Please tell me you will come to me tonight.'

I must have blushed.

'I need you,' he persisted. He did not trouble to lower his voice.

I rubbed at my eyes. 'I need sleep.'

But the booze had softened my resolve, even despite Connolly's ardent words. The doctor had never harmed me. Indeed, he had pleased me a great deal.

His posture assumed a subtle formality. 'And I want to make our love known to the others.'

'What? No...no.' This was too much. 'They are not ready to know that. My father, he...'

'We must! It is the honourable thing to do. I will want you to stay with me after this...obsession of your father's is done with. We can send him home and go on ourselves.'

Now I felt irritation building. 'You must see that I cannot leave him to survive on his own. You of all people should understand how vulnerable he is.'

'…Well.' He lowered his eyes as though I had wounded him. 'You will come to me tonight, in any event?'

I shook my head. I was no longer sure why, but he had pushed too hard. I fought the word that did not want to be said: after a moment, I won.

'*No.*' Too loud. 'No, doctor, I will not.'

His face darkened. 'You know, the parties responsible for the *Howrah* wreck could very well be among this crowd. You endanger yourself by taking a room alone.'

The piano. Damning evidence—but not conclusive. Now was not the time to reveal what I knew.

'You must excuse me,' I muttered. 'Please do not be cross.'

My face must have betrayed something, because two of the women came forward and offered to show me to my quarters. 'You ben took a bit by the rum,' said one.

One of the sealers was *away resupplying*—they did not say where, but I had noticed they referred to the rest of the world as *away*—and his house was ours for as long as we might need it. They said they extended this generosity to all visitors; someone was always away, and the houses were used alternately.

The house I was taken to was more substantial than the others we had seen among the islands: some of its walls were stone, and its interior was lined and sealed from the wind. A single candle had been left burning on a table in the front room; through an open door I could see a corridor extending further into the darkness.

'Doors are all on the right,' said the woman who had escorted me in. 'First one's your master'—she looked at me quizzically— 'and the blind man.'

'My father.'

'Ah, right. Second one's for the doctor and the convict lad.

Third's yours. Ye need to go durin the night, keep on further down the passage an there's a door what goes outside. Privy's there.'

I thanked her and shuffled down the dark corridor to the door she had indicated. Inside was a plain room walled with lining boards. An iron bed projected from the far wall, beside a window. There were no sheets and blankets in here, but more of the kangaroo hides, laid out in layers upon the flat hessian sack that did for a mattress. Another, larger hide had been nailed over the window and bunched up over a nail to one side. Outside I could make out the shapes of the night but they were elusive, unreliable. My head was spinning. I hurried to undress and climb into the bed, nesting myself deep under the warm pile of skins.

There was the sound of a night bird outside, and some scrabbling creature in the roof, then nothing.

In my sleep I heard a dog bark, and a door closing.

I may have heard footsteps.

I may have added them into my recollection later.

THE UNTHREADING OF THINGS

I woke in the darkness feeling ill, unable to tell how long I had been asleep. I felt a great urgency to get out of the bed and find a place to be sick, away from the hides that smelt of dog and fed my nausea. I was wearing a nightdress. I stood up barefoot, stomach clenching, found the heavy coat I had brought and threw it on, then dashed through the door and out into the hallway.

At first, I could see very little and was unsure where to go. The desperate desire to vomit surging in my throat, I remembered the woman's words and turned to my right. Outside, the cold breeze that struck me quelled the nausea for a moment. The sky had clouded over and I struggled to find the silhouette of a small outbuilding at the end of a rough path of granite flagstones. I stepped forward and found the door ajar; it squeaked as I pushed it inwards. The stench almost persuaded me to step out again.

All was blackness inside. I felt along the doorjamb to my

left, the side away from the hinges of the door. A small ledge, a candle on a dish and a tin of matches. The nausea was building again, fed by the stink of the privy. My fingers rushed their work, fumbling for the square of sandpaper, and I dropped the first match I tried. I took another and pinched it in the sandpaper. With a shower of sparks, the match flared and the small room was flooded with light.

I was not alone.

I raised my eyes and looked directly into the eyes of a man, above me, staring. I screamed.

There was no movement, no sound. The match sputtered and went out. The tin was still in my hand and desperately I fumbled another match and struck it.

The familiar face, convict slops. Declan Connolly hung there, suspended from the beam above the hole that was the privy. His face had darkened, his tongue bulged in the front of his mouth. The rope pulled deep under his jaw. The knot was behind one ear, tilting his head slightly on a neck made ghastly long. An upturned chair lay in the corner behind him.

I staggered and felt the world spinning and tried to scream again but could find no sound. The match burned my fingers and went out.

I flailed and found the door, smashed it open. The sickness came in a rush and I sprayed vomit heedlessly over the ground outside that hellhole, on my knees and one elbow, the other hand grabbing at my hair. I do not recall if I got up and ran, or if I crawled that way, back into the corridor.

I know I tried to remember the doors, and couldn't. I was desperate to avoid the doctor. I went past the first door, knowing it was my own, and at a guess, I went past the second and crashed open the third. In the gloom I could see Argyle's long, thin body on the right and my father's in the other bed on the left, his wild hair spilling over the sack he had used for a pillow.

Crowding thoughts distracted me. My father would be no use. I shook the master awake: he took a moment to focus. 'The convict lad!' I cried. 'He is hanging, outside, in the privy!' Argyle looked at me aghast.

'Are you having visions, miss? You went to bed a little the worse...'

'No! I am awake! Please...perhaps we can save him.'

Argyle swept back the covers and stood. He took a lantern from a small table between the two beds and lit it carefully: even in such circumstances he was solemn, methodical. He bent over my father, holding the lantern above him. I could smell what he saw.

'Drink's got him,' he said. There was no judgment in it, only observation. 'Come, show me where.'

I led Argyle down the corridor, back past the other door. There was no sign of activity there. Argyle, dressed only in a nightgown similar to my own, must have been as cold as me.

Out through the door and down the short path. A break in the cloud allowed a little starlight now. The grasses swayed in the breeze and I hated that shed with everything inside me.

Argyle pushed the door open and entered and saw Connolly. A small sound escaped him. He righted the chair and stood on it, bear-hugging the body with one arm while his free hand struggled with the noose. I shifted the boy's feet back onto the seat of the chair to take some of the weight, and his head came free from the loop. Argyle slumped to the ground, one foot straying into the putrid hole. He was still embracing Connolly, but the eyes stared dry. It was clear he had been dead for some time.

Other feet came running; the door to the back of the house

slammed shut. The *tyereelore* had heard the ruckus, and so had their men. A party took Connolly by his limbs and hauled him into the house. He was laid on a bench in the scullery. They crowded in there around the corpse and a strange sigh escaped it as the bearers laid it down.

'Fetch the doctor,' said Argyle, quietly.

I went to the room and found he was deeply asleep, composed. Beside him was the empty bed that had been the lad's. The doctor's hair was undisturbed and for a moment, stopped by a deep reluctance, I took in the image of him there. Such a curious man. When I woke him he thanked me and asked that I leave, and I realised from the sight of his bare shoulder that he was asking for privacy to dress.

'I will be there presently,' he said, as his eyes indicated the door. I went next door to check my father.

He was hard to rouse. It took several repetitions to explain to him what had occurred. The waft of alcohol was unbearable, his breath sour. He tried to hurry: but he was suffering. I told him there was nothing we could do now. I wanted him to comfort me, that was all. He did not realise it.

When we reached the scullery, the crowd separated a little to allow us in. The doctor stood over the body. His eyes found mine as we pushed our way forward. A cloth had been laid over Connolly's face. His hands reached upwards slightly in death, appearing to protest at the indignity.

The doctor removed the cloth and probed with his fingers at Connolly's neck. He pulled at his eyelids, looked in his mouth, brought his face down close to the dead convict's and appeared to sniff carefully at his mouth and nose. He gently rotated the head from side to side, feeling at the sides of Connolly's neck as he did so.

Apparently satisfied, he straightened up.

'I conclude that this was a suicide,' he pronounced. 'There is no sign of trauma other than the broken neck. History of hapolic affection following the death of his twin, a common circumstance. The chair kicked away, I am told. The choice of the privy…a matter of shame, I suspect. I shall write a report on the matter for the special constable on Preservation.' He turned to Smith. 'You will bury him here?'

He received a nod of assent, nothing more. Somewhere outside, a rooster crowed.

'Good. Be sure to place him at a remove from those Christian souls who have died in a state of grace. He has breached the fifth commandment and rejected God's sacred gift of life. This body is evidence of mortal sin.'

The doctor looked around at those assembled.

'Bring me water, please. I must wash my hands now.'

Tarenorerer, who had never taken a liking to the doctor, now glared at him in open contempt. He saw it but was unworried. He looked out the window, where the first glow of dawn had appeared.

'Now then,' he said. 'What shall we do about breakfast?'

~

My father pondered a long time over the body, a hand tracing gentle curves over the lad's head. Thoughts I could not even guess at.

Then he muttered his excuses quietly and left the room. As I watched him feel his way back down the corridor, moving slowly and in obvious discomfort, my worry for him was tinged only slightly with the familiar exasperation. My own illness had passed with the rising of the sun, leaving only a faint headache.

More confrontation. There was no alternative.

I went to his room, taking seconds to make the walk down the passageway that had taken him minutes. He wasn't there. I knew he hadn't come back past me. On down the passageway, and I saw the door to the doctor's room standing open: on the table between the beds, Gideon had arrayed his implements—the brass microscope, the case that contained his scalpels and tweezers, a mortar and pestle and a jar, in which floated a spread-eagled mouse. I stepped closer, drawn by horror, and stared through the curved glass at the tiny filigrees of its whiskers, the delicately furred snout. He'd moved fast to capture that one, I thought. I hadn't seen him venture out.

A movement reflected in the curve of the jar. I spun around. No one.

I turned down the remainder of the corridor and out the door that had led me to the privy last night. I knocked there and got no response, so I walked up a short rise, sand alternating with granite, and found my father sitting alone on a boulder. He knew my footfalls.

'Darling.'

I sighed in response. 'You're not well.'

A dry laugh. 'And for once, nor are you.' The wind in his hair, sand on his feet. Age was wasting the bulk from his thighs, and now his knees poked comically at his trousers.

'It wasn't suicide,' he said.

'What do you mean?'

'Someone killed him.'

'Father, I wouldn't raise this, but last night he was drunk and he—he more or less professed his love for me. And I rejected him, I suppose you would say.'

It wasn't that clear, of course, but how could I explain all of it?

He considered this a moment. 'Well, that may be, but he was killed. There's a fracture in the back of his skull. About six inches long. It'll be a blunt object: rounded, not edged. Jemmy or some such.'

'Why would they kill Connolly? They'd barely *met* him. He was drunk, but he wasn't causing any trouble.'

'What about the native woman? She seems to hate us all. Maybe Connolly was an easy target for her.'

'What, easier than a drunk blind man three times his age?' It was a lazy swipe. 'Sorry.'

He had turned his head slightly in response to the barb but said nothing.

'I've asked you many times but you never answer me. How are you drinking, Father?'

'What do you mean?'

'I threw out all of your booze, everyone's booze. I thought I'd stopped you. And I searched your belongings, forgive me. But I could not find a drop of liquor anywhere, and somehow you started drinking again.'

He was silent a long time.

'The doctor.'

'The doctor had a supply? But he barely ever drinks.'

'Hmm. The preserving fluid.'

'*What?*' I was too shocked to speak.

'Bearable with a little water, my darling. Stops the craving, stops the shakes, the visions.'

'How did you get it from him?'

'I just asked him. I asked him if he had anything for the symptoms. He's a doctor, after all. This was at first, you understand, when I thought perhaps I could remain sober. He said that he did, but that it was not conventional medicine.' He laughed grimly. 'I had the feeling he rather fancied the experiment.'

'*Preserving fluid?*' My face was in my hands. I could not believe what I was hearing.

'Yes. It is not…I've been…quite ill afterwards.' He grimaced. 'But you must understand. The alternative is…I could not tolerate the withdrawals. You saw how bad it became.'

My mind was racing. Other directions, places it did not want it to go.

'When did this start?'

He thought for a moment. 'When we were anchored off Hummock.'

The night in Gideon's cabin; that first kiss in the moonlight. He'd dosed my father.

'Was it every night?'

'No, some nights I was able to hold on.'

'Were you drinking it the night they threw us off Preservation and we had to come back to the *Moonbird*?'

'Er, yes, I was. Yes, he prepared me a dose that night, I remember.'

That night. The night Louisa rowed the sea chest out to us and the doctor made his first irresistible plea for me to join him in his cabin.

'And the night we were pursued and we sailed between the two islands?'

He thought again. 'Yes…yes.'

'And each time, he came to you with the preservative?'

'Yes. Early sometimes, later at other times. If he kept me waiting, I would begin to suffer.' He paused. 'Some nights I would nearly rip the jar from his hands.'

It was mid-morning now. A burial party was leaving the front of the house, down below us, carrying picks and shovels. Out here in the lonely islands, the divided twins would be separated for eternity, rotting slowly into the earth thirty miles apart.

Smoke curled from the pipe that chimneyed the scullery. Out further, past an expanse of neatly tilled potato fields, the *Moonbird* sat at anchor on a steely sea, waiting out this madness.

'Tell me again what he looks like,' said my father.

'Who?'

'The doctor.'

'Tall, you know that. Strong, very strong for a man of his age. Greying hair. Handsome in a way, I suppose, despite...'

'Despite what?' My father had turned his body towards me now, and I felt the intensity of his question as if it was heat.

'The injury to his face. He has a, his nose has been broken. Quite badly, in fact. It's crushed inwards at the bridge and it bends to the right.'

He drew in a short breath.

'Of course. Oh, of *course*. I thought the voice...Well, it has been thirty-some years. A man may change the way he speaks, but he cannot retrieve a nose spread half across his face.' His face took on a terrible urgency. 'Dear girl, I beg you to forgive me. I know you have formed...an affection—'

'No!' I found myself standing; felt the blood surge into my cheeks. 'You cannot say such things.'

He stood also, reached out for me as I snatched my hand away from his searching fingers. 'Eliza, we must find him immediately.'

I felt tears on my face. I was weeping, then sobbing, I didn't know why. Everything had gone so terribly wrong. I looked out to where the *Moonbird* rode among the skiffs of the sealers. Out past her there was another sail, a light brig, still a mile or more away but on a course towards us.

I saw the whole world of my folly now, all of its bays and capes and mountains. I clenched myself around the words and spoke them. 'He told me there was silver on the *Howrah*. Quite a lot of it, in fact. They were taking it to a bank, in secret. He knew somehow.'

'Well, then.' My father was nodding. 'There it is. The man we were sent to find. The man who caused the wreck.'

'*Figge?* It's not possible...'

'He has been with us the whole time.'

~

I rushed my father back down the slope and into the house.

The body of the convict was gone from the bench. In its place, an enormous boiled crayfish lay on its back, legs flared and tail curling up like a monstrous wasp, arching to sting itself. The doctor had snapped a spiky horn from the top of the creature's head and was cracking at it with his back teeth as he read his notebook, making emendations with a pencil. He looked up as we rushed into the room. I had no idea how the allegation could be put to him: only a blind trust that my father knew what he was doing.

'Who is in the room?' my father demanded, his voice dark and threatening.

Mother Brown spoke up. 'Why's it matter?'

'Answer me!'

She was taken aback by his tone. 'Why, your daughter is beside you. The doctor, Doctor Gideon, sits at the bench. There is Peacock, Tarenorerer, who was aboard your vessel, Meetoneyernanner, who is married to Tucker. Two children who belong to them, girl and a boy. And I am here. If you got a problem, old man, you must speak to me.'

'Where are the men?'

'Burying the lad.'

'Summon them, immediately. Must be men in the room. And send those children out.'

The children darted forward and broke some of the smaller legs from the crayfish, enduring the slapping hands of their mothers, then they bolted for the door. The doctor began to stand. 'Well, perhaps I may assist by fet—'

'*Not you!* You will remain where you are.'

I was watching the doctor closely. I knew his face well enough by now: he was calculating. But for the time being his obliging smile remained. An excruciating ten minutes ensued, during which the children ran to find the men and the rest of us stood about in that room, not speaking. One of the women came forward with a flensing knife and stabbed it into the belly of the crayfish, then ripped it down along the length of the tail so that it opened into two halves. It made a pleasant cracking sound as she pulled it open. Steam and a fishy smell issued from it.

My sightless father was spared most of the awkwardness as we waited: he did not have to make eye contact with anyone. But I watched the doctor's face. The irrelevant thought came to me with a shudder. If he was twenty-five or thirty when he had attacked my father then, like him, he would be sixty now. He still did not look it. Then I thought: why, if he had been here before, if he had somehow orchestrated the wreck, as my father clearly believed—why had the islanders not recognised him at once?

One by one the men entered, sandy dirt on their boots and hands. Some looked annoyed at having been brought back, others merely puzzled. Some of them eyed the lobster: a couple came forward and pulled a leg from it.

My father waited until they had all filed in, filling the small space of the scullery then overflowing into the larger room beyond its door. Some took chairs; the late arrivals remained standing. Eventually the crowd fell still.

'Thank you for coming back,' said my father. 'I will not delay you long. Eliza, would you indicate your presence, please?'

I spoke my name, and in doing it arraigned myself.

'And Doctor Gideon? Where are you?'

'I am here.'

'Very well. I must apologise to the rest of you, as it appears that we have brought discord into your midst. We came here because we are seeking the perpetrators of an outrage, the sinking and pillaging of a trading vessel called the *Howrah*. My judgment about this matter has been clouded, influenced by assumptions of mine that need not concern you. It now appears that I have done you all a great disservice by believing that the wrongdoers were among you.'

Confusion marked the faces of the crowd.

'It seems that we brought the responsible party here with us. Unknowingly. This man'—he gestured, accurately, towards the doctor—'is the person we were seeking. He bought passage on our vessel, travelled with us, ate with us, and he'—my father turned to face me directly—'he made pretences at friendship.'

I watched the reaction to my father's words. We had brought danger into their small society, in gross betrayal of their hospitality. Two of the men had shuffled across the outer doorway, barring it. It was close in the room: it felt near to eruption. Heavy arms came in over the top of the table, hands scooping white meat from the crayfish.

The doctor's smile had disappeared: in its place was a certain watchfulness.

'There was a shooting,' my father continued. 'At Rodondo Island. I cannot identify the victim, but he was a man trying to escape the island and we were briefly at odds with the people ashore. There was an exchange of fire. I cannot prove it but I feel sure this man fired the shot that killed him.'

'This is a calumny,' muttered the doctor. Then louder: 'The old fool is a drunkard!'

My father pressed on.

'He pushed me overboard—'

'You were drunk, *again*. You fell.'

'There was a drowning off Hummock Island, the twin brother of the man you have just buried. Convict lad.'

Gideon was taking account of every man in the room. Slowly, slowly, his eyes passed from one to the next to the next. Counting, assessing. My father could not know this, of course.

'Doctor Gideon was the only man on deck.'

'This is a blind man,' Gideon declared, his confidence unshaken, 'who was sleeping off a bender below decks. No one believes you,' he scoffed. He looked around at them all, not as an appeal but an expression of authority.

'The convict who died last night did not suicide, as this man will have you believe,' said my father. 'He had been bludgeoned, and probably dragged to the point where he was strung up. The hanging was a deliberate gesture, a message of sorts. I do not know who it is that he wishes to target with it—perhaps me.'

A man came forward and pulled the head from the tail of the crayfish, then shook it so that the mustardy head-paste poured out of it onto the surface of the table. He slid his hand through the slime and stuffed it in his mouth. No one else had spoken up to this point, but now a man at the back of the crowd raised his voice.

'What do you mean by that? Why would he target you?'
Grunts of agreement.

My father was undeterred: he could not see the murderous
look that the doctor was now directing to him. 'I investigated
this man many years ago. I was a naval officer'—here the doctor
rolled his eyes—'and I investigated his role in the loss of the
Sydney Cove at Preservation Island, and the subsequent walk
across country to Sydney. It remains my view that he killed a
number of persons, names unknown, during that journey.'

An awkward hush now descended. The doctor appeared
to have no intention of replying. The onlookers were baffled,
uncertain of their role in the stand-off.

'I am asking you to take this man into custody,' my father
continued, 'and to assist me in taking him aboard our vessel for
transfer to Sydney.'

Again, the uncertainty. A different man spoke up now, old
and stooped, his hair a shaggy white mat over his forehead.

'I don't know 'bout these dead men you speak of. You say this
feller was involved in the loss of the *Howrah*?' He looked about
himself, and there was an admission of sorts in the way he did
it. 'It is possible that other parties…were responsible for that.'

The blood rushed to my head. I wanted the moment to pass,
to have no role in it, but I could not let things stand. 'The piano,'
I said. 'It's from the *Howrah*, isn't it?'

They looked at each other. The crayfish was a ruin now,
shards of brick-coloured debris in a slick of guts and scraps.
They'd devoured pounds of meat, and a few of them were still
picking at the entrails. I stole a glance at Gideon. He seemed
relieved that the focus had shifted from him.

Smith spoke at last, as though he knew the stand-off now
required his adjudication. 'None o' what happens here is your

concern. Ye brought this man and his sins, an you cannot affix em to us. They's yours.'

His confidence evaporated as the words left him. There was disharmony now; the air was thick with it.

'Timing's right,' said someone. '*Sydney Cove* was me father's time. If it were this un'—he indicated Gideon—'he's the right age. He'd be near as old as the blind fella.'

'And it was me,' said my father, 'who organised the medical care of that broken nose. I can describe it to you perfectly. I wasn't blind then.'

Dr Gideon stood.

'Restrain him,' said my father. 'Let me take care of the rights and wrongs of it.'

That silken voice, the tone that had first caused me to take leave of my judgment. A voice that could whisper suggestions even as it spoke banalities. 'By the word of the Lord,' said that voice. 'If one of you lays a hand on me, I will not be held accountable for what I do. Choose what happens, and choose it well.'

It was a fatal misjudgment: I could see it in the faces of the sealers, the sudden tension in their bodies. They had been equivocating: now they were decided.

The tension finally broke and the long-suppressed eruption ripped the air.

Two of the sealers lunged at Gideon. He twisted from their grip, taking a wild swing at one. It missed: had it connected, I cannot imagine the damage.

There was a glint and I saw he had a fork in his hand. He struck at the other man, overhand, and it stuck in the side of his neck; the doctor had to tug it free to stab at him again. Another man hit him in the kidneys and he grunted but he was intent on what he was doing. He punched the fork into the man's face and must have hit bone, for it stayed there and the man reeled away with the handle protruding just near his eye.

A crowd of men were now pressing him against the edge of the bench while he swung madly at them with his fists. As they pressed him back his body tilted the timbers and the objects on it began to slide, the debris of the great lobster and runnels of fluid. Then the brackets snapped and the bench upended, slamming into my father, who was half-standing, and clinging to the back of a chair at the far end. Other chairs went flying and, for just a moment, the doctor and my father were caught together in the maelstrom. Then they spilled away from each other.

My father was on his back on the floor, kicking at the air like an overturned beetle, and as likely to be crushed. I reached for him and curled myself over him as the mayhem continued above.

Men were diving at Gideon, women arming themselves with implements from the scullery, shrieking. A long wooden oven peel swung through the air and a man ducked expertly under it. Gideon was the centre of the brawl, punching, kicking and lurching. I caught sight of his face in one swirl of the fight and did not recognise him at all. His eyes had rolled back and his mouth was bloodied. I thought first that a blow had split his skin, but then he spat a hunk of flesh and a man came away with the length of his eyebrow gone, blood streaming down his face.

I dived for my father again as the violence swelled and then receded. Knees and elbows and whole bodies struck my back amid a chaotic orchestra of sounds: breaking glass, screaming and grunts, the meatslaps of fist on flesh. A chair came down in splinters on me, driving a sharp end into my hip.

And then suddenly I was aware that it was over. When I raised my head I found only confusion and groans of pain, a room unused to violence suddenly ruptured by it. People were spilling out the door of the house and the terrible sounds had stilled.

The fight had ended. The doctor was gone.

CHRIST'S REDEEMING MISSION

The men organised themselves into parties and left to search for the doctor. They took with them a gruesome brace of weapons, tools of harvest turned to bloody purpose. Boathooks, poles, flensing blades, a bayonet. A man with an odd-shaped head was carrying a rock, too big to throw, too small to pummel.

They left in a fury, all trace of their earlier ambivalence burnt away, Tucker and Peterson one way, two men they called Maynard and Slack another. Wallabies darted off at their approach. The women remained, picked up the broken things and began to talk. A man named Mansell, who had told long stories of the islands to my father the night before, stood guard at the door with an iron spike. Some of the women claimed they'd seen it coming: *He weren't right in the eyes.* Big Sally wondered if the doctor had reacted as anyone would when set upon by a dozen men, but Bet Smith dismissed this with a snort: 'Had his chance to talk his way out of it. Man starts throwin punches when he can't explain hisself.'

My father and I remained among them in the house, but the hospitality had curdled. We were the ones best fitted to explain the situation, but no one wanted to hear from us. My father sat forlorn and silent, having arrived at the inevitable point where he could offer no further assistance to the pursuit. He was all obsession and no means.

The talk became argument, and the argument led them to certain conclusions. A body fresh in the ground was one thing: the mishaps that visited a seafaring society. But to have this man loose and snarling, trapped with them inside the uncompromising circle of the tide line, that was quite another thing. Now they must deal with him.

Peacock's kindly face was averted. Mansell's wife, a tiny energetic woman the others called Little Judy, had her mouth pursed in concentrated anger. The men had been gone an hour or more when Mansell appeared in the doorway.

'Mek yerselves scarce,' he hissed at the women, and two or three filed down the corridor towards the back of the house and out the door that led to the privy. The rest stood resolute.

I assumed Mansell's order did not apply to my father and me, and indeed, he next addressed us directly. 'This more o' your lot?' he asked, looking out and up the path.

I peered around the doorjamb. Masts in the bay, a brig at anchor, the same rigging I had seen on the brig that pursued us at Passage Island. They'd anchored it close in, arrogantly. A longboat larger than our jolly-boat had been pulled up on the beach beside it.

'Not us,' I shook my head.

In the foreground, approaching us, came a group of men.

They were curiously dressed, formal but not naval, and armed with muskets that they were wise enough, at least, to leave lowered. Their clothes hinted at prosperity; even those whose trousers were wet to the thighs from bringing the boat up were well turned out. At their head was a young man, square-jawed and handsome. His face was set in a resolute smile, a smile that said both *I will be pleasant* and *I will get my way.*

He smiled his way to Mansell, who now looked old and tattered. Order had arrived, apparently, in this debased society.

'Good day, sir,' the man began. 'I am James Parish, official emissary of Mister George Augustus Robinson. I carry with me the authority of the lieutenant-governor of Van Diemen's Land, Colonel George Arthur, and I am, additionally, empowered by my commission to do the healing work of our Lord and Saviour Jesus Christ.'

'Fuck,' said Mansell.

They stood in awkward stalemate for a moment, but Parish's smile never faltered. He took a hand from the pocket of his trousers and I saw that the pocket was lined with fine satin of Prussian blue. Mansell had brandished his spike when the men approached. Now he lowered it reluctantly and shook the hand.

'May I enter?' Parish asked.

'Go on, then.'

He came in, ducking under the sill. He looked around, looked at me and at my father and did not see anything there that aroused his civic instincts: just a blind man and his keeper. Tight trousers, clean boots. He tilted his hips so that one thigh projected my way. 'Where are the rest of the men?'

Mansell didn't answer, but Mother Brown did. 'There's been an upset, honey.' Something about the pomposity of his bearing had brought her sense of humour back to life. 'The boys'll be with you shortly.'

Parish mislaid his composure, just for a second. He looked uncertainly at the handful of his men who had come in behind him, and indicated with a lift of the chin that they should retreat. They stood outside in the sunshine, lighting pipes and murmuring among themselves. Mother Brown went back to sweeping broken glass off the floor, taking her time, and when she was finished she stood commandingly with her hands on her hips.

'*Fancy boy*,' she bellowed. 'You wanna come in ere and tell me your business?' The eyes of the other women indicated they knew what the business was. *George Augustus Robinson*. Parish stepped in again, and drew a rolled paper from inside his coat. From a top pocket he produced spectacles.

'Very well, then,' he said. 'I am happy to repeat this for the benefit of the men, whenever they might reappear…

'*By Order of His Excellency Lieutenant-Governor Colonel George Arthur and under the power vested in me by His Majesty the King I am hereby authorised and commissioned to take hold of, seize, arrest and remove all persons hereabouts who are Aborigines of Australia, or are of half, quarter or octoroon blood including all offspring of same and whether or not such persons are co-habiting with, or profess to be married to, persons who are the subjects of His Majesty the King.*'

'Why don't you put your paper down and talk to us in English?' came a scornful voice from the corner. It was Tarenorerer, reclining in a tattered wicker chair, with her bare feet crossed on a footstool. She was chewing at something—a twig or a straw—and it made her appear both relaxed and threatening.

Parish cleared his throat nervously. He was the only one of

his party who had spoken, and the others looked to him with obvious relief. There was no chance they would be contributing. 'It means that I am authorised to take with me all of the wives and their children. They will be resettled and given Christian catechism and the full enlightenment of English schooling.' He paused. 'It means that you are not lawfully entitled to resist.'

Shock settled over the room like a pall of acrid smoke. The children had run off cheering as the men departed on their search—I wondered now if they'd had the sense to stay away when the visitors arrived. Knowing this community, they would have been well schooled in such evasions.

'*Take* us?' Bet Smith repeated. 'You not gonna *take* us.'

Parish smiled generously. '*Take* is a strong word. I hope that I can persuade you to come with me voluntarily. You will be well fed, clothed…you will not be made to work. Only to learn.'

'Noberdy's *takin* no one anywhere,' said Tarenorerer, contemptuously refusing to rise. 'You can *take* your boat out there and keep goin, Parish, and consider yourself lucky we don't string you up like the fella last night.'

Parish blanched. 'What fe—' He took a moment to regain his composure. 'I do not want this to become a contest of wills, *Mary Anne*.'

The use of the name had the desired effect. She glared at him.

'Yes, we knew it was you. Who did you think you were mocking out there at Passage Island? The future I am here to offer these people may be…different for you. Now,' he turned to the others, brightly. 'It might assist in alleviating your worries if you come with me and meet the natives we already have on board. We have gathered people from Cape Barren, Clarke and Woody. They came willingly, I am pleased to say, and they seem very comfortable. I would not recommend you throw in your lot with *her.*'

Tarenorerer stood now, took a long step forward. Her body dominated the room.

'Why doan you tell em what's really happenin, Parish? Hey? Maybe tell em they got a choice now, but if they doan do it your way, you got soldiers comin from Launceston to put em in leg fetters? Maybe tell em *that*, tell em you gonna have em jailed, an you gonna shoot the resisters.'

She drilled her finger at the air between them as she hectored him, eyes wide. He'd tilted back, his body betraying his alarm at the onslaught.

'Mebbe tell em *that*, hey? You din come ere for your *Christ*, for your *Bible*! You come ere like a common thief, *luta tawin*!'

They were entangled in their mutual hatred, eye to eye in the centre of the room. The *tyereelore* watched on, weighing the danger this man represented against the danger of the other man, the one who was loose on their island. God and the Devil, or something. Their sympathies were with Tarenorerer, that much was clear, but she was asking a lot of them.

'You go off a minute,' Mother Brown said to Parish eventually, waving a finger at the door. Tarenorerer was silent. It occurred to me that the two women had differing claims to authority here: Mother Brown by seniority and by virtue of her relationship to Smith, but Tarenorerer had a revolutionary's fervour. The women sensed it in her.

Parish waited long enough to let it appear that it was his own idea, then left, again nodding the men ahead of him. Nothing happened once they'd gone. No one spoke. I'd never endured a longer silence in company. The only conclusion available was that they'd long seen this day approaching.

Tarenorerer addressed my father and me. 'You best go too.' Her voice was sad and kind. 'Just outside, eh.'

I took my father by the arm and led him out the front door into the westerly sun. The day hung there, ageing in the wind. To our right, the thatched roofing of the gathering place still covered the debris of the party. The piano had been moved inside, but bottles littered the ground and the dogs worked rump-high and head-down, nosing their snouts through the sand for scraps. Other dogs had gone with the men, barking elsewhere.

There was no sign of Gideon, no sign of the men hunting him, no sign even of the island's children. The newcomers knew nothing of it: that a man I'd briefly thought I could love now ran like game ahead of a maddened pack.

Parish and his crew had retreated further down the path and now stood at the top of the beach, samphire and tussocks around their shins, staring out at their anchored vessel. The sun bleached the whole scene, effacing its meaning.

I rested my hand just lightly on my father's arm, hoping the sun would warm him as it did me. Something to cling to, something to distract from the dreadful tension that gripped the settlement. I led him to the large boulder that framed the entryway to the house. It was flat on top, rising in a gentle slope so that it was possible to walk up it. I took my father up there now, wanting to look over the bay, perhaps to see some sign of the progress of the hunting parties. I helped him to sit at the top of the boulder and he did so in silence. After a few minutes I saw he had reclined, made drowsy by the warmth. I lay beside him, a child again in the sun's caress. I sank towards sleep as I lay there, each fingertip—the heels of my hands, the back of my head, my feet—feeling the heat in the rock.

Voices came to me as I lay there, disguised at first as a

dream, but making an acute sort of sense that dreams do not provide. Parish's voice was clear, infused with the same cadence as Gideon's, which I now understood to bespeak an overwhelming smugness about the world and other people.

Lying flat on the boulder, we were concealed from them. They spoke frankly.

'...timber on the western side. Perhaps only firewood. Any building materials you'd have to ship in. But there's water...'

'Two springs—I saw those.'

'So he would, would he not? I think he would be rather pleased.'

'And anchorages.'

'Anchorages.'

'Mutton fish, mutton birds. You'd not go hungry. Even with a couple of hundred to feed.'

'We can clear this lot off easy enough'—the voice I recognised to be Parish's—'but the matter that interests me is the sea all around. Currents. It is utterly escape-proof, gentlemen.'

~

I waited, the sun clouded over and the day lost its air of kindness. When I was sure the speakers had moved away, I woke my father and led him down from the rock. The missionary and his senior men had sat themselves at the benches under the thatch roof. Seeing us wander past, Parish stood and approached. He stared emptily at me. Neither of us made any attempt at an introduction.

'Would you show me these people?' I said to him. I do not know what possessed me. 'The native people you have on your boat. Perhaps I can intercede if you...'

Parish looked at me like he had not yet noticed my presence. 'Of course, Mrs...'

'Miss. Miss Grayling. This is my father, Lieutenant Joshua Grayling.'

Parish looked with pity on the stooped silent man who felt the air for his handshake. '*Lieutenant*, is it? Hello, then.' The smile of a man dealing with an imbecile.

'So you are in the government's employ, Mister Parish,' said my father slowly, and Parish nodded—nodded at a blind man—and the blind man said, 'Prestigious work, I imagine.'

This rooster had no ear for sarcasm. 'Yes it is, sir. My word it is.'

He turned to me. 'Miss, my men will row you out to our vessel. The, um, the *lieutenant* may find it easiest to stay with me.'

And so it was that I sat in the longboat with more room fore and aft of me than I was accustomed to. They rowed me out, past the *Moonbird*, the dear girl waiting at anchor like the patient friend she was.

I heard singing as we approached, native voices in stilted unison. A hymn I did not know. I looked up at the nameplate as we rounded the stern: the rower must have assumed I was not able to read.

'The *Charlotte*, ma'am,' he said. I was glad my father was not with us to hear that name spoken into the bright and pitiless daylight.

The rower's bearing was military, his dress civilian, like the rest of them. He tied the longboat to small cleats on the strakes and a ladder was lowered. I went up, conscious that he followed under my skirts.

Aboard, the beam was wider than the *Moonbird*'s and the main mast sprang from further forward. There was a hatchway under the quarterdeck and a wide, generous forecastle, but it was none of these things that struck me. It was the people sitting in supervised rows on the boards of the deck.

Several dozen natives: men, women and children, dressed in English clothes and holding hymnals as they sang. The hair and whiskers of the men had been trimmed short; the women's hair was tied back in ribbons.

The sweet piety of the singing was not reflected in the faces, which were set in exhausted obedience. They stared at the useless books without expression.

I had seen natives chained and I had seen them whipped, for you couldn't live in Sydney and not see such sights, and here I saw the same dead eyes. The people on the deck were more or less free: no fetters of any kind upon them, and the men watching them were unarmed, but the manner of their assembly was so staged that it could only be occurring against their will. The smallest of the children clung to their parents; the older ones stared sullenly into their laps and mouthed the words they had been coached to sing. The adults slumped, resigned.

I listened: I watched. The long notes were broken by a sharper sound and it took me a moment to place it: they were coughing. The cough moved around the gathered bodies like birds alighting: here then there, then again back to the first. The children had less ability to control it, and it would rack them for a full line of the music before they could hack it clear.

I watched a man holding a hymn book and I could not tear my eyes from his hand, which was a gnarled and earthy thing, a lifetime without squares of white paper.

These, then, were the souls the evangelists had collected. These were the innocents they were going to save from the depredations of settlers and sealers. Perhaps their complete despondence was only temporary: perhaps they would come to live in gratitude, fed on psalms and curtseys. Maybe this was the start of generations of happy Christian natives, and all done with the purest of motives. Maybe those in authority really did devote their time to worrying about the least, and least visible, of their subjects. I did not think so.

An officer approached me and stood at my side.

'You are concerned,' he began, as though about to discuss the weather.

'It's hard not to be, sir.'

'You must understand, ma'am, that we are sparing these people a life at the mercy of these brutes.' He nodded towards the island, and I took his comment to be a reference to the straitsmen. 'Their people are dying out. Those uns over there would terrorise em if we didn't intervene.'

'You seem very sure of that, sir.'

'Had one not so long ago, shot his woman through the breast because she wasn't plucking mutton birds fast enough. He'll happily show you the grave he dug, ma'am.'

'Miss.'

'Miss. We intervene or they die out.' The zealot's fervour, the complete absence of doubt. 'I won't be apologising for that.'

'Where are these people from?'

'We've cleared out Oyster Bay, Cape Portland, Clarke Island...' He listed their home nations as he pointed, as though they were livestock. 'Some from Cape Barren. We got to Preservation after you. See...'

He ran a finger down the rows until he came to the person he sought.

I recognised her: Drummerrerlooner, the woman Munro had called Louisa, who'd rowed the sea chest out to us after our eviction. Her gaze met mine but apparently saw nothing there. She lowered her eyes again.

'Where will all these people go?'

'Well, let's not get ahead of ourselves. We will complete this sweep of the islands. Mister Robinson is on the mainland of Van Diemen's Land negotiating with the chieftains. *Cleaning out the Augean stables*, he calls it.' He gave an admiring chuckle. 'Then we may see what we have.'

He asked me if I wished to look below decks at the natives' living quarters, and when I declined, said, 'I should apologise to you for the encounter at Passage Island.'

'Whatever do you mean?'

'Some of the crew were…over-exuberant. They have a particular view about that native woman you have with you.'

'What kind of view?'

'That she is dangerous. Surely you would agree?'

I did. I said nothing.

'She has a gift for riling them up,' he went on, and hesitated. 'Miss, there was another vessel. You may not have been aware?'

'I'm not aware. What vessel?'

'Following you. They came alongside us at Badger Island, asking after the *Moonbird*. Your vessel,' he added helpfully.

'Who were they?'

'The bosun took a note of the name, I don't have it. Smallish trading brig.'

'Perhaps they were also pursuing Tarenorerer,' I offered.

'The native woman? I don't think so,' he said, and shrugged. 'No matter. They were not hostile.'

Around us the singing had stopped and the heat of the midday sun had brought a kind of torpor. There was nothing more to see. Parish and Robinson's great civilising drive amounted to a boatload of miserable souls trapped in unrequited piety. It occurred to me that the sinners onshore were doing a better job of offering an alternative to slaughter.

~

When we came ashore again on Gun Carriage, John Smith was back inside the house, and in a fury.

He'd stationed himself there, evidently wanting to be a focal point in the search for Gideon. But the men had taken off without method, grouped by family and other allegiances. They'd armed themselves as they pleased; some were drinking: all were spoiling for a fight.

'Just as likely to shoot each other as this Gideon,' Smith fumed. 'Island's five square miles, whole east coast's heavy scrub. How they gonna find him? Did they secure all the boats? What if he swims tae one? Fuck. You two.' He collared the young men standing nearest. 'Take a walk all the way round. Any boats been pulled up, tek em out and moor em till there's none left at all, see? No boats—none—on the whole fuckin island.'

The young men ambled off. My father was seated by the fire, drinking tea someone had made for him. Other than that simple courtesy, he was afforded neither company nor conversation. We were lepers now, bringers of a plague called Gideon. Or perhaps Figge, if my father wasn't delusional after all.

There was little that could be done in the hours that followed. Argyle, who had rowed himself out to check on the *Moonbird*, was not allowed to bring the jolly-boat back ashore and had been compelled to wait until a rower was available to bring him in in the single island boat that remained in use. All of the other boats now crowded the bay, tied together in twos and fours at every mooring. The missionaries' brig was listing: its hull must have been resting on the shallow bottom. Somehow, with the draining tide, a lassitude had risen that affected all of us. We were in a world bereft of energy.

Parish's men remained outside as the evening began to descend. They lit lamps, made a fire and ate quartered kangaroo meat and shellfish that Smith took out to them. He did not offer them the hospitality of the house. He knew their business; he might not be able to undermine it but it was plain that he did not intend to make it easier.

Around dark the sealers began to file in, dejected. Some were damp from wading around the shore and through swamps. Others were sandy or covered in grass seeds. They had seen nothing, not a sign of Gideon. Smith had occupied his time up till then drawing a large map of the island in charcoal on a hide: as each party came in, he asked them where they had been and marked it off on the map.

'He in't gone,' he said to several of them. 'Hasn't taken a boat. He's 'ere, and he cannot keep this up.'

The night wore on. This time no one drank, not even my father. He had not spoken for hours and his appearance worried me. The colour had leached from his eyes and from his skin: where previously shades came and went across his cheeks, now that skin only wrapped his bones and did so without variance: his skin was tired of him. The whites of his eyes were dirty like riverbed sand. The broken veins of his nose and cheeks led to them and gave up. He lay around in ways that should have been uncomfortable but appeared not to trouble him. This apathy of his was more distressing to me than the occasions of his rage.

The fire burned low in the hearth. We put down blankets and lay on the floor near to it. Conversations came and went

301 ❧

and left confusing footprints in my mind: snatches of argument, reminiscences. Some of the fragments must have been dreams but I could not tell, I was so weary.

They were trying to get the women away. They were coming in, whispering, pleading. Crying.

What was it? *What was it?* They were going to send them away: somewhere called *Capuchin*. There was agreement that this was wise, but no one knew how to defeat the blockade created by the removal of the boats. Then an answer: they would swim. The women were the swimmers, the divers. The men could read the ocean but none of them could swim in it. The women, then: they would swim to the anchored vessels and they would slip away. Parish's men were complacent because they assumed that the boats were out of everyone's reach, not just the doctor's.

My father snored loud enough to wake himself up: the conversation stopped, he choked, embarrassed, and his eyes were startled wide, then he slept again. He could not know any of what was occurring above our heads, around the table. The men were smuggling their own lifeblood. They were desperate, angry. Seemingly defeated but not bereft of ideas.

They waited to ensure he was asleep again and then I heard a woman's voice, an urgent hiss, asking how they could leave their people behind on Robinson's brig. *The ones they already got.* Another in answer, saying they were not *her* people. 'Months go by,' she murmured, 'maybe years go by, and those ones'll come back, and our ones too, and life be normal again.'

And I heard Tarenorerer, furious, insisting there were no choices. 'Nobody make a good pact with the Devil,' she said. 'Nobody can trust these men. You can do only one thing. You take all o' your weapons, get the guns and the knives and the clubs and you surround em because they are lazy and they all sleeping in one place with no watch posted. And you storm em and you crush their skulls and shoot em and stab em and you do not stop until every single one o' them is dead, because they are not concerned that your children will be orphans, and nor should you worry for them. What's an orphan to this lot? An *opportunity*, that's what it is. An orphan is a little soul for saving. Scrub em up, teach em scriptures. Not your flesh an blood. It's a little Christian, wiped clean of the *stain*. Wanna go makin orphans, go outside and make some orphans, I tell you. An I will be right in there with you crackin heads.'

No one spoke in reply. Her speech had stopped all other consideration.

'You think about it.' She lowered her voice, as though someone had pointed us out, reminded her that we lay in the room. 'You lot live on an island far away from any white man, an when someone come after these ones to find out what happened, it'll be long enough from now, an by then you take the fucking boat out an you sink it someplace deep, an you'll have them fancy men burned and buried and the grass grown over and it'll be just wind an clouds an a greener place in the grass and you gonna say *no, they never come here mister.*

'An stop this talk about hidin an do not think for a minute of co-operatin because they lie and they cheat an they got no hope in their hearts for you: they are waiting for you all to die like you was never here. An if you give em that satisfaction then you deserve to go.'

There was a silence. Then one of them asked the very question I was dreading: *and what about these ones?* In the darkness I could feel a finger pointed at us there on the floor.

More silence, sounds of discomfort, then lowered voices, almost whispers.

'Done nothin, those ones,' Tarenorerer said. 'They's not missionaries.'

'Brought the Devil, that fella out there,' came the reply.

'Didn't know.'

'Makes no difference.'

'That ole man's just about finished anyways.'

A dog padded through the gathering and slumped itself beside me. The weight of its flank pressed warm through the blankets on the cold side, away from the fire.

'They come here thinkin we wrecked the boat.'

'What boat?'

'*Howrah*, innit? Where that pianner come off, an some o' them timbers. Ol Munro had the letterbox on *waytakupana*. Had more stuff'n what we do.'

'Not our fault.'

'What about all them people out back?'

'Same. Wasn't our fault. Just the decent thing to do.'

'Yeah, but they go home thinkin it was our fault, dun matter what we say.'

Other voices crowded in now, and the dispute rolled and tumbled between them. They would do us no violence. They figured we had our own battles to fight now, ones that were not their concern, any more than the waiting missionaries were ours.

The dog shuffled and I could smell her coat. The fire had died down. Tarenorerer had been overruled: there would be no assault on Parish's men. They would swim to Slack's boat because it was far enough that the men would not be watching it, and north enough that the tide would not rip them away. Poll and Bet Smith would go and wake the hidden children and take them to the east side and the others would rig the boat and sail it round to collect them. They would head for the Pot Boil shoal, because Parish's lot would never follow them in there. Then they would go to Capuchin, wherever that was.

The women began to file out, some rummaging around for objects in the kitchen: a cup, a plate, a hessian sack. Before long the house was submerged in a quiet that was not entirely silence because the dog breathed and so did my father, and the sea turned up small waves on the beach at the end of the path and those waves fell with a crushing sound on the heavy white gravel sand.

I could no longer sleep, I was so full of trepidation. After the moon had set and the fire was gone and there was near enough to total darkness, a shot rang out near the house. For an instant I thought *it is done* and I lay in wait for consequences. But a man clumped in ten minutes later, dragging a large roo that slid across the floor in its own blood, and that was all.

He stopped by the table and I could sense him looking around. *No women*, he would have thought. And maybe he knew enough to understand what they had decided.

I woke again in the night, sometime after the man with the bloodied kangaroo and before the first light of dawn, to discover that a huge hide of stitched-together skins—seals, I imagine—had been thrown over my father and me. It had an animal smell about it, meaty but inoffensive. I looked up and saw Argyle slumped over us in a kitchen chair, his chin in his hand. The hem of his night-dress, dirty and frayed, hung just near my outstretched hand, an embroidered edge that spoke of a fragility otherwise absent in this world. As I drifted off to sleep in the warm shadow of that hide it occurred to me that no one on the island had commented on Argyle's attire.

THE INDIAN RETURNS

The dawn revealed to Parish's men that they had been outwitted, and they were furious. The outward demeanour of piety and acceptance required of them only stoked the rage.

Myself aside, not a woman nor a child could be found upon the island. Nor had any sign of the doctor yet been seen. Parish took momentary consolation from the sight of a sail on the horizon: mistakenly thinking it was the women, he began his orders to make sail and pursue them, only to discover that the sail was incoming. It was a modest sloop, and there was agreement among the men that it was the same one which they had met with some days before.

A strange vigil came together on the bluff of granite above the house: Parish and his men, the sealers, Argyle and me: a party so riven with discord that the watching was done without exchange of a word, only occasional spitting and tapping of pipes. The weather was mild, a light south-easterly rippling the surface as it blossomed into the blues and greens of the day. I was thankful the weather was so easy: by my rough reckoning the wives had crammed about thirty people into a small working boat to make their escape.

My father had stayed behind in the house. The tremors had returned, and the pallor of his skin—visible even through the sun's leathering—had become deeply distressing to me. His hands jumped about as he tried to drink the tea I had made him. He refused food: some clenching pain or nausea was coursing through his body. My father was good at suffering—he'd done enough of it—and he merely shivered as the agonies came and went. It was only through knowing him so closely that I was aware of how bad it had become.

But I did not know what the pain meant. I knew he hadn't drunk for a day and a night, and perversely, I found myself praying that his only want was another drink. But it had never been like this before, and I dreaded it was something graver.

Smith had devised a plan to cover the low country of the island in a systematic search, believing that Gideon was still among us and could be brought in. He believed it would have the result, like a hunting drive, of flushing Gideon away from the coast and up into the high ground where he could be surrounded. Parish refused to deploy his men to the search, maintaining that it was none of his concern. It was clear he also believed the men had been complicit in the disappearance of the women, since he could not countenance the idea that they had engineered their own escape. His pretty contrapposto had been replaced by a slump of angry resignation.

All eyes were fixed on the approaching sail. The vessel tacked once, faintly, as it corrected its angle into the bay. Four men became visible on deck: two of pale skin, and two dark.

One of the darker men was small and slight: the other stood centrally, watching the watchers and turning his head at times to supervise the sailing.

'Natives,' declared Parish. 'But it's not the women.'

There were snorts from among his men.

The sloop ran straight in under full sail. It carried no dinghy, I could see, so they were not going to anchor it. The flat sand glistened in front of the sloop's pointed nose and they nudged it onto the sandbank. The occupants held on as the vessel came to an abrupt halt. All of this we watched without comment.

The four of them fussed over rigging and laid anchors on the sand fore and aft. Then one by one they dropped over the side and came ashore, stepping around the puddles left by the tide on the sandbank. They could not have known how awkward their arrival would be, but now it was plain for all to see. They walked up the beach and the crowd on the boulder, of which I was one, did not attempt to move in their direction. We just stared, dumbly.

The white men had the scarred, taciturn look of lags. Before them came the two dark men, the heavier one considerably older than the other. Up the slope of the beach, among the tussocks now, and the older man removed his hat and craned his neck to look up at us.

It was incredible, improbable that it should be him who stood there, squinting into the sun. His expression was calm, serious, unhurried. Of all of us standing about on that foreshore on that lost and troubled day in December 1830, he appeared to be the only one who understood the mood of the world and the people in it.

Srinivas.

~

A meeting was convened hurriedly in the sheltered area where I had watched a young girl play the piano just two days before.

Srinivas was watchful, polite. He waited until the men had seated themselves, until I had manoeuvred my shocked father into a comfortable position. It was put to Srinivas that he should explain himself. The straitsmen were tired and exasperated: a boatload of strangers had brought them a killer, then the missionaries had driven their women and children into hiding, and now this man was here. He was unthreatening on the surface, but they sensed our unease and fed off it.

'I am Srinivas,' he began, 'son of Prasad. I am a timber trader from the south coast of New South Wales. These two men are prisoners of His Majesty, commissioned to me under executive order of the governor. The lad is my son, Neelanjan.'

I studied the boy. He was perhaps fifteen, with a downy moustache on his upper lip. His hair was raven-black. He stood slender but resolute. I wondered what my father would make of him if he could see him there. I suspected he would see the echo of Srinivas himself, long ago.

'I sent these people, Mister Grayling and his daughter, on the *Moonbird* with the express aim of finding out what became of my trading vessel, the *Howrah*. It was under my instruction that they came among you, along with Doctor Gideon. I see he is not here.'

A murmur passed through the men. As nobody seemed willing to explain his absence, I spoke up.

'Sir, the doctor has absconded. He remains on the island, we assume. We have been searching for him.'

I saw alarm on the merchant's face, but not surprise. 'Why?'

'We believe he has killed a man. Your deckhand, Declan

Connolly. We found him hanged. There had been…antagonism between them.'

'He killed young Angus Connolly also,' came my father's voice, weak with pain. 'Drowned him. He fired upon a man in the water at Rodondo. Struck his head, killed him. And he engaged in other conduct…' His voice dropped. 'Deceptions of a personal nature.' My father's face wandered to the adamant surface of the boulder beside him, yet he addressed Srinivas in a way that was intensely personal. 'It seems the doctor is in fact the man we sought all along. Why did you inflict him upon us?'

'I did not know. I had no idea. It was never my intention,' said the merchant. The shock seemed to emanate from him in waves, and I believed him. For the first time I saw that he was deeply distressed.

I looked at us, at all of us, and realised we had arranged ourselves as though the merchant was on trial. He and his son and the two miserable lags, seated before a panel of the sealers, Smith at their head, grim and unyielding. My father and me, arrayed to one side, listening, commenting: witnesses and scribes.

'You knew this would happen. You knew who he was.' My father's voice was bitter and unconvinced.

'I'm not sure that any of us know who he is, Mister Grayling. He will be this, he will be that. People encounter him in differing ways.'

I was tiring of this nonsense. 'Why did you not tell us the boat was carrying silver?'

Again he looked surprised. Then he regained his composure. 'I did not tell you anything about the cargo. And you did not ask.'

'Why did you not tell us,' said my father softly, 'that the boat was carrying Figge? Do you still believe I wronged you all those years ago? Is that why you endangered me and, worse

310

still, my daughter, who is blameless? Why...' His voice broke and I feared he would weep. 'Why did you *do* this to us?'

'I hadn't met him, this *doctor*...I knew you would encounter the man eventually, somewhere. I did not know he would board in Sydney.'

My father's face declared his rejection of this.

'Please, Mister Grayling.' The Bengali appeared to be wrestling inside himself.

'You know that he put my father, Prasad, to a long and painful death, alone in the forest. And having cleared the way for himself, having murdered my only protector, he desecrated my body, purely because he could.' He looked at my father, whose face had altered. 'You didn't know that, did you? In fairness, you were documenting the miracle of three survivors appearing out of the bush. You were not asked to investigate the violation of a young boy.'

He looked at his hands. 'I have searched for him. I have done many other things, of course, but always that. And I have never had a clear notion of what I would do if I found him. I assumed I was not a murderer, but I felt every inclination a murderer would feel. I would see him die in my dreams, in pain that I inflicted. I would hear his last words, begging a forgiveness I would deny him. When I heard that he'd escaped Sydney under an assumed name—his names are all assumed—and that he must have perished at sea when the boat foundered in a storm... Well. Only a fool would believe it.'

'Why?' asked Smith. 'Seems reasonable to me.'

Srinivas sighed. 'This much I understand: you do not look outside for him. You look inside. He nestles himself among people, people in need. Attunes himself to what it is that they seek, and then offers it. To my father and me, to the survivors of the *Sydney*

Cove, he offered salvation. You would have to ask yourselves'—he looked at me now—'what need he had sensed in you.'

With great effort my father waved this away. 'You laid a trap for him,' he said, 'and you baited it with us. You couldn't find the man, so you conspired to have him come to you. Convinced me I should go looking for him: an invitation. *Here is your old enemy Grayling. Come and find him.*'

To my horror, Srinivas did not demur.

'Well.' My father paused to collect himself. 'He found Eliza too.'

Still the Bengali held his tongue.

'*Do you know*—' My father stood. He swatted the air with his hands until they found the edge of the table and he could steady himself. 'Do you know that he seduced Eliza, that he dishonoured my daughter while he fed my, my...*need*, and stupefied me? Do you know'—he was weeping now, broken and raw—'how it feels, sir, to have failed your child so profoundly?'

I was weeping, too, for he had spoken the truth for the first time. It was I who had been deluded. How could my father— blind, a drunkard—have so clearly identified what Gideon was doing when I couldn't see it myself?

John Smith had been watching me, his face shifting between anger and pity and impatience. 'Right,' he said. 'We're done with the lot of you. You ken be gone by mornin, thank you. Take your boat an your troubles and sail on. And you, sir'—he indicated Srinivas—'these people say you were baiting with em for whatsisname. Didnae hear you deny it. Mebbe time you baited yerself. Go on out there and announce yerself to him. If yer right about all this, yer grudges and so forth, then he'll come out for ye. An that'll be the end of him.'

I knew instantly that Smith was wrong. The man had

evaded Srinivas all these years, keeping him in a state of fevered searching, and he would continue to do it now. There was no prospect that Srinivas would meet the man out there on the island, on his own terms, and prevail. Either he would return empty-handed, or he would not return at all. It was my father— and, I was increasingly certain, me—that the man wanted.

But the discussion ranged back and forth for quite a while and nobody argued against the central idea. If Srinivas wanted Gideon out in the open there was only one way for him to achieve it.

~

They brought a meal and Srinivas ate, while his son watched him silently. The two lags had been sent back to the boat.

He ate sparingly and did not talk during the meal. No one joined him. He was so very alone: I could not decide whether he had earned such exile. When he was done, he washed his hands again and accepted a jacket and a rough hat from the sealers. They offered him a flensing knife and he tucked it into his belt. They gave him a fowling piece, ensuring he understood its workings. And when he indicated that he did, they filled his pockets with cartridges.

His face was calm through all of this.

I studied him, standing there armed and awkwardly waiting. I saw a man of modest size, of fine hands and light frame. And I had seen Gideon naked. I had clutched at his arms with my fingers, in the throes of pleasure. These moments were now my shame, but I knew that he was stronger by a great measure than this small, dignified man who, in going armed, sealed his fate. The weapons only looked foolish on him.

There was no point arming him any further: the weight would be a hindrance. The men stood back, surveyed their work and nodded to each other. Once again there was no reaction from Srinivas. He merely turned and faced me.

'Miss,' he said, 'I beg of you, accept my apology. I could not know what would eventuate. I never intended for you to come to any harm, nor your father. I cannot expect you to believe me or to forgive me. I did you wrong and no matter this business, I will not forget.'

I was surprised at the fury I felt, my unsteadiness on the cross-currents of sadness and worry for him. I lowered my eyes and said nothing; I regret it now.

He took himself outside and walked to the top of the first rise beyond the house, placed the gun at his side and waited. There was no point him heading off until the men had cleared the lowlands. The hours passed, the light turned and he stood there alone.

Clouds tumbled by. The birds went about their fraught lives. The sea attended the rocks. He was not their business. My sense of him was that he was always someone else's business.

One by one the parties came in, each leaving a single armed man behind to watch their position. They had not turned up the doctor, meaning that he could be nowhere else but on the high ground. They had ventured two thirds of the way up the slopes, then turned back, satisfied that they had cornered him. To push further, when they had positions around the peak on all sides, was to risk confusion and injuries by crossfire.

When the last of them had come in, Srinivas turned to us and said, 'Very well, then.' And he walked away.

THE PINNACLE

It was early evening by the time Srinivas set off.

Smith said we had at least three hours of light. It would take him two, he said, to pick his way up the tracks made by the livestock. Having no interest in the summit, the animals had worn contours around the peak over the years but never headed vertically towards it. Srinivas would have to break into the tussocks at some stage and improvise the rest.

I sat by his son, keeping a respectful distance. Big ants marched around in the sand: the boy watched one and flicked it away when it came too close. We watched his father's back, the light upon it. He walked with the gun's muzzle down, no haste, no state of readiness, for he was still outside the circle that the men had formed around the peak. His head was cast down. He was concentrating on his feet, but it made him look penitent. Unforgiven.

The boy had observed his father's entreaty to me, and my

graceless response. I could not guess his feelings. I wanted to beseech him, blameless in it all: to take his hand and tell him all would be well. But again, I did nothing. Distracted, preoccupied with myself, I rose and walked back the way I had come. My father was still in the chair where I had left him, holding a cloth to his mouth as though to cough or sneeze. I barely recognised the knuckles; his were the hands of an ancient man. I drew a cup of water and took it to him but he remained fixed in the position I'd first seen. I gently took the cloth from his hands and found it stained with blood. His hands were weak and shuddering.

'Father?'

He groaned. I could not see any injury to him that might be the source of the blood. I looked around, feeling panic rising in me. Maynard came forward, face betraying no reaction to this wretched spectacle. We lifted my father by the armpits and draped his arms over our shoulders. His legs made the faintest of effort at walking but we were dragging him, and there was so little of him that it was no great challenge. How had he wasted so, under my supposed care? We took him to his bed and laid him down. I covered his body with the blanket and I swept the hair back from his forehead.

'Do you have a razor?' I asked Maynard.

'No. I ken git you a good blade. Might do it.'

He went off and I held my father's hand. When he returned with the blade, a cake of rough soap and a bowl of water, we tucked a towel under his chin and I worked up a thin lather and began to scrape at his cheeks with the blade. It was crude, but I could see an improvement.

He awoke as I was angling the blade under his jaw. He was frightened and cried out and I found myself explaining why I was hovering over him with a knife at his throat. I was aware that all certainties were erased now: such was the effect that the man had had upon us. Anything could be a deception, a murderous sleight of hand. I wept inside not just that my father might be nearing the end of his days, but that he might do so doubting my love.

He settled, and I finished the haircut as he returned to sleep. When I was done, I took the towel from under his head and shook it outside then rubbed his scalp with it to remove the loose hairs. Having made sure the bedclothes were up around his shoulders I drew a chair to the side of the bed and sat in it, with my head resting just by his hand. Maynard left us there; a mumbled *pardon* drifted back as he left the room.

~

I must have fallen asleep; I do not know for how long. My neck was sore.

There was still faint light outside, and two men stood in the doorway. They made no attempt at quiet, or at excusing themselves.

'He is calling for you,' one of them said. There was no need to identify the caller.

I looked at my father. He was not conscious, but he was at least peaceful there. I followed the straitsmen without thought or hesitation: this was all inevitable. The man's giant pride, himself at the centre of the universe. Of course he would seek to confront me.

I walked the same path that Srinivas had ventured out upon hours before. The two men walked ahead of me. We had not gone far when the sky was ripped open by a gunshot. I jumped, but one of them said, half a-mutter, 'Not shootin at us. Bin takin shots at the men round the hill, keepin em down.'

'Whose gun does he have?' I asked.

'Don't know,' said the younger of the two. 'Thought it mighter bin from yer boat.'

'The gun you gave to Srinivas'—they looked at me blankly—'the Hindoo man…did it sound like that?'

They thought about this; slowed their pace slightly. 'Aye,' said one of them quietly.

'How many cartridges did you give him?' I thought of them filling his pockets. They had sent him up with a virtual armoury.

'Hmm, er…couple o' dozen,' said the younger.

Dread filled me, even as the birds skittered from our path and the dusk did its best to conjure an innocent world. The earth on both sides of the path was humped and tunnelled and I had seen enough of these islands now to know that it was the work of the moonbirds, migrants or vagrants or both. They, not the stunned and timid remnant seals, were the true occupants of the place.

The path meandered: the creatures who had made it had little regard for straight lines. As Smith had said: the track appeared to wrap concentrically around the peak, but never led up to it. Four mangy dogs followed us, snouts down and eyes furtive. Not the islanders' dogs but wild ones, opportunists. We had turned now, so that the house and the various boats in the bay were gone and we were instead looking east towards the open sea and the treacherous shoals that lay further out in the dying light: a sandpaper of white on the soft mauve expanse.

Higher, and I was looking out towards the long spit of sand that nearly connected the island to Cape Barren. The wind moaned in the grasses. The mountains of Cape Barren loomed silvery into the sky; there were green grasslands and forests and a serration of hooks and swerves in the coast. *If only he had gone there*, I thought. No one would ever have found him, and this sorry business would be at an end.

The tussocks were giving way now to exposed boulders—smooth and rounded, forming a series of lines that ran almost north-south. We were crossing them, one after another, but the lines kept coming, and some were tall enough that a man could easily appear from between them.

I was dwelling on these thoughts, alert to small sounds, when the straitsmen announced they would go no further. One of them made a gesture with the rifle he was carrying, waving the stock in my direction. I declined. I could not see what difference it would make here, and besides, I had no skill with firearms. No one had said I was being sent to kill a man.

I watched them pick their way back down the hill for a while. The occasional shots had ceased now, and there was only the wind and scattered birds to break the silence, in the vast well of air around me. I picked a comb out of a pocket in my dress and hauled my hair out of the way. There were flies about, big heavy ones. I wondered if it mattered that the light was fading.

I picked a line, a furrow between two parallel faults of granite that led up gradually in a straight line to the north, deepening as it went. I was thinking as I ascended. Not about how much further the summit was, nor where I would encounter the man, nor what would happen when I did.

I thought of my father, stung again by the cold realisation that he was nearing his end. Why, I could not say. I guessed he would be sixty, a reasonable life for anyone, particularly a man who had had such travails.

But the world would be so terribly empty without him. A world I wouldn't recognise, since my waking moments were crowded with his care. Were the things he needed within his reach? Had he been drinking, had he been sick? Were there hazards around him that I could anticipate? A curled dog he might trip over, hot water he might spill? It had seemed never-ending. But it would end.

I wanted him to make it back to Sydney, to feel his wife's presence in the air. I could not know with certainty where that memory lived for him. A grave is only a marker, and the house was long since ashes in the soil. The places she had walked in her solitude were known only to her. But anything that remained for him would be in Sydney. God knows, it was not here.

The narrow foot-track led sharply upwards, past a fallen obelisk that crossed the fault lines. I stepped up and over, and found myself in a narrow chamber that the rock had walled in. There was only the sky above and granite spearing up all around me to form a nest of rock. I stood there a moment, unsure which way to go next, and then I was conscious of a movement behind me.

I turned. The man stood there: tall, uninjured, composed. His hands were by his sides and there was half a smile on his face.

'Sweetheart,' he said softly. 'You came to me. I knew you would.'

I did not answer him: terror closed my throat.

'This is the point, you remember, the point at the centre of the spiral. No further forward motion is possible because the spiral has exhausted itself.' He gestured at the enclosing rocks with both palms by his hips, and I saw what he was carrying. 'So. This is the point.'

His left hand held a large knife: the flensing knife they'd given Srinivas. The hand was smeared with blood, up to the wrist and staining the shirt cuff that hung down out of a loose roll on his forearm. Specks of it dotted the side of his shirt where it clung to his body.

'Good heavens, I'm worrying you. Is it the knife?'

He stepped forward and I edged back. He kept coming and I retreated further, then found I had my back against the rock face, with nowhere further to go. My whole body was tensed but my mind had nothing to offer. I could not believe that dying might be so uncomplicated.

He stood only inches from my chest now. He raised his right hand, unbloodied, extended it to me.

'Give me your hand.'

My eyes scanned all around me. The sun was down now and there were shadows that offered refuge.

'Be calm. Please,' he said.

I extended my hand, palm-down. He turned it over, raised the knife and pressed the sticky handle into my palm. He closed my fingers over it to form a grip. Then he lifted the knife, and my hand, so that the tip of the blade rested against his throat, exactly where his collarbones met.

'Now. If you believe anything the Indian said, if you believe your poor addled father, you should push the knife home. Run it through me and have it stick in the bone, because if such things are true, I do not deserve to live.'

He lowered the hand that held mine. I alone held the knife now, poised so the tip trembled under my own confused power. It bounced; a prick of blood appeared. He did not flinch.

'I am Holofernes, if you want me to be. Silver and curses, as always. Take my head when you are done.'

I could not comprehend that he would surrender all that physical power to me. When I had clenched myself around him in his cabin, I had persuaded myself of exactly that illusion: that

I was mighty, that I controlled him. Now I did; yet still I did not trust the offer of his exposed throat.

'If you truly believe I murdered a man last night, do it.'

I held the blade there, wishing with all of my soul that I had the capacity to do what he asked. 'I cannot know exactly about these other things. But I *know* you poisoned my father.' I jabbed with the knife tip: blood ran more freely now.

He only sighed. 'Perhaps. Or perhaps I gave him what he wanted. Maybe I gave him succour when the world had denied him any. You give an addict the thing they crave, and maybe you delay by an hour or a day the point at which suffering will overwhelm them. Maybe you deliver a measure of peace.'

'You did it so you could fuck me in the cabin next door.'

Somewhere around his eyes I saw amusement. 'We are all of us slowly poisoning ourselves. Your father chose alcohol. The native woman is eaten by hate. Argyle...I cannot tell, but something assails him. And you, sadly, are corroded by cynicism. It eats your insides but you continue to sip at it. We all hunger for our own extinction, Eliza.'

He had made no move towards the knife, slack in my hand, so heavy now that my arm ached.

'I am tired,' he murmured. 'It's been too much, too long now.'

I wanted so badly to drive the blade home. That, or to throw it away. To end it, either way, but still I stared. At the knife. At his throat.

'Push it in.'

The darkness was advancing. In the gloom he seemed apart from the world.

'No.'

'You can end this.'

'No.'

'Very well.' He gently took the blade from me and turned it to face me. Then he lifted his arm.

There was a bang and a flash that lit the place yellow. It echoed around the rocks, around and around so loud I feared it would take my hearing with it.

His head swung away from me and sprang back. A cavity, a bright furrow of flesh and bone beside his eye, and he screamed and blood spilled from between his fingers. The knife was gone; I heard the metal bounce in the darkness behind him. The other hand flailed at the air and he ran and now I had my own hands over my face and I bawled out the terror. All tension left me as I sank to my knees and there was scuttling above me, a fierce shriek, then another explosion, another burst of painful colour.

With a thud, a figure landed beside me on the soft earth in the gully, dark and lithe like an apparition. Tarenorerer, with the giant musket balanced in her right hand.

'Fuck, woman,' she said. 'Why din't you slit him?'

She ran straight through the gully in pursuit of the man, muttering *eaten by hate my arse* as she went.

For a long time I was alone, not knowing what to do. There was nothing I could contribute to the chase, being unarmed and slower than her.

I turned uphill, driven by a different fear. It took me some effort to climb out of the chamber in the rocks. The sound of men shouting came to me on the wind but there were no further shots. The slope levelled out and I found myself on a large open flat, punctuated by boulders. The dregs of a cloud-muddied sunset hung over the strait between Flinders and Cape Barren, small islands rising from the sea as the rocks around me rose from the grass.

I stumbled over the fowling piece abandoned in the grass.

A shape ahead of me, silhouetted dark against the sky. I did not want it to be. I spun around once, hoping the men were running with me, propelled by the same instinct, but they were further down the hill, them and their dogs, pursuing the man. The silhouette took form. A pole, wedged into a pile of small boulders. Something the sealers had put up for navigation. The pole bulged in the middle. I ran harder now, my lungs burning.

A human form, lashed to the pole at the ankles and throat. Srinivas.

It must have been a single cut. He was naked, opened from chin to groin, entrails spilling from him. Other, deeper work to open his ribs. His heart was mostly cut free and it hung by one vessel outside his chest. His eyes and mouth were open, filled with unspeakable horror.

The sky spun around me now, clouds and dark velvet, studded with early stars. The wind stirred harder and the grasses whispered back and no more, no more but the world darkened forever by this act. I fell upon the boulders that held the pole and found his clothes there, and I wept over them.

EMBERS

I woke on a bed in another house, one I did not recognise. The furnishings were even more spare here. A simple glass lamp burned on a stand beside my head, the wick trailing a coil of cotton. The sharp stink of whale oil filled the room. A man sat on a plain chair in the darkened corner opposite. I jumped when I saw him, fearing that the spectre from the hill had returned. But his face was unmarked, and he had a taper in his hand from the lighting of the lamp. He spoke gently.

'Don't be alarmed, miss. I am William Slack, here keeping watch.' His speech was more formal than the other islanders', as though he had once been somewhere else, in higher company. He was my father's age, bristled and wind-beaten, but his face was not unkind. I lay silent a moment, assessing him. There was a seal hide over me, a hessian sack under my head that smelt of oily feathers.

'Where is my father?'

'In the room next door. His condition is grave, miss.'

I considered this and he waited for me. 'Can you get up?'

I went to stand, found I was still dressed in the same clothes I had worn up the hill, blood flaking dark on my right palm. I was weary but not hurt. 'How long have I been in here?'

'A couple of hours. They have not found the man.'

He led me out and across a small communal room. Nobody was about. There were signs of a finished meal, a candle burning and a low fire in the hearth. Another doorway on the far side, a darkened bedroom. Slack brought the lamp.

My father lay there, in much the same state as when I had left him. The lamp threw wild shadows at the wall beside him: the standing spikes of hair on his head were horns and fangs, his forehead a vast dome. Then all of it shrank to nothing and he was a tired old man. He opened his eyes once, still unseeing but perhaps reaching for the memory of sight, and closed them again.

As I bent and pressed my cheek to his, I heard people filing into the larger room behind us, clumping heavily on the floorboards, speaking in lowered tones. The men who'd been hunting Gideon. Argyle's voice was there among them.

Slack left the lamp on a table under the sash window and silently withdrew, closing the door. The window was open. I studied the delicate mullions that divided the panes into a grid. The breeze was warm and welcome. It wafted through the opening and the flame guttered.

I was alone with my father. His breaths were shallow, slight.

I spoke to him, low and soft. I cannot remember now precisely what I said: the terror of the hill was raw in me and I was exhausted. But I recall—or I want to believe—that I wandered through our years together, talked about how his tenderness had turned into my care of him; how I'd sorrowed for him when shame and sickness plagued him, how it was love that drove me on.

A breath would answer me when I stopped my murmuring, a tiny exchange of air between the room and his body. Enough that I could see his lip move, his chest rise and fall.

I imagined his wife, my mother, as a mountain of love and courage. I told him I was sorry for my impatience, for the deception wrought upon him by Gideon with me as his unwitting accomplice. I hope I told him he'd led a good life and would leave goodness behind.

An answering breath that had no force in it.

Several things, I now realise, mark a life in completeness: to laugh and cry, to hurt and forgive and remember and forget and to couple with another body. Perhaps, among these, to live one day through a vigil for the dying. The wrenching separation of living and dead, I now believe, is the necessary price of *having* loved. This, then, was the night that came for me. I spoke softly, the sleep tugged at me and I resisted, prayed and bargained with an unresponsive God.

A fractional movement of his throat: another breath. It held there then sighed away, fainter than the one previous, and so far from it that I began to wonder how I would know which was the last.

The lamp sputtered on in its buttery stench. My father descended far from me. I placed a hand on his chest to search for rise or fall. I listened by his mouth. I could not know if the moment would be marked somehow: a gasp, a locking of the flesh. How far apart could these breaths become? Would life finish on an inhalation, a breath kept forever?

A breath, tiny. The sigh of release.

And now I waited. It seemed forever, it seemed that I stopped breathing myself, that I lost the measure of time. No further breath ever came.

~

Somewhere before dawn I had laid my head on his chest to hear the silence where his heartbeat had been. I'd fallen asleep there, and this time the sleep had me firmly.

A noise intruded. My dreams tried to assimilate it among their troubles, but it remained stubbornly separate. I could not say how long it had been there, but it woke me eventually. A sharp crack, followed by lesser sounds. A ricochet, but not a shot.

It came again, and I realised something had been thrown into the room, clean through the open window. It rattled around on the floor and I saw it come to rest in the shadows: a stone, half the size of a hen's egg.

It took so long—too long—for my mind to catch up.

Another stone came through and bounced on the floor, a little harder than the previous one.

My father's lips were pale, slightly parted.

Then another stone. This one struck the lamp cleanly, shattering the glass. Tiny shards struck my cheek. Blue flames glowed warm beside me and I still did not understand. The oil had spilt and the flame was following it, down the side of the table and onto the floor at lightning speed, onto the trailing edge of the bedclothes and up and over my father's body.

I shrieked, ripped the furs down and grabbed him around his middle, heaved him up and out of the bed. The body was slack: there was no resistance to this violent change of circumstance. Even as wasted as he had become, his frame was too heavy for me and I crashed to the floor amid the licking flames. The oil got on me, I felt it slick under my forearm, and there followed a searing pain as the flames devoured the oil and sizzled my skin. I got to my feet, slipped once and landed on my burnt arms. Some of the skin stuck to the boards—I saw it pull away from my flesh as I pushed up from the dry floor. I screamed and hauled my father's body by the shirt towards the door.

People were rushing in; the room was bright with flame but filling with thick smoke. The fire had the curtains, it had the furniture. The bed was roaring: flames that billowed luxuriantly, that had leisure and sustenance. The smoke was too much, but then there were arms on me and the shirt was gone from between my fingers and a tangle of us fell out the door and into the living room, where the flames were eager to follow.

People everywhere, shouting, coughing, beating at the flames. Perhaps the situation could have been turned in those first few moments, but the fire was greedy in its confidence. It had found too many avenues to fuel. The door to the room where we'd been only seconds before was an inferno, too bright and hot to look at.

I knew the front door of the house was behind me but no one had left, and now I could see them bashing at the closed door with their shoulders. They ran short bursts and struck it so hard they grunted but it did not move. It was barricaded from the outside. A mad jangling music rang out in the half-light as three men hauled a piano from its position against the far wall. I hadn't noticed it there as I passed through earlier but now I could see it was the *Howrah*'s piano: the one the girl had been playing the day we arrived.

Where was my father?

Men threw chairs out of the way as the piano came through,

and others got behind it and used it as a ram while its timbers squealed and its unseen hammers struck in discordant protest. There was splintering the first time it struck, but the piano was more damaged than the door. They dragged it back to run up again, and its varnished timbers hung from its damaged frame. A fine thing, a thing that spoke of beauty, torn down like everything else.

I needed to find my father. Or I did not. He was dead; I did not know what to risk.

The second ramming succeeded. The door broke at its hinges and the night air billowed in, fanning the blaze. But the piano had crashed nose-downward, half-in and half-out of the doorway, and now its diagonal height blocked the door: they tried rocking it back and forth but its feet had caught somewhere outside. Men squatted down and heaved at the great instrument. Already some of them were falling. One lay across the back of a chair beside me, in every respect a tumbled drunk but for his clawing to find air.

The piano would not move, not for all the effort applied to it. I watched a man try to squeeze between it and the doorjamb, only to wind up stuck there himself as the flames feasted on his hair and he screamed. I could not tell how many of us were left in the room now. The air was so thick with smoke that shapes were hard to discern. I had remained low, on my knees and my blistered sticking hands, and down there I touched random limbs, boots, items of clothing discarded in desperation. Such things would glow momentarily in the flare of that hellish fire, but none of them connected to anything that might be a person, because the blackness was so deep. There were dead men around me already.

I rose again to search for the door. I sensed that the men

had given up on the piano and the doorway and had left it, were circling in the smoke for another option, calling to each other, cries of desperation: no plan. Time was at an end.

There was a great crash and the bedroom breathed out, coughed its foul hot air at us as the roof behind the door collapsed. Now the sparks were swirling bright in the black, driven by new air. Even through the bitter soot I could smell the burning of flesh, the men's or perhaps my own, and could no longer tell my pain from theirs. I was wreathed in choking darkness now, not smoke in air but tiny gasps of air in solid smoke.

Yes, it was proper to risk my living body for his dead one. This was no decent cremation.

I forced myself to go to where the bedroom door was still breathing sparks. There, by the doorway, I found the bare foot, clutched at the shin and knew it to be my father's. I crawled the length of the body and had him by the armpits. It was no more than three feet to the doorway but it felt impossible. The body seemed many times heavier now, but I had air and I was not done. I screwed the charred rug in my fist and hauled at it until I was moving, and him with me. An inch, a foot, a yard and nothing to go by but sound. I clenched my teeth against the burning. Now I was him, I was my father.

Raised up on one knee, I felt the skin tear away from my forearms again as I worked him along the floor. The end of the rug, the lip of the doorway, a threshold board. One more heave and the air changed, both hotter and colder but offering breath at least. I could see nothing, and I did not see that the bedroom had ceased to exist, was now a pile of charcoaled wreckage three feet below. We fell through an instant of clear air and landed in the ashes and embers.

The heat was worse here, a furnace scattered on the earth, and a swirl of ash seared my lungs while the coals hissed at my legs.

A shout, a clatter of timbers being thrown aside, and the grip of strong arms once again. They disentangled my body from my father's and carried him away. I was borne aloft and saw blackness and red furnaces, the starry sky and the pale glow of the sandy ground between tussocks.

~

I shook them off the moment they placed me down. It was Maynard and Slack, both eager to be gone anyway. Four men were missing, thought to be still inside; Charles Peterson, the invalid, was among them. Too slow, poor man.

I was forgotten, momentarily, on a patch of bare ground that was lit by the glow of the blaze. A crowd worked quickly around me, bringing and taking water, shovelling, dragging burning timbers off into the sand. The fire had worked through the back of the house and was now devouring an orchard, and a scattering of pens and sheds, where livestock bellowed and squealed in a chorus of agony.

I rolled onto my front and began crawling further away from the house, wanting only to escape the intensity of the heat. The cleared ground ended in a grassy rising slope, and I crawled further up, seeking darkness. There was dirt and ash stuck in the weeping slick of my arms now, and more of it stuck to my legs.

The foot of a tree, and beyond it a series of short fenceposts. Fenceposts.

No, not fenceposts. Too short, too wide. Standing boards, only knee-high.

I dragged myself along the ground to the nearest one. There were words inscribed on it. Somehow I knew what they would say before the firelight flared and I read the crude inscription.

To the Memery
7 souls washed up from the founderd bark 1830 AD
Sufer the little childern.

A crucifix, hatched with two blows of an axe. I extended a hand to touch the groove in the timber as my parched lips made names for them: *Albert and Florence; Catherine, Jane, Sarah, Violet, Frederick.*

There was nothing left to know about this place, or about its people. They had mourned the victims in private. I was tired now and in too much pain to pay heed. It was no one else's business.

~

I tried walking once or twice but my body would not co-operate. Painfully, slowly, I dragged myself back into the light where the men had gathered.

They'd laid my father on a wide timber beam between large boulders, probably a fish-cleaning bench. I bent to him and dusted the ash from his face.

Through my tears I saw a man approaching and I thought him to be wearing a nightshirt. Then the graven face was lit by the flames of the house and I saw that it was Argyle in a cotton shift.

He was speaking, quiet but firm.

'They believe it will burn the whole island. We must go, and quickly.'

FIFTEEN HUNDRED FATHOMS

It took an hour or more to get every one of the men off the island. There was only one of the little skiffs left, the others crowded together by their noses around buoys offshore.

Across a hundred yards of flat, poppled water I stood on the *Moonbird*'s deck, watching the island burn. The fire swept across the low ground, taking the house we'd first stayed in, then a collection of the lesser ones and their outbuildings before moving out to engulf the close-packed scrub and the grasses. It took livestock and tools and building materials and stored food and, in a soft yellowy eruption that billowed black smoke, a store of mutton-bird oil. *Whole season's work*, one of the men said. But how could it matter when their homes had been destroyed?

The fire took five men, their charred remains fused with the ash of the house, the incinerated surrounds. The straitsmen wept as they shovelled them out, gagging at the smell.

After the flames had devoured the settlement they tore away

across the island, muted over grassland and flaring when they found thickets. Terrified kangaroos darted ahead of the front.

Argyle and Tarenorerer stood near me, transfixed by the sight. Tarenorerer had been unable to find the man: she watched the burning land now as though she expected to see him running somewhere in the glowing darkness, a ghost made of ash and fury, mad as the flames.

Argyle had gone below, come back up with bandages and rolled them around my forearms and one of my shins, hands working gently and eyes lowered.

The daylight arrived dull as pewter; clouds had rolled in from the west and now lay heavy over the island, drifting low enough to obscure the peak of the hill. They brought rain, and the rain swept this way and that, directionless as the frantic kangaroos. The rainfall would eventually dampen the fire but for now the flames crackled low and unchecked across the early summer grass.

Smoke issued from the blackened houses, wisps of steam. The rowers laboured back and forth to other vessels moored nearby. Men sat desolate on the beach, waiting. A shift in the breeze and the smoke came our way, bitter and damp, rising high now, too. It became a column that stood taller than the peak of the island. They would be seeing it on Van Diemen's Land—word would spread, people would come. The island with its billowing cone had made a volcano of itself. There was too much for the islanders to explain; more reasons to evacuate and leave Gun Carriage to the evangelists.

The *Moonbird*'s deck gleamed in the rain. Argyle took himself to the bow and sat alone under a shelter of sailcloth pulled up over the windlass. I went to join him, grateful for his company, uncomplicated as it was. He wore a simple shirt and trousers and had combed his hair back from his forehead. He was clean, absolved of something, so that he looked older and, at the same time, newer.

'Are you all right, miss?' he asked me.

There was no answer to that, neither a great one nor a small one, so I said nothing. The rain drummed on the sail over our heads.

'Long way home,' he said after a while. 'Is it bearable now?' I failed to understand his meaning until he looked down at my bandaged arms. I nodded. We sat in silence, birds wheeling overhead. His long fingers gripped his knees. The inside tip of his right index finger bore a patch of blue ink. In its centre it was bright and new. Further out it traced the whorls in his skin and faded to nothing.

'Who were you writing to?'

He took a hand from his knees, touched the fingers absently to his lips.

'My wife,' he said at length. 'Pointless letters.'

'She will be glad to receive them, I am sure, Mister Argyle.'

His head inclined down towards the wet boards. 'She is deceased, Miss Grayling. A long time ago now.'

'Oh dear. I...' I felt a sudden panic over how to respond: the urge in me was to console this man somehow, to hold his hand or embrace him, but manners constrained me. Even to observe him in this state was an unwarranted intrusion.

'You must have wondered...'

'No, no,' I hurried. 'It is none of my concern.'

'Yes, of course. You are polite enough to not inquire. Dimity. Dimity was her name. We had no children, you see. It was the two of us, twelve years. She was my friend, I suppose, above and beyond even being my wife. That word. *Wife*. It sounds like a task, or a title, don't you think? But she was a part of me, closest I have ever known another soul. I'm not outgoing by nature, you may have noticed. But she understood.'

He sighed heavily, looked up and out at the sea again.

'*Me*—against all reason. Which is the nature of love, is it not?' The stately hands rose in a small gesture of hopelessness, then fell again to his lap. 'We were unable to have children. No prospect of it. She wept at times about that, and I wept too. But I wept for her and her…grief. That sense of wanting, like hunger. When she was most desolate, she would say that she had let me down, but that was never the case. I could have lived out my days that way, her and me.'

He gestured vaguely towards his quarters.

'So the dresses are hers. I don't know how it appears. In truth I don't care. I brought the sea chest full of everything I could find of hers, worthless to anyone else, I suppose. I hold them sometimes to summon her. The fabric against my skin is a reminder…a connection. As if she is somewhere not far away. They'd whip you for it in the township, of course. But I couldn't let her go. My body and hers.'

He swallowed.

'She wore the white dress at our wedding, the one I put on when we left harbour.'

'The empire line, with the embroidery? She must have looked beautiful.'

His eyes gleamed. 'Sometimes the smell of her comes from the cloth, even after all this time, and I remember so sharply…' His hands were tightly clenched now, in front of his mouth. It became difficult to distinguish his words.

'The last days…unbearable…never complained, not once. She was sweet, she was peaceful when she was able to be, though the pain'—he winced as if he'd been struck—'the pain was terrible. But I cannot think of that. We choose our memories, I believe. We take the recollections and assemble them and tend them like a garden. We proceed by small dignities. That is how you prevail. That is how you can stand up from your bed in the morning.'

He turned his face to me now, his brimming eyes and hollow cheeks. 'You must be feeling all these things, and choosing among them. You decide. You are fated to carry this all your days now, this loss. But you may alter its shape; that is the one grace permitted you.'

~

I put ashore in the *Moonbird*'s jolly-boat at a cove on the island upwind of the fire, where the shoreline was piled with granite stones. The back of my dress was wet from the rainwater on the thwart, cold in the breeze as I rowed. Waves appeared in miniature from unseen swells on the flat sea, rushed among the stones and were absorbed: they gleamed with the water's retreat.

I thought of the master and his words as I dragged the little boat up.

Anyone who loves intensely will believe it is they who emit the light, they who shine warmth on the other. There is a self-centredness in love, so strong that we fail to notice the loved one illuminating *us*. I understood now that Gideon had passed between me and the fierce light of my father's love. He had become an eclipsing presence that left only the finest halo of light visible around its edges, and me plunged in the antumbra. I was so fixed upon the idea that I loved my father well: I had failed to see the love he returned.

Argyle had never made the mistake of thinking it was only he who shone.

I chose three smooth stones: one for each of us, and loaded them into the jolly-boat. As an afterthought I went back, further into the grasses, until I came to a hollow filled with small coastal plants: daisies and pigface, samphire and tiny orchids. My feet began to sink into moonbird burrows: in disturbing the ground and casting seed, the birds had created a garden. I scooped among the daisies with my poor burnt hands, disturbing tiny bees, and made a thick posy. The sleeves of my dress were singed and torn: I ripped a length of fabric from the left one and used it to tie the flower stems. And so, satisfied with my foraging, I rowed back, sweat and seawater droplets burning as they found their way through the bandages.

On the *Moonbird*, Argyle had unscrewed the table from the galley, brought it out onto the deck and laid my father upon it. He took one of the Connollys' hammocks from the hold to serve as a winding sheet. We gently brought it under his body so that the two sides met above him. Tarenorerer stood alone, at a distance from us. I took her separation to be a mark of respect, that she perhaps did not consider this to be her place or her tradition. It was not mine, for that matter, but Argyle's quiet competence settled it as the right thing to do.

He took the small leather pouch that held the sail repair kit and drew twine through a heavy needle. As he began a line of stitches from my father's feet, I placed a stone between his knees. I took a bucket and washed my father's body, taking the salt and soot with sweeps of the cloth, feeling the small shifts of his flesh under my hand.

As Argyle's line of stitching followed me, I placed my father's hands on his chest—over the healing scratches where he had torn at his skin amid the tremens—and I put the second stone under the crossed palms. I slowed my work over his face, wanting to lift his sorrows and wring them into the bucket. Argyle arrived after me with his stitching, each of us silently attuned to the other's movements.

I lifted my father's head and placed the final stone, a flatter one, beneath it.

Argyle paused over the face, regarded him for a moment, then passed a stitch through the septum of his nose and tied it off. 'Tradition,' he said when I glanced my question.

I had thought about the day I would bury my father. Never seeing this, of course, but when I imagined the moment, there was always a final exchange: of apologies, promises, explanations. In my imagining, he hadn't left me like this, without a word. How would I tell him all the things that were in my heart?

I could not, not ever. It was that simple. To think otherwise was torture and madness.

Argyle took a new thread and continued his stitching over the beloved face. Over my father's forehead, closing and closing as the pale cloth swallowed him up.

~

Tarenorerer made her few brief preparations in the afternoon, when the fire had nearly extinguished itself. She found food and water in the galley and made herself a meal, then whistled to one of the nearby boats. They sent a rower who waited below us, tied off in the deep shade by the hull. It was only when I looked down from the rail that I realised there were two figures in the little boat: the second of them was the boy, Neelanjan. Srinivas's son. We had overlooked him—I suppose everyone had.

'Do you want to come aboard?' I called down.

'I think he does, ma'am,' said the rower. 'He don't speak much.'

Miss, I thought. 'Send him up.'

The lad drew the boat over to the *Moonbird*'s rope ladder and scaled it. Both hands took the rungs: he had nothing with him. When he stood before me on the deck I saw the strong resemblance he bore to his father, in all but one respect: his eyes were blue. He held my gaze, proud and devastated, eyes just higher than mine. Now we were kin, fatherless within hours of each other.

'Do you wish to come to Sydney?' I asked him, and he nodded faintly in response. And from that face that evoked at least two continents came a voice that was entirely local.

'I have been taught to crew a boat, ma'am.'

Tarenorerer waited by the mast beyond his young shoulder, obdurate as the granite. 'Where will you go?' I asked her.

'Keep movin,' she waved her fingers vaguely east. 'Robinson's mob gonna keep lookin. Batman's mob. Gotta stay ahead of em.'

She must have seen the worry on my face. 'Dumb bastards. Not that hard, eh.' And suddenly her face was alight with a smile I had never seen, beautiful teeth and a warmth in her eyes. She looked now at the island, jerked her chin faintly at the hill. 'That man…' She shook her head. 'Don't know where you found him but you wanna leave im there. If you lucky he won't foller you back.'

She placed her hands on my shoulders now, looked directly into my eyes. 'I'm sad for you, miss. Sad about your father.' The parcelled hammock lay on the ground beside us but neither of us looked at it. 'He was a good man and you're a good daughter.'

She did not address Argyle, did not look back. She strode to the gunwale—lithe and powerful and unbowed by all that had occurred—and backed onto the ladder. She carried her worldly goods, the same ones we'd found her with: a string bag and a gun.

Soon after, the boat was rowed away towards a ketch that belonged to the islanders. The rower had his head down, bent to the effort. Tarenorerer sat high in the bow of the little boat, over the dips of the oars, facing back at us. Her stare was unfocused: she was looking at me, or at Argyle, or the *Moonbird* or the water between us, or none of it.

~

Argyle and the lad prepared the *Moonbird*, after her longest layoff since we had left Sydney. They moved methodically about the deck, climbed the rigging once or twice to make adjustments, went below and returned. I stayed on the deck. Below would be too hard to bear, down among the memories, the evidence, of whom I loved and how. The captain's cabin, taken over by Gideon and festooned with dead things. My father's bed, and that small collection of his belongings that explained everything about what was left in his heart after the storm had passed through it. The hammocks of the poor Connollys. Young Neelanjan would have his choice of sleeping places.

Argyle issued instructions to the boy and me, avoiding the terminology I had heard him use with the others. The lad moved swiftly, intent on earning his place. I did what I could. When the master felt all was in readiness, Neelanjan went to the windlass and winched the anchor up. I watched over the bow as it returned from the clear green water, trailing a plume of white sand.

We followed the coast of Gun Carriage up to its northern tip then went about, running before a light northerly down the side of the island that was exposed to the open sea. Argyle was watching the shoals out to our east, a vast expanse of boiling ocean that admitted of no shape or logic. Ahead of us, a channel of calm water ran south-east towards the coast of Cape Barren Island. Argyle followed it until we were heading due east, away from the islands and into the blue. The rainclouds had attached themselves to Gun Carriage and Cape Barren, and out here was the sky from which they'd been torn, empty but for a handful of seabirds. For four hours we sailed like that, the morning peeling back as the land receded. Not a word passed between us.

My father lay shrouded at my feet and I whispered prayers over him and let the wind take them away.

At length, Argyle let out the boom and allowed it to slacken the mainsail. He waited until the *Moonbird* had settled in the water, then stood in silence watching the sky: the birds that dipped and stabbed at the water, seeking unseen baitfish. Here the sea was a deeper blue, deeper than sapphire. Argyle hauled the sounding line out of its hold in the bow, arranged the coils near the bow and threw the plumb overboard, watching the lead weights injecting bubbles into the depths.

As the coils ran off, he took the far end of the line and secured it to another coil, then another, and let the weights bump in rhythm over the side for a minute or more. When they stopped, Argyle shook his head. He motioned to the boy and the two of them hauled it all back onto the deck and re-set the mainsail.

We travelled on for another half-hour. The seawater that had flicked onto their clothes from the plumbline dried into plumes of salt. Again, the vessel was hove to and the process repeated—the birds, the sounding—except that this time the entire length of it ran noisily overboard and was stopped only by the knot the master had tied to a small cleat above the scuppers.

'We've passed the sea cliff,' said Argyle. 'Edge of the continent. Deep enough here.'

He walked to the head of the shrouded body and stood tall for a moment, the sun bright on his strong brown forearms. I sensed that I should do likewise. I stood at my father's feet. Neelanjan took up a position opposite Argyle, facing the shroud.

'All hands bury the dead,' Argyle muttered softly.

We had no ensign to lower to half-mast, but Argyle brought the mainsail down and let it lie slack.

'Feet first,' he said to me. I bent down and picked up the corners of the board at my ankles. I lifted it, as did the men, until it rested at our waists. In the end there was so little of him it was no great burden.

We manoeuvred the board so that it rested on the bulwark with the wrapped feet slightly outboard. I took the head-end from them and they stepped aside. Argyle produced a small notebook and began to read from it. The wind took the phrases, and wrapped some of them back in the swirling air to find me.

…commend the soul of our brother departed…commit his body to the deep…in sure and certain hope…Lord Jesus Christ—

The tears had come now. I did not want him to go.

The sea shall give up her dead—

I looked at Argyle, tried to understand him in his deep retreat from the world. He had blurred; I could not hold back the weeping.

…the corruptible bodies of those who sleep…changed, and made like unto his glorious body—

My hands had their task: I could not raise them to my eyes so the tears were let to run and fall. Argyle pocketed the notebook, took the board's end from me and lifted it. My father's body slid down to the sea, where it struck the surface and turned a half-circle in the lee of the *Moonbird*, then began its long journey, head-first, into the unknowable deep.

I threw the daisies on the ocean. The vague white shape grew smaller beneath them, further and bluer and less defined, until the ocean and what it had claimed could no longer be told apart.

AUTHOR'S NOTE

Srinivas and his vessel the *Moonbird* and all the characters who sail upon her are creatures of fiction.

Readers of my previous novel, *Preservation*, will recall that the wrecking of the *Sydney Cove* in 1797 is very much a matter of historical fact. Similarly, the wreck of the *Howrah* in this novel is based upon the wreck of the *Britomart*. Because I have changed the date from 1839 to 1830, I felt it was appropriate to change the vessel's name also. But the details of the incident—from the press speculation about false lights and plunder through to the various items that washed ashore on Preservation Island—are recited here as accurately as I could manage.

I have named all of the Bass Strait islands in this story as they were known at the time. There are differences, such as Forsyth Island being known then as Penguin, and modern-day Vansittart being called Gun Carriage. The 'second wave' sealers who occupied the islands in 1830 are given their correct names, as are the *tyereelore* women who lived with them. George Augustus Robinson's agents were indeed pursuing *tyereelore* women through the islands in 1830, and the sealers were taking measures to conceal them.

Tarenorerer, also known as Walyer, is a real historical figure, about whom far too little has been written. I have speculated as to her character and attitude, working from clues in the writings of George Augustus Robinson and others. But we do know that she was a woman of the Tommeginne people of Emu Bay in Tasmania/*lutruwita*, and she fought bravely against abduction, captivity and forced labour throughout her short life. She died of influenza on Gun Carriage Island in 1831, the year after this story is set.

Once again I would encourage interested readers to explore the non-fiction accounts of these islands and these people, particularly Patsy Cameron's *Grease and Ochre*, and Lyndall Ryan's *Tasmanian Aborigines*.

Any false lights that have been set by this account are my own doing.

A note on place names: these have been used and spelled in accordance with the Tasmanian Aboriginal Centre's *pulingina* to *lutruwita* (Tasmania) Place Names Map: for more about the *palawa kani* Language program and reviving *palawa* names, see http://tacinc.com.au/campaigns/palawa-kani/

A note on taxonomy: the creatures described herein, whether flying or swimming past the vessel, or ensnared by Dr Gideon, have been known by multiple names through the years. I may have taken liberties: where possible, I have tried to identify them as they were known at the time.

ACKNOWLEDGMENTS

Many books are worked into this tale, but the ones that lived on my desk were Patsy Adam Smith's *There Was a Ship*; Graeme Broxham and Michael Nash's *Tasmanian Shipwrecks* (where I first encountered the wrecks of the *Britomart* and the *Sarah*); *Grease and Ochre* by Patsy Cameron; *Me Write Myself* by Leonie Stevens; George Augustus Robinson's Tasmanian journals, collected as *Friendly Mission*, ed. N. J. B. Plomley; *One Hundred Islands: The Flora of the Outer Furneaux* by Harris, Buchanan and Connolly; and Simon Barnard's *Vaux's 1819 Dictionary of Convict Slang*.

The epigraph couplet from *Sailor's Knot* comes from Omar Sakr's wonderful collection *The Lost Arabs*, and is used with his kind permission.

Anyone who writes an historical novel learns best from the people who have lived the story. And in this instance, I have been fortunate to meet a remarkable cast of teachers.

To the people of Flinders Island I owe an ongoing debt for their willingness to share stories and thoughts about my Furneaux Island projects. Among them, I wish to thank Bill Riddle, keeper of old tales, for his astonishing *Britomart* history, and Ronald Wise for wisdom and sausages, and for introducing me to the people of The Corner on Cape Barren Island: and those families, for their willingness to talk to me.

Maikutena Vicki-Laine Green and Patsy Cameron were patient and generous with their cultural insights and practical suggestions. Damien Newton Brown, Gerard Walker, Robert Gott, Jo Canham, Chris McDonald, Ed Prendergast and Nicole Maher all read the manuscript and improved it with their thoughts.

My thanks to Sophie McKinnon for Pauline Buckby's *The Legends of Hunter Island*...and the skull; to Chris Kelly for pointing my various vessels in the right directions; to Michael Nash for his thoughts on the *Sydney Cove* wreck site; and to Clem Newton Brown and Professor John Pearn AO for sending me research.

As always, I reserve my deepest gratitude for my wife Lilly for her diligent reading of my early messes, and for her faith and love and calm counsel. Thanks also to my publisher, Michael Heyward, and all of the staff at Text Publishing for their skill and support, to Chong Weng Ho for the cover, Simon Barnard for the map and Jane Watkins for steering a steady course through strange times. And most especially to Mandy Brett, who endures the angst and hones the blade.